THE MOAT AROUND
MURCHESON'S EYE

THE MOAT AROUND MURCHESON'S EYE

LARRY NIVEN
JERRY POURNELLE

HarperCollins*Publishers*

HarperCollins*Publishers*
77–85 Fulham Palace Road,
Hammersmith, London W6 8JB

Published by HarperCollins*Publishers* 1993
1 3 5 7 9 8 6 4 2

First published in Great Britain by
HarperCollins*Publishers* 1993

ISBN 0 00 224200 1

Set in Melior

Printed in Great Britain by
HarperCollinsManufacturing Glasgow

For Marilyn and Roberta, those most patient of ladies . . .

Dramatis Personae

Sinbad:

HIS EXCELLENCY HORACE HUSSEIN BURY, Imperial Trader and Magnate; Chairman of the Board, Imperial Autonetics, Ltd. and owner of the yacht *Sinbad*

SIR KEVIN RENNER, KCMG, Captain, Imperial Space Navy Reserve; pilot of *Sinbad*

NABIL AHMED KHADURRI, Valet and Personal Secretary to Bury

CYNTHIA ANWAR, Companion to Bury

REUBEN FOX, Captain of Imperial Autonetics ship *Nauvoo Vision*

SIR LAWRENCE JACKSON, Governor of Maxroy's Purchase

RUTH RACHAEL COHEN, Lieutenant. Commander, Imperial Space Navy Intelligence

AJAX BOYNTON
JAMES SCOTT   Snow Ghost Hunters, Maxroy's Purchase
DARWIN SCOTT

RODERICK HAROLD, LORD BLAINE, DSC, GCMG, Earl of Acrux, Capt. ISN (Ret.), former master of Imperial battle cruiser *MacArthur*

SANDRA (SALLY) LIDDELL LEONOVNA FOWLER, LADY BLAINE, onetime doctoral candidate in anthropology, wife of Lord Blaine

THE HONORABLE GLENDA RUTH FOWLER BLAINE, Rod and Sally Blaine's daughter

BRUNO CZILLER, Vice Admiral, ISN (Ret.), former master of INSS *MacArthur*

DR. JACOB BUCKMAN, Astrophysicist

HIS EXCELLENCY BENJAMIN SERGEI SACHS, President of Imperial Traders Association, and Chairman of Union Express

BARON SIR ANDREW CALVIN MERCER, newly appointed Viceroy and Governor General of His Majesty's Realms Beyond the Coal Sack

ARKLEY KELLEY, Former Gunner, Imperial Marines, and Blaine family retainer

JENNIFER BANDA, Graduate Student in Xenobiology, Blaine Institute

JOCK Motie ambassadors to the Empire, representing the Mote
CHARLIE Prime family headed by "King Peter"
IVAN

CAPTAIN RAPHAEL CUNNINGHAM, ISN Intelligence case officer

ALYSIA JOYCE MEI-LING TRUJILLO, feature columnist Imperial Post-Tribune Syndicate, Special Features reporter, Hochsweiler Broadcasting Network

THE HONORABLE KEVIN CHRISTIAN BLAINE, Lieutenant. ISN

COMMISSIONER JOHN CARGILL, Admiral, ISN (Ret.)

COMMISSIONER DAVID HARDY, Bishop of the Established Church, and former Chaplain-Captain, Imperial Space Navy Reserve

LT. COMMANDER WILLIAM HIRAM RAWLINS, ISN, master of the frigate *Atropos*

COMMANDER GREGORY BALASINGHAM, ISN, master of the cruiser *Agamemnon*

THE HONORABLE FREDERICK TOWNSEND, owner and master of the yacht *Hecate*

TERRY KAKUMI, former Chief Petty Officer, ISN, engineer aboard *Hecate*

ADMIRAL THE HONORABLE SIR HARRY WEIGLE, Commander of the Crazy Eddie Fleet

The Moties:

Medina Traders Group:

EUDOXUS, Mediator
MUSTAPHA PASHA, Master of Inner Base Six
CALIPH ALMOHAD, Master of Medina Trading

East India Group:

LORD CORNWALLIS, Associate Master of Inner Base Six
WORDSWORTH, Junior Mediator
OMAR, Senior Mediator
ALI BABA, Apprentice Mediator

Crimean Tartars Group:

MERLIN, young Master
OZMA, senior Master
VICTORIA, Mediator
DOCTOR DOOLITTLE, Physician
POLLYANNA, Apprentice Mediator

Khanate Group:

HARLEQUIN, Mediator

PART 1
SNOW GHOST

I would not spend another such a night
Though 'twere to buy a world of happy days,
So full of dismal terror was the time!

—**William Shakespeare, King Richard III**

1
Interaction Nook

O God! I could be bounded in a nutshell, and count myself a king of infinite space, were it not that I have bad dreams.

—William Shakespeare, Hamlet, Act 2, Scene 2

A severed head spun across black sky. He had been a Marine: square jaw, close-cropped blond hair, glittering dead eyes. The slack mouth tried to speak. "Tell them," it said. "Stop them." Vacuum made its skin puffy, and blood made frozen bubbles on the thick neck. "Wake them. Wake them up. Mr. Bury, sir, wake up," it said urgently. The sky swarmed with small six-limbed shapes. They thrashed in the vacuum, found their balance, and swam toward him, past him, toward the battleship *Lenin*. Vacuum swallowed his scream. "Wake up," they chittered at him. "Please, Excellency, you must wake up."

His Excellency, Horace Hussein Al-Shamlan Bury, Trader and Magnate, jerked and twitched and was sitting upright. He shook his head and forced his eyes open.

The small, dark man was standing a safe distance away. Bury said, "Nabil. What time is it?"

"It's two in the morning, Excellency. Mr. Renner insisted. He said to tell you, 'The gripping hand.' "

Bury blinked. "Is he drunk?"

"Very. I woke Cynthia. She's making espresso for him. I made him take vitamins and drink some water. He was attacked outside the house. We killed all three, Excellency."

"Careless." So: three corpses. At least Renner had some excuse for waking him.

"Mr. Renner was drunk and I was asleep when the alarms rang," Nabil apologized. "Sir, they were using firearms."

"All right. The *gripping hand?* Renner's been watching too many holoflicks."

"Yes, sir. Excellency, I should be seeing to things."

"Yes, the bodies. We'll want to know all about those. The gripping hand?" Bury eased out of the water bed. His head spun with the motion, and all his joints creaked in protest. "I'll be right down. Have coffee for me, *real* coffee. Allah help you both if you woke me for nothing but a mugging."

Renner's fine new Spartan tunic was covered with blood, still wet. He had trouble focusing his eyes. He was already talking as Bury took Turkish coffee from Cynthia and sat down.

"They were waiting outside," he said. "I sent the taxi off and started for the door. Two stepped out of God knows where. One grabbed my arms from behind. One sprayed Peaceable Sam in my face. I think that's what it was; I didn't try to sniff it. Held my breath. Bit the alarm tooth and ejected my sleeve gun and sprayed him back. He fell against me. Sounded like popcorn going off all through his body. That's where all the blood came from. The guy behind me, I sprayed his feet."

Nabil was at a console, monitoring as one of Bury's agents began an autopsy on the first of the dead muggers. He looked up to say, "Mr. Renner had called in that he was coming, so the staff was waiting for him, of course. When we heard the alarm they were ready."

"Ready," Renner said. "Nabil, I haven't thanked you. Horace, he deserves a bonus, Horace."

Bury sipped at sweet Turkish coffee in a tiny cup. Renner gulped at what Nabil had given him: evil black espresso, service for four in a full-sized mug with a lemon slice floating it in. It popped his eyes open and stood his hair on end.

Bury winced, too, just watching. He said, "The gripping hand?"

"The *gripping* hand. *One* hand, *other* hand, *gripping* hand. I've been hearing it all night. I didn't haul you out of bed to tell you about a god damned mugging."

He could follow Bury's thoughts. *Drunk. Not making sense.* Then the sense came through and the blood drained from Bury's dark face. Renner said, "Hey!" and reached out to steady him.

4

Bury brushed the hand off. "Report."

Renner sat a little straighter. "I went out to look around, as usual. Dressed fancy. Well-paid pilot to a billionaire trader, carrying money and looking for fun. First—"

"You were doing Renner."

"It's the easy part of my job. Usually."

"Go on."

His lips felt numb and rubbery. Somehow he made them work. "On Maxroy's Purchase a brothel is called an 'interaction nook.' I'd heard about Ressina's. I went there. I didn't want their best girl; I wanted a native. I came away with a lady named Belinda. . . ."

Space is vast. Customs change, and every human colony is different. Some slavishly imitate the manners of the Imperial court. Others try to be like their Terran ancestors—or more likely, the way they've been told their Terran ancestors were.

The sun was setting somewhere behind the fog when they reached Shibano's Sea Cave. Maxroy people kept early hours.

Belinda was a pale blonde, tall, with a heart-shaped face. She had a thick Maxroy's Purchase accent. "Oh, it's lovely! I've never been here myself. You understand, you won't get a drink here?"

Renner had in fact chosen the place. It was a Mormon-Japanese restaurant. Maxroy's Purchase had first been settled by Mormons, and they were still a fair percentage of the populace.

Belinda was alarmed when he tried to order crottled greeps. "Do you know what you're getting?"

"I've read about this dish."

"All right." And she grinned. "I'll help you."

He'd had his doubts about alcohol-removed sake, but it tasted fine. He could get drunk later. Renner often thought of himself as a playboy-spy. Get the sense of the land, while Bury used his own means of gathering information.

Bury's means often startled him.

Bury kept track of the flow of money through the Empire. Only that. He was the same merchant prince he'd always been, with only this difference: that for the past quarter of a century, he watched for Outie maneuvering and kept the Navy informed.

Outies were worlds outside the Empire of Man. Some were

harmless, some were not. Fifteen years ago, Outie piracy had been driven from Maxroy's Purchase and from the system. It was to be expected that the flow of money through the system would have dropped off. Only Bury would have noticed that it had not decreased enough. Bury sold civilization; and the Purchase was buying too much of it.

And Bury had some time . . . and Imperial Autonetics owned three ships here . . .

The almond-eyed waiter was trying to hide a smirk when he brought Renner's main course. The dish was conspicuous, a shallow bowl over a foot across and five inches high. Customers at other tables broke off conversation to watch as he set it in front of Renner.

The creatures in the bowl might have been four-legged crabs. Their sides pulsed. Renner remembered reading that they were land creatures. They could almost reach the rim before they dropped back. Their eyes were locked on Renner's as they climbed toward him. They looked hungry and determined.

"Pick up the crottling fork," Belinda whispered. "The two-pronged fork. Use your thumb and two fingers."

It was sitting beside the bowl. Renner picked it up. Belinda whispered, "Stab just behind the head plate. Do it hard enough to set the prongs. You don't want it to drop off."

Hesitating was bad: the greeps would move. You couldn't blame them. Renner stabbed one and lifted the fork. Belinda said, "Scrape it off on the edge. You didn't stab hard enough. They bite."

Renner scraped it off and tried another. The beasts weren't fast, but it wasn't easy to center the fork. He stabbed.

"Good. Pick it up. Your left hand takes the tail. Pull hard."

Renner pulled. The exoskeletal tail came right off, exposing two inches of pale meat.

All eyes were on Renner, to watch him make a fool of himself. The naked tail writhed. Renner felt like a murderer. He said, "So, wretched sand dweller! Now will you tell us of your troop movements?"

"Actually, it was delicious. You really ought to try it," Renner said.

Bury merely looked at him.

6

"I've done this before, you know. Order something conspicuous, like crepes suzettes. Get 'em looking at me, then pick a conversation. This time I got the proprietor. He came over to lecture. 'Look at that greep. See the shimmy? On the one hand, if they shimmy too hard, they may be diseased. On the other, if they don't shimmy, they haven't eaten well. On the gripping hand, if they're too young and healthy they will escape and attempt to eat you. You would not like that.' I jumped a foot when he stuck his hand in the bowl. He liked that. 'But look here, see how it attacks my artificial finger. This is a healthy greep. Other places, they will see a tourist, and they will serve anything. Not here. Lex Shibano will not serve anything but healthy food. If it goes into your body, it must be healthy. I would—' "

"Renner!"

"Oh. Anyway, once Shibano came over, no one wanted to be near us. I guess it's one of the hazards of eating there. When he went away, the people at the next table had all lost interest. So I eavesdropped a little. Pair of men to my right were bankers, I think."

"I assume you'll get to the point sooner or later."

Renner nodded. " 'We could sell out and take a capital gain. Then again, the market's going up on Tabletop. We could hang on and make some real money.' The other one said, 'On the gripping hand, inflation's running wild on Tabletop. Let's get into something else.' "

Bury was getting older as he watched.

"I talked to Belinda. She's got ambitions, but hell, she's not stupid. She . . . see if I can get this right . . .

" 'Yes, Kevin, I could have spent my life as an honest housewife. Farm life isn't bad if you can afford to keep up the machines . . . but if I'm careful and lucky, maybe I can get to Sparta. Get rich. Then start a restaurant or something. What are my chances of getting to Sparta?'

"I didn't want to lie to her, so—"

"Go on."

"I didn't say anything. She looked down at her plate and said, 'The gripping hand is, I'll never be more than a Maxroy spill. The accent, the way I walk . . . how high can I climb?' " Renner stopped to trickle espresso past his tongue and chase it with half a glass of water.

"Gripping hand," Bury prompted him.

"I wanted a drink. I took her to the Top of the World. It's a rotating bar and restaurant at the edge of the spaceport. The people at the next table looked like prospectors. 'Prices are good for opal meerschaum and we need the money.' Second guy said, 'I hear it's getting harder to find blocks as large as we have. The price will go up.' The first one said, 'Horace Bury landed on the Purchase yesterday. If anybody can find the real source, he can. The gripping hand is, we'd better sell our stock before the price drops.' Bury, it was everywhere!"

"More?"

"I sent Belinda back to the interaction nook. She's looking for a ticket out. She thought I was it. I thought I'd better send her back. A car took off right behind the taxi. I didn't think anything of it, I just tend to notice—"

"My training."

"Right. I strolled on into the spill section. I wanted an overview, and it really felt like I was onto something. That's where I got so drunk. Local whiskey. Made from—"

" 'Gripping hand'?"

Renner sipped more espresso. "Gah! They looked like hunters. Smelled like hunters. 'Oh, I'm used to hunting snow ghosts. The furs sell for a lot, and if you know their habits, they aren't so dangerous.' One said, 'On the other hand, they did get Serge Levoy a month ago. You think they're learning, maybe? Mutating?' Another one laughed and said, 'On the gripping hand, Page, you're too lazy to do anything else for a living.' "

Bury shuddered. "Through the Coal Sack. The Mote is just on the other side of the Coal Sack. Moties must have come through the Coal Sack in slower-than-light ships."

"Not since we were there," Renner said. "Not enough time. And before that—Bury, they couldn't use that lightsail trick through the Coal Sack. Just sending that one ship to New Cal soaked up so many resources it collapsed their whole civilization."

"Gripping hand," Bury said. "Three alternatives, one dominant. Two delicate right arms and a powerful left. People don't think that way. Moties do! There's too much money on this planet. We were looking for outies. Maybe it isn't outies. Maybe it's far worse than outies."

"I don't believe it."

8

"I don't want to." Bury grimaced. "It is a pity that Nabil had to kill all three who attacked you. I think we might have learned something interesting from them."

Renner tried to look thoughtful and gave up. He finished the glass of water. "How so?"

"They wanted you alive. Not the actions of random muggers. Peaceable Sam is a gas used by police, not sold to civilians. They were skilled, and desperate, and had resources, but if they had been truly skilled, they would have succeeded."

"Desperate skilled amateurs," Renner said. "Who?"

"I trust we will know in the morning."

"Excellency?"

Bury turned. "Do you have something, Nabil?"

"The records office is closed and the computer is not responsive, so we cannot check retinal pattern identifications tonight, but Wilfred has made progress. Neither the first or second assassin had any trace of darkening in the lungs, no alcohol or drugs in the bloodstream."

"Look for caffeine."

Nabil nodded and spoke to the console.

"Mormons," Renner said. "Narrows it a bit. I'm about to fall over, Horace."

"To bed."

Renner was naked in the sauna. Despite the water and vitamins he had taken the night before, his head throbbed, and his stomach rejected all notions of food. When cold air touched him, he bellowed, "Shut it!"

Nabil smiled thinly. "You were more pleased to see me last night."

"I was still drunk. What do you have?"

"His Excellency wishes to see you. We have identified the assassins. They are crew members from *Nauvoo Vision*."

"*Nauvoo Vision*?"

"The name is Mormon. The ship belongs to Imperial Autonetics."

Renner whistled. "To Bury? Why in hell would crew from one of Bury's ships try to kill Bury's pilot?"

"Not kill. Kidnap," Nabil said. He carefully closed the sauna door.

"*Nauvoo Vision*," Bury said. "Captain Reuben Fox. A native of Maxroy's Purchase. Mormon, and recruits Mormon crew."

"Corruptible?" Renner asked.

Bury shrugged. "I have never had reason to find out. It would be worthwhile smuggling opal meerschaum if there were enough of it, but in fact it is very rare. Nothing else this world exports carries a tariff."

"What else do you know about him?"

"Very little. I do not believe I have ever met him. My Sector Commodore would have promoted him." Bury spoke softly in Arabic to his pocket computer. "It might be worth learning why, but in fact the reason seems clear enough. Fox has been a profitable captain."

"I think we should talk with him," Renner said. "And I'd better alert Navy Intelligence."

Bury grimaced. "I suppose you are correct. Especially since there may be Moties involved."

"The Governor has to know, too."

"I do not like government attention. Should I trust the Governor? If somebody on this world is dealing with Moties . . ."

"You'll be meeting him tonight, for dinner. Horace, I was hunted last night."

Nabil looked up from his console. "That is true. It is clear enough. They followed you, hoping to catch you alone or with only the woman. You left a taxi waiting when you went to the Top of the World."

"Yes—"

"We have located the driver. His cab was met at Madame Ressina's by three men with an improbable tale. They lost interest when they discovered that you were not in it."

"They really were hunting me, then. My head still hurts."

"It should, given what you drink," Bury said.

"I take my nerve restoratives. Bury, why did they want me?"

"I would presume for your keys," Nabil said, "and perhaps for instructions on how to enter the house. They carried other drugs. Serconal would have induced cooperation, or at least they must have thought so."

10

"That's illegal!" Renner protested.

Bury laughed. "Serconal is not only illegal, it is tightly controlled. It would be difficult for *me* to obtain a supply. Our enemies have resources."

Captain Reuben Fox was a dark-haired man approaching forty. He sagged and jiggled as he walked. He didn't seem otherwise unhealthy. Unlike Navy crew, civilians could neglect their free-fall exercising, and getting the muscle back was pure hell.

He seemed to be hurrying, though he wasn't making much speed. "Horace Bury! Your Excellency, I never expected that we would meet. What brings you to—I mean, what can I do for you? I and my ship?"

Bury wore his public, noncommittal smile. He appeared to be no more than an old, bearded man with a very prominent nose and a soft smile, all giving the lie to his reputation. "I often inspect ships I own. How else may I know of problems in my organization?"

"Excellency, I have no problems!"

"I know. You have a good record, trouble free. Tell me a little about normal operations of your ship."

"Let us sit down." Fox dropped heavily into a chair. Bury was in fact already seated. He was an old man, and he used a travel chair when he could.

Fox said, "We are an all-purpose cargo ship. What is often called a tramp steamer. The name comes from the days before space flight. We take orders for cargo to be brought here, and when we have sufficient cargo or passengers to make the trip profitable, we go to Darwin. Sometimes we go as far as Xanadu, and once to Tabletop, but generally only to Darwin."

"And within this system as well, I suppose?"

"Not often," Fox said. "If we have cargo within the Purchase system, we can alter our course to the Jump point and use the flinger."

Bury had glanced through computer views of *Nauvoo Vision* on the way here. The ship was versatile, a winged water-landing craft with interstellar capability but no Langston Field. There were fittings for an expanded passenger cabin or cargo hold, but either would have to be added in orbit.

The flinger (or spit gun, or AWOL tube) was a linear accelerator. A row of mountings ran the full length of the hull, and the electromagnetic rings were stored on board. Flingers were common aboard ships that ran a fixed route in heavily populated systems. They could launch lifecraft, too. Nonetheless Bury asked, "Do you make much use of the flinger? Is it really worth carrying its mass?"

"Yes, Excellency. Purchase system is short of metals. There's not much in the way of mines. Not much in the way of asteroids, either, but they'll last us the next ten thousand years. The mines have to be supplied."

Bury had noticed, in his quick perusal of *Nauvoo*'s records, that rings and fittings in the flinger had been replaced twice in thirteen years. A fitting had lost alignment and was waiting for replacement at this moment. Payments from the mines did back up Fox's claim of heavy use.

"You have a full complement of crew?"

"Three missing. I like to hire good Church members, but sometimes they backslide. We're not supposed to drink alcohol, and most of us never do, but everyone is curious . . ."

The Captain tended to explain before he was asked. It was the kind of thing Bury noticed. "Have you been Mormon all your life?"

"Not as you think Mormon," Fox said. "My ancestors had fundamental differences with the Church on Earth. They came to Maxroy's Purchase to establish the true faith. That was some six hundred years ago. We were fairly settled when the CoDominium sent us a hundred thousand transportees. Evil men and women with evil habits. They brought alcohol and drugs. The Church tried to keep control of the government, but there were too many transportees. Too many for our missionaries to convert. Some of the Elders took the true Church to the outback." Fox grinned triumphantly. "When the Secession Wars began, the false temples in the cities were destroyed, but the true Temple remained. It is the governing Temple for Maxroy's Purchase to this day, our Temple in Glacier Valley."

Bury nodded agreement. "It was much the same with the true servants of Islam. They fled from cities to country, often from world to world. Have I not heard of a *New Utah?*"

"Excellency, I've read about New Utah in history class. It is an outie world, settled from the Purchase at the same time that the Elders moved to Glacier Valley. There were close relations with New Utah, until the Alderson tram lines to it were lost sometime during the Secession Wars. Stellar geometry changes slowly, but with enough time—"

"Your crew is all Mormon, then?" Bury interrupted.

"Yes, Excellency. I am a bishop of the Church. My crew is obedient and cheerful. Don't our records show that?"

"They do," Bury said. "It is not uncommon. What do you do when you have passengers who are not of your church?"

"I know many restaurant owners," Captain Fox said. "I find Church members who are accustomed to serving gentiles, who would not want to be permanent crew. They come for one voyage." He smiled. "They are eager. What other chance has a restaurateur to see another sky? It may be unusual practice, but it works."

"In fact nothing about this ship or its practices is unusual. If three of the crew of this ship had not tried to kidnap you, perhaps to force their way into my bed chamber," Bury said, "there would be no reason to be suspicious of Reuben Fox." Cynthia moved around Bury like a tailor, dressing him. Bury stood to get his pants on, then sat again.

Renner was already dressed, elegantly but without his usual flamboyance. He sat down on the bed. "Uh-huh. Could those three have been moonlighting? Back in port, looking for a little fun, someone offers them money to break a kneecap. . . . No? I know that smile, Horace."

"I tend to notice numbers."

"Well?"

"Small Small World, Mountain Movers, Cutty on the Rocks, and others: these are the big asteroid mining concerns in Purchase system. All old. Mountain Movers is over five hundred years old. They used well-established techniques developed by the early Co-Dominium, and were cautious about upgrading." Bury's fingers were dancing while he spoke. Data flashed on-screen and were gone before Renner could quite integrate them. "But what of these?

Hannefin Mines, General Metals, Union Planetoids, Tanner Metals . . . this sequence, seven in all. What do you see?"

"Unimaginative names."

"I didn't notice that."

"Short-lived. A few years each. Um . . . they *are* in sequence. One disappears before the next is registered. Up to twenty years apart. Bury, I don't see that any of them went bankrupt."

"That would be the obvious assumption, would it not? A scam. Many names, one man. But for a hundred and ten years? And evidently they paid their bills on time. At least they've paid decent sums to *Nauvoo Vision* for cargoes delivered across the system."

"Taxes?"

"They paid their taxes."

"Offices were all here in Pitchfork River City. Check the addresses." Renner watched Bury's fingers. Sometimes the old man's hands shook; his servants learned to half-fill his cup so it didn't spill. But Bury's hands became wonderfully agile on a computer keyboard. "What does it mean?"

"No such present address . . . none of them. I'll have Nabil search out older records. It means I've been paid for nothing."

"Huh?"

"I was joking. *Nauvoo Vision*'s flinger has seen hard use. Cargoes have been launched across the system, but not targeted at asteroid mines, not *these* mines. Where, then?"

"There were extensive civilizations in the asteroids of Mote system." Renner saw Bury's hands begin to shake and said, "Just a thought. Outies is the way to bet. The rebels are back."

"I do not bet the future of humanity at any odds, Kevin." Bury leaned back, took a deep breath. "Well. We'll be a few minutes early for dinner if we start now."

"I gather that's the custom here."

"Yes. Let us see what we can learn at the Governor's Palace."

2
Receptions

The first adventurer was a nuisance. I am sure he acted against his mother's, his wife's, and the council of old men's strict orders when he did it; but it was he that found where the mammoths die and where after a thousand years of use there was still enough ivory to equip the entire tribe with weapons. Such is the ultimate outline of the adventurer; society's benefactor as well as pest.

—William Bolitho, Twelve Against the Gods

The reception line was mercifully short. Governor Sir Lawrence Jackson, a former Navy man who'd gone into politics. Lady Marissa Jackson. Renner thought she looked Eurasian. Norvell White Muller, the president of the local branch of the Imperial Traders Association. Half a dozen other local officials.

"Sir Kevin Renner," the protocol officer announced.

"Welcome to Maxroy's Purchase, Sir Kevin," the Governor said.

"Actually, I don't use the title much, Governor. Thank you for the reception. Glad to be here."

"A bit tame for someone who has been to Mote Prime, I imagine," Lady Jackson said.

There was something familiar about the Governor's voice, but before Renner could study the Governor's face more closely, the people behind him had moved up, and he was swept past the reception line and out into the main hall.

The reception hall was large and spacious. Between the big windows that overlooked the city and the Pitchfork River were "windows": holograms of scenes from elsewhere on the planet.

Here, half a dozen spectacular waterfalls plunged from orange cliffs. Silver shapes leaped and danced in the pools below the falls.

Here, a sea serpent chased a school of miniature dolphin shapes; then the dolphins turned and attacked the serpent with vicious fangs. The serpent dived to escape. The viewpoint followed it down . . . followed and closed in, until the serpent's tail seemed about to plunge out of the wall. The view shifted: the serpent was pulled tail first onto the deck of a boat, imprisoned by a tethered collar.

Renner found himself next to a pretty girl in Imperial Navy uniform. She seemed young to be a lieutenant commander. "Spectacular," he said.

"Of course holograms for palace decorations went out of fashion on Sparta ten years ago," she said. "Hello, Sir Kevin. I'm Ruth Cohen."

One of the "windows" looked out on a sparse forest carpeted in snow. Something like a thick-furred snake lifted a great, flattened head . . . no, that was a neck! The creature itself was lying flat in the snow, like a gigantic white bear rug. The narrow, pointed head lifted high and rotated to look almost backward, suspiciously, straight into the reception hall. Black-pupiled eyes bulged. The head settled; again the animal was invisible in thick snow.

"What ship, Commander?" Renner asked.

She shook her head. "Governor's office. Intelligence liaison." She glanced around to see that they were alone. "We would have met soon enough anyway. I arranged to sit next to you at dinner."

"Good." Purely business? "We'll have time to—God!"

The pointed head snapped up, the flattened bear's short legs shot backward, and it took off. It was *fast*. It might have been gliding, using its flattened torso like an airfoil. Three muffled hunters fired almost at the same moment, then turned and ran, dividing, dodging among the trees. The creature smashed into a sapling, rebounded, and collapsed. So did the tree.

"Wow!" Renner said. "What was that?"

"Snow ghost," Ruth Cohen said.

"Dangerous."

"Oh, yes. The fur's quite valuable, though. They shed their furs in the summer, but they're just as dangerous."

"You don't have a Purchase accent," Renner said.

16

She laughed softly. "You wouldn't believe what it cost my parents to—" She grinned. "Actually, if I have a home planet, it's New Washington. My father retired there. This is my first tour on Maxroy's Purchase. I've been here a year."

"Seems a nice place."

"I'm glad somebody thinks so," Ruth said.

"Governor Jackson. There's something familiar about him," Renner said.

"Could you have known him? He was Navy Reserve for a long time. Retired as a commander, I think."

"How did he get to be Governor?"

"It's an interesting story," she said. "Get me a drink and I'll tell you."

"Oh—sorry." Renner whistled to one of the circulating robots. "We seem to have Old Fashioned, Martini, and something green."

"I'll have the green one. It'll be waterwing liqueur. It's sweet, but there's a nice flavor."

Renner took two of the green drinks and sipped carefully. It tasted of ginger and something indefinable. "Not bad. I wonder if Bury knows about this."

"I'd be surprised if he didn't," Commander Cohen said. "It's a big export item. Now. You wanted to know about the Governor. He grew up here, was here before the Purchase was brought back into the Empire. He joined the Navy from school, and when he got out of the Navy, he brought a friend, another retired Navy man, Randall Weiss, and they started a freighter service to supply the asteroid miners."

"Sounds reasonable," Renner said. There had been a time when that would have been his career: finish a tour in the Navy Reserve, then go into a civilian shipping line, maybe eventually buy a ship.

"Only the Outies kept raiding their ship," Ruth said. "They took two cargoes, and the firm was about to go broke."

"Where was the Navy?"

"That was sixteen years ago."

"Ah. They were still beefing up the blockade fleet." Mote system again.

"Exactly." Ruth sipped at her drink. "That really is good, you know? Anyway. Sir Lawrence—he wasn't Sir Lawrence then of course—and Weiss decided to do something about it. They armed their ship and recruited locals and asteroid miners and anyone else they could and went out looking for pirates, or rather let the Outies find them. I guess they were lucky because they captured an Outie ship, and that gave them a bigger and better-armed ship, and they used it to hunt more Outies."

"I think I read about that," Renner said. "Didn't realize it was here. They ended up with four ships, and quite a battle."

"Yes. Randall Weiss was killed, but they pretty well smashed the Outie threat. Weiss got a statue, Sir Lawrence got a knighthood, and the local council sent him to the sector capital to represent the Purchase. Pretty soon the Viceroy sent him back as Governor."

"Good story." Renner frowned. "By God, I *have* met him, but I can't think where."

A faint gong sounded through the reception hall.

"Dinner," Ruth said.

Renner offered his arm.

The first course was a variety of sashimi. Renner looked to Ruth Cohen for advice.

"That one's yellowfin," she said. "Earth tuna grow well here. And the light gray one is a freshwater fish called dancing silver. Oh!"

"What?"

"The dark red one is cecil. It's expensive. Not exactly rare, but they don't catch one every day."

Renner took some of each. "What is cecil?"

"Big sea snake. You saw it caught, I think. In the holograms. Hmm. Kevin, I think we've been watching our dinner! I wonder if that means we'll have snow ghost?"

"Yes," Lady Jackson said from down the table. She was an ample woman who clearly liked to eat. "Do you like it?"

"I've never tasted it," Ruth admitted. "We had cecil once, though. Kevin, you're supposed to dip it in that sauce."

Renner used the chopsticks to dip the dark meat, then chewed thoughtfully. "Peanut sauce."

"And ginger," Lady Jackson said. "The Thai influence. Purchase cuisine tends to be simple. The planet was settled by Mormons, but there was strong oriental influence. The gripping hand was that we kept the simplicities of both for nearly everything."

Bury's travel chair, near the head of the table, took up the space of two normal chairs. It gave him a sense of isolation, which he welcomed, and still allowed him conversation.

Snow ghost meat was served julienne with carrots, turnips, and unfamiliar root vegetables. The dish was hot enough to wake the dead. The meat was tough. No wonder if had to be cut fine. Bury's teeth cut through it well enough, but they were harder and sharper than the teeth he'd been born with.

He asked, "Maxroy's Purchase was brought into the Empire fifty years ago?"

"Not quite forty, actually," Governor Jackson said. He was eating left-handed; his silverware had been laid out reversed.

Bury nodded slowly. "But I am told there is still considerable sentiment for the Outie cause."

Governor Jackson spread his hands expressively. He never seemed to shrug. "It's not what it seems," he protested. "Our people—especially in the outback—tend to think of New Utah as more like Heaven than a mere planet. Habitable from pole to pole, and covered with green plants and wild game."

"And it is not?" Bury asked.

"I've read the old records," Governor Jackson said. "It's a planet. More land surface than the Purchase, higher mountains, and even fewer minerals close to the surface. Stayed molten longer, maybe. The weather's more extreme. Do you care for more wine, Your Excellency?"

"Thank you, no."

"Oh, that's right, Moslems don't drink," Mrs. Muller said. "I'd forgotten."

"Probably most do not," Bury said. "Just as most Jews do not eat pork." He'd noticed that both the Governor and his wife were drinking soda water. "Governor, would there be strong reasons for the Outies to wish for trade with the Purchase?"

"Very likely, Excellency," Governor Jackson said. "New Utah is quite deficient in certain minerals and organics. There's no selenium at all, for example. They'll need food supplements."

"Just a few tonnes a year," Norvell White Muller said. "A couple of ships' worth, and the profits on those ships—" He licked his lips. "Utah Churchies would buy medical supplies, too, if the Empire would let them."

Governor Jackson laughed. "The Navy can't spare me any ships," he said. "So I can't go bring New Utah into the Empire by force—"

"You can't even get there," Mrs. Muller giggled.

"Well, we *can*, but I agree, it's not easy. Two jumps past wretched red dwarfs, and then across a big bright E-class system with only one planet and that a rock ball. There was an expedition a few years before I got here." Jackson looked thoughtful. "The Navy has records showing it wasn't always so hard."

"I believe I heard that as well," Bury said.

"Anyway, as long as I don't have Navy ships, the trade embargo is the only weapon I've got to bring New Utah in. All they have to do is join and they can have all the trade they want."

"The gripping hand is they don't want to," Renner said.

Jackson laughed. "Maybe. They've had time enough to change their minds. It's all academic because the direct Jump point disappeared a hundred and thirty years ago, during the Secession Wars. I sent them an ambassador twelve years ago, with a trade ship . . . one of yours, Mister Bury. No luck."

Stars wander, Bury thought. Jump points depend upon the luminosities within a pattern of stars. They come and go . . . why did that thought suddenly have the fringe of hair around his neck trying to stand up? Tiny six-limbed shadows flailed behind his eyes. . . .

Across the table he heard Renner murmur, "Jackson and *Weiss*?"

Governor Jackson said, "There was some traffic, I think, up until the Navy came back forty years ago. New Utah would have paid high for fertilizer. But with *what*? And the trip is just too long—"

Renner's belly laugh cut through all conversation. Into the silence Renner said, "I was trying to remember where I met you."

The Governor was laughing, too, with his head thrown back. His wife giggled.

"Governor? Sir? I watched your hands," Renner said. "Like this?" He pushed back his chair and stood; never mind that they were in the middle of dessert. Right hand up, closing: "On the one hand, high price for fertilizer." Right hand dropped to near the hip, closed again. Bury nodded. "On the other hand, they don't seem to have anything to pay with," Renner said. Left hand out, fingers closed in pairs, like a hand with three thick fingers. "Gripping hand, it's too far anyway. Did I get that right?"

"Why, yes, Sir Kevin. My wife's tried to break me of the habit—"

"But the whole planet's doing it. Did you learn it here, or on Mote Prime?"

Bury's vision swam. He pulled the diagnostic sleeve out of his chair arm and inserted his arm, hoping nobody would notice. Orange dots blinked, and he felt the coolness of a tranquilizer injection.

The Governor said, "I was sure you wouldn't recognize me. Couldn't remember where you'd met me, hey? . . . Bury? Are you all right?"

"Yes, but I don't understand."

"You were an honored passenger, and Sir Kevin was the Sailing Master, and Weiss and me, we were only Able Spacers. I was sure you wouldn't know me. But we went down to Mote Prime, and we stayed till Captain Blaine decided we weren't needed and sent us back. Weiss, he picked up that habit from the aliens, the Moties. One hand, other hand, gripping hand, and they shrug with their arms because their shoulders don't move. I learned it from him. We were on the holoscans a lot when we were fighting the Outies, and I've been on since Sparta made me Governor, and I guess . . . The whole planet, eh?"

Renner said, "All of Pitchfork River, at least. Top to bottom, hill to spill, they've taken up that three-sided Aristotelian logic. You're not just the governor, you're a holo star too."

The Governor seemed embarrassed, but pleased. "That's the way it is in the outlying worlds. Sir Kevin, Excellency, I was purely *delighted* to meet you again after so long." As equals, he didn't say.

"So that's all there was to it," Renner said. He sprawled back in the big RelaxaChair in Bury's study and let the massage begin as he lifted a glass of real cognac. "Jackson and Weiss got successful and become tri-vee stars. Local boys made good. So everybody copied them. Wow! And to think we knew them when." He laughed suddenly. "Weiss must have driven his Fyunch(click)

crazy, imitating him like that! It's supposed to go the other way around."

"Naive." Bury let himself sink cautiously into his chair and touched the button twice for coffee.

"How so naive? You heard the Governor."

"I heard him explain away a peculiar habit," Bury said softly. "I did not hear an explanation of why there is too much money in this system."

"That's true," Renner admitted.

"He has been to Mote Prime," Bury said. "The Governor himself. He and Weiss had money to buy and outfit a spacecraft. If there ever was a man better suited to hide captured Watchmakers. Or an Engineer, or—"

Renner laughed. "Bury, that's bizarre!" He leaned back into the massage chair and let it work as he remembered the miniature Moties. Small aliens, not really intelligent, but able to manipulate technologies beyond anything Renner had ever seen. Oh, they'd have been valuable, all right! And they'd destroyed the battle cruiser *MacArthur*.

Still. "Horace, you've been clinically paranoid since long before I met you. Blaine let the Watchmakers get loose on his ship, but Christ, it was impossible to get Moties into *Lenin!* The Marines didn't let anything through unless it went through molecule-by-molecule inspection!"

"Not impossible. I did it myself." Bury's hands kneaded the chair arms.

Renner sat bolt upright. "What?"

"It would have worked." Bury waited as Nabil came into the room with an ornate silver coffeepot and thin cups. "Coffee, Kevin?"

"Sure. *You smuggled out a Motie?*"

"We did that, didn't we, Nabil?"

Nabil grinned mirthlessly. "Excellency, that is one profit I am pleased that you never collected." It was a liberty Nabil would not normally have taken; but Bury only shivered and sipped at his coffee. He was wearing the diagnostic sleeve.

"Bury, what in hell?"

"Have I shocked you after twenty-five years? The Watchmakers were potentially the most valuable thing I had ever seen," Bury said. "Able to fix and repair and rebuild and invent. I thought it

22

madness not to keep a pair. And so we arranged it, a pair of Watchmakers in suspended animation, hidden in an air tank. My air tank on my pressure suit."

"On your *back?*" If Bury was lying, he was doing it well. But Bury *did* lie well. "You don't have Watchmakers. I'd know."

"Of course I do not," Bury said. "You know part of the story. *MacArthur* was lost to us, the Watchmakers were running wild throughout the ship, changing the machines for their own use, killing Marines who peeped into their nests. We crossed on lines between *MacArthur* and *Lenin*. Long spiderwebs of line with passengers strung like beads. The universe was all around us and the great globe of Mote Prime below, all circles, the craters left by their wars. The huge globe of a ship came near. I could feel the wealth and danger on my back, Marines ahead, and the risk of running out of air too soon. I had accepted that risk. Then—"

"Then you looked back. Like Orpheus."

"The sun happened to shine directly into the faceplate of the man behind me."

"You saw tiny eyes—"

"The djinni take you, Kevin! It's *my* nightmare, after all! Three pairs of tiny eyes looked at me out of the faceplate. I hurled my briefcase at them. I reached around and wrenched one of my air tanks loose and hurled it after. The suit dodged—clumsy, it was a wonder they could get it to move at all—dodged the briefcase and was in perfect position when the air tank smashed the faceplate."

"I've had this nightmare twice myself, I've heard it so often. Bury, it would have served you right if you'd grabbed the wrong air tank."

"It was not the worst of my fears. The faceplate smashed and a score of Watchmaker class Moties blew out and thrashed in the vacuum, and with them came a tumbling head. That was how they got past the Marines. And I would have taken that air tank past *Lenin's* Marines."

"Maybe."

"And maybe I was not the only one. Two Able Spacers were on Mote Prime. We all saw how useful Watchmakers were when properly used by the Engineer class of Moties. Did one of them find yet another way to conceal Watchmakers? Or Engineers or *Masters?*"

23

"It's hard to disprove, Bury, but you really don't have any reason for thinking so. By the way, don't tell that story to anyone else."

Bury glared. "I haven't told *you* for twenty-five years. Kevin, we do have something useful. *If* this three-hand way of thinking spread because there are Moties around—of whatever class—*then* I know who is guilty. The Governor says that he and his companion spread that. He would be lying, covering up."

"Maybe not. He might really believe—"

"Kevin—"

"Or maybe it was Weiss. All right, all right. We still don't know about the money flow. We don't know where the cargoes went when Captain Fox used his flinger. We need to find out."

"You must report to the Navy first. In case we should disappear."

"Right. And then I'll find a way to chase Outies, and you find a way to chase Moties, and I'll be in Scotland before ye. Now I'm going to bed. When I was in the sauna, I swore I'd go to bed sober."

". . . Yes."

3
The
Maguey Worm

Men have died from time to time, and worms have eaten them, but not for love.

—Shakespeare, As You Like It, Act 4, Scene 1

Ruth Cohen led the way downstairs into the cellar of Government House. Two Marines were seated at the far end of a long, blank-walled corridor. One stood to attention. The other remained at his console.

"Identity, Commander, please." He waited as Ruth stared into a retinal pattern reader and put her hand on the Identiplate.

"Ruth Cohen. Lieutenant Commander, Imperial Navy. Unrestricted access to security systems," the box said.

"Now you, sir."

"It won't know me," Renner said.

"Sir . . ."

"I know the drill, Sergeant." Renner looked into the box. A red light danced about in his eyes.

"Pattern recorded. Subject unknown," the box said.

The Marine touched buttons on his console. A door swung open to reveal a small antechamber that looked much like an airlock. As Renner and Cohen entered the antechamber, the Marine dictated, "Lieutenant Commander Cohen and subject identified as Kevin Renner, civilian, Imperial Autonetics, entered security rooms . . ."

The inner door opened when the outer door was closed and

25

locked. Renner couldn't help thinking of the weapons the Marines could use on them while they were locked into the comfortably furnished suite. There was a conference table, good chairs, and a couch, all identical to security rooms Renner had seen on a dozen planets. "Seems like home," he said.

Ruth Cohen held herself stiffly. She set her recorder on the table and wiped her palms on her skirt. Renner read her nervousness. "You all right?"

"Maybe I don't interview captains all that often."

Renner grinned. "Don't look like one, do I? There's a price for this, you know."

"What?"

"You'll have dinner with me tonight."

"Captain . . ."

"What are they going to do, fire me?" Renner demanded. He made faces at the recorder, which wasn't on. "That for you. And no report until Commander Cohen agrees to go out with me."

"Suppose I refuse?"

Renner stared. "Then I make my report."

"Oh." She smiled enchantingly. "In that case, I'd be delighted to have dinner with you."

"Hot damn! How do you feel about—"

"I won't touch crottled greeps. Why is it everyone who's seen a crottled greep wants to watch someone else coping? Captain, does it strike you that you and I shouldn't be seen together very much?"

"You're right," Renner said. "Heckfire."

"So I guess that's that." She sat at the table. "Ready? Okay. Recorder's on." She dictated date and time. "Report of Kevin Renner, Captain, Imperial Navy Intelligence. Case officer, Lieutenant Commander Ruth Cohen . . ."

Renner waited until she had finished the introduction and header, then sat at the table. "Captain Sir Kevin Renner, KCMG, Navy Intelligence, Special Assignment. As stated in previous reports, we brought the Imperial Autonetics yacht *Sinbad* to Maxroy's Purchase because of the suspicions of His Excellency Horace Hussein al-Shamlan Bury, Magnate. Bury's financial analysis indicated there might be irregularities. Imperial Autonetics has a startup factory here, and owns three ships, so there was no problem about cover stories.

"Two days after we arrived there was an attempt to kidnap me—"

Ruth Cohen involuntarily drew in a deep breath.

Renner grinned. "Glad you care." He leaned back in his chair and stared at the ceiling for a moment, then began to talk. He told about the attack, then what had preceded it.

" '. . . healthy greep. Look how it shimmies.' Commander, if you keep laughing in the middle I'll never get done."

"That's not fair!"

"Sure it is." Renner continued with his night in the capital. At appropriate points he inserted recordings of what they had found out about the three attackers, Captain Reuben Fox, and the history of *Nauvoo Vision*.

"Mormons," Ruth Cohen said. "Three of them. It's hard to believe they're ordinary robbers."

"Yeah, I noticed that," Renner said. "One Mormon going bad is unfortunate. Three at once is a conspiracy. Not to mention that Bury is sure that Captain Fox is covering up."

"General conclusions?" Ruth prompted.

"Of my own, none, but His Excellency Horace Bury believes there may be Moties loose in the Purchase system. I do not. I think the Outies are back."

Ruth nodded grimly. "I don't think I believe in Moties either," she said. "But the regulations are clear enough. This interview gets off to Sector Headquarters soonest. Discussion?"

"Bury's paranoid," Renner said. "He *always* sees a Motie threat. But he could be right, and if he is, the Governor's in a conspiracy against the Empire."

"Captain, this report will go directly to Sector Headquarters. They may not know about you and His Excellency."

Renner grinned. "Okay. Horace was born rich. His father made a massive fortune in interstellar trade after the Empire annexed Levant. Bury extended it. He's a hundred and sixteen years old, and he understands the flow patterns of money. A powerful force in the Empire is Horace Bury.

"He . . . um. He committed acts which put him afoul of Empire law, details classified, twenty-six years ago. We had both visited Mote Prime as part of the official expedition. I was just getting out of the Navy, having served as Sailing Master of the INSS battle cruiser *MacArthur* of ill fame."

"The only ship ever destroyed by aliens," she remembered.

"Other than blockade battles," Renner said. "But essentially yes.

27

MacArthur was destroyed by Motie Watchmakers. It's a class of Motie animal. Not intelligent, and they have *four* arms, not three. All kinds of people have speculated about that, including the Moties at Blaine Institute. Anyway, I was getting out, and Bury was facing a hangman's noose. He made a deal. For twenty-five years he's been holding down rebellion and Outie action all across the Empire, largely at his own expense, and I'm the guy the Navy assigned to watch him. He's dedicated, too. I've never caught him doing anything that would get in the way of his mission." Except once, he remembered.

"Why Outies? Vengeance? Outies gored his ox?"

Renner sighed. "Horace doesn't give a damn about Outies. Outies take up time and resources. Anything that distracts the Empire from dealing with Moties is a threat to the human race and the children of Allah. Moties frightened Horace once. Nobody does that twice. Horace wants them extinct."

Ruth Cohen looked puzzled. She glanced at the recorders. "Captain, if the Moties did break out, would they be that big a threat?"

"I don't know," Renner said. "It's not impossible. It isn't that their technology is so much better than ours, as that their instinct for technology is beyond anything we know. Humans are better at *science*, but once the principles have been discovered, the Moties—the Browns, anyway, the Engineers—are better at turning them to practical use than any humans who ever lived.

"Example. They'd never heard of the Langston Field when we arrived at Mote Prime, and before we left their system they'd made improvements we never thought of! Another example: the magic coffeepot we got off *MacArthur*. By now that technology is all over the Empire, even here. I'm sure some variant of the coffeepot is used to get the alcohol out of the sake I was drinking night before last."

"Thank you. Have you other observations?"

"Yeah. My own plans. Bury's paranoia can be useful sometimes, but I don't like seeing him so nervous. He might do something . . . hasty. Anyway, I trust he'll be busting his arse to find what he thinks are Moties. That leaves me free to track Outies, if *that's* what we're facing. I want to *show* Bury that the Moties are still safely bottled up.

"We can't trust anyone but Bury's people, so we don't have any troops. Can't use the local cops. But there are some . . . mmm, avenues. Where has Captain Fox been sending his cargo pods? Is there an Outie base in the asteroids? Why the peculiar flow of money? Imperial Autonetics is constantly being picked at by embezzlers. Robbing a corporation, it's like robbing a machine, for some people. Here, it doesn't look like anyone's being robbed."

She was smiling again. "Is that bad?"

"Well . . . it's odd. Something is hidden but nobody's being robbed."

"What will you do?"

"I'll do Renner." He grinned at her. "I'll spend money. I'll make passes at pretty girls, and ask shopkeepers about whatever they're selling, and buy people drinks and generally get them talking. Maybe . . . yeah, maybe I'll look into where opal meerschaum comes from."

She was looking at him, frowning. "Alone?"

"More or less. I'll keep Bury's household posted as best I can. This is what I do."

"Anything else to report?"

Renner shook his head, and Ruth turned off the recorders. "I always did wonder about the regulations about Moties," she said. "What do we do now?"

"First, you get this recording off to Sector. You do understand that no one on this planet sees it first?"

"Give me a little credit—"

"Oh, I've always known that beauty and brains go together. There are implications, you know."

"Lots of them," Ruth said. "Kevin, have you thought this through? The True Church of Jesus Christ of the Latter Day Saints has power. And a lot of members. If you're threatening it . . ."

"They'll have plenty of gunmen. Sure. Now think about what we could be doing to threaten that Church."

"I did. So far I got nothing."

"Me either," Renner said. "So I'll keep poking around."

Shopping centers had never come into vogue on the Purchase. Big and little shops were scattered through the city, a sudden surprise among the houses.

Here: four huge rock slabs leaned against each other at the tops, with window glass in narrow triangles where the rock didn't meet. The boutique was a block from the Pitchfork River, in a neighborhood that had once been fashionable and was now getting to be again. Kevin Renner glanced in and saw a squarish chunk of white rock glittering with opal colors.

He walked in. Chimes sounded above his head.

He paid little attention to the cookware, lamps, rifles. Here was a row of glittering white pipes with amber bits, and one, isolated, that was fiery opal in a black matrix. Some were carved in intricate fashion: faces, animals, and one flattened tube shaped like an Imperial skip-glide fighter.

A short, muscular, balding man emerged from somewhere aft. His eyes scanned Renner in genial fashion. He said, "The pipes."

"Too right. What kind of prices do these things carry? The black one, for instance."

"Oh, no, sir. That's a used pipe. Mine. After I close up, then it comes out of the case. It's there for display."

"Um. How long . . ."

The old man had it out on the counter. It had been carved into a face, a lovely woman's face. Long, wavy hair ran down the bit. "I've been smoking Giselle here for twenty-six years. But it doesn't take that long. A year, year and a half, the matrix will blacken up nicely. Longer for the larger pipes."

"Longer if I like switching pipes, too. How—"

"You'll find you smoke just the one pipe at home, sir. Opal meerschaum doesn't go stale after a few thousand puffs. Briar is what you'll take on trips."

Interesting. You took the cheaper pipes on trips, of course, and the little ones. Big pipes were more awkward but smoked better. But most of the pipes in view were pocket-size.

"Do you keep the bigger ones somewhere else?"

"No, sir, this is all we have."

"Mmm. That big one?"

"Nine hundred crowns." The proprietor moved it to the counter. It was an animal's head, vaguely elephantine.

"That's high. I've seen better carving," Renner said.

"On opal meerschaum?"

"Well, no. Is it difficult to carve?"

The old man smiled. "Not really. Local talent. It may be you'd want to buy a blank, like this." It was bigger yet, with a bowl bigger than Renner's fist and a long shank and short bit. "Take it to another world. Give it to a better carver."

30

"How much?"

"Thirteen fifty."

It wasn't Kevin's money. Very little of what passed through his fingers was Kevin's money. There would be a Navy pension, and he might be in Bury's will ... but this would be charged to expenses. Nonetheless Kevin shook his head and said, "Wow."

"Higher on other worlds. Much higher. And the value goes up as you smoke it." The man hesitated, then said, "Twelve hundred."

"Would you go a thousand?"

"No. Look into some other stores. Come back if you change your mind."

"Rape it. Sell me that. Do you have tobacco, too?" Kevin handed over his pocket computer and waited while the proprietor verified the transfer, wrapped the pipe, handed it across. And added a tin of local tobacco, gratis.

Kevin knew what he wanted to ask next ... and suddenly knew that he didn't have to. He just grinned and let silence stretch until the old man grinned back and said, "Nobody knows."

"Well, how does it come in?"

"Private fliers. Men go out and come back with the stone. Are you thinking that they could be made to talk?"

"Well ... ?"

"There are criminal elements in Pitchfork River. They don't control the opal meerschaum and never have. My suppliers say they don't know where it comes from; they always bought it from somewhere else. I've heard it so often I'm beginning to believe it. I helped finance some geologists once, when I was younger. They never found anything. Money into a rat hive."

"Too bad."

"You won't find a shop that sells only the opal meerschaum. It's sporadic. There hasn't been a new source in twenty years, that's why it's so high. Some of us think it comes from the north. The north is more geologically active, and the fliers mostly go out in that direction."

"But he was willing to bargain," Renner told his pocket computer, set to RECORD. "Two other dealers offered me deals, too. That's three out of four. I think they're expecting a new source anytime now. That would drop the price. It would fit the cycles you noticed, slow rise in price, peak, steep drop, every twenty years or so."

He put the computer away. The taxi settled and let him out. He was in a narrow wedge of manicured forest, in Tanner Park, and a bridge was in view of the north.

Across the bridge: the spill. It wasn't quite a slum; but the houses crowded too close, and potholes and broken lightstrips weren't repaired at once, and the crime rate was high. Renner hadn't wanted to get out of a taxi here. He strolled through the streets, looking for what there was to see.

That sign: THE MAGUEY WORM, on a tall concrete building painted in garish murals. Surely that was where he had fried his brains, night before last? Not that it mattered much. Renner went in.

Midafternoon. Not much of a crowd: four at the bar, two at a big table, all men. Working men, by their look: comfortable, durable clothes. Renner ordered waterwing liqueur and settled back to soak up atmosphere.

There are those who prey on tourists. . . .

But nobody made a move. He might have been invisible.

Renner unwrapped his package. Carefully he filled the bowl of the pipe with tobacco, then lit up.

Staring is a universal insult, and nobody was; but others had become aware of his existence. Renner said aloud, "The old guy was right. That's a terrific smoke." It was true.

"I wouldn't know," the bartender said, and a brawny guy two chairs down said, "Amen." He was wearing several layers of clothing, like the hunters of two nights ago. Geared for cold, wearing it all because it was the easiest way to carry it.

Renner looked disconcerted. "Oops. I should have asked—"

"Smoking's allowed in the Maguey Worm." The bartender jerked his thumb upward, at the high ceiling and slowly turning fans. "Go ahead, it'll give the place a bit of class. I'm told you should be drinking skellish with that, for the taste. Or B and B."

"Pour me a skellish, then, bubble on the side. A round for the house. You, too."

"The house thanks you," the bartender said. "Amen," said six customers, and the house became busy.

One of the hunters raised his glass to Renner. "You were in here—what, two nights ago?"

32

"Wednesday," the bartender said. "We don't get a lot of off-planet trade here." His voice was friendly, but it held a question.

Renner shrugged.

The hunter came over to Renner's table. "Mind? . . . Thanks." He sat and looked pointedly at Renner's pipe. "He sure ain't broke."

Renner grinned. "I got lucky once." The trick is to imply that *anyone* can get lucky. "I'm a rich man's pilot. I can play tourist when I'm on a planet, while Bury busts his ass making more money."

"You want local color, you came to the right place. I'm Ajax Boynton."

"Kevin Renner."

"Sir Kevin," Boynton said. "Saw you on tri-vee. Hey, fellows, we got a celebrity."

Renner grinned. "Pull up a chair. Tell me tall tales." He waved to the bartender, who had politely moved out of earshot. "Another round."

Four more joined him. Two ordered straight orange juice. It cost as much as liquor. They introduced themselves as the Scott brothers, James and Darwin.

"I take it things are slow?" Kevin asked.

"A little," Darwin Scott said. He shrugged massive shoulders. "Snow ghost hunting's a chancy thing. Get a good one and you make money, but you don't always."

"Then what?"

"Then you wait for somebody to stake you," Ajax Boynton said. "You looking to invest some money?"

Renner looked thoughtful. "Truth is, I'd like to own a snow ghost fur and I'd like to shoot it myself. What would it cost me?"

"Five thousand buys a quarter share," Boynton said. "Ten thousand buys forty percent."

"Why—"

"With ten thousand worth of gear we have a better chance of getting a ghost."

"Oh. Plausible."

"Still interested?"

"Sure, if I get to come along."

Boynton looked annoyed. "Hunting ghosts isn't dude work. We lose people."

"You keep saying that. With IR gear, and—"

"And sonar, and the best damn acoustic gear we can come up with," James Scott said. "And we lose people, because it's a long way north. The aurora mucks up electronics. And—"

"And ghosts move fast," his brother said. "They dig in near tree roots, where you can't get a good sonar map. They stay down in the snow so the IR doesn't spot them. And they can swim under snow faster than you can walk. Forget it, Mister."

"Let's see, now. I back you for ten thousand worth of gear, which I leave behind when the ship lifts. A good ghost fur costs . . . what? Straight from you, no retailer."

Darwin Scott said, "I'd get around twenty thousand."

Renner's sources were accurate. "So call it another twenty thousand when I get back, and call that incentive to bring the greenhorn back alive. Total, thirty thousand." They were trying to maintain poker faces, but he surely had their interest. "Just that, and you keep your sixty percent, but I expect you to indulge yet another whim."

Three men sighed. Renner said, "See, I can't think of any reason not to hunt snow ghosts where I might stumble across some opal meerschaum, too."

Three men were hiding smiles. Ajax Boynton said, "Me neither. If you've got a place in mind, I'll tell you if there are snow ghosts there."

"Let's find a map."

4
Snow Ghost

Have you not seen how your Lord lengthens out the shadow?
He could have kept it motionless if he liked.
Yet We make the sun its pilot to show the way.

—al-Qur'an

Is this wise?" Bury sipped at coffee and examined the map projected on the wall. "It will certainly not be comfortable."

Renner shrugged. "I like comfort. But hey, if I can get a snow ghost fur, it'll sure keep me warm enough."

"So will synthetics, and they are much cheaper. Why the area between the glaciers?"

"Oh, Hell, Bury. How do you know Reuben Fox is hiding something but he isn't stealing and can't be bribed? Brains and instinct and technique. It took me all afternoon. We talked. The Scott brothers switched from orange juice to tea . . . the Maguey Worm has a magic coffeepot variation. Gilbey makes a liter of tea and then lets the caffeine filter out through the wall. Takes five minutes."

"More Motie influence."

"Right off of your ships, Horace! Anyway. I pointed at various parts of the map, all of it in the region where the northern lights play, but that's fairly large. Snow ghosts? Yes. No. Maybe. They'd never live here, they've been hunted out there, my brother got one here a year ago."

"I wish you had a fast-forward switch, Kevin."

"By and by, Boynton said he'd heard opal meerschaum came from under the Hand Glacier. The Scott brothers said it didn't, it

35

had been searched by an uncle or something, and besides, the place had been hunted out of snow ghosts twenty years ago. So I went on pointing, and every place I pointed, the Scott brothers thought I might find a snow ghost there."

"Ah."

"There's something in the Hand. The Mormons know about it and Boynton doesn't. For that matter, it might *be* opal meer-schaum. Under the glacier. You wait till the glacier moves; that's why the market's so sporadic."

"Given the geology I would not be surprised, but what is that to you?"

Renner spread his hands. "One hand, it's cold and miserable. Other hand, the source of opal meerschaum is a big secret, and we're looking for secrets. Gripping hand—" Bury suppressed a shudder. "Gripping hand, *they're* interested. What is Horace Bury after? Opal meerschaum? Something else?"

"And you trust your companions, whom you met in a bar—"

"I had Ruth Cohen check on them. Boynton and the Scott brothers are well known, no trouble with the police except that Boynton gets drunk when he has a good hunt. The Maguey Worm is one of half a dozen places where ghost hunters hang out looking for a stake."

"Still—?"

"You have a better lead?"

"I have leads. And a different manner of searching." Bury gestured to indicate his travel chair. "Certainly you are better suited to follow this than I am. Kevin, communications will not be reliable in that area. The crew on *Sinbad* can attempt to keep track of you, but it is not likely they will succeed."

"No guts, no glory." Renner grinned. "Besides, I'll have Boynton and the Scott brothers looking out for me. They each get an extra five thousand if I get back alive. Ten each if I have a snow ghost. What can go wrong?"

The glacier ended in sharp edges bordered in bare rocky ground. The bare spots ranged from a few meters to several kilometers before vanishing into the snow. They flew past a cluster of buildings nestled against the glacier edge. Two buildings stood out, one wide and low, the other taller and more massive. Mist and steam rose from all the clear-ground areas to the thick cloud cover above them, so that it was hard to see the town.

"Zion," Ajax Boynton said.

"Looks interesting," Renner said. Maybe four thousand population, maybe less.

"For us," Darwin Scott said. "That's one of the True Temples. But there won't be any ghosts near there. No opal meerschaum, either."

"Not there," Boynton agreed. "But that stuff's got to be near here somewhere."

"Why?"

"We know the jade comes from here."

"We know people say so," James Scott said. "But I never met anyone who'd found any."

"You have, too," Ajax Boynton said. "Ralph. Ralph . . . hell, I forget. Came to the Maguey and bought for the house."

"Yeah, and the next day bought a ticket for Tabletop," James Scott said. "I'd forgotten him. Okay, so you can get lucky."

"Never did understand that," Boynton said. "Ralph—Plemmons, that was his name. I didn't know him all that well, but I sure never figured him to leave the Purchase." He looked down at the map display on the flier's navigation screen. "Fifteen more klicks south, then twenty east. I know a good place."

Renner studied the rugged ground below. It rolled with hills, mostly covered with thin forest. Those bumbershoot trees needed a lot of room. The area near the glacier was obscured with mist, but away from it the air was clearer. Brush and treetops thrust up through the snow in the clearings. "Just where do you land?" he asked.

"You land on a lake," Darwin Scott said. He touched the light pen to the area Boynton had indicated. The bush plane banked slightly and changed course. "A *shallow* lake."

"Why shallow?" Renner asked.

"Snow ghosts aren't the only things that eat people," James Scott said. "Boynton here lost a partner to a freshwater cecil. You sure this isn't the same lake?"

"Hell, no. I told Brad that lake was too deep," Boynton said.

Fifteen minutes later James Scott took manual control of the plane. He brought it in low and circled a patch that was clear of trees.

All three hunters used binoculars to study the lake. The snow cover was undisturbed. "No blow holes," Boynton said. "Looks okay."

Scott brought the plane in low and let it settle onto the frozen lake. He circled the perimeter several times before he taxied out to the lake's center. "You want to flatten the snow," he said. "All around your camp. Pack it tight."

"Whose partner got eaten in his sack?" Renner asked.

They just looked at him. "Nobody's *that* stupid," Boynton said.

The Scott brothers unfolded the tent and inflated it. It was larger than the flier. Darwin Scott said, "Ajax, are you trying to break the man?"

"Actually, I bought it," Renner said. "It looked comfortable."

Darwin Scott looked at the tent and laughed. His breath made a thick plume in the cold air. "Comfortable. Renner, you're not *supposed* to be comfortable when you hunt snow ghosts."

Renner's pocket calculator beeped softly to indicate that *Sinbad* would be overhead. He held the calculator to his ear, but there was only static. Renner shrugged and spoke into it. "I don't expect anyone to hear me. Nothing to report. We're on snow buggies about thirty klicks from camp, and we haven't seen a thing. There are a lot of caves under the glacier edge. Too many. It would take a year to explore them.

"Nobody cares if we go toward Zion, except Boynton gets disgusted at how candy ass I am wanting to go to a town instead of hunting a ghost. I told him if there was an opal meerschaum source, there had to be people nearby. So I'm looking for a town bigger than it should be.

"But when we start to go much more than forty kilometers south of Zion, the Scott brothers start to twitch. That's where we found that interesting fissure in the Hand Glacier. Could be just my imagination, of course."

Renner put the computer back in the pocket of his parka and gunned the snow buggy to catch up closer to Darwin Scott. The wind was cold on his face. He pulled the parka up tighter around his nose, adjusted the goggles, and wondered if he'd ever be warm again despite the electric heaters in his boots and gloves.

His suspicions were starting to feel silly, and he didn't know why. *Attitude problem. So what if it's a blind alley? Keep smiling, pretend you're having fun. Get yourself a fur. Impress Commander Cohen.*

They drove south for another fifteen minutes, then Scott slowed to a stop. When Renner pulled alongside, Scott took out snowshoes.

"We take it slow from here. And no talking." Scott pointed to the forest edge a kilometer away. "Maybe in there. Good ghost country."

"Wouldn't they hear us coming?"

"They heard," Scott said. "They'll be watching. Most will run away from two guys with rifles. They'd all run from four."

"They can tell we're armed?"

Scott shrugged. "Some say so. I believe it."

"You said most will run."

"A hungry one might not. Now, no talking. They don't like talk. Don't know why."

It took Renner a few minutes to get the hang of snowshoes. These were shorter and wider than skis. Renner learned to walk with a shuffle, using the poles to help push along. James Scott tried to help him, but he couldn't suppress the grin. The weight of the heavy rifle slung on Renner's back was some comfort when they went past a bloody patch of snow strewn with bones. Big bones, larger than a cow's. Or a man's.

Renner thought enviously of Ajax Boynton back in the tent with tea and brandy. Boynton hadn't believed there were any ghosts in this area.

They reached the edge of the woods and Scott gestured Renner off to his left, briskly.

They'd been making good time. *That* was his problem: James and Darwin weren't holding back anymore. Maybe his impression had been wrong. Maybe they'd simply decided to indulge the greenhorn. Maybe they weren't hiding anything at all.

They moved farther into the woods. It was a strange place, dotted with bare-limbed maples from Earth, and bumbershoots, and a tall whippy thing with fuzzy bark that grew twenty meters above the snow, then drooped again, some drooping so far that their tops were beneath the snow. As they moved farther in, the trees were spaced closer, some only three meters apart. Whatever underbrush there might be was buried under snow.

His snowshoes kept trying to plunge through. It would be easy to break a leg.

Darwin Scott stopped at intervals to thrust a long pole into the snow. The top of the pole had meters and a jack for earphones. Darwin listened, then waved them onward.

Snow mounded on underbrush could be snow mounded on a ghost, Renner thought. He'd seen a holoflick of a ghost in action; he knew its shape. But he kept seeing shapes that might be ghosts . . . and he'd point, and James would shake his head and grin.

Four two-chamber hearts the beast had. The explosive bullets were pointed, to do less damage to the fur. A bullet in the torso might kill. One in the head would kill, but would damage the trophy, and the head was harder to hit.

James stopped. Pointed. Darwin nodded vigorously.

The mound was quite shallow. Kevin Renner stared (his gun not raised, not yet), but the shape wouldn't . . . yeah, you could find symmetry there, and if the ground dipped beneath the beast and its legs were folded along the torso . . . then . . . James and Darwin were both aiming at the mound, but they waited. Which end was which? Kevin swung his rifle forward and fired twice into the center of the mound.

The head came up, three feet off the ground on a thick neck. It wobbled, turned to look at him. Kevin's peripheral vision caught both Scott brothers running full out, while Kevin backed away, ready for the charge. Darwin shouted, "Run!"

The beast reared to its feet. Lumbered toward him. Faster than it looked, and Renner turned to run, but the beast's foreleg collapsed and it skidded through the snow. It tried to rise again, and Renner had a clear shot past its shoulder into the torso. He fired again.

The snow ghost stayed down. Its head was up, weaving. Trying to focus its eyes. Then the head dropped into the snow.

They built a frame to hang the beast. James and Darwin skinned it, carefully, while Renner followed his footprints back to the snowmobile. He got back dead tired. The brothers had the beast open and were cleaning out the abdominal cavity. He'd have been interested in the makeup of the alien beast, but the brothers' knives had chewed its innards into unrecognizability.

He rested while the Scotts relayed back for the other vehicles.

It was the last rest he got that day. He helped roll up the fur,

40

bloody side out, and roll plastic around it. They cleaned the carcass and dressed the meat and packed it into two snowmobiles. The roll of fur rode prominently on top of Renner's buggy.

Darwin clapped Renner on the back. "Now we can go back. Good shot, man. Looks like you blew one of the hearts and the hydraulic shock took out the rest."

"I want a long rest in a spa." Renner felt wiped out.

Darwin looked concerned. "Can you drive? We can leave one buggy and come back for it."

"No, I'm all right." There wasn't enough room left in either snow buggy for two people and the remains of the bear. Renner felt pride washing back his fatigue. They hadn't planned on this big a kill!

"You'll get your spa in Zion," Darwin said. "Tomorrow."

"Hey, why so soon? We could take another ghost tomorrow. And I'm still wondering where the opal meerschaum—"

"Mr. Renner, that rug should be treated before it starts to rot. The meat should be *sold* before it rots. You don't hang snow ghost meat, or any other red meat animal native to the Purchase. Has to be eaten fresh."

"Oh."

They covered five or six miles before the snowmobile came back for them. Renner wondered why they hadn't simply camped . . . and didn't ask. Walking was something he did to let his mind get organized; and he'd had a number of interesting thoughts.

Boynton swore at the size of the carcass. "I still don't believe it. This place was hunted five years ago. How would it have time to grow so big?"

The brothers had only grinned and kept working. There was certainly work enough for four. They'd laid a fire; they'd cut wood and built a platform to hang half the carcass over it. The sunset afterlight was dwindling and the cooking meat smelled wonderful, and Renner was going to hurt tomorrow.

It was a matter of pride. You ate the meat when you killed a ghost, they'd told him. You opened cans when you'd failed.

"It feels like I've been diddled, and I don't know how or why," Renner told his pocket computer. No way of knowing if it was getting through. "There should be more to it. But we're going back to Zion tomorrow unless I see some way around it."

41

He closed the computer. He was ravenous. The meat would take another hour to cook through. Would it taste as good as dinner at the palace?

Less well seasoned, maybe, less well cooked, but fresher. And there was the "sauce": exhaustion and hunger. Four men would be hard put to make a dent in that much meat.

That much meat. He flipped the computer open. The ship would be halfway to the horizon, dammit. "The ghost was well fed. Why didn't it attack like the one we watched at the palace? I didn't blow a heart open. It lived too long. It acted . . . drugged. The Scott brothers didn't seem weary enough, either. If I'm not seeing mirages . . . there'd have to be a lot of men involved. This is big."

They collapsed the tent and loaded it with the fur and the snow buggies into the cargo compartment of the plane. The snow ghost meat was lashed to the struts holding the landing skids. Boynton climbed in and sat in the pilot's seat.

"Hey," Darwin Scott said.

"Oh, Hell, I'll fly," Boynton said. "I didn't do anything else to earn my keep. Son of a bitch, I'd never have believed that big a ghost would be in here. Farther south, yeah, but not just here."

"Why didn't we land farther south?" Renner asked.

"Lakes are too big," Boynton said. "Lots of warm streams from the volcanoes. Most lakes don't even freeze, and they're all deep. You want to go down there, you land here and take a long trip on a snow buggy." He spat through the window. "Which I had intended to do. Son of a bitch."

James laughed. "Renner? I wanted to see how you moved before we got into real danger. I didn't expect any snow ghost, not there."

The Scott brothers climbed in. James took the right-hand seat next to Boynton.

"I'm a pilot," Renner said.

"Next time," James Scott said. "This is tricky, with the plane loaded down . . ."

"He's right," Boynton agreed. "You ever fly one of these things? . . . Didn't think so. I'll check you out in Zion. Right now we ought to get that fur somewhere it'll be properly treated. That's a good fur."

Renner strapped in behind James Scott and waited until Boynton had the plane airborne. "Hey, Ajax, take us over the woods where I shot the ghost."

Boynton grinned. "Right. Want to have a look myself."

"We really ought to be getting in," Darwin Scott said.

"Hell, the man wants to see the place," James said. "Would myself. Good shooting, Mr. Renner."

"We'll just circle and go on," Darwin Scott said. "That's a good fur."

"It is that," Boynton agreed.

There had been light snow that night, but Renner could still make out their snow buggy tracks in places. The area where they had stopped was clearly marked, and so were some of their snow-shoe tracks.

"Must have been a lot of wind through here," Boynton muttered.

Renner frowned. Boynton was right. There was very little snow caught in the trees here. In the woods near the lake where they'd landed, there had been a lot more. Here there was less in the trees, more on the ground. Mmm?

"Right down there," James Scott said. "Here, I'll take it a moment." The plane banked and turned in a tight spiral so that Renner could see down to the scene of his triumph.

Boynton was on the high side of the plane. He craned up and looked off to the left. "What the hell . . . ?"

"What?" Renner demanded. He craned past Boynton.

"Tracks?"

South of the forest the snow looked chewed. Snowmobile tires, men's footprints, the blurred circle where a helicopter must have come down and taken off. A hell of a lot of activity. Renner said, "Okay, take us—"

Darwin Scott drove his elbow into Renner's stomach. Renner gasped, and a sickly sweet smell filled his lungs. He sat back with a sappy grin on his face. "Peace . . . Sam," he said.

"What the hell?" Boynton demanded.

"Gentile friend, you have seen nothing," Darwin Scott said.

"Gentile. Church business?"

"He is not a gentile," James Scott said. "Lapsed, but he was born to the Church."

"I must think on this," Darwin said.

A part of Renner's mind told him that Boynton was acting strangely, and so were the Scotts, but he didn't really care. When

43

the plane banked slightly so that his head rolled, he saw that Darwin was holding a pistol. Renner giggled.

"Use the spray," James Scott said. "I have the controls."

"Hey, I don't want to be no giggling idiot," Boynton said. "Look, if this is Church business—hell, give me the skin and my share of the gear, and it's quits for me. I'll say we got a ghost, and the dude wanted to hunt some more, so we split up. You took the dude off to a place you didn't want me to know about. After that it's up to you."

"It would even be true," Darwin Scott said. "We must think on this."

"While you're thinking, where the hell are we going?" Boynton demanded.

"Outside Zion there is a small lake," Darwin Scott said. "Land on that."

5
The True Church

Come, come, ye Saints, no toil or labor fear; but with joy wend your
*   way;*
Though hard to you this journey may appear, Grace shall be as
*   your day.*
'Tis far better for us to strive, Our useless cares from us to drive;
Do this, and joy your hearts will swell—All is well, all is well!

—Hymns of the Church of Jesus Christ of the Latter Day Saints

A tiny red light danced in Ruth Cohen's eyes, then the massive
door opened before she could touch the bell. The butler was
dressed in a traditional manner. Ruth hadn't seen anyone in
that costume except in Government House and tri-vee shows.
"Welcome, Commander. His Excellency has been expecting
you."

Ruth glanced down at her best civilian dress and grinned wryly.

The butler took her overcoat and handed it to another servant.
"His Excellency is in the library," he said, and ushered her down
the hall.

Bury was in his travel chair, not at the desk but at an elaborately
inlaid game table. "You will forgive me if I do not stand? Thank
you. Would you care for a drink? We have an excellent Madeira.
Not from Earth, I fear, but from Santiago, which many say is not
greatly inferior."

"I would really prefer coffee."

Bury smiled. "Turkish or filtre? . . . Filtre. Cynthia, the Kona, I
believe. And my usual. Thank you." Bury indicated a chair.
"Please be seated, Commander. Thank you."

Ruth smiled. "Your hospitality is a bit overwhelming."

Bury's expression didn't change. "Thank you, but I am certain that a vice admiral's daughter has seen better. Now, what can I do for you?"

Ruth looked pointedly around the paneled room.

Bury grinned mirthlessly. "If anyone can listen to me without my knowledge and consent, some very expensive experts will regret it."

"I suppose. Your Excellency, Kevin—Sir Kevin invited me to dinner. Now I'm probably not the first girl he ever stood up, but there's a matter of his reports as well. And when I called here, no one seemed to know where he was." She shrugged. "So I came looking."

Bury's lips twitched. "And I presume you have left messages with the Imperial Marines in case you also vanish?"

Ruth blushed slightly.

Bury laughed. "Renner said you were clever. The truth is, Commander, I was about to call you. I don't know where he is either."

"Oh."

"You put a very great deal of expression into that syllable. You are fond of my—impetuous—pilot?"

"I don't have to say."

"Indeed."

"And he was supposed to make reports—"

"I have them. Recorded," Bury said. "Renner concocted a scheme for exploring the outback with three snow ghost hunters. He was suspicious of two. They left three days ago. I have received no coherent message since."

"You have a ship in orbit."

"Indeed, and Renner's pocket computer was programmed to remind him of the times when *Sinbad* would be above the area in which they would be hunting. At least once we received garbled signals that we assume were from Renner."

"You didn't go look for him?"

Bury indicated his travel chair. "That is hardly my way. What I did was invite Captain Fox to dinner."

"Have you learned anything else about our . . . problem?"

"A great deal, but nothing about Renner," Bury said.

Renner was glad of the blindfold. A blindfold could mean they didn't intend to kill him. On the other hand, it might mean that they wanted him to think that.

On the gripping hand: the snow ghost. They'd made massive efforts to keep him alive up to now.

His mind was clearing; the drug had worn off to that extent. But he couldn't walk.

He was strapped to a gurney and carried from the lake where they landed to a closed vehicle. The only time anyone spoke to him was when he tried to ask where he was. Then a voice he hadn't heard before said, "We understand that two doses of Peaceable Sam within a few hours produces a terrible hangover. You'd best be quiet." He decided that was good advice and concentrated on remembering everything he could.

The snow tractor drove for about ten minutes, then he was outside briefly. They went in, and down in an elevator, and presently he felt smooth acceleration.

Subway train? They're really organized. He had about decided he was wrong when he felt deceleration and heard the sounds of electrically operated doors. Someone started to speak and was shushed.

They carried him to another elevator, which went down a long way, then he was rolled down a long corridor with only gentle turns, then to another elevator, and after that he was maneuvered around often enough that he lost all sense of direction.

"So," a new voice said. "Let us see what you have brought us. Remove the blindfold and straps."

Renner blinked. The room was large, and completely enclosed, doors but no windows. He was at one end of a long conference table. They indicated a chair and helped him sit in it. His legs still didn't want to do what he told them to.

Four men sat at the other end of the table. Bright light glared past them into Renner's face so that he could see them only in outline.

The Scott brothers stood next to him. One held a spray can. The other had a pistol.

They'd dressed him in someone else's clothes and removed

47

everything he'd been carrying. Renner felt for the alarm tooth and bit it.

There was a chuckle from the end of the table. "If you have a transmitter that can send a message from here, I will buy it from you no matter what it costs."

"One hundred thousand crowns," Renner said.

"I appreciate humor, but perhaps we are short of time. Have you anything serious to say before we fill you with Serconal?"

"You've been busting your asses to keep me alive. You had to find a decent snow ghost, herd him north into the forest, wait till he killed something, drug him, hover over the trees on a helicopter to shake the snow down to cover him up . . . Twenty or thirty men, a dozen snow buggies, and a helicopter. Indeed, I'm honored."

"What do you think you've found, Mr. Renner?"

"Better you should ask, 'What does Horace Bury think we've found?' Me, I thought it was more piracy. Then again, you go to too much trouble; it can't be cost-effective. Religious motives. I'm feeling a little light-headed."

"I expect you are. Mister Scott . . ."

Darwin Scott took a bottle of scotch from Renner's pack and set it on the table with a glass. "They tell me this stuff helps."

Renner poured a hefty shot and drank half of it. "Thanks. Coffee does it even better. What do I call you?"

"Ah—Mister Elder will do."

Renner tried to grin. "Like I said, religious motives. You understand I thought this out last night after I realized the ghost was drugged. I still don't understand all that. You'd have done better just to leave things alone. Bury never cared about your opal meerschaum, and nobody's actually robbing anyone."

Mister Elder's shadow shifted restlessly. "It's a problem. Many of my people do not feel they earn credit in Heaven by doing nothing. You still have not said what you suspect."

"I think you've got a periodic Jump point to New Utah."

The men looked at each other.

"There's an old description of New Utah system. A good yellow star, and a neutron star companion in an eccentric orbit. New Utah must have had billions of years to build up an oxygen atmosphere after the supernova. The neutron star hasn't been a pulsar for at least that long."

Renner's head felt clearer. Coffee would have been better, but the drink had helped . . . and he'd had time to think last night. He said, "For most of a twenty-one-year cycle, the neutron star is way out beyond the comets. Quiet. Dark. When it dips close to the major sun, solar wind and meteors rain down through that godawful gravity field. It flares. The Jump points depend on electromagnetic output. You get a Jump point link that lasts maybe two years. That's when you import opal meerschaum, among other—"

"Enough. It bothers me to be so transparent, Renner, but this is a very old secret. The soil isn't right on New Utah. The True Church would die without periodic fertilizer shipments."

Renner nodded. "But the gripping hand is Bury. He thinks you're dealing with Moties. If he goes on thinking that . . . Bury's crazy. He'll drop an asteroid on you and explain to the Navy later."

"An asteroid!"

"Yeah, he thinks that way. Maybe he'll decide that takes too long and just use a fusion bomb. Whatever he does, it'll be drastic. Then he could clean up New Utah without interference, without the Navy ever knowing."

"He has abducted Captain Fox," Elder said.

"If Fox knows where I am, Bury will know."

"He does not. But—"

"But he does know where your Jump ships hang out," Renner said. "You've got a problem. Maybe I can help."

"How?"

Renner looked pointedly around the room. "As you said, it's an old secret. I'm surprised you kept it this long."

"There have been few with Horace Bury's resources seeking it."

"Resources, brains, and paranoia," Renner said. "I guarantee you he won't believe anything you can tell him about what happened to me. Doesn't matter who tells him, either. If I don't get back, he'll think Moties were involved, and he'll know just where to look. I take it I'm under the Hand Glacier? You've got a spaceport around here. A secret one. Bury'll find it."

"Is there anything you do not know?"

"Come on, it all fits once you get the key part about New Utah." Renner hesitated. "Then again, I don't truly know that you aren't

49

dealing with Moties. If you're doing that, you've betrayed the human race, and you *should* be nuked."

Slowly Mister Elder said, "How can we persuade you?"

"Easy. We'll clear that up in a couple of hours. I'll tell you then. Meanwhile, let's think about talking Bury out of whatever mischief he's planning. I'd better do that pretty quick."

"And after that?"

"Then we talk to the Governor. Look, right now you haven't done anything to get you in that much trouble."

"Only enough to be hanged for high treason."

"Technically," Renner agreed. "But if they hanged everyone who trades with relatives on Outie worlds, they'd run out of rope. The only people killed so far were yours."

"This is madness." A voice with a whine in it. "Elders, brothers, this man knows *everything*. We can't just let him go."

"Better what I know than what Bury suspects," Renner said. "Understand something. His Excellency will make *sure*, I mean really sure, that there aren't any Moties involved. Once he's done that, he'll be so relieved, it won't be hard to get him to talk to the Governor.

"What's the Governor got against you? A little trading with Outies. Nothing serious. Jackson will be glad of a chance to convince the Church that the Empire's no real threat. He's been looking for someone to negotiate with. And look, if New Utah is dying for lack of *fertilizer*, they *should* be in the Empire. We'll make them another offer while the Jump point's still open."

The leading Elder stood. "This must be discussed. Is there anything else you need?"

"Yeah. There's some coffee in my backpack." Renner got to his feet. He tried rotating his hips, a standard back exercise. He didn't fall down. "I seem to be recovered. Now, you've been wary of launching your ship while Bury's on the Purchase. Correct?"

"Yes."

"Take me to it. Show me that ship, no arguments, no phone calls, take me there *now*. *All* of you."

"I didn't give them time to fool with the ship. They couldn't have done much anyway. They led me right to it. I saw everything, outside and in. There's nothing of Watchmaker manufacture. Horace, I know the Motie touch! There's no mistaking their hand.

50

They make one widget do two or three jobs at once, they don't know from right angles, you remember.''

Bury was silent, head bowed, eyes hooded in shadow.

"I found two variants on the Motie coffeepot. One takes the caffeine out of tea. The other must have been added in the last month, the joins are still new. It filters the hydrogen fuel. There's a layer of Motie superconductor under the reentry shield. All three carried the Imperial Autonetics logo.''

Ruth Cohen was perched at the edge of her chair. "They took you there right away?''

"I damn well made them. Three different elevators, but I took the whole entourage with me. They cooperated. I'm as sure as can be that they didn't phone ahead. Mister Elder had to threaten the guards with damnation when we got there, and then they made calls while I inspected the outside, but I was inside within five minutes. Bury?''

Bury's head came up. "Yes?''

"Do I have your attention? I wasn't sure. Look, if you had access to Watchmakers and Engineers, and you—''

"I'd kill them. You know that.'' There was no force behind his words. He looked old, old.

"Assume, just assume that they're allies. Pretend you trust them. Wouldn't you set them loose on a ground-to-orbit ship? A little improvement in a space shuttle can double the cargo capacity! For a smuggler, that's golden! But it was an old ship, refurbished, and the engineering was entirely human and not very good at that.

"These people are not in contact with Moties, Mr. Bury.''

Bury didn't move.

Ruth Cohen used the stylus to make notes on the face of her pocket computer. "Kevin, I believe you, but we still have to be sure.''

"You'll take care of that,'' Renner said. "They've got a ship on station at that wavering Jump point. Send a small ship with a couple of Navy people to inspect that ship. Go yourself. When they signal that it's clean, we talk to the Governor.''

"It will work,'' Ruth said. "Governor Jackson would look very good if he could persuade New Utah to come into the Empire without a fight, and this might just do it. Fertilizer! Well, they're not the first world to have a soil problem.

51

"All right. Between the regulations about Moties and your reputation, we won't have any trouble getting Captain Torgeson to send a scout ship out to the Jump point. One of the local Church people ought to go, so there won't be a fight."

"Ohran," Renner said. "The one who called himself Mr. Elder is a high-ranking bishop named Ohran. Send him." Renner poured himself a brandy. "And that takes care of that. Mr. Bury—damn it, Horace!"

Only Horace Bury's sunken dark eyes moved. They burned. "They're not here *now*. They're still corked up behind the blockade for *now*. For a quarter of a century I have left it to the Navy to keep them that way. Kevin, I've remembered too much. I've always known how dangerous they are. I manage not to think about it unless I'm asleep. Kevin, we must visit the blockade fleet."

"What? At Murcheson's Eye?"

"Yes. I need to *know* that the Navy is on duty. Else I will go mad."

Ruth Cohen spoke. "Your Excellency, your dossier indicates that your . . . that the Secret Service may take exception to your plans."

Bury grinned. "Let them hang me, then. No, I don't mean that, and of course you're right. I'll have to be persuasive in a number of places. We'll have to go to Sparta."

"Sparta." Ruth Cohen sighed. "I'd like to see Sparta someday."

"Come with us," Renner said.

"What? Kevin, I'm assigned here."

"We can get those orders changed. I can requisition people at need."

"What need?" she asked suspiciously.

"Well . . ."

"I thought so."

"Actually there is a very good reason," Bury said. "Kevin, you propose to convince the Governor to condone high treason. I do not doubt your ability to justify that on Sparta, but it will do no harm to have another Navy officer confirm our story." Bury drained his coffee. "So. Commander, if you will see to the investigation of the ship at the Jump point, Nabil will make *Sinbad* ready for the voyage."

"That'll give me some time," Renner said. "I'm going back to the spill."

"Surely we have better wines and whiskeys here." Bury glanced significantly at Ruth Cohen. "And better companionship as well."

"Oh, easily. But that miserable wimp Boynton still has my snow ghost fur. I'm going down to the Maguey Worm and take it back."

PART 2
SPARTA

Treason doth never prosper: what's the reason?
For if it prosper, none dare call it treason.

—*Sir John Harington*

1
Capital City

For forms of government let fools contest;
Whate're is best administered is best.

> —Alexander Pope, "Epistle III, Of the Nature and
> State of Man with Respect to Society"

A.D. 3046   Imperial University

The Imperial University was founded in CoDominium times as the University of Sparta and enjoyed close ties to several Earth institutions including the University of Chicago, Stanford University, Columbia, Westinghouse Institute, and the University of Cambridge. In exchange for the privilege of appointing a majority of the regents, the first kings of Sparta endowed the University of Sparta with extensive lands in the hill regions south and east of the capital. Much of that land was subsequently leased to commercial institutions, so that the University enjoys a large income not under political control. The name was changed to Imperial University during the early years of the First Empire.

The capital has also expanded to engulf lands previously granted to the aristocracy, some of whom retain estates now surrounded by city buildings.

The study at Blaine Manor looked like what the designer had imagined were the rooms of an Oxford don in the nineteenth century. The furniture was leather and dark wood. Holograms of

books lined the seven-meter walls, and a rolling ladder stood in one corner. Roderick, Lord Blaine, Earl of Acrux, DSC, GCMG, Captain ISN (Ret.), frowned at it as he went past. Nobody ever used it except to maintain the hologram generators. He'd sworn a dozen times to have the place redecorated to something more functional, but so far nothing that appealed to him was satisfactory to Sally, and it did show images of real books in his library. As usual he looked over some of the titles. Macaulay's *History of England* stood next to Gibbon. Crofton's *Guide to the CoDominium*. Savage's classic *Lysander the Great. Ought to read that one again. . . .*

Blaine crossed the study and went into the small office off to one side. "I thought I heard a door slam."

Sally Blaine looked up from the computer. "Glenda Ruth."

"Another fight?"

"Let's just say our daughter is not entirely happy with the rules at Blaine Manor."

"Independent sort. Reminds me of someone I used to know."

"*Used* to know? Thank you."

Rod grinned and put a hand on her shoulder. "Still do. You know what I mean."

"I suppose—you didn't come in here to talk about Glenda Ruth."

"No, but maybe I ought to have a word with her."

"I wish you would, but you never do. What's up?"

"Got a message. Guess who's coming to visit?"

Sally Blaine looked back at the computer screen and scowled. "Thank you very much. I've just managed to straighten out our social schedule. Who?"

"His Excellency Horace Hussein al-Shamlan Bury, Magnate. And Kevin Renner."

Sally thought. "It'd be nice to see Mr. Renner again. And . . . Bury comes with him, I seem to remember. Watchdog. I suppose—"

"I won't have Bury in our home. He was one of the instigators of the New Chicago revolt."

Lady Blaine froze.

He squeezed her shoulder. "Sorry."

"I'm all right." She patted his hand, then ran fingertips up into the loose sleeve of his dressing gown. Smooth, ridged, hairless. "Your scars are real."

58

"You spent weeks in a prison camp, and you lost your friend."

"It was a long time ago, Rod. I can't even remember Dorothy's face. Rod, I'm glad you didn't tell me then. Nine months on *MacArthur* with Horace Bury. I'd have spit in his face."

"No, you wouldn't. You won't now. I know you. I suppose we'll have to see him, but we'll keep it to a minimum. I gather Bury's done some good work for the Secret Service."

"Let me think about it. At the worst we can take them to dinner. Someplace neutral. I *do* want to see . . . Sir Kevin?"

"Right again, I'd forgotten. I want to see him, too." Blaine smiled. "For that matter, so will Bruno Cziller. I better tell him his crazy navigator is in town. Tell you what, love. Since the news came through the Institute, I'll invite them to the Institute. They may regret that. Everyone and his dog will want to interview them."

When Sally turned around, she was smiling broadly. "Yes, the Institute. We have a surprise for His Excellency, don't we?"

"What—hey! He'll think he's back in *MacArthur*. We'll test out his bioheart!"

WARNING

You have entered the controlled zone of the Imperial capital.

It is strictly forbidden to remain in this star system without permission. Notify the Navy ships on patrol at the Alderson entry points and follow instructions. The Navy is authorized to use deadly force against uncooperative intruders.

Transmit your identification codes immediately

YOU WILL RECEIVE NO FURTHER WARNING MESSAGES

Cruising through Sparta system could make a man nervous.

The sky was no different, except in that all skies are different. Stars formed new patterns. The little K0 star Agamemnon was a bright white flare growing to become a sun. The companion star Menalaus was a fat red spark. Asteroids sparkled well below *Sinbad's* path, and then tiny crescents that showed as ringed and banded gas giants in the screens.

That was how star travel was. Cruise outward, find the Jump point, Jump across interstellar distance in a wink. Blast across space to the next Jump point. Then cruise inward through the new system, new planets, toward a new world with different climate, customs, attitudes . . .

But Sparta was the capital of the Empire of Man.

The black sky was as peaceful as it would have been anywhere; but there were voices. Alter course. Increase deceleration. Watch your exhaust vector, *Sinbad!* Warning. Identify. Those gas giants, so peculiarly and conveniently close to Sparta's orbit with their massive atmospheres of spacecraft fuel and industrial chemicals, were surrounded by great naval installations massively guarded. Ships guarded the score of Jump points that led everywhere in the Empire. Eyes watched *Sinbad* as Renner brought the yacht inward.

Renner maintained his cool as best he could. His image was at stake . . . and Ruth was having a wonderful time, but Bury needed calming. Horace Bury didn't like being watched, particularly by weapons that could tear the skin off a continent.

Sparta was white on blue, the colors of a nearly typical water world. Renner glimpsed the curled shape of Serpens, the mainland; the rest was one tremendous ocean with a few dots of island. The planet's near vicinity swarmed with ships and orbital junk, growing thicker in geosynchronous orbit.

Customs kept changing Renner's path to avoid collisions as he moved inward. He didn't see much of what he was avoiding, though he did come in view of a tremendous wheel-shaped space station. Most of this was military stuff, he thought. Most incoming ships had to park on the moon; but Customs knew Horace Bury.

They knew him well, and not as an agent of the Secret Service. They were beginning their search of *Sinbad* as Renner took the shuttle out of its bay and started his descent.

It was his first sight of Sparta, and Ruth's, too. They watched avidly as the world came close.

Water. Sparta seemed all ocean, what he could see through the clouds. The shuttle moved into darkness and he saw only a smooth black curve.

Then: rough edges on the horizon. Then: lights. Islands, myriads of them, all tiny, all glowing; and a shape like a coiled snake on fire. Sparta was tectonically active, but lava had boiled up preferentially on this limb of the planet. Serpens, the Australiasized mainland, had one terrific harbor: the land was stretched into a mountainous rugged helix. Mountain ridges were dark patches in the luminescence. Farmland was rectangular patterns of tiny lights. There was a lot of it. Cityscape blazed; there was a lot of city, too. Even the water crawled with tiny moving lights.

The capital of an interstellar Empire was bound to be crowded.

He steered wide of Serpens, circling the coast as he shed speed. The radio was quacking at him; he tried not to say anything amusing. He'd never found a Customs officer with a sense of humor, not on any world.

He was low enough to see phosphorescent wakes behind some of the hundreds of ships. There were barges floating on the water, houses and bigger habitats. Population: 500 million, most of it gathered in this one spot. It struck Renner that if he flew a sonic boom straight across the mainland, Bury would be wiped out by the fines.

"Horace? How are you doing?"

"Fine, Kevin, fine. You're a good pilot."

Bury had been affable with Customs, but when they hung up, Renner had heard esoteric cursing. Now he asked, "What did Customs do to get you so upset?"

"Nothing. You know where to land?"

"They're telling me yet again. Black water, just ahead of us. We'll come down outside the harbor and spiral in like a big boat. I wonder where they'd put me down on a rough day."

Bury said nothing for a bit. Then, "On Sparta I am a second-class citizen. Only here, but forever. Department-store clerks will serve me, and I can bribe a headwaiter and hire my own car. But there are parts of Sparta I may never see, and on the slidewalks . . ."

"You're getting mad before anyone's insulted you. Oh, well, why wait till the last minute?"

"I've been to Sparta before. *Why in Allah's Merciful Name couldn't Cunningham see me today?*"

"Maybe he thinks he's giving you a day's rest."

"He's making me wait. Damn him. My superior. Bless you for not using that word, Ruth, but I knew what you were thinking."

Ruth said, "It's a technical term."

"Of course."

— — —

61

On Serpens the flat land had been occupied long ago, as farmland or baronial estates. New buildings such as the Imperial Plaza Hotel tended to cling to the sides of cliffs. The Plaza stood eighty stories tall on the low side, sixty-six on the high.

Bury's agent had rented the lowest of the suites, the seventy-first floor. It had been fully furnished, and servants were in residence; but only two were awake when they arrived.

Through the picture wall they could see a vastness of sea and islands and a hundred shapes of boats and ships, and Sparta's gross red sun easing clear of the water. It was five in the morning of a twenty-hour day. By ship's time it was close to noon. "I feel like a serious breakfast," Renner said. "Coffee. Real cream, not protocarb milk. Restaurant probably isn't open, though."

Bury smiled. "Nabil—"

The kitchen staff had to be awakened. Breakfast took over an hour to appear, while they emptied their suitcases and settled in. Lots of luggage. No telling how long they would be on Sparta. How persuasive would Bury need to be?

Maniac. But was he wrong? It might be *vital* that a Master Trader send himself to inspect the Crazy Eddie Fleet on patrol at Murcheson's Eye. But if the Secret Service wanted something else from him . . . well, they had something on Bury. Probably something political.

They'd all learn tomorrow.

"Every little boy and girl wants to see Sparta," Renner told Ruth. "What do we want to see first?"

Bury said, "The Institute doesn't open until noon. We'll have four hours to play in, I think. I expect I'll drop in at the Traders Guild and make some waves. Ah, here's Nabil."

Breakfast featured two species of eggs and four varieties of sausage and two liters of milk. The fruits all looked familiar. So did the eggs: chicken and quail. Life on Sparta (Renner now remembered reading) had never really conquered the land. There wasn't enough land to make it cost-effective. The planet had been seeded with a variety of Terran wildlife, and an ecology established itself with little native competition.

"They eat two meals on Sparta, breakfast and dinner. We should eat our fill," Bury told them.

"The milk's a little odd," Ruth said.

"Different cows eating different grass. Mark of authenticity,

Ruth. Protocarb milk always tastes the same, every ship in the universe."

"Honestly, Kevin, I *like* protocarb milk."

The coffeepot was tall and bulbous. Bury looked underneath it. "Wideawake Enterprise," he said.

"You don't sound happy about it," Ruth Cohen said.

"Motie technology," Renner said. "Probably common here."

"Very common here," Bury said. "Nabil, do we have a computer?"

"Yes, Excellency. The call name is Horvendile."

"Horvendile, this is Bury."

"Confirm," a contralto voice said from the ceiling.

"Horvendile, this is His Excellency Bury," Nabil said.

"Accepted. Welcome to the Imperial Plaza, Your Excellency."

"Horvendile, phone Jacob Buckman, astronomer, associated with the University."

A moment passed. Then a somewhat waspish voice said, "This is Jacob Buckman's auxiliary brain. Dr. Buckman is asleep. Your Excellency, he thanks you for the gifts. Is there sufficient urgency to wake him?"

"No. I am at the Imperial Plaza and will be on Sparta for a week. I would like an appointment when convenient. Social hours."

"Dr. Buckman has meetings Wednesday afternoon and evening, and nothing else."

"I suggest Thursday afternoon and dinner Thursday night."

"I will tell him. Do you wish to record a message?"

"Yes. Jacob, I'd like to see you before one of us dies of old age and sloppy medical techniques. I told your machine Thursday, but any time will do. Message ends."

"Is there anything else?" Buckman's voice asked.

"Thank you, no."

"I will inform Horvendile when the appointment is confirmed. Good day."

"Horvendile."

"Your Excellency."

"Appointment with Dr. Jacob Buckman at his convenience, highest social priority."

"Acknowledged."

"Thank you, Horvendile. Now get me an appointment with the president of the Traders Guild."

The contralto voice said, "That is His Excellency Benjamin

Sergei Sachs, chairman of Union Express. When did you wish to see him?"

"As soon as possible."

There was a pause. "His computer reports this morning is free. Shall I ask for an immediate appointment?"

"Yes, Horvendile." Bury sipped coffee. "Where will you go?"

Renner shrugged. "Doubtless we'll think of something. Are you sure you'll be able to see the president of the ITA on such short notice?"

Bury's smile was thin. "Kevin, I control seven seats on the board. Not a majority, but more than enough to veto a candidate for president. Yes, I think Ben Sachs will see me."

"His Excellency will be delighted to see you at any time, Your Excellency," the ceiling said. "If you wish, he will send a limousine."

"Please ask him to do so. Thank you, Horvendile."

* * *

The exterior facade of the clubrooms of the Imperial Traders Association alternated phases of opulent ostentation and quiet elegance. It had recently been redecorated in plain white marble. The severe lines extended into the lobby, but beyond the Members' door were the familiar walnut-paneled walls and original oil paintings Bury remembered from the last time he was there.

The President was waiting for him in a private conference room and stood when Bury drove his travel chair into the room. He was a large man, impeccably dressed in a dark tunic and matching trousers. A yellow sash broke the monotony of colors. "Excellency. Good to see you. All well, I take it?"

"Yes, thank you, Your Excellency. And yourself? . . . Splendid." Bury indicated his travel chair. "Sparta gravity."

"Of course. Some days I wouldn't mind getting around in a travel chair myself. What can I do for you, Excellency?"

"Thank you, nothing. I have only come to see my colleagues and enjoy my club."

"I'm glad you can find the time. But if there is anything at all we can do . . ."

"Well, perhaps there is a small favor you could do for me."

"Your Excellency has only to name it."

64

"How well do we get along with the government this year?"

Sachs shrugged. "Probably as well as we ever do. Of course they will never love us."

"It may be that you could help me. I wish to visit the blockade fleet off Murcheson's Eye."

Sachs's eyes widened. "The Navy has never been fond of us."

Bury snorted. "They hate us."

"Many do."

"I hope to persuade the Navy," Bury said. "What I must be sure of is expeditious service from the bureaucracy when I need the formal documents."

Sachs grinned broadly. Clearly he had been expecting a more difficult task. "Ah. That should be no problem. Your Excellency, I think you should meet the Honorable George Hoskins, our Vice President for Public Affairs."

"George Hoskins. Of Wideawake Enterprises?"

"Yes, Excellency." Sachs looked thoughtful. "His company does compete with yours, but then nearly everyone does! Have you met him?"

"I never had the pleasure."

"Then I must introduce you. I will send for him."

Bury touched the keys of the shorthand ball built into his travel chair. After a moment a voice spoke quietly in his ear:

"Wideawake Enterprises. Founded in 3021 by George Hoskins (now the Honorable George Hoskins, PC), formerly of New Winchester. The company's first product was a coffee-filtering system based on Motie technology. Imperial Autonetics asked for an injunction prohibiting sale of the Wideawake Coffeepot on the grounds that IA had exclusive license to exploit Motie technology, but this was rejected by the Imperial Court of Appeals on the grounds that all Motie technology had been obtained by the Navy, and any unclassified knowledge was therefore public domain.

"IA investigation revealed that Hoskins had a brother-in-law aboard INSS *Hadley* at the time that the ship's coffee-making system disappeared, and that the redesign which made the coffeepot easier to reproduce was primarily the work of Harvey Lavrenty, married to Hoskins's daughter Miriam.

"Aggressive marketing combined with a readiness of the civilian economy to accept the Wideawake Coffee System resulted in unprecedented sales and—"

Bury switched off the voice. He remembered the rest. Two years and a million crowns to master the secrets of the magic coffeepot. Nearly 50 million to expand and reconvert factories. The Navy had bought coffeepots as fast as Imperial Autonetics could make them and paid well; but the real money would have been in selling to civilians. Then Hoskins and Wideawake burst on the scene.

Imperial Autonetics had done Hoskins's advertising for him. Civilians had been hearing about the Navy's magic coffeepots for two years. IA remained second in sales to this day.

Bury said, "I look forward to meeting the Honorable Mister Hoskins with great pleasure."

The Honorable George Hoskins was a round, cheerful man, expensively dressed. He had a wide smile and a handshake of great enthusiasm. After introductions, Sachs excused himself and left them in the conference room.

Hoskins bubbled. "You're a legend, you know, throughout the Empire. Can I get you coffee?" A wide-open face that showed every thought, and guilt was not there. A man who never remembered a crime. Horace Bury at least knew when he had something to hide!

"Thank you. I'll serve myself," Bury said. "Would you care for some waterwing liqueur?"

"Here?"

"I had a case sent over." Wherever *Sinbad* set down, Bury would buy several cases of something distinctive. They made easy gifts.

There had been a time when Turkish coffee wasn't available at the ITA, but that was before Bury controlled seven seats on the board. Now there were three varieties. Bury chose a Mocha-Sumatra mix and sipped while Sachs perched at the edge of a massage chair.

"I'd give half my fortune to visit Mote Prime," he said. "What's it really like?"

Bury had heard that question too often. "Light gravity. Sunset all the time, from the red sun in daytime and Murcheson's Eye at night. The air is slow poison, but masks were all we needed. Architecture straight out of nightmares, and nightmare shapes moving through it. I was frightened all the time, and you know, they did murder three midshipmen who strayed out of open territory through no fault of their own."

"I know. Still, we should go back. What they could teach us!"

Hoskins was among the most enthusiastic supporters of that faction, the Traders who wanted open contact with the Mote. Small wonder. Still—could he be talked around?

"You made your fortune in Motie technology, Mister Hoskins. You counted coup on me, in fact. Has it crossed your mind that someone might take new Motie technology and do the same to you? Some Motie entrepreneur?"

Hoskins chuckled. "Oh, Excellency, how would they—*Motie* entrepreneurs?"

"You have read of the Motie Mediators? They are assigned to study important visitors. Study is not strong enough. They learn everything they can, until they *think* like the subject of their attentions.

"One was assigned to me."

Hoskins had been listening with a puzzled expression. Now it changed to alarm. "There will be Moties who think the way you do?"

"It seems likely. Worse, from your view. They will think the way I did in those times, when I was younger and more aggressive." He did not add that his Fyunch(click) was certainly dead by now.

"It's tough enough competing with you," Hoskins said. "A Motie who thinks like you and has Motie technology would be—formidable."

Bury smiled in satisfaction. "I hoped you might see it that way. Now there is another matter. What are the disturbing rumors I hear concerning the Blockade Fleet's budget?"

Hoskins shrugged. "Certainly many of the stories we have heard about waste and inefficiency were not rumors. Have you seen the series by Alysia Joyce Mei-Ling Trujillo in the *Capital Update?*"

"Summaries."

"Ms. Trujillo has found corruption, inefficiency, waste—more than enough to justify an investigation."

"You want to cut the Blockade Fleet budget?" Bury asked.

"Certainly. When did we ever support larger appropriations for the Navy?"

When we run into Outies. When our trade ships are threatened by pirates. "I see. This is serious, then."

"Serious enough that they're sending a new Viceroy to New Caledonia," Hoskins said. "Baron Sir Andrew Calvin Mercer. Do you know him?"

"No."

"Sorry, of course you wouldn't. He spent most of his time in the Old Earth sector. Would you like to meet him? He's introducing our guest speaker at the dinner tonight. I can arrange to have you at the head table if you like."

Tonight? And the University this afternoon. A busy day, but this was urgent. "I would be honored," Bury said.

Bury settled into the limousine.

"Imperial Plaza to collect Sir Kevin Renner," he told the driver. "Then to the Blaine Institute."

"Yes, sir."

The limousine's bar held local liquors, rum, and vodka, and a Mote-technology thermos of coffee made by Nabil before Bury left, but he selected a bulb of fruit juices. A bottle of evil-tasting tonic rested beside the thermos. Bury poured a shot glass full and drank with a grimace, then killed the taste with fruit juice.

A small price to pay for a clear head and good memory at my age. He reached for his shorthand ball and let his fingers play over the keys. He had mastered the modern practice of conversing with computers, but he often preferred keyboards. They made the machines seem less human. He liked that.

"Sir Andrew Mercer, Baron Calvin," the computer said into his ear. "Distantly related to the Imperial family on his mother's side. Widower. Two children. Lieutenant Commander the Honorable Andrew Calvin Mercer, Jr., serves aboard INSS *Terrible*. Dr. Jeana Calvin Ramirez is Associate Professor of History at Undine University on Tanith.

"Appointed a junior officer in the Department of Commonwealth Affairs upon graduation from New Harvard University in 3014 and has remained continuously in the civil service from then to present. Inducted as a Commander of the Imperial Order, 3028; Knight of St. Michael and St. George, 3033. Succeeded to status of civil baron on the death of his father in 3038.

"Series of staff offices until appointed Lieutenant Governor of

Franklin in 3026. When the Governor was killed in an Outie attack, Mercer became Acting Governor and was confirmed in post of Governor in 3027. Rapid promotions thereafter. Was Chief of Mission with rank of Ambassador in the negotiations leading to the reincorporation of New Washington in 3037. Privy Counselor after 3038. Secretary of State for Trans–Coal Sack Affairs, 3039 to present. Member of board of directors, Blaine Institute, 3040 to present.

"Appointment as Viceroy, Trans–Coal Sack Sector, to take effect upon his arrival at New Caledonia."

"More," Bury muttered. "Motivations and ambitions?"

"Moderate personal wealth. Prefers honors to increase in fortune. Has written two articles purporting to prove that his family held title of marquis during the First Empire. He hopes to regain the title."

"Evidence?"

"Calvin has become a client of Haladay Genealogical Services, and a member of the Augustan Society. He has made no secret of his ambition. Haladay is a subsidiary of Confidential Services, Inc."

"Enough," Bury said. Moderate personal wealth, and he wouldn't become Viceroy until he reached New Caledonia. He wouldn't be traveling in any lavish style. Bury smiled thinly.

2
Tourists

*We have explained in various ways all things to men
in this Qur'an; but of all things
man is most contentious*

—Al-Qur'an

The bus was supposed to land on the hotel roof at 0830. Kevin and Ruth got there five minutes early. A dozen others waited for the tour to start.

The rooftop was still shadowed by the mountains to the east, but south and west the harbor was in bright sunshine. Even this early the vast harbor bay was lined with the wakes of both big ships and sailing craft. A warren of small boats, power and sail, many of them multihulled, jammed much of the docking area nearest the hotel. Most appeared to be yachts, but there were also square-hulled junks covered with laundry and children.

The tops of the mountains to the east and north were hidden in clouds.

Renner pointed. Far to the south they could see where the continent ended in steep mountains. "Blaine Institute is down there. According to the maps it's over a hundred kilometers to the ocean."

"One benefit of empire," Ruth said. Renner raised an eyebrow. "Clear air. Out in the new provinces they're still burning coal."

"True enough. Bury makes a fortune bringing in fusion plants and power satellites. It helps if your customers have to buy—"

"They don't have to buy from Bury. And even if they did, hey, it's worth it!"

Renner took a deep breath. "Sure."

The bus landed on the hotel roof at exactly 0830. When Kevin and Ruth got on, a small man with a round face and red-veined nose looked at them quizzically. "Sir Kevin Renner?"

"That's me."

"Durk Riley. I'm your guide, sir. And you must be Commander Cohen."

"Did we order a guide?" Ruth asked.

"Nabil," Renner said.

"I've reserved you seats, sir." Riley indicated three places near the front of the bus. "Always like to have Navy people with me. I put in nearly forty years. Retired as coxs'n about twenty years ago. I'd have stayed in, but my wife talked me out of it. Civilian life's no good, you know. Nothing to do. Nothing important. Well, I don't mean that the way it sounds."

Ruth smiled. "We understand."

"Thank you, ma'am. I don't usually talk so much about myself. Sure glad to see Navy people. You Navy, Sir Kevin?"

"Reserve. Sailing Master. I went inactive about the same time you retired."

Kevin and Ruth took their seats and settled back. Riley produced a hip flask. "Little nip?"

"Thank you, no," Kevin said.

"You're thinking it's a bit early. Guess it is, even for Sparta, but with the short days we tend to do things a little different here."

"Well, why not?" Kevin reached for the flask. "Good stuff. Irish?"

"What they call Irish most places. We just call it whiskey. Better strap in."

The sky was as crowded as the sea. The bus rose through a swarm of light planes and heavy cargo craft and other airfoil-contoured buses, curved wide away from an empty area a minute before some kind of spacecraft came whistling through it, and went east toward the mountains. It followed the tiers of houses and estates up into the clouds. They broke through cloud cover to see that the black mountaintops went up high above them.

"That's pretty," Ruth said. "What do you call those mountains?"

"Drakenbergs," Riley said. "Run down most of the length of the Serpens. Serpens is the continent."

"Barren up here," Renner said.

The Serpens had a sharp-curled spine, black mountain flanks bare of life. Sparta hadn't developed foliage to handle that soil, and it held too much heavy metal for most earthly plants. The tour director told them that and more as they flew along the spine of the continent.

The bus dropped back below the tablecloth of clouds and followed the curve of the mountains to where they dipped into the ocean, dropped to half a kilometer altitude, and headed south across the harbor.

"That's Old Sparta to the left," Riley said. "Parts date back to CoDominium days. See that green patch with tall buildings around it? That's the Palace area."

"Will we go closer?" Ruth asked.

" 'Fraid not. There are Palace tours, though."

Boats of every size moved randomly across the calm water. They continued south. The calm water of the tremendous harbor changed from green to blue, sharply. The sea bottom was visible, still shallow; the boats were fewer, and larger.

"It doesn't show," Ruth said.

"Yeah." Renner had guessed what she meant. "They rule a thousand worlds from here, but . . . It's like the zoo on Mote Prime. Sure it's a different world, sure there's nothing like it anywhere in the universe, but you get used to that when you travel enough. You expect *major* differences. But it's not fair, Ruth. We look for worlds like Earth because that's where we can live."

Riley was staring. Other heads had turned from windows. *Zoo on Mote Prime?*

"Defenses," Ruth said. "*There's* a difference. Sparta must be the most heavily defended world of all."

"Yeah. And all that means is, there are places the bus won't go. And questions Mr. Riley won't answer."

Riley said, "Well, of course."

Ruth was smiling. "Don't test that, all right? I *know* you. We're on holiday."

"Okay."

"I don't know anything about Sparta's defenses anyway," Riley said uncomfortably. "Mr. Renner? You were on the Mote expedition?"

"Yup. Riley, I didn't keep any secrets, and it's all been declassified. You can get my testimony under *What I Did on My Summer*

72

Vacation, by Kevin Renner. Published by Athenaeum in 3021. I get a royalty."

There was a storm to the east. The bus flew west and dropped even lower (the ride became bumpy) to fly above a huge cargo ship. Big stabilizer fins showed with the roll of the waves, waves the size of small hills. There were pleasure boats, too, graceful sailing boats that rolled as they climbed up and down the water mountains; their sails were constantly shifting along the masts.

The bus skimmed over a big island patterned in rectangles of farmland. "That's the Devil Crab," Riley said. "Two sugarcane plantations and maybe a hundred independents. I'd love to be a farmer. They don't pay taxes."

Renner jumped. "Hey?"

"Population's dense on Sparta. The cost of land on Serpens is . . . well, I never tried to buy any, but it's way up there. If the farmers didn't get some kind of break, they'd all sell out to the people who build hotels. Then all the food would have to be shipped in from far away, and where would the Emperor get his fresh fruit?"

"Wow! No taxes. What about these guys below us?"

"They don't pay either. Transport costs are high, and the produce isn't as fresh when it gets to Serpens. The Serpens farmers can still compete. Even so, this is the way I'd go. Lease an island a thousand klicks from Serpens and raise beef. There's no room to raise red meat on this part of Serpens."

They veered away from another rocky island that seemed to be covered with a patchwork of concrete slabs and domes. "There's some of the defense stuff," Renner said. "Battle management radars, and I'd bet there are some pretty hefty lasers in there."

"It's a good guess, but I wouldn't know," Riley said.

Presently the bus turned north and east and flew toward the narrow hooked spit that enclosed the harbor from the west. "That was the prison colony back in CoDominium days," Riley said. "If you look close, you can see where the old wall was. Ran right across the peninsula."

"There? It's mostly parks," Ruth said. "Or—"

"Rose gardens," Riley said. "When Lysander II tore down the old prison walls, he gave all that area to the public. There's the rose festival every year. Citizen fraternities compete, and it's a big deal. We do tours every other day, if you're interested."

"Where's Blaine Institute?" Ruth asked.

"Off east. To the right there. See that mountain covered with buildings?"

"Yes—it looks like an old painting I saw once."

"*That's* the Blaine Institute?" Renner said. "Captain Blaine's richer than I suspected. And to think I knew him . . ."

"Did you, sir?" Riley sounded impressed. "But that's the Biology section of Imperial University. The Institute is the smaller area next to it." He offered his binoculars. "And Blaine Manor sits on the hill just east of that. Would you like a tour of the Institute?"

"Thanks, we'll be there this afternoon," Ruth said.

The bus crossed the narrow spit and then stayed well out over the harbor. The sun had burned off most of the cloud cover over the city. The skyline was a jumble of shapes: in the center and to the south were massive square skyscrapers, thin towers, tall bulidings connected by bridges a thousand feet above street level. North of that were lower granite buildings in a classic style. In the center were the green parks of the Palace district.

Renner looked thoughtful. "Ruth, think about it. *The Emperor* is over there. Just lob a big fusion bomb in the general direction of the Palace . . ."

He stopped because everyone on the bus was looking at him.

"Hey! I'm a Naval Reserve officer!" he said quickly. "I'm trying to figure out how you keep someone else from doing it. With this many people on Sparta, and visitors from everywhere, there's bound to be crazies."

"We get our share, *Sir Kevin*." Riley emphasized the title so everyone would hear it.

"We do check on people coming to Sparta," Ruth said. Her voice had dropped. "And it's not all that easy to buy an atom bomb."

"That might stop amateurs."

"Oh, all right," Ruth said. "Drop it, huh? It's a depressing thought."

"It's something we live with," Riley said. "Look, we have ways to spot the crazies. And generally professionals won't try because it won't do them any good. Everybody knows the royal family's never all in the same place. Prince Aeneas doesn't even live on this planet. Blow up Serpens and you'll get the Fleet mad as hell, but you won't kill the Empire. One thing we do not do—sir—is tell everybody on a random tour bus all about the defenses!"

"And one thing I don't do," Renner answered, and his voice had dropped low, "is guard my mouth. It would prevent me from learning things. Even so: sorry."

Riley grunted. "Yes, sir. Look over there. Those are the fish farms." He pointed to a series of brightly colored sea patches divided by low walls. "That's another good racket. Fish from offplanet don't do well out in Sparta's oceans. You want sea bass or ocean cat, it'll come from here or someplace like it."

The limousine was waiting at the hotel. Bury wasn't smiling. When they were airborne, he looked to Ruth. "What did Kevin do this time?"

"Eh?"

"The Secret Service asked me to verify that this was indeed my pilot, Sir Kevin Renner. Asked *me*."

"Oh," Ruth said. "Well, he did talk about lobbing an atom bomb at the Palace."

Bury did not look amused. "I would prefer not to be thrown off this planet."

"It wouldn't help my career much," Ruth said. "Look, maybe I better talk to them."

"You need not bother," Bury said. "Once they were certain of his identity they lost interest."

"Now I know I want to see your file, Kevin," Ruth said.

The limousine stayed low over the outskirts of the central district. Massive granite buildings stood next to parks.

Ruth stared through binoculars. "Department of Public Health," she read. "Stock Exchange. Wow, that's the Colonial Office! It doesn't look big enough."

"Nor is it," Bury said. "That building houses the offices that might be of interest to the general public, and the secretary of state. The computer and most of the offices are scattered all over the city. Many are below ground."

"Maybe someday they'll build a new building and put everything in one place," Ruth said.

Bury chuckled. "That *is* the new building. You would not suppose its cost, most of it paid for by taxes on interstellar trade."

"It doesn't look new," Renner said.

"No government building looks new," Bury said. "They are deliberately done in classical styles. Some show Russian influence."

"I see plenty of skyscrapers and tall walls, though," Renner said.

"Certainly. Sparta is the financial center of the Empire," Bury said. "Land near the city is very costly. Only the government could afford anything as inefficient as classical architecture. Ah. To illustrate—"

He pointed. "The Blaine Institute."

The Institute looked south at ocean beaches. The complex of buildings rose up the side of a steep cliff. Balconies broke the steep lines, and halfway up was a large flat roof dotted with small trees and picnic tables.

The limousine landed on the roof. Two ramrod-straight young men opened the doors and helped Bury into his travel chair. The ocean breeze was brisk on the rooftop. Sunlight danced on wavetops below. Ruth stretched and took a deep breath. She turned to Renner, but he wasn't looking at her.

Renner stared at a large elderly man in police uniform coming toward them. "Kelley," he said. "Gunner Kelley."

"That's me, Sir Kevin. Your Excellency."

"By damn, it is you. Ruth, this is Gunner Kelley. Imperial Marines. He was in *MacArthur*. Kelley, this is Lieutenant Commander Ruth Cohen."

"Pleased to meet you, ma'am."

"I thought that was a police uniform," Renner said.

"Well, it sort of is," Kelley said. "I'm security chief here at the Institute. But there's not a lot of need for that, so I've got plenty of time to greet visitors. The Earl will be glad to see you."

"Earl?" Renner said. "Isn't Blaine Marquis of Crucis?"

"No sir," Kelley said. "Not yet. The Marquis isn't as young as he used to be, but he still gets to Parliament." He gestured. One of the uniformed staff opened the door to the interior. Another guided Bury's travel chair.

The inside corridor was short. Scenes from Mote Prime decorated the walls. At the end of the corridor was a semicircular reception desk. The receptionist wore a skirted version of Kelley's uniform, and a businesslike sidearm. She held out thick badges on a tray. Their names and pictures were already on the badges.

"Welcome, Your Excellency. Sir Kevin. Commander Cohen," the receptionist said. "If you'll just thumbprint the badges . . ."

When Renner touched his thumb to the badge, it glowed softly green.

"Thank you. Please be sure to wear these at all times. Enjoy your stay."

There were three elevators beyond the reception desk. Kelley passed them all and indicated a fourth around the corner, marked PRIVATE. Renner noted buttons for thirty-eight floors. Kelley used a key before punching the button for twenty-four.

When they were inside, Renner frowned. "I thought you said there wasn't much need for security."

"No, I said there wasn't much need for a security chief," Kelley said. "And there isn't. I've got a good staff."

"Do you often have trouble, then?" Bury asked.

"Not too much, Your Excellency. But we have had some threats. There are people who don't like Moties. Don't want us studying them."

The twenty-fourth floor was paneled in dark wood, and thickly carpeted. The walls were hung with photographs. Ruth stared at one of them. "Kevin—Kevin, that's *you.*"

Renner looked. "Yep, in the Museum on Mote Prime. That statue—that was the time machine."

"What?" She started to laugh, changed her mind, and looked more carefully.

"Didn't work."

"Ugh. What are those things attacking? The, uh, time machine?"

"Evil, aren't they? The Moties told us they were mythical demons defending the structure of reality. Later we found out they were Warrior-class Moties. You would not want *those* loose in the Empire."

Kelley led them to the end of the corridor, knocked, and opened a walnut door. "My Lady. M'Lord, your visitors."

*　　*　　*

Rod Blaine stood as the others entered. He was far enough away that he didn't have to shake hands. "Welcome to the Institute, Your Excellency. Delighted to see you again. Kevin, you're looking good. Civilian life must suit you."

Bury managed to stand and bow. "My Lady. Lord Blaine. And may I present Lieutenant Commander Ruth Cohen. She is traveling with us."

Kelley excused himself and closed the door.

77

"My Lady," Ruth said. She bowed to Rod.

Rod took her hand and kissed it. "Welcome to the Institute, Commander." Her ears were turning pink. *Easily flustered*, Rod thought. Traveling with Kevin Renner should have cured her of that.

Bury sat carefully. "If you'll excuse me . . ."

"Oh, certainly," Sally said.

"It's been a while," Rod said. "Kevin, how have things worked out for you?"

"Not as bad as I thought they would. By the way, Ruth knows our dread secret. Most of it, anyway." Renner turned to Sally. "We heard about your uncle. Sorry. He was a good man, even if he did force me into a career of espionage."

Sally nodded. "Thank you. Uncle Ben never would take care of himself."

Ruth looked wide-eyed. "Uncle Ben—that would be Senator Benjamin Fowler. Kevin, the *Prime Minister* recruited you into the Secret Service?"

Renner laughed. "No, Lord Blaine did that. Senator Fowler declared an emergency so my discharge wasn't any good."

"What can we do for you, Excellency?" Rod asked.

"Why, nothing, really . . ."

"Your Excellency, it has been a busy day, and while I understand the custom of circumnavigating the subject before mentioning it, Lady Sally and I have a great deal more work to do."

"Ah. Thank you, my Lord," Bury said. His smile didn't seem forced. "I hope to persuade you to use your influence with the Navy. My Lord, the blockade is now a quarter of a century old. We do not agree about the Moties. You see opportunities where I see threats. Yet you agreed to bottle them within their own solar system. As did you, my Lady. We are all agreed that the situation cannot continue forever."

"Yeah, we can accept that," Rod said. "We bought some time."

"What do you want from us?" Sally asked. She was no longer trying to be polite.

"More time," Bury said firmly. "My lady, I must know that the blockade is effective. I wish to look for myself. I wish to talk to those closest to the problem. I want to look for alternatives, to see what we—what the Empire of Man—can do to be certain that the Moties will not free themselves and explode through the Empire."

"That's a big order," Rod said.

Bury said nothing.

"Horace wants Navy clearance to go have a look at the Crazy Eddie Squadron," Renner said.

Bury nodded in tiny motions. "Precisely."

"Not our decision," Sally said quickly.

Bury looked steadily at Rod Blaine.

Rod spread his hands without shrugging. "As Lady Sally says, it isn't our decision. We gave up our seats on the Commission years ago, when we moved the Institute to Sparta. But consider this, Excellency. How could anyone *prove* that the Moties are safely locked up?"

Bury ignored Blaine's tone. "I must see." The trader looked terribly old, terribly tired. "I have defended the Empire. I have ignored the real threat while I confined myself to thwarting treason and Outie plots. Nuisances. I will continue to do so, but I must know that the real border is defended. You think I can never be satisfied. You may even be right. But I must see for myself. I have earned that right."

Rod looked at Sally.

"Earned it," Bury insisted. "I doubt that the Empire enjoys a more effective intelligence team than Kevin Renner and me. And I tell you, Lord Blaine, I must see!"

"You've made your point," Rod said. "I understand that you find this a serious matter." He looked at Sally again. "We have some developments here, too."

Sally cleared her throat. "Rod, we've got a meeting . . ."

Rod glanced at the clock on the wall. "Sorry, I'm letting the time get away. Excellency, we're delighted to see you, but we do have a meeting with a parliamentary committee. Would you like to see what we're doing here?"

"I sure would, Captain," Renner said. "I mean, my Lord."

Blaine chuckled. "Good. We thought you might." He looked up at the ceiling. "Fyunch(click)."

The ceiling answered. "Sir."

"Ask Jennifer to come in. I'm sure you'll all like your guide. She's a graduate student in xenosociology, and she's been dying to meet the other people who've been to the Mote."

"Rod—"

Blaine waited until the door closed behind Renner. "Yeah."

79

"I do not want that man out there! Our son is in that fleet."

"I thought of that."

"He's a traitor," Sally said. "All right, we use him, but he doesn't have any real loyalty to the Empire. Money." She sniffed. "That's all he cares about. He'd sell us to the Moties for enough money."

Rod nodded thoughtfully. "I expect it would do no harm to have a few words with our friends in the Palace." He grinned.

"That's an evil look."

"His Excellency is due for a shock."

"Yes—are you sure you want to tell him?"

"Sally, we'll be announcing it in four days. Bury will know. We might as well get some mileage out of telling him. Hell, he may know already."

"No, I don't believe that."

"Anyway—Sally, he committed treason a quarter of a century ago, but he's right this time. The blockade bought time, but it's no solution. Sooner or later, either we'll have an Empire of two intelligent species, or a war of extermination. Sally, the Empire's going to have plenty of people who think like Bury. At least he's been there! Maybe he could be useful."

"I'd sooner convert hive rats to the Church," Sally said. "But you're right, he'll find out sooner or later, and he's a good test case. I want to see his face. We'll know how good his spies are then!"

* * *

Jennifer Banda was an inch over Renner's height, lean and dark, with just enough length of hair to suggest a white ancestor. When they were introduced, she was polite to Ruth Cohen, deferential to Renner, and almost fawned on Horace Bury.

Watusi genes, Renner speculated. If she's not dark enough, it's Sparta's weak excuse for a star.

"What would you like to see?" Jennifer had asked, and when no one knew what to say, she continued, "We can start with some of the specimen collections. There's sort of a meeting in the grad-student lounge in about an hour. Would you like to go to that?"

"Yes, please," Renner said quickly.

" 'About,' " Ruth Cohen said, mimicking the odd way that Jennifer had pronounced the word. "Vancouver, New Washington."

Jennifer Banda turned, startled. "Yes—"

Ruth grinned. "I'm from Astoria. Glad you weren't playing basketball when we had to play Vancouver."

Renner watched Jennifer moving ahead of him to the elevators. Nice sway to the girl. Good muscular control . . . and New Washington gravity had about .93 standard gee. She must have been one hell of an athlete. She must also have had a hell of a time adjusting to Spartan gravity, but clearly she'd done it.

The elevator opened onto a corridor lined with display cases. Jennifer led the way past them. She turned at the far end to find Renner ambling at leisure, peering at Mai Tai parasol fungi and huge-headed glider snakes and ponds of oddly colored water with microscope screens attached. . . . He sighed and moved briskly to join them.

At the far end was a conference room with refreshments, a large table, and a hologram wall.

"We've got specimens from four hundred Imperial worlds and thirty Outie planets," Jennifer said. "Too many. There's no room to set up live demonstrations, so mostly we have holograms. Wanora!"

"Ready," the ceiling said.

"My sequence one, please."

"Certainly."

A series of holograms formed at the far end of the room.

"These are from water worlds," Jennifer said. "Just about every one alike. Four fins, a head, and a tail. Like us."

Another series of holograms formed. "Then there are forms evolved from planets without much water. Theory says they crawled out earlier. Six- and eight-limbed forms. The Tabletop Crazylegs with eighteen. But again all symmetric."

"You have holograms of—how many do you have?" Bury asked.

"Excellency, we try to be *complete*."

"Do you have the Levantine Honeypot?"

"Mmm? Wanora! Levantine Honeypot."

The holograph display showed what looked like a grossly misshapen barrel, with bright flowers at its top. Small birdlike creatures fluttered around it. Abruptly, slender tendrils shot up from

81

the edge of the barrel to entangle one of the fliers and drag it out of sight.

"What *is* that?" Ruth Cohen asked.

"I confess it's new to me," Jennifer said. Text was scrolling across the screen: *"Kaybo Sietzus.* Local Anglic name is the Levantine Honeypot. Largely sessile carnivorous animal.

"The Honeypot is one of the largest known animal life-forms to display radial but not bilateral symmetry. Its biochemistry was thought to be unique until 3030 when Ricardo haLevy described the life cycle of the Tabletop Ground Hag, whose larval form uses similar enzyme processes."

"Ugly thing," Renner said.

"They're not very common," Bury said. "Never more than one in an oasis. Usually none at all. They can't move fast, and dogs like to eat them." He read quickly. "Interesting. When I was in school, the Honeypot was used as an example of why panspermia wasn't true. Totally unique and all that. I hadn't heard there was anything like it. I take it that the Blaine Institute accepts the panspermia theory?"

"Most of us, Excellency," Jennifer said.

Bury chuckled at the note of surprise. "Traders do not spend all their time reading commodity price reports."

"Clearly."

"Panspermia?" Ruth Cohen said.

"An old theory, from before CoDominium times," Jennifer Banda said. "The notion is that life is so improbable that it can happen only once in a galaxy."

"Omnia cellula e cellula," Renner muttered.

Ruth frowned at him.

"Sorry. A phrase they taught in school. All cells come from cells. No spontaneous generation of life. It was an early experiment in scientific discovery."

"Right," Jennifer said. "So the theory is that eventually all successful life-forms evolve a means of reproducing across interstellar distances. When we got out into space, we found there were organics all over the place, and they could cross interstellar distances by hopping rides with comet clouds. Sometime back then, I guess during the early days of the First Empire, a scientist named Sir Fred Hoyle postulated that an intelligent entity was deliberately sending biochemical messages through the galaxy."

"You don't believe that, do you?" Ruth asked.

Jennifer shrugged. "Not really, but you know, for all that people keep saying Sir Fred must have been off his head, we've never been able to disprove it. Space is just *rich* with improbable organics." She paused for a moment. "I think the Moties believe it."

Bury looked at her critically. "How could you possibly know that?"

"Oh. Sorry. I've been trying to think like a Motie so long sometimes I forget. I mean, I think the Moties will believe it."

The holograms continued. A score of worlds had jet black plants. "It's based on selenium and it's a lot more complicated than chlorophyll," Jennifer said. "But again we can find copies in interstellar organics. If this stuff gets rooted first, chlorophyll doesn't have a chance because the black plants use yellow sunlight better.

"Dry worlds are different. More limbs, usually. But still symmetry," Jennifer said. "Always symmetry. That's the puzzle. If only you'd brought back some seeds or something from Mote Prime!"

Renner laughed (and Bury didn't). "Admiral Kutuzov went to great lengths to prevent that. Jennifer, we pretty well accepted that all the asymmetrical forms were derived from the Engineer class, and they evolved the three arms after they were intelligent."

"Yes, they believe that, too. But of course they don't remember."

Bury looked at her quickly, but she had turned back to the holographic displays.

3
Jock

When We said to the angels:
"Bow before Adam in adoration,"
they all bowed but Iblis.
He was one of the djinni and rebelled
against his Lord's command.
And yet you take him and his offspring
as your friends.

—Al-Qur'an

This way," Jennifer Banda said. She ushered them into a twenty-fourth-floor windowed room that ran most of the length of the Institute. A dozen people in their twenties sat at tables or poured themselves coffee from an Imperial Autonetics urn. One wall of the room was French doors leading onto a veranda cantilevered out over the beach area far below. The brisk wind smelled of seawater.

"Quite a view," Ruth Cohen said.

Kevin Renner nodded absently. The atmosphere was odd. A dozen graduate students. They all knew that Kevin Renner and Horace Bury had been to Mote Prime—and they were all looking at each other, or out at a spectacular view that they had certainly seen before.

"McQuorquodale. *Philosophic Journal*, about six months ago," someone said. "Studies of a hummingdragon in motion."

"But it's not my field."

"It'll still be on the test. Depend on it."

Jennifer led them out to the balcony. Renner went to the rail and looked over, then noticed that Ruth Cohen had stayed near the door.

"Acrophobia?"

"Maybe a little." She sat at a table near the wall, and after a moment Bury wheeled his travel chair to join her. Renner leaned against the railing and enjoyed the view while listening to the conversations behind him.

A female voice waxed eloquent about the importance of parasites in ecologies, while her male companion pretended interest. Renner remembered similar conversations when he was that age and sympathized.

Two students at the next table sipped tea. "I still say it isn't fair. I'm in political science, for God's sake. I'll never need to know anything about organic chemistry that I can't find on the computer."

"That's what you get to prove next week," another said. He chuckled. "I offered to help, Miriam Anne."

Renner took a seat between Ruth Cohen and Jennifer Banda. "Nice place." He scratched his head. "Okay, I give up."

Jennifer Banda raised an eyebrow.

"This is Blaine Institute, the primary center for the study of Moties. Here are two people who've been on Mote Prime. And no one's interested in us."

"Polite," Jennifer said. "They were warned not to bother you."

"Ah." It was the explanation Renner had expected, but he still felt something was wrong.

"We've all studied your flick, Sir Kevin. And every Imperial Autonetics report that mentions the Mote."

"Commendable," Bury said. "And of course you had the Moties to study. I presume holograms were made of everything they said."

Jennifer's answer was drowned out as the girl at the next table choked on her drink, then set it down with exaggerated care.

"What have you learned?" Bury asked.

"Well, we've compiled a general history of the Mote," Jennifer said. "As much as Jock and Charlie could remember."

"Jock and Charlie?" Ruth asked.

"Jock and Charlie and Ivan were the ambassadors from Mote Prime," Jennifer said. "Admiral Kutuzov couldn't refuse them. But you have to remember, they don't represent the whole system; not even the planet. Just one government, or even one extended family, among maybe tens of thousands."

"King Peter," Bury said, "Of course he wasn't really a king and the government wasn't really a monarchy, but that is the name they chose in hopes that it would sound familiar to us. They knew us that well, even then."

Jennifer nodded. "They certainly learned more about us than we did about them. They sent three ambassadors, a Master and two Mediators. Ruth, you know about Masters and Mediators? Moties are a differentiated species with a lot of different castes. The Masters give the orders and the Mediators talk for them. Anyway, they called the Master 'Ivan'—probably because Admiral Kutuzov was in charge of the expedition and they thought the Russians were Masters in the Empire—and the Mediators got the names Jock and Charlie. Ivan died first, but he never talked much except through the Mediators so we didn't learn much from him. Then—anyway, as His Excellency said, we made holos of everything we could. Of course, once you get back a couple of cycles there wasn't much detail."

"Cycles," Ruth said. "I saw a lot about that in school. It's about all I remember about Moties."

"Too right," Renner said. "Everything about the Mote was cycles. Civilizations rise and fall."

"Sometimes incredibly fast," Jennifer said. "And they tried everything! Industrial feudalism, communism, capitalism, things we never even thought of. Anyway, we got lots of stories, what we'd call folk legends, but not much *history*."

"There couldn't be," Ruth Cohen said. "It takes continuity to make history. I can feel sorry for the Moties."

"I pity them, too," Bury said. "Who could not? They die in agony if they can't become pregnant and give birth. Endless population expansion, endless wars for limited resources. Sometimes I fear that only I can see how dangerous that makes them. Jennifer, we visited Mote Prime. A world crowded beyond description, with complex competitions for power and prestige. We were told it would collapse soon, and I believed them. We also saw signs of a civilization in the asteroid belt. Jacob Buckman told me that many of the asteroids had been moved."

"I'm surprised he noticed," Renner said.

"He lost interest in them after he found out," Bury said.

Jennifer laughed. The couple at the next table had fallen silent. They were joined by two other students who also pretended not to listen.

"We learned nothing important about the asteroid civilization," Bury said. "That has always concerned me. Perhaps you know more, now?"

"Not a lot," Jennifer said. "The—our Moties had never visited the asteroids. Jock believed that the Trailing Trojans were in an ascendant imperial phase, but he was never certain."

"The industrial feudalism on Mote Prime will long since have collapsed," Bury said. "Other systems will be emerging. Or perhaps nothing but savagery."

"Oh, surely not," the girl at the next table said.

"Circles," Renner said. "You didn't see them."

"Circles?" Ruth Cohen asked.

Before Renner could answer, the girl at the next table stood and bowed slightly. "Miriam Anne Vukcik. Political history. This is Tom Boyarski. May we join you?"

"Please do," Bury said.

"Circles?" Ruth asked again.

Renner said, "The circles were the first thing you saw from orbit. Craters everywhere, big and little, and all old, all across Mote Prime. Seas and lakes. One lopsided crater skewed by an earthquake fault line, one across a mountain range . . . you get the idea."

"The great asteroid war. Our Moties didn't remember anything about it," Miriam said.

"They think in circles, too. Cycles. Rise and fall. Population growth and then a war. They keep their museums to help the next civilization get itself together. They don't even try to stop it anymore. They're too old. It's been going on too long."

Miriam said, "Crazy Eddie—"

"Yeah, Crazy Eddie tries to stop it."

"I don't think I understand the Crazy Eddie myth-figure. We have plenty of legends about the coming of the Messiah, and about holy madmen, but no human culture ever pinned all its hopes for the future on a savior who had to be crazy."

"Don Quixote?" Ruth Cohen grinned.

Jennifer nodded agreement. "Good point."

"Humans try the impossible. It's part of our nature," Tom Boyarski said. "Submitting to the inevitable is a big part of Motie nature."

"But Jock really liked *Don Quixote*," Jennifer Banda said.

"They *liked* the Persian story about the man who told the king he could teach a horse to sing," Tom said. "And maybe they understood intellectually. But not at a gut level." He laughed. "That's all right. We know a lot about them, too, but deep down they're still a big mystery."

"And always will be," Miriam said.

"No," Tom said. "Next time, we'll know more about what to study. Next time we'll find out."

"Next time," Bury said. "You are planning a new expedition to the Mote?"

Tom looked startled, then laughed. "I don't have the funding." For a moment he must have considered; but he wasn't young enough to suggest that Horace Bury *did*. "No one is," Tom said. "No one I know of, anyway. But sooner or later there's got to be one."

Jennifer Banda's pocket computer chimed. She looked embarrassed, but she stood up and said, "Excuse me, people. I was told to take you back to Lady Blaine's office."

Bury set his chair in motion. Renner stood up. "You don't understand, and that's the truth," he said. "Crazy Eddie is supposed to *fail*."

✳　✳　✳

Instead of the receptionist, there was another woman, younger and blond and expensively dressed, in the receiving area outside Lady Sally Blaine's office. Renner had seen a picture of Glenda Ruth Fowler Blaine, but he wouldn't have needed that. She had the same finely chiseled features and penetrating eyes as her mother.

"Sir Kevin, Your Excellency," she said. Her eyes twinkled. "I thought I'd introduce myself before my parents made it all formal." Her smile was infectious. "Kevin, I'm delighted to meet you! Your Excellency, did you know my brother was named for your pilot?"

"No, my Lady—"

She nodded. "Kevin Christian. We mostly call him Chris. Mom

doesn't like us chattering about family. Did they ever tell you, Kevin? But you guessed anyway. Kevin, I still have the christening cup you sent. Thank you, and thank you, too, Your Excellency! There wasn't anything like that for sale for years."

"It was crafted in our laboratories, my Lady," Bury said. His smile was genuine. "I'm pleased that you remembered."

"It still delivers the best-tasting milk on Sparta." Glenda Ruth pointed to the wall clock display of the dark and light areas of Sparta. "They're waiting for us. Uh—I'm not supposed to tell, but I hope you're prepared for a surprise." She held the door open for Bury's travel chair.

There was something about Jennifer Banda's smile as she and Glenda Ruth ushered them into Lady Blaine's office. Both Blaines were wearing that same conspiratorial smile. The air of mystery was getting on Renner's nerves.

There was another occupant.

He stood up slowly from his oddly designed travel chair, and bowed. A hairy, grinning, hunchbacked dwarf, not just short but grotesquely misshapen, too. You don't stare at a dwarf, and Renner was in control of his expression, but he lost it all when the stranger bowed. His backbone jutted, broken in two places.

The mind would always misinterpret that first sight.

It stood four and a half feet tall. It was hairy. The brown and white markings were still visible, though they had shaded mostly to white. There was one big ear on the right side, and no room for one on the left; the massive shoulder muscles ran right up to knobs at the top of the misshaped skull. There were two slender right arms. The dolphin-grin was simply the shape of its face.

Renner gaped. For a moment he couldn't take his eyes off it . . . and then he remembered Bury.

Horace Bury's face was all the wrong colors. He'd opened the case in the arm of his travel chair, but his hands were shaking too badly to deal with the diagnostic sleeve. Renner slipped it into place. The system began feeding Bury tranquilizers at once. Renner studied the readings for a moment before he looked up.

"Captain, that was nasty. I mean my Lord. My Lord Blaine, you could have killed him, dammit!"

"Dad, I told you—"

Earl Blaine nibbled his lip. "I hadn't thought. Your Excellency . . ."

Bury was furious, but he had it under control. "An excellent joke, my Lord. Excellent. *Who are you?*"

The Motie said, "I'm Jock, Excellency. It's good to see you in such health."

". . . Yes. It must be, considering. I find it *stunning* to see you in such health. Did you lie to us? Mediators die around age twenty-five, you said. All Moties die if they cannot be made pregnant, and the Mediators are mules. Sterile, you said."

Renner said, "Between the legs."

Bury looked. "Male? Allah's . . . blessing. Lord Blaine—Lady Blaine—this is a stunning achievement. *How?*"

Sally Blaine said, "Fyunch(click), give us Charlie 490."

There was a holowall. Understandably, Renner had not noticed it. Now it showed what looked to be shadows of a CAT scan, the interior of something not human. A Motie, of course. The hips: one intricate and massive joint in backbones as solid as the bones of a human leg. Mote Prime had never invented vertebrae.

The camera zoomed within the abdomen. A white arrowhead pointed to tiny tadpole-shapes clinging to the abdominal wall.

"That," Lady Sandra Fowler Blaine said, "is the C-L worm. We did gene-tailoring on a symbiote in the digestive tract. Now it secrets male hormone. It was already secreting something a lot like it. This wasn't the first thing we tried, but we tried all *kinds* of things, and this didn't get enough attention. Ivan died before we were ready. We think Charlie was killed by the physiological change, female to male. He was too old."

Bury's color was better. "You've broken the Motie breeding cycle."

"We've repaired the cycle, Your Excellency," Lady Blaine said coolly. "It's broken in Mediators. Child, male, female, pregnant, male, female, pregnant, that's how it goes with Motie classes. But Mediators are sterile mules, so they're only male once, and they die young.

"We only had three Moties to test, but we could ask questions. When a Motie's been male awhile, the single testis withers and the Motie goes female. Giving birth excites cells in the birth canal, and more testes form, but only one grows to term."

"He's carrying more than one of your worms," Renner pointed out.

"We worried about that, but it's not a problem," Glenda Ruth said. "The kidney flushes the extra hormone. This is an old, well-established Motie parasite. It had already evolved practically to symbiote stage. It won't overbreed inside its host. The hormone itself inhibits that, and the worm long ago developed other mechanisms to protect the host."

Bury's eyes flicked to Renner's. They must have been thinking exactly alike: *there'd be no problem transporting the symbiote.*

Bury said, "What next, my Lady?"

Sally nibbled her lip. "We don't know. Kevin? I think you understood the Crazy Eddie concept better than most of us. Would they *want* this?"

"Of course they will!" Glenda Ruth said.

Sally looked at her daughter coldly, then turned back to Renner. "Does this make them fertile?" Renner asked.

"No. Not Mediators, anyway," Sally said.

"Keepers," Renner said.

Bury nodded. Keepers were sterile male Masters, less ambitiously territorial than most Motie Masters. The title came from the Keepers of the Museums and other public facilities, and three Imperial midshipmen had died to find that out.

Renner grinned suddenly. "Mediators would want it. Masters would want it for their enemies. But you don't know it works on Masters."

"No. But it does work on Mediators. And if we had a Master to test . . ."

"Kevin," Bury said.

"Yeah?" Bury still looked sick. Renner glanced at the clock face on the travel chair. A dull orange light glowed on its face. "Yeah, you've got to get ready for dinner at the Traders Guild. My Lord, my Lady—"

"We should speak further on this." Bury seemed to have trouble manipulating his lips. "Later. You have a, an exceedingly powerful . . . tool."

"We know it," Rod Blaine said. "We won't forget. How long will you be on Sparta, Kevin?"

"Say two weeks. Maybe three." *As long as it takes,* Renner thought. *Now, if not before.*

"Kevin, let's have dinner," Glenda Ruth said. "I mean, no one can get mad if a girl has dinner with her brother's godfather." She looked at her mother and smiled sweetly. Can they?"

Renner was sleeping like a baby, but the door chime snapped him awake. He asked, "Horvendile, is Bury present?"

"His Excellency has just entered."

Ruth stirred. "Kevin? What is it?"

"I think I should go hold Bury's hand."

Nabil passed him at the door to the parlor. Renner asked, "How is he? Is he likely to want to talk?"

"He ordered hot chocolate," Nabil said.

"Okay. Two."

The travel chair was in the middle of the rug. Bury was looking straight ahead, motionless, like a stuffed dummy. Presently he said, "I was affable."

"I'm impressed. What was His Highness like?"

"He will not become 'His Highness' until he assumes his duties as Viceroy." Bury shook his head slightly. "We were at the same table, but several seats apart. Later, many crowded around him in the clubrooms. I formed the impression of intelligence and charisma, but that would be apparent from his career. Really I learned nothing I had not known, but at least we have been formally introduced, and I detected no signs of distaste."

"So what's next?"

"I persuaded him to come to dinner Thursday. It was the only time slot he had. He can listen to me and Jacob reminisce."

"That'll tell him if he wants to travel with us to New Cal."

"Yes. Horvendile, determine Lord Andrew Mercer Calvin's preferences in food and entertainment. Kevin, we must go. These happy lords never really saw the problem, and now they think they have a solution!"

"You've got to admit, they've got a piece of one."

"Hoskins sees profit from the Mote. The Blaines will want to try out their new toy. The graduate student, Boyarski, wants to play tourist. He was right. There will certainly be another expedition, if the blockade doesn't fail first."

"I know. What people know how to do, they do eventually. Look at Earth."

"There's another thing. The Blaine girl will want to go to the Mote. With her family's influence—"

"Yep. She'll inherit power all right. Glenda Ruth. Nice of her to remember our present."

"Kevin, of course she remembers, because she knows it gives you pleasure that she does. As she was delightfully at the edge of informal familiarity with me."

It took Renner a moment to see what he meant. "Oh, my God. Raised by Motie Mediators. She's going to make one hell of a diplomat."

Nabil brought mugs of chocolate. Bury used his to warm his hands. "The Crazy Eddie Squadron. If they know how *important* their work is. The expedition to the Mote, when it comes, would have to go through the blockade."

"Forget it, Horace. The Navy obeys orders."

"They swear an oath." Bury tapped at the keyboard in his chair. The wall lit.

"I solemnly swear to uphold and defend the Empire of Man against all enemies foreign and domestic and to extend the protection of the Empire to all humans; to obey the lawful orders of my superiors, and to uphold and defend as sovereign the legitimate heirs descendant of Lysander the Great; and to bring about the unity of mankind within the Empire of Man."

"You see? Their oath would force them to halt the expedition, if I show it to be a danger."

"Forget it, Horace. Oaths are one thing, courts-martial are another. But look at it this way. If worse came to worst—say, if an expedition actually went and brought back a Master and his household. Or if a Motie ship got through the Jump points *and* as far as New Cal *and* as far as, oh, personal conducted interviews with the interstellar news media. It could become politically impossible to just wipe them out. You've had such thoughts, haven't you?"

"I have. A Motie household with a Mediator to swear that they left their Warriors—and Watchmakers—home."

"But now we could sterilize them without hurting them. It's *better*, Horace. Now, why don't you go to sleep. The Secret Service expects us to be bright eyed and bouncy tomorrow."

The look Bury gave him would have imbued a stone statue with pity, or at least fear.

4
Veto

The Yeoman First Class was clearly impressed. Bury guessed that she'd never before met an Imperial Magnate; she was certainly unfamiliar with his titles. Even so, she worked at being casual, and at covering the fact that Bury was kept waiting ten minutes past the time of his appointment.

"Captain Cunningham will see you now, Your Excellency," she said. "I'm sorry about the delay. We've been really busy this week, I've never seen anything like it." She got up and opened the door to Cunningham's office as Bury directed his travel chair.

In twenty-five years Bury had only had three case officers. He had no trouble recognizing Captain Raphael Cunningham. They'd never met, but there had been hologram messages. Cunningham looked like a child: a head round as a bowling ball, ringed in fluffy white, and a button nose and pursed mouth. Bury knew everything published about Cunningham's background and career; additionally, what he knew of the officer's childhood and family connections might or might not have startled his case officer. Presumably the Navy understood that Horace Bury left little to chance.

His investigations had been disappointing if unsurprising. There were few levers on Raphael Cunningham. His forty-year Navy career was not particularly distinguished, but it was certainly unblemished. Bury's agents suspected that Cunningham had not been entirely faithful to his wife, but they couldn't prove it.

Fools, Bury thought. The Navy cared more about appearances than reality.

It was an effort to stand in Sparta's gravity, but Bury managed it without a grimace. He bowed slightly; he had learned long ago to wait for some gesture before offering his hand to any Imperial officer.

Cunningham's smile was broad, and he came from behind his desk to go to Bury. "Excellency, it's a pleasure to meet you after all these years." His handshake was firm but brief.

So, Bury thought. *I am kept waiting for ten minutes, but his secretary apologizes. He will meet me halfway. A very correct man is Captain Cunningham.*

"Excellency, I confess I never expected to meet you."

"Regrettably, my work does not permit me to visit Sparta often."

"I took the liberty of ordering coffee." Cunningham touched a square inlaid on his desk, and an orderly came in with a tray. He put a large Navy mug on Cunningham's desk, and a smaller cup of black Turkish coffee at Bury's elbow.

"Thank you." Bury raised his cup. "To our continued cooperation."

"I can certainly wish for that," Cunningham said.

Bury sipped his coffee. "Of course, *cooperation* may be too strong a word. Given the costs and rewards . . ."

Cunningham frowned slightly. "I expect I don't know all the costs, but as to rewards, I confess some puzzlement, Excellency. We don't have much besides honors to give. Your work in the Maxroy's Purchase affair merits commendation, but you have refused additional honors. May I ask why?"

Bury shrugged. "I am certainly not unappreciative of Imperial honors, but perhaps they have less—utility—to me. I thank you for the offers, but there is something else I desire a great deal more."

Cunningham raised an eyebrow.

"Captain, you will long have known that I consider Mote Prime the greatest threat to humanity since the Dinosaur Killer struck Earth sixty-five million years ago."

"We differ there. Your Excellency, I like the notion that we're not alone in the universe. Different minds, with insights different from ours. Was it the *MacArthur* thing? The little Watchmaker creatures swarming all through the ship?"

Bury repressed a shudder. *Cunningham likes Moties. A change* of subject was in order. "My record shows that I am not a fool. I believe it is no more than a simple statement of fact that the Empire has never had a more effective intelligence officer than me."

"I can't quarrel with that. Can't offer counterexamples, anyway. Bizarre, the way you can— I gather you see patterns in the flow of money. Is that the way of it?"

"Money, goods, attitudes. One can see changes in local attitudes by changes in a world's imports or the inflation rate. I followed these matters long before I joined your office," Bury said. "Twenty-five years ago I was—persuaded—to aid the Empire. I seek Outie plots and heresies and treason so that the Empire may concentrate on the real threat. The Moties! Of course you've read my report on Maxroy's Purchase."

Cunningham smiled. " 'Gripping Hand.' But the Moties hadn't busted loose after all, had they?"

"No. Not this time, Captain, but—how can I put this? I—"

"You were frightened."

Bury glared. Cunningham raised a big, thick-fingered hand. "Don't be offended. How would anyone have reacted? Little bitty lopsided faces looking out of a pressure suit, crawling up a rope just behind you. Christ! Anyone else might have wound up in a mental institution. You—" Cunningham laughed suddenly. "You wound up in the Secret Service. Minor differences."

Bury spoke low. "Very well. I'm frightened again. I'm frightened for the Empire of Man."

"So much so that you can't do your work? I must say, Your Excellency, that I don't see supervising a long-term naval blockade operation as . . . requiring your special expertise."

Cunningham already knew. Bury said, "When I was brought into the Secret Service, I had no choice. Since then conditions have changed. Do you believe you could force me to do your will now?"

Cunningham stiffened. "Excellency, we have never *forced* you into anything. You go where you will."

Bury laughed. "A pity Senator Fowler is not alive to hear you say that. In any event, my status has gradually become that of a volunteer."

Cunningham shrugged. "It always has been."

"Exactly. And you agree that I am valuable to the Empire?"

"Of course."

"Invaluable and inexpensive, in fact," Bury mused. "So. I will continue to be. But now I want something."

"There is no need to be so aggressive. You want a ticket to the Blockade Squadron," Cunningham said softly.

"Precisely. Did you learn from Blaine or the ITA?"

Cunningham laughed. "The Traders don't talk to us. You're serious about this, aren't you?"

"Captain—" Bury paused. "Captain Cunningham, one of your most effective agents is concerned about a potential threat to the Empire. I am as serious as any other of your madmen. I do not ask for funds, I am quite capable of paying my own expenses. I control seats on the ITA Board, and I have—influence—with several members of Parliament."

Cunningham sighed. "We're worried about the blockade, too."

"Oh?" There *was* something! Bury would not lose face by reaching for his diagnostic sleeve; not yet.

"There's a threat to the blockade, yes. Of sorts. Maybe we can deal. Have you read the recent news stories by Alysia Joyce Mei-Ling Trujillo?"

"You are the second person to ask me that in as many days. No, but I shall as soon as I return to my rooms."

"Good. Excellency, that—investigative reporter has been giving us pure holy hell. I won't say she hasn't found some reason to, but God damn it! The Crazy Eddie Squadron has been out there forever. Blockade duty is the worst kind of duty the Navy can assign. Constant possibility of danger, but mostly boredom. Nothing happens, and nothing happens, and then—"

"You were there?"

"Fifteen years ago. Worst year of my life. I was lucky, it was just a training assignment. Some ships and crews are stuck out there for years! Have to be—if we rotate them too often, there's nobody with experience. Leave them too long though, and—Hell, Excellency, it's no wonder she's found people screwing things up. Everybody's tempted. I'm surprised it's not worse. But she's making us look very bad."

Bury knew he should have read this Mei-Ling's articles last night. He'd been too upset. "Her dispatches come from New Scotland, don't they? What has she found? Bribery, inefficiency, price-fixing? Nepotism? Old-boy networking—"

"All of that. We've got no choice, we have to give her a ticket to visit the Squadron. It occurred to me that it would be no bad thing if you took her there."

Bury mulled it. "The more she learns, the more damage she can do."

"She might. Or she might see dedicated Navy men holding the line against a credible threat. And I am told you have means of persuasion. We can give you very complete files on the young lady. And her family. And friends."

Bury smiled thinly. He had no doubt that this room was secure, and that his travel chair would be subject to magnetic fields that would erase all possible recordings of the conversation; in fact he hadn't even tried making one. He said, "And for two or three months there would be no dispatches at all."

Cunningham nodded. "By the time she sees New Scotland again, we'll clean up most of what she's complaining about."

"I will do my best. We haven't met, of course. She may detest me on sight."

Cunningham smiled. "If you can't charm her, Kevin Renner can. We're agreed, then? Then I want to talk to Sir Kevin, and with luck the rest is formality."

"Formality?"

Cunningham shrugged. "Lord Blaine has asked that he be informed. Surely he would have no objections? I understand you have known him for many years."

"More than twenty-five years, Captain," Bury said; and he felt a cold chill in his stomach.

❋   ❋   ❋

It was standard practice to interview intelligence officers one at a time no matter how closely they might work together. They'd been polite enough to bring Renner and Bury in by separate entrances. Renner glimpsed Bury's travel chair as it wheeled into the reception room. Then he was ushered into Cunningham's office.

Cunningham stood. "Greetings, Captain. Trust you're well."

"Fine." Kevin looked wryly at his expensive civilian clothes. "Didn't know the rank showed."

Cunningham frowned a question.

"Forget it." Renner sat in the visitor's chair and took out a pipe. "Mind?"

98

"No, go ahead." Cunningham glanced at the ceiling. "Georgio, exhaust fans if you please." He tapped keys below a screen that faced away from Renner. "Georgio" set a brisk breeze moving. "Now, Captain, if you could just clear up a couple of points about Maxroy's Purchase . . ."

". . . I'm sure aren't worth worrying about," Renner concluded. "My formal opinion's on record. Governor Jackson not only can handle the situation, he'll have New Utah voluntarily in the Empire in ten years without anyone firing a shot."

Cunningham scratched at the computer entry pad with his stylus. "Thank you. Excellent report of a very creditable job. I can tell you privately that the Admiral's pretty well decided to endorse your report."

"That ought to make Jackson happy."

Cunningham nodded. "Now. What can you tell us about this latest scheme of Bury's?"

Renner spread his hands. "My fault. I came staggering home at one in the morning, dead drunk and covered with blood, shook the old man awake and told him, 'The gripping hand!' Dammit, the whole planet was talking like they've got three arms! Time I finished talking, we were both convinced the Moties were in Purchase system."

"But they weren't."

"No. But they might be somewhere else. I'm with Bury. I want to know the blockade works."

"It works."

"You can't verify that."

"Captain—"

"When did you last visit the blockade? Spend long enough to be sure it's puncture proof? Who was minding the store while you were there? Have you seen clips of the Motie Warriors?" Renner waved it away with a slicing gesture. "Never mind, Captain. The point is, Bury's determined. I haven't even tried to talk him out of it. I don't want to."

"In other words, he'll go whether we like it or not?"

"Let's say he's determined. Besides, what harm can it do? There aren't many secrets he doesn't know, and of all people he's unlikely to give the Moties anything. For that matter, if the blockade personnel ever needed a pep talk, you wouldn't find anyone better than me and Horace Bury . . . mmm . . . with a tranquilizer drip, maybe."

"I take it you intend to go along, then?" Cunningham glanced at the readout screen inlaid on his desk. "You've three times requested retirement and then changed your mind. God knows nothing's stopping you."

Renner chuckled. "What would I retire for? I like what I'm doing, and this way someone else pays the bills. Sure I'll go. I'd like to go back to the Mote."

"Nobody's planning *that!*"

"Not now, maybe, but you'll have to one day."

"You've been with him a long time. Is he—all right?"

"He's death on Moties. He can smell the money currents between the stars. Your office never made a better deal."

"I mean loyal."

"I know what you meant," Renner said. "And the answer is yes. He wasn't always, maybe, but he is now. And why shouldn't he be? He's put this much of his life into making the Empire stronger. Why throw it away?"

"Okay." Cunningham looked up. "Georgio. Call Admiral Ogarkov, please."

After a few moments a voice boomed, "Yes?"

"As we agreed, sir," Cunningham said. "I recommend we give Bury clearance to visit the Blockade Fleet. He may solve the Mei-Ling Trujillo problem for us, and he and Sir Kevin may pep up the Crazy Eddie Squadron. It can't hurt to let him try."

"All right. Talk to Blaine."

"Admiral—"

"He won't bite. Thanks. Good-bye."

Cunningham made a face.

"You don't get along with the Captain?" Renner asked.

"Earl. Don't have that much to do with him," Cunningham said. "He's not Navy. Was once, I know, but he hasn't been for a long time. Georgio, polite mode. I'd like to speak with Lord Blaine. The Earl, not the Marquis. At his earliest convenience. I think he's expecting the call."

✳　　✳　　✳

Bury had hooked up his diagnostic sleeve as soon as he left Cunningham's office. Cunningham's secretary was trying not to stare. He wanted to tell her that he wasn't upset—that he only expected to be upset.

Would Blaine say no?

He practiced deep breathing until his pulse was steady, then fingered the control ball.

"Alysia Joyce Mei-Ling Trujillo. Present age twenty-seven standard years. Feature columnist Imperial Post-Tribune Syndicate, special features reporter, Hochsweiler Broadcasting Network. Highly rated.

"Born New Singapore. Parents Ito Wang Mei-Ling and Regina Trujillo. One older brother. Ito Wang Mei-Ling is the founder of Mei-Ling Silicon Works, New Singapore, publicly traded, current price thirty-one and one-eighth."

Bury fingered in two questions.

"Six million shares, of which he retains forty-five percent. Adding the mother's name is not customary on New Singapore.

"Alysia Joyce attended Hamilton Prep on Xanadu and graduated cum laude in journalism from the Cornish School on Churchill. When she arrived on Sparta, her account in the local branch of the Bank of New Singapore was opened with a letter of credit for three hundred thousand crowns. She worked as a volunteer research assistant to Andrea Lundquist of Hochsweiler at a nominal salary of fifty crowns per week until her news analysis series was sponsored by Wang Factoring."

Bury nodded as he listened. New money. Oriental princess out to save the Empire with her father's money and her mother's name.

Bury glanced down at the telltales. Blood pressure, heartbeat, adrenaline level: all acceptable. Why not? Mei-Ling was an investigative reporter, no different from any other. She thought her wealth protected her, and surely did not think that it also made her vulnerable. Her family was worth a hundred million crowns. *Only* a hundred million crowns.

What was she doing that the Navy feared? No time to read everything now, that would have to wait, but he could begin on the summaries.

"Digest: Series filed from New Caledonia by Alysia Joyce Mei-Ling Trujillo. Series title: 'The Wall of Gold.' "

Bury listened intently, but there was little to surprise him. Markups on maintenance and repair. Luxury supplies sent to the blockade squadron, most obtained without competitive bids. Imperial Autonetics coffeepots, heh heh.

Graft . . . she'd already gotten four men arrested. And several fired from the Navy shipworks on Fomor.

On Levant, bureaucrats were expected to support themselves by bribes and extortion and favors. It was a different system, a mere matter of viewpoint, and not the black-versus-white ethical situation perceived by the Imperial Navy.

This kind of thing wouldn't destroy the blockade . . . not if it were being run by Levantines. Bury's people had a sense of proportion.

Then again, too much graft could bleed any military effort white. Then any kind of enemy could charge through the tissue-thin corpse. According to Trujillo, the grafters were interfering with supplies to the Blockade Fleet! Freeze-dried food stocks, blackbox replacements. One David Grant, high in the Planetary Governor's office, had taken half a billion crowns to replate the blockade ships with Motie superconductor. The scheme existed only in spurious computer memory, praise Allah. There was no superconductor plating in the blockade—and shouldn't be on ships that must regularly descend into a red supergiant star! But what might that stolen money have bought to strengthen the fleet?

What if she was right?

He *had* to speak to Trujillo. He'd go to New Scotland no matter what Earl Blaine said; and then perhaps there would be a way into the blockade. He should learn that anyway, to probe for ways *out*. So search for a handle on Mei-Ling Trujillo. Two hundred million crowns would buy control of her father's company. Who owned the outstanding stock? Bury tapped keys. Might as well find out.

The computer scrolled . . . and here:

"Ito Wang Mei-Ling has retained the services of Reuben Weston Associates."

Hah. Most people had never heard of Reuben Weston, but those who had knew his group as one of the most effective—and expensive—public relations firms in the Empire. They specialized in building contacts at Court. A New Singapore electronics company wouldn't need that kind of service; a provincial mini-tycoon with ambitions to increase his rank most certainly would.

And Bury might help the man . . . but not until he knew how Mei-Ling Trujillo felt about her father. And he could do nothing while marooned in this anteroom. *What was taking Renner so long?*

✳   ✳   ✳

Cunningham hung up. "Blaine won't have it," he said.

"Damn," Renner said.

"Yeah. What is it? They were together on the Mote Prime expedition—"

"No. Something from before. Rumors—" Renner stopped.

"Something I should know?"

"Evidently not. Well, Bury's going to be disappointed, and what happens after that . . . I don't know." *But he sure won't give up easily. . . .*

5
Passengers

For he possessed the happy gift
Of unaffected conversation;
To skim one topic here, one there,
Keep silent with an expert's air
In too exacting disputation.

—Alexander Pushkin

Watching news broadcasts over many years had taught Kevin Renner this much: styles mutated like crazy on Sparta. He knew his clothes didn't look funny because Cunningham's secretary had steered him to Cunningham's tailor. His problem was in identifying a maître d'. A maître d' should stand out.

He watched the other customers.

She was a lovely statuesque blonde wearing a pantsuit with shoulder frills, but the four young men ahead of Renner weren't ogling her, just waiting to catch her eye. None of the other women in his view wore shoulder frills. She walked briskly to a small waist-high desk. The space above the desk was a faint rainbow blur from where Renner was standing, but from her viewpoint it would be a data display with a mug shot for identification.

She led the four away, then came back for Renner. "Good morning. Table, sir?"

"A table sounds useful. Kevin Renner, and I'll be joined by a Bruno Cziller."

She didn't have to tap keys; she just looked. The computer was programmed to pick up names. "Welcome to the Three Seasons, Sir Kevin. I'm very sorry, we don't have your table just yet. Admiral Cziller hasn't arrived. Would you care to wait in the lounge?"

"I'll wait here, thank you." He could see empty tables. He watched her lead another couple past him. Higher rank? But they didn't walk that way. They were trying to keep up and still watch faces without being caught. Celebrity hunters.

"Kevin?"

"Captain!"

Cziller wrung his hand. He looked old, softening in the face, but his hand was still a vise. His voice had turned husky. "Call me Bruno. I've never seen you in civvies. My, you do like colors!"

"Is it—"

"No, you look fine. Hey, I studied your report on Mote Prime, the one with the funny title. Did you ever think you'd be playing tourist with another species?"

"Never did. I owe it all to you."

The statuesque maître d' led them to a table next to a floor-to-ceiling window, with a terrific view out over the harbor. Renner waited until she was gone, then said, "She gave away some tables before she let us have one. I wondered why."

"Rank."

"Well, that's what I thought, but—"

"Serves you right for getting a knighthood. You had to have a window. Wouldn't do to have you sitting with the misters. Sparta's very rank conscious, Kevin."

"Uh-huh. The computer says you married."

"I'd have brought Jennifer, but . . . her sense of humor isn't . . . mmm . . ."

"Isn't there?"

"Right."

"Okay, and I'd have brought one Ruth Cohen, but she's taking a quickie training course at where she works. How are you holding up otherwise?"

"I get the impression I'll last awhile, but—no, never mind."

"You sick, Bruno?"

"Not sick. But the last time I went off planet, my doctor gave me pure hell, and so did Jennifer, of course. Wasn't the gravity, that was fine, but the longer day had me exhausted half to death. I came back with walking pneumonia. I can't travel anymore. I'm getting cabin fever. It's a small world, Kevin."

"Mmm. You could be in a worse place. You get all the news that's fit to broadcast, and all the museums worth visiting—"

"Not all. Tell me about the museum on Mote Prime."

"*That* was different. They took us there in big limousines they made just for us. The other cars were all teeny, and they collapsed flat. Even the limousine could fold smaller. The museum was all enclosed. One big building. Artificial environments inside. In one room it was raining buckets. Moties wanted to lead us in anyway."

Cziller laughed.

"We saw too much to take it all in. There was stuff we should have noticed. There was a wild Porter. Tame Porters are like two-fifty centimeters tall, with two arms, and they carry things. This thing had three arms, and tusks and claws. It was a little smaller."

A tubby robot wheeled up, took a drink order, and produced whiskey screwdrivers. A live waiter followed. A local seabeast was on the menu, and Renner ordered that. The other offerings were Earth life, uninteresting.

He said, "One whole floor was a mockup of a ruined city. There were big five-limbed rats and a camouflaged predator and a lot of other stuff, a whole ecology evolved to live in ruined cities. We didn't see the implications right away. We may not know them all yet. . . . No telling what they've been learning at the Institute, of course. But Horowitz swore that the city rats are related to the Warriors. We haven't ever seen a live Warrior yet, but we had the *Time Machine* sculpture and a silhouette of the Warrior aboard the colony ship they sent to New Cal—"

"War. Continual war."

"Yeah. With their population problem it's hardly surprising. Bruno, do you suppose it's possible to find the man who invented the condom? He deserves a statue somewhere."

Bruno laughed a long, throaty laugh. "I've missed you, Kevin."

Food arrived. Kevin listened while they ate, a habit so old that he'd have had to concentrate *not* to listen. At the next table some lordling was complaining bitterly about . . . what? Fishing rights up in the upper Python River. His family had had exclusive rights, and they'd been rescinded. Something about the salmon breeding cycle: some lowborn bureaucrat had decided that the Dinsmark family wasn't keeping the upstream route sufficiently open.

His companion was insufficiently sympathetic. Kurt Dinsmark wouldn't have had fishing rights anyway, he was a younger son. . . .

And on the gripping hand, Renner thought, *they're talking privi-*

leges instead of duties. How common is that? "We pay the nobles one hell of a stiff fee for running civilization," he said.

"I rarely hear it put that way. So?"

"Oh, I like to keep track of whether they're doing their job. In fact, it's part of *my* job, which is nice, because I was doing it anyway. But what I'm hearing about is privileges."

"Give 'em a break. They're off duty. There was another museum."

Renner nodded slightly. "Yeah. That one's hearsay, and from Moties at that. The Moties killed the midshipmen who stumbled onto it. This one wasn't your ordinary museum. The idea was to help the survivors rebuild civilization."

"Heh." Cziller drained his glass. "If I hadn't got stuck trying to rebuild New Chicago . . ."

Renner made sympathetic noises. "Understand you did a pretty good job, though. Hey, I just had a thought. I'm on duty myself in a couple of hours, but . . . do you get nostalgic for spaceports? And spacecraft?"

"Sure. The new port is in the old crater where the Halfway Dome blew up, and sometimes I go out there just to— What's your thought?"

Renner put down his fork, fished out his comcard. "Get me Horace Bury."

He set the comcard on the table while he finished his meal. It took a while, but presently the card said, "What is it, Renner?"

"I had a thought, Excellency."

"Praise Allah, my training has not been for nothing."

"We're taking Buckman and Mercer up for dinner tonight. Would you consider another guest? It's Bruno Cziller, retired as admiral. He was my captain before he handed me to Blaine. Turned *MacArthur* over to Blaine, too. The Earl's first ship. I've been trying to tell Bruno about Mote Prime, but hey, why not let him listen while you and I and Buckman reminisce? An appreciative audience can be a good thing."

Momentary pause. Bury too was rank conscious. "Good. Put him on, please."

Renner passed the comcard across. Bruno Cziller said, "Excellency?"

"Admiral, we'd be delighted if you could join us for dinner tonight aboard *Sinbad*. The next Viceroy of Trans–Coal Sack will be present. Jacob Buckman is the astronomer who traveled with us to the Mote. We became friends on that trip. You'll hear as much about the Mote system as you can learn outside the Institute."

"Capital. Thank you, Excellency."

"Will you be accompanied?"

"Thank you, no, Excellency. Mrs. Cziller has appointments for the evening."

"Admiral, I'm handing you over to the computer to order your dinner. We'll want a chance to put food stores aboard."

Cziller's eyebrows went up. Renner said, "Bury's got a good chef. Test him out."

Cziller nodded, and did. Presently he passed the comcard back. "Kevin, you never used to be subtle."

"I may have picked up something in a quarter century with Bury. Mercer will be happier if a higher rank is there. And Bury might tell you how he spent his time on Mote Prime. He's never told me."

"Oh?"

"Moties scare him. He'd rather not remember. It's worth a try. Besides, I've got to get to the spaceport early to get the shuttle ready. Why don't—"

"Why don't I come with you to supervise."

"Right. And now I have another thought."

"Expound."

"A month ago we thought we'd found Moties loose in the Empire."

Melon arrived, and Kevin talked while they ate. He had Bruno Cziller chortling. "Now Bury wants to visit the blockade, be sure it's leakproof. So do I, Bruno. Maxroy's Purchase was scary."

"And?"

"Rod Blaine has vetoed it. I'd like to give Bury a shot at changing his mind."

Bruno Cziller was studying him like a lab specimen, or perhaps like the man across from him at a poker table. "I'm the man who gave the Earl his ship and his Sailing Master. I also wished a prisoner on him. Horace Bury was traveling as a prisoner on *MacArthur*. Do you know why?"

"Nope."

"After twenty-five years?"

"I might not have liked it. I've got to live with him, Bruno."

"The question is, why should I get involved?"

"I haven't thought of that part yet."

The coffee arrived. "Real cream," Renner said.

Cziller smiled faintly. "I'd be glad to get used to basic protocarb milk if I could go to space again."

Renner studied his coffee for a moment. "Look, shall I tell Bury you already turned me down, so you don't have to go through this twice?"

Bruno said, "Yes." And they moved on to other matters.

"Smooth," Jacob Buckman said.

Horace Bury looked up in momentary puzzlement, then nodded. The transition to weightlessness had been quite smooth, but Bury was used to Renner's skillful management of the shuttle. He felt tiny accelerations, then the chimes announced they were docked with *Sinbad*. The connecting hatchways swung open. A crewman brought a towline from *Sinbad* into the shuttle and made it fast. "All correct, Excellency," he said.

Bury waited a moment to allow Nabil and his assistants to go ahead, then disconnected himself from his couch. It was good to fly free of the travel chair. "Welcome," he said. "Does anyone wish assistance?"

"Thank you, Excellency," Andrew Mercer Calvin said. He unsnapped his seat belt and allowed himself to drift into the center of the passenger bay. He grasped the towline and tugged himself toward the ship.

Bury followed. As he did, the connecting hatchway to the pilot's compartment opened. Cziller and Renner came out. "My congratulations, Kevin," Bury said. "Dr. Buckman remarked on the smoothness of our ride."

"Not my doing," Renner said.

"Guess I haven't lost all my skills," Cziller said smugly.

In fact there was little for humans to do beyond giving directions to the computer. Or— Bury wondered. Had Cziller flown by direct control? Would Renner have let him, given who their passenger was? *Yes. Yes, he would.*

They clung to a score of handholds while *Sinbad* spun up. Then

Bury led the way into the interior, moving smoothly if not quickly in 60 percent of standard gravity. *Aaah.*

"When I was twenty-six years old," he said to nobody in particular, "the natives of Huy Brasil took exception to some of my policies. They attacked me in the desert east of Beemble Town. I beat them into town, doubled through some alleys, and was back in the desert heading for my shuttle. I outran them all. Sometimes I do miss being young."

"Amen," Cziller said.

"I had to outrun an earthquake once," Buckman said. "I got downstairs and out of the observatory before it shook down on me. I think I could still do it. I run every day." He stopped walking. "Roomy. I knew you were rich, Bury."

Sinbad's lounge was big. Two recessed rails ran down the center, chairs and couches on either side. "Please be seated, and consider this your home," Bury said. "Hazel will take your drink orders."

Bury tended to employ women of great beauty. It wasn't his first priority, but it could help a business transaction to run more smoothly. Mercer was looking at Hazel when he said, "Bury, I like your ship."

"Thank you. It's roomier than it seems. I can attach a pod the size of this lounge and open up that entire oval area in the floor, which is the hull side, of course. The cabins don't become any roomier, but you don't have to spend all your time in them."

Mercer laughed. "I'm surprised you bother with hotels."

"Not always our choice," Renner said. "Customs isn't always as efficient as they were today."

"Ah. Hazel, what do you suggest?"

"We have a good stock of wines, my Lord."

Mercer smiled broadly. "Just what I've missed on Sparta. Dry sherry?"

"Me, too," Cziller said. "Kevin, do you always live like this? I haven't had a decent sherry in five years." He stretched. "Got good legs on this ship?"

"Not bad," Renner said. "She's no battle cruiser, but we can pull a full gee for a long way. The drop tank fits behind the add-on cabin, and it almost doubles our delta-vee."

"And of course you won't have a Langston Field generator in Sparta system," Cziller prompted.

"The Navy approves licenses for private ownership of Field generators sometimes," Renner said. "Outside the Capital. One of Bury's engineering ships will meet us."

"As well," Bury said smoothly. "We were running low on Sumatra Lintong coffee."

Bury watched Mercer and thought he detected envy. He asked, "Will you be leaving for New Caledonia soon, my Lord?"

"There's a Hamilton Lines passenger ship in three weeks," Mercer said. "Or I can go with the Navy relief squadron next month. Haven't quite decided."

Bury nodded in satisfaction.

※　　※　　※

At point six gee, food stayed on the plates, wine stayed in the glasses.

Mercer had had an ulcer in 3037 and a recurrence in 3039. Modern medicine could make those go away, but nothing could cure a high-pressure lifestyle. And Bury was old, and so was Buckman. For them *Sinbad*'s chef had prepared a mild chicken curry.

Cziller had asked for sea grendel, an air-breathing Spartan seabeast on the endangered species list. Sea grendels were being raised in a small bay on Serpens. They were for sale, but the price was high. Renner got it, too. He didn't have to order. His tastes were known: he would eat anything he couldn't pronounce.

"Good," he said. "Really good. Were they hunted to extinction?"

Cziller finished chewing and put his fork down with a broad smile. "Haven't had that since we were invited to the Palace. No, it wasn't overharvesting. The orcas have learned to hunt sea grendel, but that's not it either. Mostly, there's a lot of ocean down there and not much land. The last passing of Menalaus was too close, the ocean got too warm for them, the West Sea thermal plant was stirring up the water, the fish they were eating went into a decline, and suddenly sea grendels were very scarce. Might have been worse but old Baron Chalmondsley got interested in them. Now the University's on top of the problem. Hey, Kevin, what did you eat on Mote Prime?"

"Mostly ship stores, and protocarb milk, but the Moties found us a few things. There was an interesting melon. We didn't bring anything back, of course." Renner set his fork down. "Anything.

111

My Lord, we could have covered *Lenin*'s hull with souvenirs. What would you have brought back, Bury?"

I'll put that back in your teeth, Kevin. "I thought of taking Motie Watchmakers. I thought they would make wonderful pets. That was before they destroyed His Majesty's battle cruiser *MacArthur*. After that I tried to persuade the Admiral to cremate everything."

"My files say you made a fair profit from the superconductors and the filters," Mercer said.

"I would have vaporized them."

Renner asked, "What would you have brought back, Jacob?"

"Information," the astronomer said brusquely. "That, the Admiral didn't prohibit."

Cziller nodded. "Buckman's Protostar. Kevin, did you get anything named after you?"

"Nope."

"What would you have brought back?"

"Artwork. I wanted the *Time Machine* sculpture long before we knew what those demons were. I wanted a certain painting . . . the one my Fyunch(click) called the *Message Bearer*. Another thing we should have noticed. There's a Runner subspecies, and they're still kept around. When the cycles turn and all the Moties' sophisticated communications collapse, there are still the Message Bearers."

"You said information, Dr. Buckman," Mercer said. "I understand the Moties were not permitted to bring any sophisticated record storage devices, but surely you collected your own."

"What I could," Buckman said.

"Of course the Moties themselves are pretty sophisticated record storage devices," Renner said.

"One reason they haven't developed information technology much," Buckman said. "Things fall apart so often."

"More wine, my Lord?" Bury asked, and signaled Hazel to open another bottle.

He could have had fresh fruit shipped up; but Bury wanted to show off *Sinbad*'s kitchen. Dessert was an array of cakes served with fresh espresso. Bury watched Mercer with satisfaction. A Navy wardroom offered nothing like this. The best accommodations on a Hamilton Lines passenger ship could only rival *Sinbad*, and the liner made calls on four planets before reaching New Caledonia.

112

"Of course if this young pup Arnoff has his way, it'll be called Arnoff's Protostar," Buckman said.

Renner laughed. "What? Hey, it was your discovery. I mean, Jock might argue they ought to call it Jock's Protostar, but as far as humans go—"

Mercer said, "Excuse me? I've studied the Mote expedition records, but I must have missed that one."

"Not surprising," Renner said. "Look, from Mote system you get a good look deep into the Coal Sack. While the rest of us were dealing with the sudden fact of an intelligent species older than we are, Dr. Buckman found a curdling in the Coal Sack. He was able to show that it's a protostar. It's a thickening of the interstellar gas that's about to collapse under its own weight. A new sun."

"Jacob, what is this?" Bury asked.

"Oh, this young idiot believes I got it all wrong, that the protostar will ignite any day now."

"But surely you would have known," Bury protested. "You had *MacArthur*'s instruments for observation."

"Some of the data were lost when we abandoned ship," Buckman reminded him. "Only they weren't."

One of the reasons Bury liked Buckman was that their interests were so different. He was a man Bury couldn't use. Bury could relax when Buckman was around.

In fact, Bury was paying more attention to Mercer. But he noticed how Renner's hands suddenly gripped the table's edge. Renner said, "What?"

"Some of the observation files were beamed to *Lenin*," Buckman said. "There were Watchmakers all through *MacArthur* then, and the information came all in one dump. About a year ago they were doing upgrades on *Lenin* and the files turned up." Buckman shrugged. "Nothing I thought was new, but this fellow Arnoff thinks he's got enough for a new theory."

Renner said gently, "Jacob, wouldn't you like to live to see it become a star?"

Buckman shifted uncomfortably. "Well, I'd look foolish, but . . . it's impossible anyway. Sometimes it seems unfair. My Fyunch-(click) believed that the fusion burn will begin within the next thousand years. I've reviewed my observations repeatedly since, and I think he's right. I came that close."

"A Mediator. Your Fyunch(click) wasn't really an astronomer.

Male, wasn't it? A male would be too young to have had practice at anything."

"Mediators learn to think like their targets. My Mediator was an astronomer, Kevin, at least by the time we separated."

"Uh-huh. Does the Navy know about this Arnoff's theories?" Renner asked.

"I suppose someone in the Bureau of Research watches astrophysics file updates," Buckman said. "Why the Navy?"

"Gerbil shit! Doctor, you have *got* to learn to look outside your specialty!"

"Kevin?" Bury demanded.

"If the protostar ignites, we get new Alderson paths," Renner said.

"It won't happen," Buckman protested.

"A moment," Mercer said quietly. "Sir Kevin, could you explain?"

"I may have to lecture."

"Please do so."

"Okay. Ships travel along Alderson tramlines. Tramlines form between stars, along lines of equipotential flux. I won't explain that, you got it in high school, but it means they don't form between all pairs of stars. Not all the tramlines are useful, because if the flux densities aren't high enough, they won't carry anything big enough to have a drive aboard.

"The Mote sits out there with the Coal Sack on one side and the big red supergiant Murcheson's Eye on the other. The Eye is big and bright. So bright that the only useful tramline from the Mote is not only to the Eye, it terminates inside the supergiant. Tough on Moties trying to use that tramline. The blockade is there to make it even tougher.

"When Buckman's Protostar ignites, it'll create new tramlines."

"To where? Who would I ask?"

"Damned if I know," Renner said. "Dr. Buckman, maybe. It depends on the energy levels after ignition."

"But the Moties could escape." Bury had his diagnostic sleeve on. It showed him staying remarkably calm, considering. As if he had always known, always known they would get out.

"Yeah," Renner said.

Mercer caught Hazel's eye. "Another of that excellent brandy, please. Thank you, Bury. There's no better at the Palace. Now. Sir

Kevin, let me get this straight. For a quarter of a century the Empire has spent billions of crowns to maintain a blockade to contain the Moties, as an alternative to sending in a battle fleet to exterminate them. Now you say that if Dr. Buckman's theory is incorrect, that blockade will be ineffective. Suddenly. Is that a fair statement?"

"As I always feared," Bury said. Renner was nodding, teeth bared.

"Nonsense," Buckman insisted. "That star won't collapse in our lifetimes, I don't care how good your doctors are!"

"I find that comforting," Mercer said. "You will understand that as the new Governor General of the Trans–Coal Sack Sector, I will automatically become chairman of the commission that sets policy regarding the Moties? I'd thought the Motie policy fixed and settled. The political questions regarding New Scotland and New Ireland are more than enough to renew my ulcers." He sipped at the huge snifter Hazel had brought him.

"Jacob." Bury sounded very old. "You once had a different notion about the protostar."

"Oh, I don't think so."

"It was long ago, and memories are fallible," Bury said. His hand strayed to the input ball of his chair, and his fingers played complex chords with the buttons. The inboard wall of the lounge became translucent.

Two images formed. Bury and Buckman, both twenty-five years younger, dressed in shipboard clothing fashionable that long ago.

"Buckman, you really must eat," Bury's image said. "Nabil! Sandwiches."

"The Navy people only let me use the telescopes at their convenience," the younger Buckman said. "Computers, too."

"Are either available now?"

"No. Of course you're right. Thank you. Only—Bury, it's so damned *important*."

"Of course it is. Tell me about it."

"Bury, do I know astrophysics?" Buckman's image didn't wait for a reply. "Not even Horvath thinks he knows more. But the Moties—Bury, they've got a lot of new theories. Some new math to go with it. The Eye. We've been studying the Eye since Jasper Murcheson's time. We've always known it would explode one day. The Moties know *when!*"

Bury's image looked apprehensive. "Not soon, I trust?"

115

"They say A.D. 2,774,020 on April twenty-seventh."

"Doctor—"

"Oh, they're trying to be funny, but dammit, Bury, they're a lot closer than we were, and they can prove that! Then there's the protostar."

Bury's image raised an eyebrow.

"There's a protostar out there," Buckman said. "Forming out in the Coal Sack. I can prove it. It's about ready to collapse."

The younger Bury smiled politely. "I know you a little, Jacob. What do you mean by *now*? Will you have time to eat?"

"Well, what *I* meant was sometime in the next half a million years. But the Moties have been watching it a long time. My— student—how do you say it?"

"Fyunch(click)," Bury's younger image said. (Eyes flicked toward the living Bury. Could a human being have made that sound?)

"Yeah. He says it'll take a thousand years, plus or minus forty."

A younger Nabil came on-screen with sandwiches and an old-fashioned thermos.

Bury touched his controls and the wall faded out. "You see, Jacob? You were led to your theory. Left alone, what might you have thought?"

Buckman frowned. "Not the Moties. Their math."

"Observation reports, too," Renner said. "Theirs."

"Well, yes . . . yes, of course. But Kevin, you're . . ."

"What?"

"You're suggesting my Fyunch(click) lied to me."

"It never would have crossed my mind," Bury said gently, "that my Fyunch(click) would not lie to me. Kevin's played jokes on him, of course. Lady Blaine's certainly lied to her. It's on record."

"Yes." Buckman was not happy. "Then Arnoff's right."

"Jacob? Come with me aboard *Sinbad* to Murcheson's Eye. You can get new data. If you can't destroy this Arnoff's reconstruction, you can refine it, improve it, until half of civilization thinks it's yours."

"I'll come," Buckman said quickly.

"This dithering is a bad habit, Jacob," Renner said.

"I'm getting tired of reviewing old data anyway."

"When does Arnoff say is the earliest this—event—could happen?" Mercer asked.

"Last month," Buckman said.

Mercer looked puzzled. "Then it could already have happened and we would not know. I think you said your protostar was light-years from any observer?"

"Oh," Cziller said. "No, my Lord. It has been known since Co-Dominium times that Alderson tramlines form as nearly instantaneously as anything can be in this universe."

"There's a propagation speed," Buckman said. "We just don't know what it is. No way to measure it." The astrophysicist looked thoughtful. "All the really interesting events happen in the last dozen years."

"Now. They could be happening now," Renner said. "You know what this means? It may be important to have a ship from the Crazy Eddie Squadron pop into the Mote system long enough to get data on the protostar."

"Allah be merciful," Bury said. He straightened visibly. "Well, my Lord, I promised you an entertaining dinner."

"You've kept that promise," Mercer said.

"Now may I offer you more? I have long intended to go to New Caledonia. I would be more than pleased to have you as a guest for the journey."

"That's generous," Mercer said. "I'd like to accept."

"But you do not?" Bury asked.

Mercer sighed. "Excellency, I'm a politician. Successful, I think, but still a politician. I don't know how it happened, but you have made a very powerful enemy."

"Captain Blaine," Renner said.

"Earl Blaine. Precisely. I need not tell anyone in this room just how powerful the Blaine family is. As the first members of the Imperial Commission, they set the policies on our relations with the Moties. The old Marquis has a standing invitation at the Palace. Frankly, I can't afford to have their opposition."

"No argument there," Cziller said.

Mercer shrugged. "Excellency, I can see great benefits to having your friendship, and a comfortable and expeditious journey is probably the least of them, but what can I do?"

"Let me get something straight," Cziller said. "His Excellency's—uh, strong distrust—of Moties is well known. My last assignment was in BuPolDoc—excuse me, the Navy's Bureau of Policy and Doctrines—and Bury, you had half a dozen expensive Imperial Autonetics PR types trying to convince everyone in the Navy."

"I suppose I became something of a joke," Bury said.

"Not that, Excellency. Hardly that. But maybe we stopped giving your holos quite as high a priority when they mentioned Moties. Kevin, I never knew you considered Moties a threat. Your video report sure doesn't come across that way."

Renner nodded. "I had a wonderful time on the Mote expedition, and I guess that's what showed. That report was for the media. I didn't make it for the Navy. For that matter, I have to calm Bury down sometimes.

"Even so, at Maxroy's Purchase I was the one who ran around shrieking, 'The Moties are coming!' I'm not *blind*. A couple of points, okay? I love Mediators. Especially my own Fyunch(click), and I suppose that's just my natural narcissism. We all felt that way. Every so often I have to remind myself that everyone who thinks he likes Moties actually likes Motie Mediators. They're the ones who do all the talking. But the Masters make all the decisions, and they only talk to and through Mediators. Clear?"

"A point worth noting," Cziller said. "My Lord, did you know that the Blaine children had Motie nannies when they were growing up? It wasn't generally publicized."

Renner said, "Yeah. Second. I like Bury. Tastes differ, but I like Horace Bury just fine. You didn't know that, did you, Bury?"

Bury felt his cheeks warming. "You've never said that."

"Yeah. But he's *dangerous*. Check his record. The Moties are likewise *dangerous*, and I don't mean Mediators now, I mean a dozen species that think like robber barons and build like idealized engineers and carry a ton of stuff on their shoulders and do their farming with an inborn green thumb and fight like God knows what. We've never seen Warriors fight, but if they're as good at war as Engineers are at tinkering, yuk."

"One must not forget their sexual cycle," Bury said.

"Yeah. If they don't get pregnant, they die horribly. Is that a population problem, or what?"

Cziller waved that away. "We don't need *that* lecture. Everybody knows it. We know how they solve it, too. Wars. It's why we had to lock them up in the first place. Damn! I suppose it is . . . scary, to think of Mediators lecturing at Blaine Institute and raising little Blaines. There was a Master, too, but I hear he died early."

"The Blaine children. We met young Glenda Ruth. She was grateful for a present I provided."

Cziller looked thoughtful. "My Lord, you said you could see advantages to His Excellency's friendship."

"Well—"

"Pardon me, my Lord. I wasn't arguing. I can see advantages, too." Cziller looked grim. "Look, I'm as loyal as anybody, but I'm not blind. The Empire just isn't as efficient as it was thirty years ago. When the Moties were first discovered, Merrill was Viceroy out there behind the Coal Sack. Old Navy man. He had a battle fleet together before Sparta even knew there was a problem. You couldn't do that now, my Lord."

"No, Admiral, I probably couldn't," Mercer said.

"You can't even get Sparta to react that fast," Cziller said. "It's like we've got fat in the arteries. My Lord, if the Moties really are dangerous, and that damn star really is about to let them out, you're going to need all the clout you can get. Blaine and Bury together wouldn't be too much."

Mercer nodded. "I can't argue, but I can't think what to do, either. I don't know why the Earl so thoroughly disapproves of Trader Bury."

"I do," Cziller said. "Damn all, I promised Jennifer I wouldn't get into this. Excellency, would you ask your computer to help me place a call? Blaine Manor."

"You can get through?" Renner asked.

"Once. I can't abuse the privilege or they'll change the codes on me." He turned to Bury. "Excellency, I think it's about time you and Rod Blaine had a talk about New Chicago."

Ice ran up Bury's spine, and he saw his indicators jump.

6
The Seeds
of Treason

Each man must for himself alone decide what is right and what is wrong, which course is patriotic and which isn't. You cannot shirk this and be a man.

—Mark Twain

The informal luncheon room of the Drakenberg Club was paneled in walnut, then decorated with a theme Renner didn't recognize: pictures of men in strange uniforms, carrying odd implements that included oversize gloves for one hand, and a small white ball.

The club steward ushered him to a table. Glenda Ruth Blaine was already there. The steward bowed formally. "My Lady, your guest."

"Thank you, William," she said. "William, this is my brother's godfather, Sir Kevin Renner."

"Ah. Pleased to meet you, Sir Kevin. Shall I send the waiter, my Lady?"

"Please." Glenda Ruth waited until the steward was gone, then flashed a hefty grin. "Made his day, we did. William does love rubbing elbows with the aristocracy."

Kevin Renner sat. He couldn't help thinking what a remarkably pretty girl Glenda Ruth was. Not beautiful in the fashion-magazine sense. Something else, something about her infectious smile. Of course she was only seventeen standard years old, but she seemed older. Influence of the Moties? Her mother hadn't been a lot older, no more than twenty-five, when she'd gone to the Mote world. Renner tried to remember what Sally Fowler had been like.

He indicated the half dozen forks at his place. "Bit fancy for lunch?"

Glenda Ruth winked at him. "Stuffy place, but it was the only one I could think of where you can't possibly grab the check."

"Is that important?"

Her smiled faded slightly. "It might be. Daddy doesn't want us accepting favors from Horace Bury. We're guessing you have an expense account."

"I do, but this isn't business. Or is it?"

She shrugged. "It might be. I took Admiral Cziller's call. After he talked to Daddy, I called him back."

"Yeah, I suppose you would know him."

"You could say that." She chuckled. "I called him Uncle Bruno until I was ten— Here's the waiter. Champagne cocktail for me. Kevin?"

"Bit early for drinking. Coffee, please."

"Yes, sir."

Glenda Ruth was grinning at him again. "You don't need to be so adult."

"Eh?"

"They know how old I am. My champagne cocktail won't have alcohol in it. Of course some kids just slip in vodka from a flask."

"Will you?"

"I don't even *own* a flask."

"Motie influence?"

"No, none of them ever mentioned it."

Hmm? But she *didn't* drink. But— "Yeah. They wouldn't see the point. They eat, drink, *breathe* industrial poison. If you aren't tough enough, you die. Why go looking for more?"

She nodded. "That sounds right."

Kevin looked around the room. Typical aristocratic luncheon place. Expensive women and very busy men. He didn't really notice them. He looked away from the table so he wouldn't look as if he were staring at the girl he was with, and the truth was that he very much wanted to stare at her. She was far and away the most attractive woman in the room. Probably the most expensive, too, Kevin thought. Her clothes were simple enough, a dark wool afternoon dress that fit perfectly, emphasizing her femininity without being overtly sexy. The skirt was just knee length, slightly conservative by current fashions, but that tended to emphasize the calves and ankles. Her jewelry was simple, but included a matched pair of earrings of Xanadu firestones worth enough to buy a house on Renner's home planet.

"Quite a long way from Maxroy's Purchase," Renner said.

"Or from New Caledonia."

"True. How long were you there?"

"I barely remember it," Glenda Ruth said. "Dad thought Kevin Christian and I ought to grow up on Sparta instead of in the provinces." She shrugged. "I suppose he was right, but—I worry about the Moties, now that Mother and Dad aren't on the Commission."

"They're not on the Commission, but they still have plenty of influence," Renner said. "As Bury and I found out."

"Yeah. Sorry about that."

"So. What did you want to see me about?" Renner asked.

"Crazy Eddie."

"Uh?"

"You said back at the Institute that we don't understand Crazy Eddie. He's supposed to fail?"

"Yes, I guess I said that."

"I've only known three Moties," she said. "I think I understand Crazy Eddie, but I'm not sure. You knew a lot of Moties—"

"Not for long. Not very well."

"Well enough to understand Crazy Eddie."

"Not understand, exactly."

"You know what I mean. There were a dozen stories about Crazy Eddie. Most were recorded, and I have them. There was the story they told you, for instance." She took out her pocket computer and scribbled on it for a moment. An image rose out of the tablecloth.

Renner had taken this sequence straight from *MacArthur's* records as beamed to *Lenin*. A twisted shape in brown-and-white fur, a Motie Mediator, was speaking. "Renner, I must tell you of a creature of legend.

"We will call him Crazy Eddie, if you like. He is a . . . he is like me, sometimes, and he is a Brown, an idiot savant tinker, sometimes. Always he does the wrong things for excellent reasons. He does the same things over and over, and they always bring disaster, and he never learns."

The image jumped a bit. Renner had edited this for *Summer*

Vacation. "When a city has grown so overlarge that it is in immediate danger of collapse . . . when food and clean water flow into the city at a rate just sufficient to feed every mouth, and every hand must work constantly to keep it that way . . . when all transportation is involved in moving vital supplies, and none is left over to move people out of the city should the need arise . . . then it is that Crazy Eddie leads the movers of garbage out on strike for better working conditions."

Glenda Ruth turned it off. Renner said, "I remember. My introduction to Crazy Eddie. Once we knew what to ask for, we got more. Jock Sinclair's Motie spoke of melting down your supply of screws to make a screwdriver. Father Hardy's Mediator talked about a religion that preached abstention from sex. We didn't know how bizarre that was, for Moties."

"Yes, but you know, we never did learn much more about it," Glenda Ruth said. "So why did you say that Crazy Eddie is supposed to fail? Don't the Moties admire Crazy Eddie? Jock certainly does."

"You'd know more than me. But yes, I think they all admire anyone *mad* enough to think all problems have solutions. Which doesn't mean that they expect the universe to cooperate."

"No, of course not. But I still wonder."

"The Cycles," Renner said. "It's all they have for history. Crazy Eddie thinks he can change all that. End the Cycles. Of course they admire him. They also know he's crazy, and it won't happen."

"But maybe we have the solution now. The parasite."

"Yeah, I've wondered about that," Renner said. The waiter brought coffee, and a tall champagne glass with something sparkling and pink for Glenda Ruth. Kevin ordered absently, his mind far from food.

"You knew two Mediators," Renner said. "Of course you didn't get to know Ivan."

"No. He was—more aloof. Masters are."

"And the Mediators speak for them," Renner said. "That's more obvious on the Mote than it would have been to you. But it's something you don't dare forget. Take your parasite. Jock can't make any deal that's binding on Masters back on the Mote."

"Yes—"

"There's also the question of how your parasite would get to the Mote. I doubt the Navy will let any ships go there."

"I talked to Uncle Bruno this morning," Glenda Ruth said.

"Eh?"

"The protostar. When it ignites, the Moties will come out. We have to do something before that happens. I'm sure Admiral Cziller is talking to all his classmates right now."

"Will something happen soon?"

"Of course not. Sparta isn't like that. It will have to be discussed in the Navy, then at the Palace, then the politicians will get in the act."

"Fortunately it may not collapse soon. Or does Jock know something?"

She shook her head. "He doesn't know, and he wouldn't have known. Ivan may have known things we weren't supposed to find out, but Jock and Charlie never did. And Ivan was no astronomer. He wouldn't be. Keepers aren't usually curious." The waiter brought lunch. Glenda Ruth talked all during lunch, drawing Renner out, until he realized he had told her nearly everything he'd ever thought about the Mote.

She's a damned good listener. Cares what you say. Of course she would—it's hard to tell what's an act and what isn't. Maybe none of it is.

She waited until dessert before she said, "Bruno said he wished he could go with you. To the Mote."

"We're not going to the Mote. Just to the Crazy Eddie Squadron—maybe not there, if your father doesn't lift his veto. You know he's blocking the trip. Can you talk to him?"

"I can talk. It won't help. They don't much listen to me. But I'll try—if I get Daddy to say yes, can I go with you?"

Renner managed to set the coffee cup down without spilling any.

*　　*　　*

Glenda Ruth looked defiantly at her mother. "Aaall right. You won't let Kevin and Horace Bury go. Fine. I won't go with them. I'll go with Freddy."

"Freddy!"

"Certainly. He has a ship."

"Pretty good one, too," Rod Blaine said. Sally's look silenced him before he could say anything else.

124

"You are *not* going halfway across the galaxy with that—"

Glenda Ruth cocked her head. "Freddy? You can hardly complain about his social standing. His family is as prominent as ours. About as rich, too. We went out beyond the moon for a week during Spring vacation. You didn't search wildly for an appropriate insult then."

"Did—" Sally caught herself. "It's a bit different, being in a small ship for months."

"If it's my reputation that worries you, we can take a chaperone. Or one of my friends from the Institute. Jennifer. And her mother."

"That's absurd. Jennifer can't afford that."

"I can, Mother. I'll be eighteen in two weeks, and I'll have my own money. Uncle Ben left me quite a lot, you know."

Rod and Sally exchanged looks.

"What does Freddy's father have to say about this?" Sally demanded.

"For that matter, have you asked Freddy?" Rod asked. "I know you haven't asked Bury."

"She doesn't think she has to ask anyone," Sally said.

Glenda Ruth laughed. "Freddy will be glad to take me anywhere, and you know it. And his father doesn't care what he does, if he won't join the Navy."

"Which he won't," Rod said.

"Because he knows he wouldn't be any good at it," Glenda Ruth said.

Sally shook her head. "I don't see what you see in Freddy Townsend—"

"You wouldn't, Mother. He's not a hero like you. Or Daddy. But I like him. He's funny. And Jock likes him."

"You must like him a lot if you're willing to be cooped up in that yacht of his for several months," Rod said. "And I don't think you would for a trip to Saint Ekaterina. Widget—"

"Please don't call me that."

"Sorry, Princess."

"Go ahead and wriggle, my Lord, but you'll have to think of me as an adult soon or sooner. Two weeks to practice, My Lord Blaine."

Blaine recovered fast, but for an instant he'd been jolted. Then, "Glenda Ruth, I know why Bury wants to go to New Caledonia. He wants to inspect the Blockade Fleet. But why you? Freddy's ship can't go to the blockade point! It's inside a star, and last time I looked there wasn't any Langston Field on that yacht."

"I want to see my brother. I don't have to visit the Blockade Fleet for that. He gets to New Cal twice a year."

Sally snorted. "Brother. What you want to do is go to the Mote."

"Chris would, too," Rod said. "But neither of you is going to do it."

"She's persuasive," Sally said. "And so is Chris. Together—"

"Separately or together our children aren't going to talk the Navy into *that*," Rod said. "Prin—Glenda Ruth, this is silly. You're upsetting your mother. You are not going to New Caledonia."

"I am, yes. I don't want to start a big fight, but really, how can you stop me? In two weeks I'll have my own money." She grinned. "Of course I could marry Freddy . . ."

Sally looked horrified, then laughed. "Serve you right if you did."

"Anyway, I don't have to."

"You've already been accepted at the University," Sally said.

"Yes, and I'll go, but not just now." Glenda Ruth shrugged. "Lots of kids take a *wanderjahre* before starting college. Why not me?"

"All right. Let's be serious," Rod said. "Why?"

Glenda Ruth said, "I'm worried about the Moties."

"Why should you be worried about the Moties?" Sally asked.

"Politics. Growing up in this house, I've seen a lot of politics go past my nose. When the Parliament starts debating the cost of the Blockade Fleet, anything can happen. Anything! Suppose they think it costs too much? They aren't going to just pull the fleet back to New Cal. You know they won't. They'll—" She caught herself.

"They'll what?" Sally asked.

Her voice was no more than a whisper. "They'll send for Kutuzov."

Sally frowned and looked to Rod.

He shrugged. "The Admiral retired long ago. He's pretty old. As old as Bury, I guess. Last I heard he was still active in Saint Ekaterina politics, but he doesn't come here."

"He's organized Mankind First," Glenda Ruth said.

Rod frowned. "I hadn't heard he was behind that group. How sure is this?"

"Freddy told me, but I had a chance to back it up. Sir Radford

Bowles spoke for Mankind First at a University of Sparta symposium. Freddy took me. I got in an argument with him at the tea afterward. I watched him. He's picked up some of Admiral Kutuzov's mannerisms."

Rod shook his head, smiling. "I tore the first Motie probe apart, so the Humanity League wanted my hide. Now this Mankind First outfit wants to use Blaine Institute research to wipe out the Moties! I can't win."

"It's not you who can't win," Glenda Ruth said. "It's the Moties who'll lose. And there's no reason."

"There aren't any Moties," Rod said.

"Dad—"

"Not the way you say it. There are plenty of Moties, all right. A planet full of them. More in their Trojan Point clusters and the moons of the gas giant. But there's no single Motie civilization, Glenda Ruth. Never was, never will be. Every Master is independent."

"I know that."

"Sometimes I wonder if you do."

"Dad, I know more about Moties than you do! I've read *every-thing*, including your debriefings, *and* I grew up with Moties."

"Yes. You had the Motie *Mediators* as friends and companions. Sometimes I wonder if that was such a good idea," Rod said. "Your mother didn't like it much."

"I went along," Sally said. "Glenda Ruth, you think you know as much about Moties as we do. Maybe you're right. Maybe you aren't, though. You've only known three of them. Only two at all well. And you want to gamble with the lives of the whole human race—"

"Oh, Mother, stop that. How am I gambling with anything? I can't even get to Mote Prime. Dad knows that."

Rod nodded. "Pretty hard to do. The Blockade Fleet's there as much to keep the Imperial Traders out as to keep the Moties in. You sure won't get to the Mote in Freddy Townsend's yacht."

"Then I can go to New Caledonia?"

"I thought you weren't leaving us any choice."

"Dad, Mom, I'd rather have your blessing."

Rod Blaine asked, "Why?"

"If all else failed, I could come running to you for help. Something could go wrong. I'm not crazy enough to think it couldn't."

"Rod—Rod, is that ship safe?" Sally asked.

Glenda Ruth grinned.

✳ ✳ ✳

The limousine landed on the roof of the Blaine Institute. Three security guards politely helped Bury into his travel chair and escorted him to the elevators. There was no receptionist. As Bury entered the elevator, a guard took out badges and handed them to him and Renner.

So. Formally correct. Bury wished that Admiral Cziller had come to the meeting. Cziller understood. Bury wasn't sure why, but it was clear. And both Blaine and Renner respected him.

The elevator door opened. Two more uniformed guards ushered them down the hall to the Blaine office suite. There was no one else in the corridor.

The guards opened the doors without knocking.

Both Blaines were present. Bury felt relief. *This is an impossible task, but it would be doubly so without her. Whatever I can say to him she can veto. Only Allah can persuade those who will not listen, and He doesn't do that.*

Lady Blaine was pouring coffee. She had not spoken to Bury or Renner, and there was no shaking of hands.

The Blaines wore kimono-like garments in strong contrast to the formal tunics Bury and Renner were wearing. Bury had seen clothing similar to those kimonos in the streets of Sparta, and even in restaurants. They were acceptable for receiving guests, but they were neither friendly nor formal.

Bury had never seen Roderick Blaine in short sleeves. Smooth, hairless scar tissue ran from the knuckles up his left arm into the sleeve; and when Bury understood why, he knew he had lost.

He accepted coffee. It was excellent . . . it was Jamaica Blue Mountain. Bury held the cup before his face for an extra moment, to gather himself. "Very good. Sumatra, perhaps, mixed with local black?"

The Blue Mountain's entire coffee crop had been reserved for Sparta, the Palace and the nobles, for half a thousand years. Bury recognized it—but he wasn't supposed to.

The Earl said, "Kevin, I take it you're with him."

Renner nodded. "Yes, Captain. I came with him. I want to see the blockade fleet in action. I want to know if they're ready for something totally off the wall. Captain, we did some talking last night, and things came out. Have you spent any amount of time talking to Jacob Buckman, the astronomer?"

"No, of course not. Who would?"

"I would," Bury murmured.

"Forgive me, your Excellency."

Renner laughed. "Two green monkeys. What kind of company could either of them find aboard a working battleship?"

Bury glared. Renner continued, "None of us knew why Bury was aboard. I suppose Jack Cargill did, but all you said to us was that His Excellency was a guest, and he was not to leave the ship. I never quite knew—"

Blaine said, "All right. Did Buckman say anything worthy of note?"

"We thought so," Renner said. "Some old data on Buckman's Protostar surfaced from *Lenin*. Do you remember the curdle in the Coal Sack, twenty light-years in and a light-year across?"

Sally Blaine looked puzzled. Lord Blaine nodded without enthusiasm.

Get to the point, Bury wanted to shout, but he sat tight-lipped. He had agreed to let Renner begin the conversation.

"It's a protostar, an unborn star," Renner said. "Buckman's Motie said it'd ignite around a thousand years from now. Buckman confirmed that. Now there's a young guy who thinks he can prove that it'll happen much sooner, and he's using observations from *MacArthur*."

"So? It'll still be Buckman's Protostar."

"It'll be a T Tauri star, Captain. Very bright. The second question is when. The gripping hand is, is the blockade fleet ready to deal with several new Jump points?"

Blaine's lips moved silently. *New Jump points*— "God's teeth."

The coffee trembled in Sally Blaine's hand. "Kevin Christian—"

"Yeah," Blaine said. "All right, I owe Cziller an apology. How valid is this?"

Bury said, "My Lord, it was a very late night. I summoned up this Arnoff's work and went over it with Jacob at my shoulder. He pointed out equations and compared them to his own. I understood nothing, but I know this. They use the same observational data, but Jacob used additional data, older data, which he took from Motie astronomers.''

"That could have been faked." Blaine sat at his desk. "Which would mean they were ready for us from the first moments they saw us. They saw how the protostar could be used. Before we did."

"They knew about the Alderson Drive," Renner said. "They call it the Crazy Eddie Drive. It makes ships vanish. But they already knew how to build it, and they won't have forgotten."

"Cycles," Sally Blaine said. "They play on them. Use them. We can ask Jock—"

"We will," Blaine said, "but we know what answer we'll get. Buckman was given doctored data."

Bury shrugged. "Moties lie to their Fyunch(click)s. Who should know that better than we?"

Sally nodded grimly. "They don't like it—" and she saw Bury's flicker of a smile.

Rod Blaine finished his coffee before he spoke again. "All right, Kevin. You've made your point. A good one. The government has to do something about this. I'll call the Palace as soon as we're done here. That still doesn't tell me why you. Why Bury. Why *Sinbad*."

"A piece at a time," Renner said. "Okay? First, you have to send Buckman. We need new observations, and someone to interpret them."

No interruption came. He said, "Second, New Cal system has to be ready. However the Moties get out—and this includes anything they might try, Captain, protostar or no protostar—they'll have to come through New Caledonia. That's where the crucial Jump point leads, as far as I can tell from a first cut.

"We met Mercer, the new Governor General. Had him aboard *Sinbad* last night. He's a politico, Captain. Sharp, but still a politico. Not a Navy man. He's got the sense to listen, but you still have to talk slow and repeat yourself and use simple words. He has to have things explained to him."

"So?"

"We'd have time to work on him if he rides with us to New Cal. Once we get there, there's a certain large-mouthed reporter named Mei-Ling Trujillo who's doing her best to cut the funding for the Crazy Eddie Fleet. The noise she's stirred up, Cunningham already wants to send her to the Fleet. She's got the clout, she might find something she likes, and at least it would shut her up for a while.

"Fourth, there's Bury. If you haven't seen the record, I can tell you. He's been one hell of an effective agent for the Empire. More than me. Now one of your best agents sees a threat to the Empire and wants to investigate. So do I."

"I see." Blaine looked at Bury. His expression was anything but friendly. "It seems we made a good decision about you, all those years ago."

"As it happens, my Lord."

"I still don't trust you."

"Do you trust me, Captain?" Renner demanded.

"Eh—"

"And while we're on the subject, trust who to do what?"

"Sure I trust you," Blaine said. "You think the whole Spartan nobility is working for you. Okay, I don't mind being supervised. Maybe it makes the Empire stronger. But—Excellency, I'm not sure you want the Empire stronger."

Bury said, "If twenty-eight years of service—" and ran out of words. If twenty-eight years of holding back the darkness wasn't sufficient, then . . . there was nothing to be said.

"You see?" Blaine was trying to be reasonable. "We don't have to send Buckman, Kevin, in case you've arranged things so he'll only go with Bury."

"No, Captain, it's just that way. He's—"

"We can send Arnoff. Or a host of others. Kevin, I have good reason not to trust Bury, and damned little reason why I should."

Renner's voice rose. "Captain, for twenty-eight damn years we've been out working for the Empire—"

"Kevin, you can't possibly convince me you haven't enjoyed it," Sally said.

"Well, all right, so I did." Renner sipped his coffee. "Captain, let's talk about your arm for a minute."

Blaine took a count of three. Then, "Why in blazes would you want to talk about my arm?"

"Well, you're wearing short sleeves, for one thing. And I now recall that when you came back aboard *MacArthur* at New Chicago, you were wearing a big padded cast. How'd you get those scars? Did it have anything to do with the revolt?"

Blaine said, "Why don't you stick to the subject, Renner?"

Bury was wishing the same thing with all his heart. It was hopeless. Bury hadn't tried to shut Renner up in a very long time.

Renner said, "Nobody wears short sleeves to meet someone he doesn't like. I think your scars may have something to do with your attitude here. Was it a burn-through? You don't get those anymore."

"Yeah. New Chicago. The Langston Field took a torpedo, got a hot spot, burned right through the hull. The flame fused my arm to the sleeve of my pressure suit."

"And now they're plating all the Navy ships with Motie superconductor."

"Ye-ess. You understand, it doesn't mean we don't get killed anymore. We don't get *hurt*. Burn-through in the Langston Field, the whole hull warms up. Till it gets too hot. Then it isn't a superconductor anymore, and everyone fries."

"And the sleeves?"

The Earl was rubbing the bridge of his nose. It hid his expression, a bit. "I . . . suppose I was being belligerent. I wasn't going to mention it myself, but I was damned if I'd let His Excellency forget. Petty of me. Kevin, I wouldn't let an old grudge get in the way of Imperial goals. I thought you knew. Bury was a prisoner on *MacArthur*. He was suspected of instigating the New Chicago revolt."

"And you were in one of the prison camps," Renner said to Sally Blaine.

"And a friend came with me, and she never went home," she said. Her eyes narrowed. "And he's guilty as hell. He pushed a whole world into revolt just to bloat his already bloated fortune!"

"Um," said Renner, "no."

"We had the proof," the Earl said. "We showed it to him. We used it to make him work for us— What?"

Lady Blaine had put her hand on her husband's scarred wrist. She said, "Kevin. What do you mean, no?"

"I've known him more than twenty-five years. Bury breaks rules for enough money, but there *wasn't* enough money. There couldn't have been. New Chicago isn't rich. Never was, was it?"

"Well, it was once . . . come to think of it—"

"Captain, we've *stopped* revolts. You know what causes revolts? Bury knows. Crop failure! It's an old tradition: when the crops fail, the people depose the king. Trust me, if New Chicago was ready for a revolt, then it probably wasn't worth robbing, not to the likes of Horace Bury."

Blaine said, "All right, Bury. Why? We never asked."

"I wouldn't have answered. Why should I testify against myself?"

Blaine shrugged.

"You will listen?" Bury demanded.

Blaine looked at him quickly. "Yes, Excellency."

Bury spared a glance for his diagnostics. He'd set them high; he didn't want to be too calm. Nothing had triggered. Good . . .

"Thirty-five years, my Lord. You would have been twelve when I entered New Chicago politics. Of course I was not acting for myself."

"For whom, then?" Sally demanded.

"For Levant, my Lady. And all the other Arabs that Levant represents."

"You were ALO?" Blaine asked.

"My Lord, I was the Deputy Chairman of the Arabic Liberation Organization."

"I see," Blaine said carefully.

"So my life was forfeit in any event," Bury said. "If you had found out." He shrugged. "ALO membership was covered under the amnesty, in case you're wondering."

"I'm sure," Blaine said. "But what in the devil was the ALO doing on New Chicago? It wasn't an Arab planet."

"No," Bury said. "But it had once been a source of ships. I take it you know little of New Chicago's history."

"Almost none," Blaine admitted. "I was only there to fight, and Lady Blaine has painful memories."

Bury nodded. "So, let me tell you a tale, my Lord. New Chicago was settled late, well after the formation of the First Empire. It was far away beyond the Coal Sack, an insignificant world, settled by North American transportees but administratively part of the Russian sphere of influence. That is significant because the Russians favored a planned economy and what they planned for New Chicago was that it would be a source of ships for the future expansion of the Empire."

"Figures," Renner said. "Edge of the frontier."

"What's your point?" Sally Blaine demanded.

"A source of ships," Bury continued carefully. "The people of the First Empire were largely transportees. *Not* trained astronauts. Spacesuit and habitat technology had not moved as fast as spacecraft technology using Alderson Drive and Langston Field. Metals on New Chicago are easily available. Foundries could be built. The settlers had decent gravity and reasonably Earthlike conditions. The regions of exposed ores are east of the good farming land, and there's a dependable east wind to carry away the industrial stenches. My Lord, *nobody* knows more than I do about New Chicago."

"Local asteroid belts."

"Yes, exactly. Spacesuits and habitats were improved. The sons of transportees were trained as astronauts. *Of course* the next generations began mining their own local asteroid belts. New Chicago had built their foundries and shipyards and taught their people the skills, but meanwhile all the settled solar systems were building their spacecraft in the asteroids. New Chicago was geared for a boom that would never come.

"Then the First Empire came apart. New Chicago did very well out of the Secession Wars."

"Oh," Lord Blaine said.

"Do you see it? New Chicago's boom period came during the first crisis. That was when my grandfather made his first contact with the place. He was one of the founders of the ALO."

"I still don't get it," Sally said. "What did the ALO want from New Chicago?"

"Ships."

"Why?"

"Everyone needs ships. Certainly Levant and the other Arab worlds did. Then, later, when the Second Empire was proclaimed, there was another reason. New Chicago was new to the Empire. Here was a source of ships that were never in any Imperial registry."

Lord Blaine looked puzzled.

"Untraceable?" Sally asked.

Bury nodded. "An Outie world geared to make spacecraft, desperate for custom."

Sally looked up at the ceiling. "Fyunch(click)."

"Ready."

"In what class was Levant admitted to the Empire?"

"First. Full self-governing, with interstellar capability."

134

"With New Chicago ships?" Blaine asked.

Bury shrugged. "Any planet when the life support fails."

"But that was long before the revolt," Blaine said.

"Certainly, my Lord. That was in my father's time. Now think back thirty-five years. Today you see the Empire as successful. I invite you to see it as we did then."

"Which was how?" Rod Blaine said. He saw that Sally was nodding to herself.

Lady Sally was trained in anthropology. Can that be useful? "My Lord. Your Second Empire was only beginning. It had proclaimed itself Christian, and if you do not recall the history of the Crusades, I assure you that we Arabs remember! You had already incorporated Dyan into the Empire, and promoted Jews to high positions in your military and navy. Why in the Name of Allah the Merciful should any of us have trusted you?"

"Calm down," Renner said.

Bury glanced at the glowing graphs. "I'm *fine*. So, my Lord, at last you know. Yes, I helped instigate the New Chicago revolt, and to you it must have been from the blackest of motives. That would have been an Outie world, with an economy based on building spacecraft and a thirst for customers. Unregistered ships, in case Levant should need them. In case the negotiations with the Empire failed, or in case the Empire collapsed under its own vaulting ambitions. Empire of Man, indeed! We might well have been forced once again to proclaim jihad with no armies and no navies and nothing but the courage of our young men for weapons."

"And now?" Blaine asked.

Bury shrugged. "The Empire has been successful. You do not like us. Socially we are second class, but legally we have the rights you promised. Our planets are self-governing, under people of our own religion. The threat is now from the Mote, not from Sparta. There is no more need for the Arab Liberation Organization, and for the past dozen years I have presided over its liquidation."

"You're the Chairman, Horace?" Renner demanded.

"Not in name."

"Sure. You're not the formal president of the Imperial Traders Association, either. Holy catfish."

"Kevin, *we* presided over the liquidation of Nassari's group. He would not give up his ambition. I caused—"

"You made *me* dig up data on him and turn him in to the

135

Imperials. Sure. You couldn't hardly tell them, 'Nassari isn't taking my orders anymore,' now could you?"

"I did what I had to do, Kevin." Bury turned to Blaine. "You see? We had a way to get unknown spacecraft for ourselves. New Chicago no longer has a place for such schemes, but another world might, or an asteroid belt, or an Oort cloud near an old supernova. If men want spacecraft, or if *Moties* want spacecraft of human manufacture, then—then you must have Horace Bury, the spy."

Into an uncomfortable silence Earl Blaine asked, "Your Excellency, just what are your plans, specifically?"

"Plans or ambitions?" Bury demanded.

"Eh?"

"I don't know enough to have specific plans. But already I have found out more about the Motie threat than Mercer knew. Or you, my Lord. I have abilities, I have money, and among Allah and my doctors and this chair I have energy. I propose to employ them all in the Imperial service."

And he waited.

"I'll withdraw my objections," Blaine said, ignoring a small sound of protest from Lady Blaine. "That's all I'll do, but I expect it will get you to the blockade fleet. God knows what you expect to accomplish there. Don't waste any more time than you have to."

"Thank you, my Lord," Bury said.

✳ ✳ ✳

Sally waited for the door to close. Then she demanded, "Why?"

"You heard it all."

"But Rod, what's changed? The revolt on New Chicago, the bloodbath, the prison camps, he caused it all! He raped a world and he killed Dorothy!"

"I might have done the same in the service of the Empire. I might have been in *Lenin*'s crew when Kutuzov burned Istvan down to bedrock. Bury's not just an opportunistic bandit anymore. He was defending his homeland."

"*Levant.*"

"Mmm? But it's *his* world. The key is loyalty. He was an enemy; now he's an ally. He's protecting the Empire to protect Levant.

The enemy of my enemy is my friend. He sees the Empire as friends, the only hope against the Moties."

"He could be turned again."

"Hah! Yes. We set Renner to watch him, and Renner's been doing that for a quarter century. Maybe there's something that could turn Bury's loyalty. But not at the blockade. He won't accomplish anything there, barring a pep talk and some politics, but he won't do any damage. The blockade stands between Levant and the Moties."

"If Bury could see Moties as we do . . . Rod? How do you see Moties?"

Rod didn't answer.

"They destroyed your ship, and you'll never forget. I think you loved *MacArthur* more than you have ever loved me. But we've found the solution!"

"Have we? It works on Mediators. We don't know about Masters. We don't know if Masters would accept it even if it does work. They'd call it a Crazy Eddie answer."

"It will. It has to."

"Sally, we depended on the blockade. A few years from now we might not have a blockade . . . or a hundred years, maybe, or one. And you know how long it will take Sparta to decide to *do* something. Renner and Bury—"

She nodded slowly. "Action, not talk." She looked at the ceiling. "Fyunch(click)."

"Ready."

"General instructions, all department heads. List essential equipment and personnel for transfer of the Institute to New Caledonia."

"Acknowledged."

PART 3
THE MOAT AROUND MURCHESON'S EYE

To the question, what shall we do to be saved in this World? there is no other answer but this, Look to your Moat.

—George Sevile, Marquis of Halifax

1
New Ireland

The foolish will now ask and say:
"What has made the faithful turn away
*   from the qiblah toward which they used to pray?"*
Say: "To God belong the East and the West.
He guides who so wills to the path that is straight."

—al-Qur'an

Hyperspace links only specific points. The time required to travel from one Alderson point to another is immeasurably short; but once that Jump has been made, the ship must proceed through normal space to the next Alderson point. This can take weeks to months depending on the Alderson geometry, ship speed, and logistics.

Sinbad was faster than most passenger liners, and Bury had arranged to be met by other ships of his fleet carrying supplies and fuel, so that *Sinbad* could go by the most direct route possible; and even so the trip lasted long enough to put everyone on edge. They remained polite; but everyone was glad that *Sinbad's* size allowed some privacy.

Yet Renner observed that the odd friendship between Bury and Buckman remained as strong as ever; and if the new Viceroy was tiring of being told stories of Imperial trade on the one hand, and the follies of Imperial science policy on the other, he showed no signs of it. Renner had long since taken to excusing himself quickly after the evening formal dinner.

He was glad to be able to announce the last Jump. "It'll be about midnight ship's time," he said. "Take your sleeping pills and you may sleep through it."

"I wish I could," Ruth Cohen said. "And I don't think I'll ever get used to Jump shock."

"You can sleep through it, but you won't get used to it," Renner said. "It's not something you can get used to. Anyway, this is the last for a while."

"One of my ships should be waiting," Bury said.

Renner nodded. "Yes, sir. They'll have been waiting awhile. We had a message saying it passed through three weeks ago."

Bury grimaced. "A costly rendezvous. Ah, well. Thank you, Kevin."

✳ ✳ ✳

A thin, reedy voice rang through the ship, first in Arabic, then in Anglic. "Prayer is better than sleep! Come to prayer! I witness that the Lord our God is One God. I bear witness that there is no God but Allah, and Mohammed is the Prophet of Allah. Come to prayer. God is great! Prayer is better than sleep!"

Ruth Cohen sat bolt upright. "What in the world . . . ?"

The ship was in free-fall. The Velcro covers had held her snugly in the bed, and she'd got so used to gravity changes in the past few weeks that taking the spin off the ship hadn't awakened her. *Must have been done smoothly.* She realized she was alone in the bed. *And I really did sleep through the Jump, too.*

Kevin Renner floated in from the adjoining cabin as the thin singsong finally ceased. "Shh."

"But—"

"Horace has visitors. Partners, or relatives, both maybe, from Levant on the supply ship. Bury has Nabil play muezzin when he wants to look like a conventional Moslem. Sorry I couldn't warn you, we only found out when we docked ships, and I was busy then."

"But—"

Renner grinned. "They wouldn't appreciate that *Sinbad*'s pilot sleeps with a concubine."

"I am *not*—"

"Well, I know that, and you know that, but they won't know that. Anyway, I take it back. They won't be shocked that I have a concubine. They might not be thrilled by your name."

"Name."

"You're from Dyan."

"I'm not from Dyan, I'm from New Washington."

"*I* know."

"And I am a Navy officer, on assignment." She looked down at her translucent harem set and tried to grin. "Well, not on duty *just* at the moment—Kevin, this is *not* funny."

"Well, maybe not. At least it wasn't hard to figure the direction."

"Kevin—"

"Point toward Earth and you're facing Jerusalem and Mecca both. No difference from here. Same qiblah."

"What has this got to do with anything?"

"I read up on it once," Renner said. "When Mohammed first went to Medina, he preached that the Jews and the Believers were one people, all descended from Abraham, and they'd all have one Messiah. Maybe himself, but that wasn't established. One God, Allah, who was the same as the Jewish Jehovah. Mohammed venerated the Torah. Prayed toward Jerusalem."

"Jerusalem? Kevin, why are we discussing this?"

"So you won't brood about being insulted."

"I still don't like it."

"Of course not. Neither does Bury. You're a guest. If you insist on acting like one, Bury will cooperate. God knows what it would cost him, though."

"Oh." Ruth pulled a sheet up to her chin and wriggled farther down into the covers holding her to the mattress. "All right. Tell me more. Are you making all this up?"

Renner smiled. "Nope. I'm told that in Medina there's a famous mosque, called the mosque of the Two Qiblahs—"

"Qiblah. Direction?"

"Yeah, aspect. Direction the mosque faces. Mohammed sent letters to the Jewish leaders inviting them to join him. They wouldn't. They said you had to be a son of Jacob to inherit the kingdom and get all the benefits of the prophecies, and Arabs didn't qualify since they were only sons of Abraham."

"And nobody cared about the daughters."

"Not a bit. But for a couple of years they faced Jerusalem, not Mecca, to do their prayers. But when the Jews rejected his offer, Mohammed brooded about it. One morning, Mohammed was in

143

the middle of his prayers, facing Jerusalem, and all of a sudden he swung round to face Mecca. Everybody else did, too, of course. And that's why Arabs and Jews fight."

"I never heard that."

"True, though." Renner looked thoughtful. "Good thing, too. Can you imagine what would have happened to Europe if the Jews and the Moslems had been on the same side? Anyway that's the story of the Two Qiblahs. Now for the fun part."

"Fun part?"

"For the next two weeks we have this ship pretty well to ourselves. The supply ship isn't the only one Bury had meet him here. He's got a hospital ship that would make the Navy's doctors drool kittens. In about three hours, Horace and the Viceroy and Buckman are going to board *Mercy of Allah,* and by the time we get to New Ireland they'll be new men."

"Wow. Aren't you included?"

Renner grinned. "What's the matter, don't like the old one?"

"Well, my opinion's on record, but it doesn't seem hardly fair."

"But who'd keep you company? Actually, I got rebuilt just before we went to the Purchase. Time enough for touch-ups when we're in orbit and I don't have piloting duties. But we'll be pretty much alone with the staff most of the way into New Ireland."

"I suppose it's just as well. I'm not sure I want to be around a Kevin Renner with more energy than you've already got."

NEW CALEDONIA: Star system behind the Coal Sack with F8 primary star cataloged as Murcheson A. The distant binary, Murcheson B, is not part of the New Caledonia system. Murcheson A has six planets in five orbits, with four inner planets, a relatively wide gap containing the debris of an unformed planet, and two outer planets in a Trojan relationship. The four inner planets are named Conchobar, New Ireland, New Scotland, and Fomor, in their order from the sun, which is known locally as Cal, or Old Cal, or the Sun. The two middle planets are inhabited, both terraformed by First Empire scientists after Jasper Murcheson, who was related to Alexander IV, persuaded the Council that the New Caledonian system would be the proper place to establish an Imperial university. It is now known that Murcheson was primarily interested in having an inhabited planet near the red supergiant known as Murcheson's Eye, and as he was not satisfied with the climate of New Ireland, he demanded the terraforming of New Scotland as well.

Fomor is a relatively small planet with almost no atmosphere and few interesting features. It does, however, possess several fungi that are biologically related to other fungi found in the Trans–Coal Sack sector.

The two outer planets occupy the same orbit and are named Dagda and Mider in keeping with the system's Celtic mythological nomenclature. Dagda is a gas giant, and the empire maintains fuel stations on the planet's two moons, Angus and Brigit. Merchant ships are cautioned that Brigit is a Navy base and may not be approached without permission.

"Which we won't need to do, thanks to Bury's supply ship," Renner said, wiping the screen. "We're good all the way to New Ireland."

NEW IRELAND: Second planet of the New Caledonia system. New Ireland was terraformed by First Empire scientists under the influence of Jasper Murcheson and was the original site of the Trans–Coal Sack branch of the Imperial University until the campus was moved to New Scotland.

The inhabitable areas of New Ireland are comparatively small and confined to the temperate-zone areas adjacent to the single major sea. Climate in the inhabitable zone is warm and pleasant. The soil is fertile and there are few insects or other predators. Crop yields are high.

New Ireland joined the Secessionists and continued the war long after both New Ireland and New Scotland had become isolated from their respective allies.

Little industry has been rebuilt since the destruction sustained during the Secession Wars. This was originally due to opposition from New Scotland, but is now apparently the choice of the New Irish Parliament. Consequently New Ireland remains a backwater with tourism as the major source of hard currency.

New Ireland, and particularly the region known as Derry, is fiercely sought by Imperial Navy crews as a place for shore leave.

Sinbad's B lounge was an add-on pod the shape of a lima bean. Ruth Cohen had set the wall transparent. Andrew Mercer found her reading at a viewscreen, with stars blazing around her and the Coal Sack behind her. The blackness in the other direction was New Ireland's night side.

He'd been watching the Coal Sack on and off ever since *Sinbad* arrived in New Cal system. He preferred not to let himself know that the view made him uneasy. The vast black blot stretched across thirty degrees of sky, in the shape of a hooded man with one glowing red eye. Murcheson's Eye, the red supergiant, had a yellow fleck in it: the Mote. And Ruth was a child in the arms of the Hooded Man, her face eerily lit from underneath by the computer screen.

Mercer moved around her to see over her shoulder.

"Greetings, Your Highness," Ruth said.

"Not for two more hours. I don't become Viceroy until we land."

"But you've been in the New Cal system for three weeks. And I know you've been reading reports and sending instructions."

Mercer shrugged. "Two weeks of that was in the hands of Bury's djinni." He stretched. "Do I look different?"

"As a matter of fact, yes. Not much, but I can tell. I wonder how long Bury will keep *Mercy* here?"

"A while, I gather. He plans on some touch-ups. Thinking of taking a turn in the tank?"

"I just might once we settle in. It's not an opportunity I'll get very often. So tomorrow's the big day. Why New Ireland instead of New Scotland?"

"Actually, Sir Kevin suggested it. After I thought it over, it did seem a good idea to have the formal installation on New Ireland. Patch up the old wounds. Let the New Irish know they're accepted. Even if I can't begin work until we get to New Scotland."

"Well, Trujillo got here first."

"Eh?"

Ruth scrolled back to the beginning of the news squib. Mercer read over her shoulder.

— — —

Dateline Montenth 32, 3047. Derry, New Ireland. Mei-Ling Trujillo.

His Highness arrives tomorrow. Not only is this the first official visit of an Imperial Viceroy to New Ireland since the wars ended, but Arthur Calvin Mercer will be formally installed as Viceroy for His Majesty's Domains Beyond the Coal Sack in the New Ireland Parliament building.

The Government clearly expects this to be a big deal and has gone all out to bring in official guests to witness the event. There will be three days of official holiday. The New Cal branch of the Imperial Traders Association has arranged for fireworks and is paying for an all-day banquet.

There's no question that among the best people of New Ireland the installation will be the biggest show since INSS *Terrible* bombarded Derry and ended New Ireland's secession eighty years ago.

At tomorrow's ceremony the Fleet will be represented by three ships, the largest a light cruiser. It seems none of the others in the New Scotland naval yards is spaceworthy. When His Highness has had enough pomp and ceremony and wants to get to work, he might start by looking into the Yardmaster's records.

Meanwhile, for most of New Ireland it's business as usual, and an unusual business it is.

For fifty-six years the province of Derry has been visited by the Navy on leave. They were not always welcome; but they have always been the source of money, and money heals many wounds. Today Derry is famous for its welcome.

The scars from *Terrible*'s visit have long disappeared. Elsewhere on the planet, much of Murcheson's careful terraforming has also disappeared, leaving vast desert regions. But from the top of Romance Crag, Derry still looks like farmland, miles of it in all directions. The town is not one clump; it stretches arms along the crests of the hills, with farmland below.

In the streets it is quite different ...

The whores have a wholesome look. I questioned several, and I always had the feeling that they were laughing at me. Uncorrupted. Part of the answer is that I was never able to find one twice. "We come for a little day trip, and maybe we make some money. Then it's back to work with the pigs and the corn," Deirdre told me.

She knows who her father is. Jaynisse doesn't. Both thought it an odd question.

If you walk the streets of Derry, you'll find there aren't any brothels, but there are whole blocks of hotels that will provide rooms

147

by the night or by the hour. Most of them have splendid room service.

It is estimated that the average Able Spacer will leave three months' pay on Derry. If you count in the petty officers, the average Navy man spends nearly eighteen hundred crowns here. It is, by the way, very much an average. The Navy people save for their visit here, but they also gamble heavily.

Navy men—I haven't found any women spacers who'll admit being interested in Derry—tend to spend heavily, but it isn't all wine and women. "I always go to the Dream Palace," the midshipman I'll call Carlos Meredith told me. "You can bring your own game cassettes and interface them and play the locals. Anything new from Sparta, the locals love it. I usually win for the first day."

Then he finds a girl and goes off to sleep and comes back the next day and loses what he has left. "The locals are pretty quick with a new game."

Ruth glanced up at Mercer. "There's more, but here's the tag." She skipped to the end of the file.

They find a lot to worry about in Government House, but in the Fleet there's only one topic of conversation. Will the new Viceroy close down Derry?

"Humpf," Mercer said.

"Sir?" Ruth asked.

"She can't mean that. No columnist could be dumb enough to think my first act would be to close the one thing that makes blockade duty tolerable."

"Oh."

"Not much work for you here," Mercer said. "No Outies anywhere, and I can't see how the Secret Service could learn more about the Mote. Maybe you'll find a plot on New Ireland."

"It may not be that funny. There aren't many active anymore, but the Rebel Alliance still exists, you know."

"They threw a bomb at Governor Smelev. But that was twenty years ago. I think the worst we have to worry about on New Ireland would be getting too far behind on our shots."

The intercom saved Ruth from having to answer. "They finally called," said Renner's voice. "All personnel, strap in. Ruth, come forward. You don't know how to steal a spacecraft until you can land it."

* * *

The inauguration ceremonies had begun at noon and lasted six hours. The celebrities had gone their own ways. Now trucks were moving between the barricades that lined Skid Street. The sun was still well up.

Kevin and Ruth strolled along the main drag. Here was the Falling Ship, a hotel made up of two-story buildings laid in squares, flowerbeds between, aerial ramps linking the roofs. Kevin wondered what they were charging for rooms with a view of Skid Street. A taller hotel could have made considerably better profits on a day like this . . . but nothing stood tall on New Ireland, not even the Palace.

The trucks were opening like flowers. Ruth and Kevin stopped to watch one unfold. In minutes it had become a bakery, and merrymakers were swarming to buy fresh bread. Kevin bought a loaf, tore off two pieces, and handed one to Ruth.

They ate. "All *right*. You don't get this on shipboard," Ruth said. "Let's find some fruit."

"Crudités?" Renner dropped what remained of the loaf and guided her to a vegetable stand. The trucks had all looked alike; now all the suddenly blooming stands were different, and the trucks within had vanished. They munched carrots and a head-sized radish as they walked.

"I smell meat," Kevin said. "That way."

"It's not all sex here," Ruth said.

The sudden market already swarmed with women, young and middle-aged, varying between comely and beautiful, but generally good-looking. Men in Navy uniforms stopped to talk and found ready companionship. "I never did get shore leave on New Ireland," Kevin said. "We all knew it was what we wanted. Family cooking, fresh food, and wholesome sex. Hard to say which a Navy man wants more, after a year eating bioplast and yeast steaks. And marijuana. Even a little borloi. They told me you can get drunk, too, but you have to go looking for liquor, and it isn't in the rituals, if you follow me. No bars."

149

"And you're finally in Derry, but there's a woman hanging on your arm."

"I'll tough it out somehow. And there's dinner. What the blazes is it? Or was it?"

A carcass roughly the size of an ox was roasting over a fire. Right here in the street? Yes, but the fire was sitting on ribbed metal, the fold-down side of another truck. New Irish kept things neat. The burly proprietor cut them two slices and sealed them in plastic. They walked on.

"Speaking of sex," Kevin said, "what did you think of Trujillo?"

"I guess that look never goes out of style."

"Eh?"

"No makeup. You probably thought she was careless. Look like a mouse, but wear a thin dress and no underwear. It turns men on. Worked on you, didn't it?"

"Point taken."

Ruth sighed. "It only works when you're young. Maybe I will take Bury up on his offer. Look, jugglers."

"Did you like her?"

"Trujillo? I'm not supposed to like her. She's no friend to the Navy. But the real answer is I didn't get much chance to talk to her."

"You will."

"Kevin?"

"Weeks ago she requested passage to the Crazy Eddie Squadron. We all decided she could ride aboard *Sinbad*."

"Oh."

"Bury's idea. He wants to convert her into a Motie hater." Renner chuckled. "Fresh blood for His Excellency. Mercer heard Horace's spiel so often he was ready to scream if anyone mentioned the Moties. He already sent a letter of invitation."

"Hmm. And you won't say whether she turns you on. I think I'd better do some shopping. Or should I bother?"

"Meaning?"

"Meaning we both know this doesn't last forever. Getting tired of me?"

"Not yet. Want out?"

"Not yet." She nodded thoughtfully, then smiled. "We'll leave it that way, then."

Renner took out his pocket computer. "According to Ms. Trujillo's article, the Brick Moon serves artichokes eighteen different ways. Room service in the hotel next door. Interested?"

"Mmm. Dammit, you've got me thinking like you."

"How so?"

"I want to see how the clerk acts when he sees you walk in with off-planet competition."

2
The High Commission

The art of putting the right man in the right places is first in the science of government; but that of finding places for the discontented is the most difficult.

—Talleyrand

NEW SCOTLAND: Third planet of the New Caledonia system. Originally lifeless with extensive atmosphere of methane and water vapor, New Scotland was terraformed by massive infusions of genetically engineered microbes.

The original colonists lived under domes ...

New Scotland's major city was dominated by the Viceregal Palace. It stood in the center of a series of concentric rings; much like medieval cities on Earth, New Scotland's growth was controlled by the city's defense technologies.

Renner sent the small landing craft in a wide circle to dissipate its speed. "There are some changes." He pointed to smaller built-up complexes out beyond the final ring. "All that's new since I was here. They must think the war's finally over, to build outside the Field protection."

"The Moties have done that much good," Ruth Cohen said. "They've got New Scotland and New Ireland thinking 'us' about each other. Except at football games."

"They do get a bit rough, don't they? Better than throwing bombs at each other . . . well, some better anyway." But Moties wouldn't build like that, he thought. Wouldn't build what they couldn't defend.

The flier completed its circuit of the city. Renner brought it to the landing area outside the black granite complex of Government House. Bored Marine guards noted Ruth Cohen's Navy uniform and Renner's expensive business clothes, perfunctorily took their identity cards and inserted them into computer readers, glanced at the screen, and waved them through into the courtyard. They got inside through an unlocked French door leading into a maze of corridors. Renner tried to lead the way to the Commission meeting rooms, but soon became lost. Finally he stopped looking. "Ah. Here's a guard."

They were directed to a different part of the building. Ruth Cohen giggled.

"The last time I was here it was for a meeting in the Council Chamber," Kevin said. "The big hall with a dome. Anybody could find that. How was I to know they'd put the Commission off here in the Annex?"

In contrast to the Grand Council Chamber, the Commission's meeting room was strictly functional. There was no throne. The Viceroy's place was merely an armchair at the center of the big table. The council table was massive. It might have been wood, but Kevin didn't think so. Chairs for advisers stood behind the table. In front there were seats for an audience of fifty or so. Large viewscreens, now blank, dominated both side walls.

They had barely got into the room when a tall, balding man dressed in dark, conservative business clothes thrust forward and held out his hand. "Kevin. By God, you look good." He paused to look at Renner. "Colorful, too."

Renner frowned for a moment, then grinned. "Jack Cargill. Good to see you." He turned to Ruth. "Commander—I guess it's 'admiral,' now, isn't it?"

Cargill nodded.

"Ruth Cohen, meet Admiral Cargill. Jack was Exec in *MacArthur*," Kevin explained. "Are you still with the Crazy Eddie Squadron?"

"No, I'm on the High Commission."

"Gosh. You're important. And to think we shared a cabin once."

"Here's another Commissioner you know," Cargill said. "David." He indicated a heavyset, balding man in clerical attire.

"Father Hardy," Renner said. "Hey, it's good to see you again. What have they done, loaded the Commission down with *MacArthur* crew?"

"No, we're the only ones," David Hardy said. "And I'm not sure in what capacity I'm here."

Renner noted the large pectoral cross on Hardy's cassock. "Everybody's been promoted. Bishop, eh? Do I kiss your ring, my Lord?"

Hardy grinned. "Well, you're welcome to, but you're certainly not part of my flock."

"Sir?"

"I'm missionary bishop to Mote Prime. Of course we don't have any converts."

"Sure of that?" Renner asked.

"As a matter of fact, no," Hardy said. "I never did learn what happened to my Fyunch(click). Not that he was a convert, exactly. Anyway, I might be here as the Church's representative, or as the only semanticist ever to visit Mote Prime—ah." He turned toward the door as it opened. "Here's someone you need to meet again. I'm sure you recognize him."

A tall naval officer in uniform. He looked young to be a full lieutenant, but then Kevin Christian Blaine's father had been a lieutenant commander when only a couple of years older, and captain of *MacArthur* a year after that. The aristocracy got promotions, but they were also weeded out of the service if they couldn't keep up. *Or used to be,* Renner thought.

"Your godson, I believe," Hardy was saying.

"Well, not that I exercised many of the duties of the office," Renner said. Blaine's handshake was firm. "And this is Ruth Cohen. How are you, Kevin?"

"Very good, sir. And I really appreciated the things you sent for my birthdays. Some of the oddest stuff—holos, too. You sure got around, Sir Kevin."

"Kevin Renner, galactic tourist." Renner reached into a sleeve pocket and took out a message cube. "On that score, your sister sent this. She's on her way, in case you didn't know."

154

"Thought she might be. I wondered if she might be coming with you."

"It would have been a bit crowded, and she had a lift. The Honorable Frederick Townsend decided to visit New Caledonia."

"Ah."

"He probably thinks it was his idea," Renner guessed.

"You've met Glenda Ruth, but not Freddy," Kevin Blaine observed. It took Renner a moment to realize that he wasn't asking.

The room began to fill. A half dozen Navy officers in uniform, led by a commander who wore a ship's miniature badge indicating he was master of a medium cruiser. They waved to Blaine, but stayed to themselves on the other side of the room. A group of civilians sat in adviser chairs and put their pocket computers on the arm-desks. Another knot of Navy officers came in. They had white shoulder boards indicating administrative branch and sat near but not with the combat officers.

"The accountants," Cargill said. "Here to convince the world that not one cent has ever been wasted."

"Can they do that, sir?" Ruth asked.

"No." She seemed to expect more, so Cargill said, "No matter how you slice it, blockade duty is long stretches of utter boredom. Spiced up with random moments of sheer terror, of course, but that doesn't make up for the boredom. Of course the men are going to misbehave. Officers, too. We're just damned lucky to have troops who'll do it at all."

The large double doors at the end of the room opened wide to admit Bury in his travel chair. Renner clucked in disapproval: Bury's doctors wanted him to spend more time exercising. Bury was accompanied by Jacob Buckman and Joyce Mei-Ling Trujillo.

"She's wearing underwear today," Renner said. Ruth made a face at him. If Blaine and Hardy heard the remark, they didn't comment.

Joyce Mei-Ling Trujillo was in fact quite well dressed, in a thin silk afternoon dress that would have been fashionable on Sparta. She carried a pocket computer large enough that she needed a bag for it. Ruth Cohen sniffed. "Doesn't trust the central computer system to keep records for her."

"I've found journalists are often like that," Kevin Christian Blaine said.

155

"Experience?" Renner asked.

"Quite a lot. The Navy likes me to do their talking."

Bury, Buckman, and Trujillo took places in the first row of the audience seats. Blaine glanced at his watch. "I'd best be getting to my post."

"Me, too," Cargill said. "Dinner tonight, Kevin?"

"Yes, please. Anyplace special, or shall I ask Bury to invite you up to *Sinbad*?"

"*Sinbad*, if you can swing it."

The double doors were thrown open again, and a palace functionary came in. "My lords, ladies, and gentlefolk, His Highness the Viceroy."

Everyone stood. There was no other ceremony, but Mercer looked a bit self-conscious as he took his place at the center of the big table. He was joined at the table by Cargill and Hardy, and two others Renner hadn't met. Their place cards named them as Dr. Arthur MacDonald and Sir Richard Geary, Bart. Renner took a seat near Bury and scribbled on his pocket computer.

Arthur MacDonald, Ph.D. Professor of cultural biology, University of New Scotland. Holds Blaine Institute Chair of Xenobiology.

Richard Geary, baronet. Investor. Member of Board of Regents, University of New Scotland.

There was more, but Mercer was tapping on the table with his gavel. "I call this meeting of the Imperial Commission to order. Let the record state that this is a public meeting. If there is no objection, we will record the names of attendees. . . ."

There were various chirps like a hundred crickets as the palace central computer queried everyone's pocket computer to get the meeting attendance list. Renner's computer beeped twice and then rattled. Heads turned. Renner grinned.

Mercer turned to the Commission secretary. "Mr. Armstrong."

"Thank you, Your Highness," Armstrong said. His voice was thick with the accent of New Caledonia. "In deference to our guests, His Highness has changed the meeting agenda to omit the opening formalities and routine business. We therefore proceed directly to Item Four, the report from the blockade squadron. His Highness has requested that the fleet prepare a summary report covering the principal activities of the squadron through the years, as well as a more detailed report of current actions. The report will be presented by Lieutenant the Honorable Kevin Christian Blaine, executive officer of INSS *Agamemnon*."

Chris Blaine stood near the large screen that dominated one wall of the room. "Thank you, Mr. Secretary. Your Highness.

"The blockade force is formally known as the Eleventh Fleet, or Battle Fleet Murcheson's Eye. The mission of Battle Fleet Murcheson's Eye is to intercept any and all ships entering the Empire from the Mote—to enforce the blockade decreed by this Commission. Blockade duty is hard duty, and the officers and men of the Blockade Fleet are proud of our record of one hundred percent success. We have achieved that success in spite of many very real difficulties."

Renner's thoughts chased each other:

I wonder who wrote that for him?

Still, the Crazy Eddie Squadron would have driven me nuts.

Heyyy . . . He dared not speak his next thought. *Chris doesn't sound that bloody convincing, does he? Why not? Raised by Mediators—*

He doesn't believe what he's saying.

Blaine gestured, and the wall screen lit up to show a wide-angle view of a dozen blobs ranging in color from black to dull red in a bright red glowing background. "The Alderson point from the Mote lies within the supergiant star. Ships can't stay on station very long, so there's a continual circulation of ships from outside the star to the blockade station. They stay until they're too hot, then they go outside to cool off.

"Motie breakout attempts can happen at any time."

Four new blobs, all dead black, popped into existence on the screen. Imperial ships became floodlight beams as fusion drives lit within the red-hot murk. The screen showed the beginnings of a space battle. Bright threads sprang between the ships. Torpedoes raced out.

"You're shooting with no warning!" someone said. Renner looked around to see Joyce Mei-Ling looking embarrassed, clearly not having meant to speak aloud.

Blaine said, "We wouldn't be telling them anything they don't know, Ms. Trujillo. The best time to hit the Motie ships is during Jump shock, when their automated systems are shut down. If we wait until they've recovered enough to communicate, we might not be able to catch them at all. The rules of engagement acknowledge that."

"A question, Lieutenant."

"Yes, Your Highness?"

"Suppose they wanted to negotiate. To surrender?"

"They may well try to," Blaine said. "But how could we know? They cannot come through with no Field. The star would cook them. We can't wait until they get out of the eye, or we'd lose them entirely. This was debated in the first meeting of the Commission, and the rules of engagement were adopted then. They haven't been changed because there's no way to change them, Your Highness. The way to surrender is not to come through."

Mercer nodded thoughtfully. "Proceed, Lieutenant."

Renner glanced over at Bury. He was watching, fascinated, but seemed calm. Probably tranquilized to the eyes.

"Motie breakout attempts have ranged from the simple to the ingenious," Blaine said.

The screen showed a kaleidoscope of actions. Single ships; armadas of ships; cluster ships that came apart like grenades and scattered; ships that came out at enormous velocity, tearing meteor trails through orange-hot gas. . . .

"Now, this one was a beauty," Chris Blaine said with what had to be pride. They watched an iceball two kilometers across emerge from the invisible Alderson point. "Four days after I joined the Crazy Eddie Squadron, at the noon watch . . ." The squadron chased after it. The comet-head left a comet-trail of itself as it plunged through the rarefied star-stuff. It dwindled, evaporated, exposing black beads: ships in Langston Field bubbles that raced off in random directions to be chased down by squadron ships.

"Of course we can't send all our ships against any single attempt," Blaine said. "There always has to be a reserve. Since there's no possible way the information could get back to the Mote, I suppose it's safe to say that sometimes that reserve has gotten critically thin."

Chris sounds better, surer. This part he knows, Renner thought; *it's the cover-up he doesn't like.* "He's pretty good," he said to Ruth Cohen.

"Given his training, he damned well ought to be," Ruth replied.

The presentation continued. There were clips of the men amusing themselves on long watches. Then more battle scenes.

"Lately the Moties have a new trick," Blaine said. "They're sending what we've termed 'token ships.' These are unmanned ships, really only the framework of a ship, just an Alderson Drive and two tanks and a fusion motor. With this one, the sixth, we held off to see if it would *do* anything."

It didn't. They saw an absurd stick-figure of a ship pop into existence at low velocity and immediately begin to melt.

Mercer cleared his throat. "Commander, do you have any theories on why they would send such things?"

"No, Your Highness. They come one at a time; no Field, they're easy to shoot down. No attempt to send messages. If they wanted us off guard, why send anything at all? It's as if they *want* us to be alert. We've speculated that they may want to locate the Alderson point more precisely—at their end, in Mote system—but they know that well enough to send ships through at point one percent of lightspeed. *We* can't do that."

"Hah," Renner said. Everyone looked in his direction. "I think I know—"

"Yes, of course," Buckman said. He stood up. "Sir Kevin is right."

"Jacob—" Bury said. His voice was surprisingly strong.

"Oh. Um. Yes, of course. Cal—Your Highness, should I explain?"

Mercer was nodding gloomily. No surprises here. "Please do, Dr. Buckman."

"They're not trying to locate the Alderson point, they're proving that it's still there."

"Still there?" Jack Cargill sounded shocked. "Excuse me, Dr. Buckman, but why the devil shouldn't it be there?"

"Because it will move when the protostar collapses," Buckman said. "Renner, you seem to be good at talking to amateurs. Maybe you ought to tell them."

They listened as Kevin Renner talked. Kevin watched their eyes for bewilderment or comprehension, watching—he didn't realize it at first—for Kevin Christian Blaine's surprise or disbelief. But Blaine's eyes widened in a slap-my-head *Eureka!* reaction: old knowledge falling into place. *Oh, Lord, he believes it.*

✳   ✳   ✳

"I see," Bishop Hardy said. "I think I understand. But as the least technical person on the Commission, perhaps I should summarize and the experts can tell me if I've left anything out."

"Please," Mercer said.

"We are now convinced that the Moties deceived us about their stellar observations, particularly regarding the protostar. They convinced Dr. Buckman that the protostar will not ignite for from centuries to millennia. It now appears that it may collapse and ignite at any time. Might even have done so already."

"Yes," Buckman said. His voice was grim. "I have to give young Arnoff credit. He was right."

"When it ignites," Hardy said, "the Eleventh Fleet will be guarding an entry point that no longer exists."

"Well, may not, and will have moved a considerable distance in any case," Buckman said. "I've been working on the geometry, but with much of the data suspect it's hard to be exact. Everything depends on the violence of the collapse and the brightness of the new star."

"Yes," Hardy said. "In any event, their first warning would be when the Jump point in Murcheson's Eye moves. Meanwhile, we expect at least one more unguarded Alderson point leading from the Mote into normal space rather than to the inside of a star. And since Alderson Path events happen nearly instantaneously, all this will happen before any light from the protostar reaches us—or reaches the Mote. And therefore you have concluded that the Moties are hurling these cheap probes, these *tokens*, through periodically to see if the old Point has moved."

"Precisely," Buckman said.

There was a long, low whistle from the skipper of *Agamemnon*. "Your pardon, Highness."

"Not at all, Commander Balasingham, I nearly did the same myself," Mercer said. "The situation appears serious indeed. One question. The Navy has ways to determine the location, and thus presumably the existence, of Alderson points without sending ships through them. Don't we?"

"Yes, Your Highness," Commander Balasingham said. He nervously stroked his thick mustache.

"So why the tokens?"

"Disturbances?" Renner said.

"Sir Kevin?"

"Back when I was a navigator, finding an Alderson point was one of the trickiest things we could do. It's never easy, and it's impossible during heavy sunspot activity or during a battle, because Alderson events are very responsive to thermonuclear fluxes."

"You think there may be thermonuclear bombs going off in the Mote system?"

"It wouldn't surprise me, sir."

"Nor me," Bishop Hardy said.

Joyce Mei-Ling Trujillo had sat quietly during all this. Now she came to her feet. "May I ask . . ."

"Please," Mercer said.

"You're suggesting that the Moties are about to get out."

Renner said, "Right."

"But that's—" She looked at Bury, who was staring ahead with unseeing eyes, his breathing carefully controlled. "Shouldn't we do something?"

Everyone spoke at once. And Bury's eyes flicked up at her. Rage and despair, and a sudden twitch of a mad smile.

Mercer tapped on the table with his gavel. "Of course Ms. Trujillo is correct," he said. "We should do something. The question is what? And I'm not certain that subject needs debate in a public meeting."

"Why not? Who doesn't belong here?" Trujillo demanded.

"Well, you for one," Commissioner MacDonald said. "I dinna believe we need the press here. Your Highness, I move that we adjourn this public meeting and go into executive session."

"I expected something like this," Joyce Mei-Ling Trujillo said.

Commissioner MacDonald seemed astonished. "That's more than I did."

"Cover-up all the way. Corruption in the fleet, so hide it with something else. Mr. Bury, your reputation precedes you."

Bury glared. Mercer said, "Madame, I was well aware that the Moties had lied to us. That was a secondary purpose for this meeting. I . . . would have thought we'd have more time. These 'tokens'—"

"Your Highness, I've found enough evidence of corruption that they can smell the stench on Sparta. In a sense I've caused this commission, and in the first meeting you want to go into executive session! So far as I am concerned, the council has evaded the question of corruption in the Crazy Eddie Fleet. Do you really expect me to go along with this *massive* sense of urgency?"

In the moment before anyone could explode, Kevin Blaine caught Mercer's eye. "Excuse me, my Lord, but she does have a point."

Looks of fury turned on Blaine, but MacDonald said, "In what fashion, Lieutenant?"

"Urgency. Let us look at this as a gambling situation. What's the expected return here, the pot odds? The Moties persuaded Dr. Buckman that Mote system could be bottled up for between five hundred and two thousand years. If they thought that lie was worth telling, the expected date must be conspicuously sooner. It can't be much more than a hundred years, could it? That gap wouldn't be worth hiding.

"Call it thirty to seventy years. We've eaten thirty. Twenty years left, with a fat margin of error. Why the rush?" Blaine turned to Trujillo. "Right?"

"And we know it hasn't gone off yet!"

"Well, not last month. There'd be some delay before we heard from the Crazy Eddie Fleet. The Jump point from the Eye to *here* would move. But the urgency is because of these token ships. They indicate that the Moties are ready *now*. The margin of error could still be large, of course," Blaine was talking directly to Trujillo now, "but we're in a maniacal rush so we can get *something* into place. *Anything.* Ultimately we'll move some ships from the Crazy Eddie Squadron so they can sit on their asses for twenty years. Or forty, fifty—"

"Or twenty days," Bury muttered.

"And why shouldn't the press be watching that?" Mei-Ling demanded. "Nothing said here can get back to the Moties. You're only keeping secrets from the public!"

"What's said here can get back to Outies," MacDonald said. "And to traitors who might well like to see harm come to the Empire while our strength is massed against the Moties. It's no been so long since the New Irish threw bombs at the Governor General, you know. Madam, I've no doubt of your loyalty, but I do believe you have heard aye more than is safe already. I would no care to see any of this on the tri-vee. Were it left to me—"

"Commissioner MacDonald has a point," Mercer said. "Miss

Trujillo, I must ask you to hold what you have heard here in strict confidence."

"Suppress a good story?" She smiled thinly. "I wonder if you can make me do that?"

Commissioner MacDonald said, "Your Highness, the law is very clear regarding threats to the Empire. Is this no a state of emergency? You have but to declare one."

"Even that can't stop me from writing about corruption and this council's evasions," Trujillo said. She paused to let that sink in. "But I'm willing to cooperate. Of course there's a condition."

"What is your condition?" Mercer asked.

"Let me find out the rest of the story."

"What?" MacDonald was outraged.

"Let me finish," she said. "I'll take whatever oath you like— oath of the privy council, isn't it?—and promise not to publish anything, including what I've already heard, until you agree it's safe. But I want to *know*. I want to be in on the whole story, Moties, corruption in the fleet, all of it."

"Hmm." Mercer looked around the room, then down at the screen set discreetly into the table in front of him. "It would appear that you are the only problem guest, Ms. Trujillo. Everyone else here is already under one or another obligation to keep the secrets of the Empire."

"Him?" Trujillo pointed at Horace Bury.

"As a condition of my accompanying him on his journey to this system, His Excellency and all his crew consented to the conditions of the privy council," Mercer said. "It would have made for an uncomfortable trip without that."

"I see. All right. Anyway, I've said I'll take your oath."

"Commander Cohen?" Mercer said. "I make no doubt the Navy has already done a thorough investigation of Miss Trujillo. Has your service any objections?"

"I don't think so. Joyce, you do understand what you're doing? You are voluntarily placing yourself under the restrictions of the Official Secrets Acts. The penalties can include exile for life on any world of His Majesty's choosing."

"Yes, I know. Thank you for the warning. But this is the only way I'll ever find out, isn't it? And if the Moties really are coming out, that will be the biggest story ever."

"If the Moties really are coming out, it will mean war," MacDonald said. "And you'll be under wartime restrictions."

"Are you objecting to including Ms. Trujillo in our official family of advisers?" Mercer asked.

"No, my Lord. Not really."

"All right," Mercer said. "Let's get on with it. Mr. Armstrong, if you'll do the honors."

The Commission secretary fingered his own computer controls. "Miss Trujillo, if you will face His Highness. Raise your right hand and read from the screen in front of you."

✳ ✳ ✳

"First things first," Mercer said. "Admiral Cargill, I presume you've sent a standby signal to every ship in the system? . . . Thank you. So just what ships have we?"

"It's bad timing," Cargill said. "We've got three frigates in transit from the Crazy Eddie Squadron to New Cal—"

"God is good," Bury muttered. The other three turned to him, and he grinned like a death's head. "They came through. The Jump point hasn't moved since . . . two weeks ago?"

"Yes, but the ships themselves are all in need of repair. Not a lot of use. Then, a sovereign-class battleship with three general-class battle cruisers and assorted light escort ships jumped out to the Eye three hundred hours ago. There's no way to recall them except to send a messenger ship after them. Nothing else closer than the Crazy Eddie Squadron. Doctor, do we have any damn idea where we'd want to put a second fleet?"

"This is only a first cut," Buckman said.

After a moment Cargill said, "Cut away."

Jacob Buckman tapped at keys. A string of numbers appeared on all the consoles. "There. And maybe there."

"Uh . . ." Renner looked at the screen. "Right. We'll almost certainly get a Jump point at MGC-R-31. That's a smallish star eleven light-years toward the hem of the Hooded Man figure. Eight light-years from the Mote. Then we might get one at MGC-R-60, a brighter star a little nearer the Mote, but that one would lead into Murcheson's Eye. Beyond that . . . Jacob? Something in the Coal Sack itself?"

"Probably not, but even so, Murcheson's Eye dominates."

"So it's just this . . . red dwarf," Mercer said. "Well, we've got to put *something* there, and I prefer it be now. So what do we have?"

"There's Balasingham's *Agamemnon*," Cargill said. "A *Menalaus*-class cruiser. Good ship. I presume you're ready, Balasingham?"

"Admiral, we can boost out as soon as I'm aboard," Commander Balasingham said. "I sent up orders to round up the crew and refuel as soon as I understood what Dr. Buckman was saying."

"Then there's the *Atropos* frigate," Cargill said.

"Sir, I took the liberty of asking her skipper to put that ship on full alert, too," Balasingham said.

"Good," Cargill said. "Unfortunately, Your Highness, except for some messenger boats and merchantmen, there isn't anything else. The battle cruiser *Marlborough* is in the Yards, but it will take a minor miracle to get her out in under a month."

"Nothing coming in?"

"Not for a month," Cargill said. "We'll send messengers out to scrape up what we can find, but—"

"The upshot is that we've little enough to send to watch the new Alderson point," Mercer said. "Two ships."

"Three, Your Highness," Bury said.

Mercer looked at him sharply. "Horace, are you all right?"

Bury tried to laugh. The sound that came out was more ghastly than humorous. "Why should I not be? Highness, the worst has happened. The Moties are loose."

"We don't know that," someone said.

"*Know?*" Bury demanded. "Of course we don't *know*. But it is— easier to think that way. Highness, there is no time to waste. Let us take whatever we have to the new Alderson point. Kevin, I presume you and Jacob know where it will appear?"

"Close enough for government work. It isn't a point, it's an arc four light-minutes long," Renner said.

"We go, then. *Agamemnon*, *Atropos*, and *Sinbad*."

"Why *Sinbad*?" Commander Balasingham asked. "She's not even armed!"

"You might be surprised," Mercer said. "Jacob, will you go with them?"

Buckman nodded. "I expected to. And I'd much prefer to work aboard *Sinbad* than a Navy ship. I remember trying to work aboard

MacArthur. Everyone felt entitled to get in my way, block my sightings, move my equipment—"

"Renner, you can't keep up with us," Balasingham said.

Renner shrugged. "We won't be all that far behind. At worst, we're witnesses, we can report back. Your destruction will make prime-time news."

Bury scowled. "I suppose the Trujillo woman . . . yes, of course. She would have gone with us to the Eye, after all. We should be on our way now. Now. Allah is merciful. We may yet be there before the Moties. We *must* be there before the Moties."

3
Communications

In the name of Allah, most benevolent, ever merciful.
Say: I seek refuge with the Lord of men,
The King of men,
From the evil of him who breathes temptations into the
  minds of men,
Who suggests evil thoughts to the hearts of men—
From among the djinns and men.

—al-Qur'an

On their last night together, Kevin told Ruth, "I'd take you with me if I could find any kind of excuse. Good or bad."

"Would you?"

"Yeah. We're crowded as hell, you know. We've dropped part of the kitchen, we're carrying a drop tank . . ." She wasn't buying it. "Love, when we get back into the Empire, it'll make the news. Contact me then? You've got my work number."

"I gave you mine." She looked down at her sleeves. The three rings of a full commander had just been sewn on. "Of course we're likely to be in different solar systems."

And it really felt like good-bye.

From New Scotland to the Jump would take nearly two weeks. *Agamemnon* and *Atropos* started later, but were moving at two gravities of thrust; they would Jump just ahead of *Sinbad*. *Sinbad* could beat them there with the drop tank's extra fuel, but Kevin refused to subject Bury to more than one gee. He would have preferred less.

This trip wasn't like the voyage from Sparta. *Sinbad* felt like a different ship. Attitudes had changed.

With Mercer gone, the kitchen storage region could carry cargo more appropriate to their mission. It didn't matter much. *Sinbad*'s kitchen was styled to feed Horace Bury: to create small, healthful meals rich in flavor for a man whose taste buds were almost dead of old age. Now that program served Renner, too. Renner could diet between suns, when fresh food was unavailable anyway. Blaine, a lord's son but also Navy, expected no better. Buckman never noticed what he ate, and as for Joyce Mei-Ling Trujillo . . .

"Ms. Trujillo, are you getting fed all right?"

"Lieutenant Blaine asked me that, too. I eat whatever's where the story is, Mr. Renner. I'd say you set a fine table, but—have you ever eaten streaker rat? By the way, you'll be calling me Joyce eventually, won't you? Start now."

Perhaps Bury derived some satisfaction from what Joyce didn't know she was missing. He made no great effort to avoid her; he wasn't agile enough. In her presence he could be affable, but he called her Trujillo.

And so the ship was settling down, and Kevin Renner was enjoying his freedom.

Freedom. Ridiculous. He was surrounded by people, by walls, by obligations . . . and yet this was his place of power. Horace Bury's ship; but then, he was Bury's superior officer in the Secret Service. *Sinbad* went where he willed . . . except that with the Empire of Man at stake, his will had best take *Sinbad* straight through to MGC-R-31.

Over the past quarter of a century Kevin Renner and Horace Hussein Bury had evolved routines and rituals. One was coffee after dinner.

"She is attractive enough," Bury said. He sipped at the thick, sweet brew. "I know planets where she could be sold at a high price." He chuckled softly. "Not as many as there once were, thanks to our efforts. Perhaps we could arrange to use her as bait. . . ."

"She'd be good at that. For a good enough story she'd volunteer," Renner said.

Bury fingered his beard and waited.

"Only guessing," Renner said. "I really haven't spent much time with her at all."

"So I noticed."

"Yeah. Well, put it down to complications. We've got all the time in the world just now, but that could change. Or not. Most likely thing is we spend a boring six months in an empty solar system until an Imperial fleet comes in and chases us out.''

"If so, Miss Trujillo will be desperate for distractions," Bury said. "I would presume from anyone willing to provide them.''

"Hmpf. Truth is, Horace, it feels good to be—unencumbered.''

"The Devil he blew an outward breath, for his heart was free from care.''

Renner grinned. "Something like that." *And maybe she wants something I can't deliver. . . .*

"I cannot say Allah has not been merciful. It would not do to presume too much on His mercy," Bury said.

"And that's the truth. We'll be to the I-point soon enough. What's happening there could tear everybody's leisure all to hell.''

*   *   *

"I still don't understand," the Honorable Frederick Townsend said. "And I don't think I ever will.''

"I'm sorry," Glenda Ruth said. She looked around the ship's lounge. *I think I know every rivet and seam. Hecate* was not much larger than a messenger ship. She was fast, but not overly comfortable. Freddy Townsend had bought her for racing, not for long-distance cruising. Compartments had been added for ship's stores and one servant, but everything was cramped. "I should have gone with Kevin—''

"You needn't start that again, either," Freddy said. "I suppose you could have gone with them, but why? I'm glad to do you the favor. I like doing things for you. As you must know. But—" Freddy looked up in irritation as Jennifer Banda came into the lounge. "Dinner in half an hour," he said. "Guess I'll get washed up.''

Frederick Townsend insisted on dressing for dinner. It had seemed a bit silly at first, but at least it broke up the monotony. The ship was mostly automated, with only the ship's engineer, Terry Kakumi, as crew. The only servant was George, a retired Navy coxswain who served as cook, butler, valet, and sometimes piloted the ship as well. Having one nearly formal meal each day gave everyone something to do.

169

Jennifer waited until Freddy had left the lounge before she spoke. "I walk into something heavy?"

Glenda Ruth shrugged. "No heavier than usual. Glad you came in, though."

"You're driving that boy crazy," Jennifer said. "Sure you want to do that?"

"No, I'm not sure I want to do that."

"Want to tell me about it?"

"Not really. *Yes*. What Freddy is too polite to say is, 'You went to bed with me when we took the trip after graduation, so why won't you sleep with me now?' "

"Oh. I didn't know. I mean, I know what's happened since we left Sparta. Or what hasn't happened. Glenda Ruth, no wonder he's going nuts! I mean—" Jennifer stopped.

"I *know* what he had every right to expect."

"All right, so why? Bad experience the first time?"

"No." Glenda Ruth's voice was very low and small. "Not a bad experience." Silence; then, "You've studied Moties."

Jennifer smiled. "But I was raised by an all-human orchestra."

"Right. I picked up attitudes from the Moties. Consider that I can *refuse* to mate. From twelve to seventeen years of age I just plain enjoyed that. Then, consider that I can *refuse* to get pregnant."

"Freddy?"

"Yes. *Sure*. I've known him since we shared a crib. And we had just under a month . . . which was just about right for both of us to get to know our bodies. Something I wasn't likely to learn from Moties. Jennifer, I wish to hell I could tell *him* all this."

Jennifer was folded up like a stick figure into her web chair. "Ruth, I haven't heard a problem yet."

"Sometimes it takes a while before I feel the vibes. Particularly with vague, murky attitudes. You know?" Glenda Ruth was turned away, looking at the universe in a picture-window display. "My parents don't think it's right to take a bed partner before I'm married, or at least engaged, but they're not sure, so I can live with that. Freddy's parents *are* sure, but I can live with that, too."

Glenda Ruth turned around. "But Freddy's maybe half sure his parents are right, and it was two months after the trip before I realized it, while I was *dancing* with him, and what it amounts to is this. By the way, I really appreciate you listening."

"Okay."

"And understanding. Only a damn Motie expert could listen to this and not try to send me to a confessor. Okay. If I sleep with Freddy, it's because we're going to get married or it's because I'm a slut. I'm not sure I want to marry him, and I'm not sure I don't. Either way would be okay, but I'm hung up, *so* . . . ."

"No man would understand that line of argument, counselor."

"Freddy's not stupid. He'd know, he'd understand, if I could *say* it right. So I'm still thinking. Damn."

"He'd marry you—"

Glenda Ruth grinned. "Like a shot. But—look, all my life—"

"All eighteen years."

"Well, it's a lifetime to me." *Poor Charlie didn't last much longer,* Glenda Ruth thought. "All my life I've had someone who could tell me what to do. Had the *right* to tell me. Now I don't. Now I've got my own money, and I'm legally an adult. Freedom! It's wonderful. The last thing I need is a husband."

"Maybe it's better this way. You sure keep the Honorable Freddy attentive!"

"Oh, damn, it does look that way, doesn't it? *He* hasn't seen it, but—"

"It'll be all right. Last jump tonight. We'll be on New Scotland in three weeks. Freddy can find another girl." Jennifer grinned. "Don't like that either? Honey, you are in what the Navy calls an untenable position."

❋   ❋   ❋

Her cabin was small, like all the cabins on *Hecate*. The only spacious cabin belonged to Freddy. Of course he'd expected her to share it.

Why don't I? she wondered. *I lie awake thinking about it. It's not like I don't have my pills, or Freddy has some kind of disease. It's not like I didn't—all I'd have to do is go tap on his door.*

Maybe I'd lose him. Can't he be replaced? I can pick any stranger out of a crowd and know if he's sane, trustworthy, intelligent, horny, crosswired, docile. I hear women say they don't understand men, and I want to snicker—

There was a sharp wrenching sensation, and she felt sick and confused. Somewhere in the back of her mind she knew the ship

171

had made an Alderson Jump, and she was in the grip of the disorientation that always followed. Her father had told her there were a dozen explanations of Jump shock, all inconsistent with each other, but no one had ever been able to disprove any of them.

Gradually control returned. She moved her fingers, then her hands and arms, until they did what she wanted them to. Freddy always recovered faster than she did. She resented that. *Not fair.*

And now they were in New Caledonia system. Maybe Freddy would drop her off and go on to New Ireland. . . . She had just settled in to try to sleep when her intercom chirped.

"Glenda Ruth."

It was Freddy, of course. What in the world did he want? Hah. Well, why not? If he could stand her in this condition. It wouldn't take long to get cleaned up. She tapped the intercom button.

"Hi. Look, I hate to disturb you, but we've got a message for you."

"What?"

"There's a trader ship here, the *New Baghdad Lion.*"

"Here?"

"Here. Waiting at the Jump point. They say they have a message for the Honorable Glenda Ruth Fowler Blaine. They need your identification code."

"Oh. All right, I'll be right there. You're on the bridge?"

"Yep."

"Be right up. And—Freddy, thanks."

"No problem. Bring your computer."

This sounded urgent, but she took the time to get dressed, the baggy trousers gathered at the ankles that were standard for low gravity. She also took time to put on an Angora sweater, comb her hair, and dab on lipstick. The ship was under slight acceleration, just enough to hold her slippers to the carpet. She made her way forward. Freddy was alone on the bridge.

He indicated the copilot chair. "They're standing by for your code."

She plugged her personal computer into the ship's system. "Clementine."

Yes, dear. The words scrawled across her computer screen.

"We're supposed to identify ourselves," Glenda Ruth said. "This is me. Now prove it to them."

Password.

"Damn it all, you know it's me. All right." She sketched rapidly with the stylus; not words, but a cartoon.

Right you are. There was no sound, but she knew the computer was sending an encrypted message that could be decoded using her public key. It hardly mattered what the message was, since only messages encrypted with her secret key could be decoded with her public key. The public/secret key system made for positive identifications as well as secure communication.

"Acknowledged," a voice said on the ship's speakers. It was a voice thick with Levantine accent. "Greetings to Miss Glenda Ruth Fowler Blaine. Please prepare to record an encoded message from Lieutenant Kevin Christian Blaine."

"Ah," Freddy said. "Standing by. Ready. Got it. Thank you, *New Baghdad Lion.*"

"You are welcome. We have been instructed to offer you fuel."

"Fuel. Why would we want more fuel?" Freddy asked.

The Levantine voice was unperturbed. "Effendi, His Excellency told us to offer you fuel. We offer it. It will not take long to transfer. Shall we do so?"

Freddy looked to Glenda Ruth. "Now what?"

She shrugged. "They're bigger than we are, and if they wanted to do us any harm they'd have done it. Why not let them top off your tanks?"

"Lot more than topping off," Freddy said. "All right. *New Baghdad Lion,* we accept your offer with gratitude." He punched an intercom button. "Terry, that merchantman's going to pump us some hydrogen. Give them a hand, will you? You have the con."

"Aye, aye. I relieve you," the engineer said.

Freddy shook his head. "But just what is all this in aid of?"

"Maybe this will tell us," Glenda Ruth said.

The message had been encrypted using her public key. She set Clementine to decoding it.

Kevin Christian Blaine to Glenda Ruth Fowler Blaine. The rest does not break in clear, the computer informed her.

"Hah. Use Kevin's special code."

Willco. She adjusted her earphones and waited. Everyone was assured that the public-key/private-key system was secure against everything. *Maybe we're just paranoid.*

She heard, "Sis, we have a problem. The Moties could be loose by the time you get this."

Freddy was watching her. "Ruth, what's wrong?"

"Nobody's dead. Shh." In the boredom and the interpersonal dominance games, she'd had weeks to forget that she was frightened for the Moties. Now—

Her brother's voice said, "We're taking three ships to the incipient Alderson point, the I-point, at MGC-R-31. Two Navy ships, and Bury's *Sinbad*. I've been put aboard *Sinbad* as liaison. I'm the senior Navy officer aboard, but I catch vibes from Renner. He can show he ranks me if he wants to. Maybe by a lot. The other Navy officer who came out here with *Sinbad*, an Intelligence lieutenant commander, decided she was needed back on New Scotland.

"I don't think of a lot we can do there by ourselves. The Moties have had a quarter century to prepare for this, and we're just now realizing we have a problem. I can't think three ships will have any surprises for them.

"The pot odds say we'll get there with ten to twenty years leeway, but there are complications. Odd things happening. It might be a lot sooner. There's even a chance it happened already.

"Sis, I sure wish we had the latest the Institute has developed. So does Mr. Bury. If you can get that to us, it might change things. I've attached our best-guess coordinates for the I-point. We thought about waiting for you, but we don't know just how long we have before everything happens. Bury arranged for the ship that gave you this message to refuel yours. Let them, if you haven't done that already. Try to get to the I-point before the Moties do.

"*Sinbad*'s crowded. Bury's got Nabil and three women including Cynthia, no change in the relationships. There's me, Dr. Jacob Buckman, and Joyce Mei-Ling Trujillo, the newscaster. She's interesting. Intelligent and wants to prove it, female and doesn't have to. Commander Cohen decided she was needed on New Scotland just after Trujillo was invited aboard, and that leaves Renner loose. Interesting patterns here.

"You may get here and find nothing's happening at all. Some of the blockade fleet may be en route already, but of course it'll take them months. If things last that long, maybe there won't be a problem, or maybe Mom's Crazy Eddie project will work just fine and we can think on how to use it.

"Or it may be all over before you get here. If they send through a big fleet with Warriors . . ."

If they do that, you'll talk to the Master in charge. If we have the symbiote, maybe she'll listen. If you live long enough to talk, Glenda Ruth thought. *If.*

And her brother's voice ran on: "Anyway, we're going for a look. It will probably help if you can get here pretty quick, but you do what you think best.

"Love, Chris."

She reset and heard the message through again. "Freddy?"

"Yes, my love?"

She let it pass. "Freddy, we're being given fuel so that we can go direct to"—she punched in the coordinates from Kevin Blaine's message, and the navigation screen lit up—"*here,* instead of going to New Scotland first."

Freddy studied the display. "That's a wretched red dwarf system. There's nothing there."

"There will be."

"Glenda Ruth, do you know what you're doing?"

"I think so. It's no trivial thing, Freddy—"

"All right." He turned to the computer.

"No trivial thing at all. I don't exaggerate, do I? So. The fate of the Empire and the fate of the Motie species"—he hadn't paused— "it's all on our shoulders. I didn't even bother to ask Jennifer, she's worked up to this her whole life, but *you*—"

He'd finished typing in the course change. A warning note sounded, then they felt gentle acceleration. *Hecate* was now on route to MGC-R-31. Freddy relaxed in his chair, tired, not looking at her.

Didn't wait. Didn't need to think it over. Just trusted me and moved.

And she saw that it would break him. He would heal, over the years, almost; but his view of women of his class would be colored by a period of terrible frustration while his life was bent to one powerful woman's missionary urge.

She made a bet with herself, no trivial thing at all, and said, "I'll be moving into your cabin, if your offer's still open."

He looked up, and searched among possible answers while hiding his surprise. She held her expression solemn, a bit uneasy. Freddy nodded and smiled and took her hand, and still feared to speak.

✳   ✳   ✳

Chris Blaine reminded Kevin of someone. Of Captain Roderick Blaine, of course, but of someone else, too . . . and he finally got it as Chris paused at a window. Kevin had seen Midshipman Horst Staley looking out at Murcheson's Eye blazing against the Coal Sack, like a single coal red eye within a monk's hood, just before *MacArthur* jumped to Murcheson's Eye itself.

And Chris took his fill of the Hooded Man, then moved on aft to get breakfast, while Kevin mused at his station.

Why Horst? Horst Staley, who had learned too much on Mote Prime and died for it, twenty-eight years ago. They could never have met. They certainly weren't related. Chris Blaine looked like his father, square face, fine blond hair, tiny Irish nose . . . his father's was broken, of course . . . whereas Horst Staley had been enlistment-poster handsome, triangular face, long, heavy muscles, and sloping shoulders. . . .

"Ah."

Horace Bury looked up. "What?"

Chris Blaine was just coming into earshot; Renner could hear his voice. He said, "Just a vagrant thought."

As they approached their stations, Renner heard Trujillo's voice, cheerful and musical and not quite audible; then Blaine's voice raised above the hum of the ship's systems. "If you hadn't been digging for scandal, the high brass wouldn't have heard about the token ships for years. They look so harmless!"

"I can't take credit for that. It was the scandal I was after."

They were both finishing breakfast bars. Joyce Trujillo's assigned chair was out of the way, with a view of several screens but no controls. Blaine took his place as copilot. Renner waited a few minutes, then asked, "Chris, how're we doing?"

"Seventy hours en route and up to speed. I'll wind down the thrust"—*tap*—"now. Then we can drop the external tank and coast till we're approaching the Jump to the red dwarf. Two hundred seventy hours, unless the Jump point's moved, in which case all Hell lets out for lunch."

"I'm inclined to keep the tank and refill it. Better safe."

Blaine nodded.

During the next five minutes the thrust dropped from a standard gravity to .05 gee, just enough to pull spilled liquid out of the air. Renner waited it out, then said, "Lieutenant, you have the con." And he went aft for coffee.

He was unsurprised to find that Bury had floated after him. He asked, "Turkish?"

"Please. You have left—left Blaine in charge of my ship. Is that wise?"

"We're barely beyond Dagda's orbit in New Cal system in free fall, near as dammit. What could happen? Outies? Helium flash in the motor? He's Navy trained, you know."

"Yes."

"Like me."

"Yes. Kevin, what was it you didn't want him to overhear? Or was it the Trujillo woman?"

"Oh . . . something was nagging at me, irritating me, and I finally got it. You wouldn't remember Midshipman Horst Staley. He was an idealized Navy officer, handsome, imposing, the kind you put on posters. So's Blaine, but he's doing it consciously, like a signal."

"Yes, after all, he was raised by Moties. What think you now of Trujillo?"

"All sex and all business, generally not at the same time. She can turn it on and off. What are the rules this trip, Horace? Sex or no sex?"

"Blind eyes, I think. Poor old Trader Bury notices nothing. But she is staying to business?"

"Yeah. Projects availability, but. I like it, actually. I like flirting." Bury did not smile. Renner said, "Give her a break, Horace. Her dad told her about Traders, merchant princes, but she doesn't know any. She'll learn about Traders from you."

" 'Your reputation precedes you,' " Bury quoted.

"I doubt she meant that as viciously as it sounded." Renner sighed. "It's going to be a fun trip. Trujillo offended you first chance she got, you *hate* Blaine, and if everything goes right, we'll get there in time to find a Motie armada coming out at us."

In the pause that followed, Renner finished brewing two bulbs of Turkish. Bury took his and asked, "How can you say that I *hate* Kevin Christian Blaine? He is your godson. He is my guest."

"Horace, you haven't been overtly rude, but I know you. And look, if I had to . . . Igor! Tonight we will make something quite different, *quite*."

"Yes, Doctor Frankenstein! Yes! Yes!"

"Tonight we will create the infidel least likely to be welcome aboard a teeny tiny spacecraft with Trader Horace Bury. We will give him the following characteristics, *hnpf hnpf hnpf!* Anglo-Saxon. Christian. An Empire Navy man. Related to the same *Roderick Blaine* who once held Bury prisoner aboard a Navy warship. And lastly, *hnpf hnpf hnpf!* He will be raised by Motie Mediators!"

Horace dropped the accent. "Lastly, he is a manipulative son of a dog."

"I'd say that goes with the Motie training."

"Yes, Kevin, but he tried to manipulate *me*. Does he think me a fool?"

"Mmm."

"It was not Joyce Trujillo who discovered the significance of the token ships!"

"I'll be dipped. Horace, he's chasing her."

"Eh?"

"I didn't see it. She's a career woman six years older than he is! Even so, that's it. He let her see him manipulating you for her benefit. I wonder if she'll buy it?"

Renner hadn't even decided if he *liked* her. That was not always the most interesting question. Perhaps, somewhere in the back of his brain, he had considered Joyce Mei-Ling Trujillo to be his by default. Blaine was too young, Buckman and Bury were too old, and Kevin Renner was captain of *Sinbad*.

The problem lay in what she might want. Not money, nor entrée into certain levels of society; he could do that. But secrets . . . she loved secrets, and Kevin Renner's were not his to give away.

Blaine was too young, and he was a classic model of a Navy man—but Kevin Christian Blaine had been raised by Motie Mediators. Why was that so easy to forget? Renner began to watch him.

Sinbad in free fall could not be spun up. Chris Blaine was used to a bigger Navy ship. He was clumsy for the first couple of days. So was Joyce; she had not spent much time in space. Then they got oriented more or less together. Simultaneously, in fact. . . .

You had to concentrate to see it, how often they occupied the same space. In any of the narrow passages they might pass without brushing. Joyce was still a bit clumsy, but Chris could eel gracefully past her, close enough to link magnetic fields, but without touching her at all. Like dancing.

The morning before *Sinbad* began deceleration, Joyce Trujillo looked different, and so did Chris Blaine. They both seemed a bit embarrassed about it, and they couldn't seem to avoid body contact.

✳   ✳   ✳

Two centuries ago, Jasper Murcheson had cataloged most of the stars this side of the Coal Sack. He had numbered them in some haste for his *Murcheson General Catalog,* then filled in details at leisure.

Half those stars were red dwarves, such as this orange-white dot called MGC-R-31. Murcheson had collected more detail on the hotter yellow dwarves, those that might have habitable planets and particularly those that did. MGC-R-31 had a brown dwarf star companion at half a light-year's distance; Murcheson hadn't even known that much.

Kevin Renner knew it the moment he popped into the system. He knew because some unseen nearby mass had skewed his Jump point by several million miles.

It should be located, fast. It would move the I-point, too! Buckman and Renner set to work at once.

It was good to be in MGC-R-31 system, good to have something to do, to have an excuse to lock that door.

A week of Bury's strained good manners and Blaine's and Trujillo's body-contact formality had been getting on everyone's nerves . . . or maybe only on Kevin Renner's. Buckman's needs gave him an excuse to do something about it. Renner had a section of *Sinbad*'s lounge partitioned off to become Jacob Buckman's laboratory.

It was cramped for Buckman, very cramped for Buckman and Renner; visitors were impossible. They preferred using it that way to everyone's popping in and out of the small bridge compartment. The others tried not to interfere.

Search for a brown dwarf. First observe the red dwarf, find its plane of rotation. By then Buckman had calculated a series of distances and masses that might account for the shift in the Alderson point. Look at one locus of points, observe again, calculate again . . .

Dinner appeared from somewhere. Renner would have ignored it, but Buckman hadn't even looked up. Better to eat, and make Buckman eat too.

And breakfast . . . but by then they were done. Renner sighed in relief. He opened the door to the lounge and announced, "Nothing. We're here first."

"Allah is merciful," Bury said.

"How sure are you?" Joyce Trujillo asked.

Chris Blaine said, "Good question. You can't know where the Alderson point is going to be."

"I do know that there is no new Alderson point in this region," Buckman said. "As to where the incipient point *will* be, I've had to change the locus because of the companion. Not much. Brown dwarf stars don't radiate much. It's still an arc along *here*, still about a million klicks long. I moved it by a couple of light-minutes. And it isn't there."

The arc Buckman's cursor made across the screen stretched away from the orange-white glare of MGC-R-31, toward the Coal Sack and an off-centered red peephole into Hell: Murcheson's Eye.

Renner touched a button on the console. "*Agamemnon*, this is *Sinbad*. We get a clean sweep. Do you? Over."

Agamemnon had popped out a few minutes ahead of *Sinbad*, separated by no more than the gap between Earth and Earth's moon. Now they were a few tens of thousands of miles apart, while *Atropos* moved ahead toward the hypothetical I-point. *Agamemnon*'s response came immediately.

"*Sinbad* this is *Agamemnon*. Affirmative. I say again, affirmative, there are no signs of any ships in this system. We are definitely here first. Is Lieutenant Blaine available?"

"Right here."

"Please stand by for the skipper."

"Right."

"So that's that," Joyce Trujillo said. She was all business now, as Blaine was all officer.

"For the moment," Bury said. "They will come. But now—now I believe Allah has given us this chance. We may yet lose it, but we have the opportunity."

"God is merciful," Joyce said. "He will not do everything and thus take away our free will and that share of glory that belongs to us."

"Biblical?" Renner asked.

She laughed. "Niccolò Machiavelli."

"Arrgh! Joyce, you have done it to me again."

Buckman said, "Horace? I've listed it as Bury's Infrastar. Your ship, your crew, your discovery."

Seconds late, Bury reacted. He smiled with effort and said, "Thank you, Jacob."

"Here's the skipper," the comm set announced.

"Blaine?"

"Yes, sir. We're all here."

"Some of my officers are suggesting this is a wild-goose chase."

"I would like nothing better, Commander," Horace Bury said. "But I do not believe that."

"Don't guess I do either. We're wondering what to do next. I don't mind admitting this isn't a situation I was trained to deal with," Balasingham said.

"Nothing complicated about it," Buckman said. "Renner has us on a course to coast along the arc over the next . . ."

"Fifteen days."

"Fifteen days. Your other ships have our data."

Chris Blaine took over. "Sir, we've sent the data to *Atropos*, so he'll take up station ahead of us. The I-point will be in this region. I suggest that *Agamemnon* stay behind, that is, between us and the path back to New Caledonia. Maybe they can intercept. As for us, we make repeated passes until the I-point appears."

"All right," Balasingham said. "For now, anyway. The Viceroy's sending more ships." Short pause. "What if a Motie fleet comes through shooting?"

"Then we do what we can," Bury said.

"And maybe the horse will sing," Renner muttered.

Bury shrugged. He seemed amazingly calm. "The Moties have no control over the protostar. This will be as Allah wills, and Allah is merciful."

* * *

If Buckman turned off his intercom, as he frequently did, the only way to find out what he was doing was to bang on his door and risk his acerbic comments about disturbing his work.

He had left the compartment door open this morning. Buckman had been constantly in his laboratory or the adjacent lounge for over thirty hours. Kevin Renner and Chris Blaine had alternated waiting just outside the lab door, and it was Chris's turn. He'd been there an hour, with nothing to do. Then he heard a shout.

"By God!"

Chris went to the compartment door. Buckman was hunched over a console. His grin was wide.

"What is it?" Chris asked.

"It's happening."

Chris didn't ask *what*. "How far away?"

"I'm only getting a flux reading. It's not stable yet, but it will be. It's tremendous! By God! Blaine, this is the best record of a new Alderson event anyone has ever got! Now we can set up for the visuals."

"How far away, Doctor Buckman?"

Buckman shook his head vigorously. "It's wobbling back and forth! The new star must be pulsing. It's traversing the arc. Half a million kilometers of sweep. More. We could conceivably Jump while *it* passes *us*, if it was anything like stable yet."

"I'll tell the other ships."

"It's strong enough that even Navy instruments should pick it up, but go ahead." Buckman went back to his console.

Blaine used the lounge intercom. "Kevin. Buckman says this is it. I'll alert *Agamemnon*."

* * *

"Agamemnon this is *Sinbad.* Alderson event detected in our vicinity. Buckman data attached to this message. Suggest you con-

verge on probable Alderson point location. I am also sending this message to *Atropos*. Blaine.''

They waited. Two minutes later the answer came. "*Sinbad* this is *Agamemnon*. We are under way at three gee, I say again, three standard gravities. We'll move toward you, but I will remain between the I-point and the exit to New Cal.''

"Doesn't take him long to make decisions," Renner said. "He's about twenty light-seconds behind us, but he's not going where we are. He can get to the New Cal Jump point in"—he typed rapidly—"about five hours, starting now. And *Atropos* is ahead of us. I don't know the best tactics.''

"Depends too much on what comes through," Chris Blaine said crisply.

"What is it? What's happening?" Joyce eeled out of her cabin, hurriedly adjusting her clothing. "Moties? They've come through?''

"Not yet," Blaine said. "They will.''

"Yeah," Renner said. "Dr. Buckman, have things stabilized at all?''

"Beginning to, yes, Kevin. Do you see how the I-point comes *fast* toward us along the arc and *slow* going back? I expect we're seeing irregular pulses on the protostar.''

"Yeah. *Boom* and it settles down, *boom* and it settles down, *boom*. When the protostar stops flaring . . .''

"Well, for the next hundred thousand years it won't quite.''

"Eases off, then. The I-point will be ahead of us, won't it? Closer to *Atropos* than us, and still wobbling a bit.''

"At a guess, Kevin. This is a first in every way. The collapse of Buckman's Protostar into Buckman's Star.''

"It's all guesses, but give *Atropos* about four and a half hours. At one gee we'll take about eight.''

"But you and Buckman don't think we have four hours," Blaine said.

Renner said, "I know, can't push much more than a gee without killing Bury.''

"Do not worry about me," Bury said from behind him. "I will be in my water bed. Nabil is bringing it to the lounge now.''

"One and a half, then. No more," Renner said. "Okay, as soon as you get in it—''

"Stabilized!" Buckman shouted.

"How do you know?"

"A ship came through. There's another! A light-second or two apart."

Renner brought the images up on his screen. "About three light-seconds ahead of us. Closer to us than *Atropos*—three ships." Renner's fingers were dancing. An alarm wheeped; Renner slapped the volume down. *Secure for acceleration.* "Four ships. Five."

Sinbad's motor lit. Objects drifted aft.

"They're well separated. The star must be still flaring, the I-point's still drifting."

"Mercy of Allah," Bury muttered. "Quickly, Nabil, get me into my water bed."

"I must secure it to the deck," Nabil said calmly. The little old assassin moved easily under what had become half a gee of pull.

"Six. Seven," Renner said. "Seven so far. Blaine, you'd better get *Atropos* on line."

"Roger. Doing it."

"What's happening?" Joyce Mei-Ling demanded from the lounge door.

"Secure for acceleration, dammit!" Renner shouted. "All hands, secure. Nabil, let me know when it's safe!"

"The bed is secured. If you do not turn too much, I can put him in it when we are under way."

"I'll hold it at one gee until you've got him set. Everyone secure? Buckman, you holding on to something? Here we go."

Sinbad eased up to one gee. "They're scattering," Renner said.

"Must have come through with different velocities," Blaine said. "It's just drift so far."

"Sure."

"They will scatter," Bury said. "Of course they will. Seven ships. They have been preparing for this for years. Kevin, can we intercept them all?"

"Not likely. Moties can't take as much gee stress as we can, but there's no way three ships can chase down seven. Not given that much head start."

"*Sinbad* this is *Agamemnon*. What's happening, Blaine?"

"Seven Motie ships so far," Blaine said. "Beyond us, and drift-

184

ing in seven directions. I'll squirt up the data we have." He pressed keys, and the computer sent out what it had. Data twenty-plus seconds out-of-date would be better than nothing.

Nearly a minute went by. "Blaine, they'll have plenty of time to recover from Jump shock before we get there," Balasingham's voice said. "Assuming each one accelerates along its present course, and giving them anything like the performance Motie ships had at the blockade point, we aren't going to catch more than four. Five tops, and that assumes we can cripple them without too much of a fight, which is assuming a lot. *Damnation*—"

Pause; then Balasingham said, "I think it's time to change tactics. I'm ordering *Atropos* to move toward the I-point and prepare to chase Motie ships. That gets him close to you. I'm taking *Agamemnon* back to block the way out of this system. Our entry point won't have changed enough to matter. We'll never catch them all, but maybe we can bottle them up in here."

"Not bloody likely," Blaine muttered. "But I suppose it's the best thing to try."

"Captain Renner," Balasingham continued. "You were given sealed orders when you left New Scotland. To be opened on my instructions. My orders said to have you do that when the situation got beyond my control. I hereby instruct you to open those orders.

"You'll find that your Reserve commission as Captain is activated, and you're in command of this expedition with the titular rank of commodore. I don't know what you can do, but I sure can't think of anything. I'm ordering Commander Rawlins in *Atropos* to put himself under your direction.

"Sir, I am now changing course to guard the Alderson point to New Caledonia. If you want me to do something else, tell me what it is. *Agamemnon* out."

"God's navel," Renner said.

"Kevin, have I heard correctly?" Bury demanded.

"Apparently," Renner said. "I heard it too."

"Moties," Joyce said from somewhere aft. "Chris—"

"Later."

"Yes, but—Chris, they're *Moties!*"

"Joyce, it's a great story, but there's no time!" Chris shouted.

"Captain, the first two Motie ships are under acceleration. They must be automated; Moties wouldn't have recovered yet."

"Wonder what kind of computer they trust to work that soon after a Jump?" Buckman muttered.

Chris Blaine examined the computer screen. "Continuing in their original directions. My guess is they'll all do that."

Renner said, "Scatter and lose us. Only seven ships, and I don't see any more . . . in fact I've lost one. I'd have thought they would send more."

"Me, too," Blaine said. "Maybe they couldn't."

"Spacecraft are expensive," Bury said. He sounded comfortable enough under 1.5 gravities. "Many resources, of different kinds. A complex society."

"Which may mean they've got problems," Renner said. "Jacob, where in the Mote system will their end of the tramline be?"

"Fairly far out. Well beyond the orbit of their gas giant, Mote Beta."

"We never looked at the Trojan civilizations," Renner said. "Maybe we should have."

Half an hour later it was clear enough. Chris Blaine went back to explain to Joyce and Bury: "There are seven Motie ships. Five are under full acceleration in five different directions. One of them is lost, to us and *Agamemnon* and everyone else. Maybe we'll find it. Maybe not."

"Mercy of Allah," Bury muttered. "And the seventh?"

"The seventh is headed directly toward us, Excellency."

Bury fingered his beard. "They will want to talk, then."

Joyce Mei-Ling was staring at the viewscreen. Suddenly she pointed at the Motie ship. As they watched, a laser beam blinked on and off.

"As you said, Excellency. If you'll excuse me . . ." Blaine went back to his duty station and turned to Renner. "Apparently they want to talk."

"So do we," Renner said. "We'll never catch any of the others. *Atropos* may, but *we* won't."

"One of the others looks to be heading for the Jump point to New Cal," Blaine said. "*Agamemnon* will be there first, though."

"Meanwhile, that ship is coming to us," Renner said. "Hah.

186

They're modulating that beam. Let's see if any of it makes sense—"

"Imperial ship, this is Motie vessel *Phidippides*," the speaker said.

"I've heard that name," Joyce Mei-Ling Trujillo said.

"We come in peace. We seek His Excellency Horace Bury. Is he aboard?"

Joyce said, "Phidippides was the first Marathon runner. Delivered his message and died."

Renner and Blaine looked at each other, then at Bury flat in his water bed with a screen above his face. Renner looked at the sensors before he spoke. Bury's heartbeat was steady, brain waves indicating he was fully awake. Okay.

"Horace? It's for you."

4
The I-point

*Foreign relations are like human relations. They are
endless. The solution of one problem usually leads to another.*

—James Reston

The Honorable Freddy Townsend woke slowly, savoring each moment of relaxation. He felt eyes on him and turned over. "Hi."

"Hi, yourself."

Nobody puts a big bed aboard a racing ship. It only leaves room
for accidents. Freddy had moved the double into *Hecate* for that
earlier voyage with Glenda Ruth. He'd left it aboard for this trip . . . of
course, why not? It had seemed so empty, until now.

"Chocolate," she said. "Is there any chocolate aboard?"

"You shall have your desire if I have to grow the beans myself,"
Freddy proclaimed.

"If you find any aboard, lock it up. We're likely to need it."

He stared. Then he reached for her, a tentative gesture. Glenda
Ruth laughed. "I won't vanish, you know."

"I can barely follow you, and you always know what I'm thinking. That worries me. If you know so much about—people—from
what the Moties taught you, what do *they* know about *us*? Everything including what we don't know ourselves?"

"Maybe not that much," she said.

"But you're not sure."

"I only knew three Moties. And they had to be the smartest ones
available. I mean, who would you send as ambassadors to another
race? To an empire that threatened your whole race?"

"Yeah, you're probably right." This time he took her firmly by the shoulder and pulled her toward him.

It would take them six days to cross to the Jump point to MGC-R-31.

On a later splendid morning Glenda Ruth said, "You should let Kakumi teach you some fighting techniques."

Freddy wasn't quite awake yet. He woke slowly and carefully. "Terry? I don't know that he knows any. Inuit are nice peaceful folk who really know machines."

"Taniths aren't. There was three hundred years of tooth and nail. Terry Kakumi's half Tanith."

"Mmm . . ."

"And maybe five percent Sauron superman, Freddy. He's bound to know something."

Freddy sat bolt upright. "Rape my lizard! Kakumi's been my engineer—Glenda Ruth, how would you know that? You barely know him!"

"I started watching him because I don't want Jennifer hurt. It looked like she and Terry were, um, courting."

"Four years, five, he's kept this ship healthy."

"He's a good man, Freddy, but I noticed things. I've watched him *move*. He tried to cook for us once?"

"Ugh. I should have warned you. In a race there's just the two of us. I take precooked. It's better."

"They were perfect soldiers, the Saurons. March for a week without sleeping. Tolerate any sunlight level, any gravity. Breathe any atmosphere, never mind the stench. Sleep anywhere, wake instantly." She paused. "Eat anything organic. Anything."

"Oh. I guess that figures. Okay, so he's part—Sauron. There are Sauron loyalists, you know. Kakumi was six years in the Navy. Honorable discharge as an engineering petty officer."

"It doesn't matter."

"Some places it does," Freddy said. "I'm glad they didn't know when we were racing in the Ekaterina system. I'm glad *I* didn't know. I'd have been too nervous."

"You won, though."

"Sure. Didn't know you . . . You *don't* follow racing. Damn, sometimes you scare me."

"Pooh."

"Yeah, pooh. Let's both take lessons." They'd been in New Cal system for four days; another six would take them through the Jump point to MGC-R-31. Six lessons in how to be a Sauron soldier?

"Oh, Freddy, that's . . ." She stopped.

"You weren't going to say . . . ?"

"No, not because I'm a girl and you're a boy! *Mediators* don't fight. Sure, let's both take lessons."

Terry Kakumi looked hard and round, a little taller than Glenda Ruth but more than half again her weight. When *Hecate* was racing and all needless mass had been stripped out, he slept in the engine compartment. Now there were bulkheads installed to make a cabin for him just forward of the engine compartment, but he hadn't done much with it.

"Bare as the engine room," Freddy told Glenda Ruth. "I suppose it makes sense—are you sure about his ancestry?"

"Want to ask him?"

"No, I don't think so—"

"Of course he may not know."

Freddy tapped on the engine room compartment door.

It opened. "Aye, aye." Kakumi saw Glenda Ruth, came out into the companionway, closing the door behind him. "Need me to relieve George on watch?"

"No, we're on course. Wanted to ask you something, Terry. You were Navy, you must have learned how to fight . . . ?"

Kakumi nodded.

"Or knew already. Anyway, you knew when we left Sparta we'd be trying to get to the Mote. Well, it might be dangerous. We're wondering if you'll give us some lessons?"

Kakumi looked at Freddy, then Glenda Ruth, and shook his head slowly. "Wouldn't be a good idea. Four days or so, you'd learn just enough to get in trouble. If there's trouble, you talk, I'll fight." He grinned, making small wrinkles at the corners of his eyes. "Better than if I talk and you fight. Jennifer's good at talking, too. Do we know for sure if we're going to the Mote?"

"Not yet."

"Too bad."

"Well. I suppose you're right," Freddy said. "About learning just enough to get killed. All right."

"Let's go look at the charts," Glenda Ruth said. She took Freddy's hand and led him away. When they reached the bridge, she was laughing.

"What?"

"Think about it. Why he closed the door."

"Huh? Oh. Jennifer."

"Interesting that he's that sensitive."

* * *

"Excellency, greetings!" The lopsided Motie face bubbled with enthusiasm . . . somehow.

"Salaam. I see that you know me."

"Of course."

Face had been a new concept to the Moties. Renner remembered that rigid, twisted smile. Motie faces weren't evolved to send messages. The creature must be signaling with body language and intonation: *Glad, glad to see you! How long it has been, how much like coming home!*

Bury's indicators were twitchy but not ominously so. "My Fyunch-(click) must be long dead."

"Oh, yes, but she taught another, and that one taught me. I've been Fyunch(click) to you since my birth, yet we meet for the first time. Please tell me, was the coffee-tasting event a success?"

For an instant, Bury gaped. Then, "Yes, indeed. Your teacher's teacher was quite right, the Navy had never considered that a man who doesn't drink wine might still teach them something of discrimination."

"Splendid! But it must seem that I'm talking of some past Dark Age. Let me say in some haste that my task is to persuade you and yours not to fire on us. We come in peace. We carry none of the Warrior class."

Bury nodded in satisfaction. "Astute of you to say so."

Renner and Blaine exchanged glances. Chris Blaine grinned slightly.

"What?" Joyce demanded in a fierce whisper.

"Warriors," Blaine said. When she raised a questioning eyebrow, Chris raised a palm to cut her off. "Later."

The Motie continued to project confidence. "Excellency, our first ship, which we have named *Gandhi*, wishes to carry an ambassa-

191

dor to your nearest peopled world. She is accompanied by a Mediator, of course, one who can speak to your political authorities. Meanwhile, we aboard *Phidippedes* wish to accompany you and yours into Mote system."

Bury's passengers stared at their alien communicant. Buckman grinned in anticipation. Joyce scrawled something on her pocket computer. Renner checked again: only Bury was in camera view. "Buckman, cut thrust to half a gee," he said.

"You sure?"

"We're not chasing anything anymore, and Horace has to talk, and that was an order."

Bury ignored the byplay. To the Motie he said, "Me and mine?"

"I was told to invite any ship I found here to follow me home, but particularly the craft with Horace Hussein Bury aboard."

Bury's dancing dials had settled; he must feel himself in control of this situation. "And why should we go with you?"

"Ah. For you, Excellency, to be here at all is to be aware that matters have altered. Until today every ship we sent through the Crazy Eddie point was under sentence of death. We know that none have returned from that alien country. Today new paths between the stars have opened. Your battleships can no longer stand between your systems and ours. Will you not try negotiation instead? Negotiation and trade." The creature didn't rub its hands together when it mentioned trade, but the suggestion was there.

"Perhaps you should speak to our commodore," Bury said. A tap of the button set the camera and monitor screen turning . . .

Toward Kevin Renner. Kevin said, "Hi."

"Kevin, hi! I don't remember 'commodore.' Are you actually in command of that ship?" Just a bit awestruck, she was, with no intention of showing it. "You've come a long way."

"Uh-huh. Did another human's Fyunch(click) train you, too, maybe?"

"I inherit no training from your Fyunch(click), Kevin, but Bury's Mediator observed other humans. You can't ever know too much about the people you deal with."

"And who did I learn *that* from?"

"Exactly. And how are Spacers Jackson and Weiss, if you know, sir?"

These personality changes were disconcerting. Renner said,

"He's Governor Jackson of Maxroy's Purchase, if you please, and just loving every bit of it."

"All *right!*"

And Weiss was dead and they both knew it and neither would ever mention it again.

Off camera, Chris Blaine made a suggestive throat-cutting gesture. Joyce looked up from her recorder in alarm. "Keep it talking," she mouthed soundlessly.

Renner studied the lopsided visage a bit longer . . . knowing how little it was gaining him, while the Mediator used these seconds to study his *face*. He said, "Make up a name for yourself, for my convenience."

"Eudoxus."

Bury smiled thinly; Joyce's eyes narrowed, then popped wide. When Renner raised an eyebrow, Bury said, "A classical trader and explorer. Discovered the Golden Wind of the Arabs."

"Okay. Eudoxus, for the moment I command every Empire ship in this system. I listen to Horace Bury, so you're talking for his benefit, too. Now, you've sent seven ships through from the Mote. Some we've captured, some are running. One has an ambassador aboard, and you want her transported to where she can contact the Empire. Is that about it?"

"Two ambassadors, Kevin. She and he. An older Keeper to teach the younger, younger to last longer."

Keepers: sterile Masters. "Prudent. You sent no other Classes?"

"Mediators, of course. And there were working Classes aboard some ships for maintenance, until the Curdle collapsed. Then we spaced them. We feared you would feel threatened.

"However, I have an Engineer pilot aboard, and so does *Gandhi*." The creature's left hand came up in haste. Something must have showed in Renner's face. "She can be spaced if your big ship takes ours in tow."

"Watchmakers?"

"Of course. They are very valuable."

Bury's needles jumped, then settled back.

"We'll call you back in an hour. Until then . . ." Kevin considered. "Don't do anything drastic. I'm going to free fall. You match course with me and then cut your thrust. Keep station ten thousand klicks away. Can you cause your other ships to gather here?"

"I can call them, but they will not obey. Three have instructions to hide within this system." The Motie shrugged. The shoulders didn't move. "I tell you nothing you would not expect. Let me repeat my offer. Come with us."

"I'll call you back." Renner switched off. He closed his eyes tight and heaved a massive sigh. Then, "Talk to me. Horace?"

Bury laughed. "How did Eudoxus know that we know of their Warriors? Answer: she did not. But we might know, and if she did not say, 'We have no Warriors,' no more would be said at all. We would bend every effort to destroying every ship, every Warrior Motie." No laughter now. "An astute analysis, and the correct conclusion, to admit it immediately."

"Um-humm," Renner said. "I was working on that."

"Can they know us that well? Already?" Joyce Mei-Ling asked in wonder. "Kevin—Captain Renner, how did it recognize you?"

"What else?" Renner asked.

"She still doesn't know how *MacArthur* died."

"Yeah, and you could hardly tell her how the Kaffee Klatch ended, could you?" Kevin grinned at Joyce's puzzlement. "All right, Joyce. Eudoxus recognized me because the Moties took pictures of everyone they met. Made extensive records of what we did, too. Memorizing everything they know about every human who ever went to the Mote would be part of Eudoxus's training."

"Their memories are that good?"

"At least that good. As to the Kaffee Klatch, the Watchmakers had reworked *MacArthur*'s coffeepot months after we thought we'd cleaned them out. They were loose in the tween decks areas, all over the ship, and when we discovered they were there, they fought us. Before *that* was over, *MacArthur* was abandoned and Horace was ready to exterminate the Moties. But his Fyunch(click) never knew any of that."

"Eudoxus expects to manipulate me. Poor Horace Bury," Bury said thickly, "he'll risk anything to master the wealth of Motie technology."

"She knows now, Horace. She saw Kevin twitch when she mentioned Watchmakers. It may have been a mistake to leave the visuals on. Horace, I wonder just how much the Moties know about your Arab nationalist sentiments? Anyway, what shall we do?"

"An ambassador. *Gandhi!* Ludicrous."

"We don't have to blow the Motie ship up, though. Do we?"

"Perhaps if we could destroy all seven . . . but we can't do that, Kevin. Consider: what if one of the seven was a decoy, say a token ship mounted on a small comet head? Poof, gone. Evaporated. We would only find six, never the seventh. And three have instructions to hide. With a whole system to hide in. A system we have not explored any better than they have. Who knows what resources are here? And you may be sure that *those* ships have fertile Masters, probably pregnant."

"Yeah."

Joyce Trujillo said, "But in that case, if we could find six— Oh."

Kevin noticed the look of annoyance Chris Blaine cast on Joyce Trujillo. But why . . . ?

No time to worry about that. Kevin said, "Yeah. Six ships, and what if there's no iceball? Talk or fight, and we can't start shooting until or unless we find them all, and we've lost at least one already. So talk, and they want us to go with them to the Mote. That may be a good idea. The question is, can we leave them here? *All* of the Mote ships, with *Agamemnon* on guard, until more ships from the blockade squadron come through from the Eye?"

"Can we not? Consider further," Bury said. "These ships are unarmed. There has been no hint of a threat, but if one of these does not report back . . ."

"The threat is certainly implied, sir," Chris Blaine said. "Look at the record. The first couple of ships the Crazy Eddie Squadron dealt with were probably unarmed. The rest had any weapon you can think of. Excellency, she knew *you'd* see the threat. With strangers she would have been more explicit."

Renner said, "We have to let Eudoxus report back, and we learn more if we go with her." He got a confirming nod from Bury. "All right, whether or not *Agamemnon* is enough, she's all we have, because I don't fancy taking *Sinbad* into the Mote system without a reliable way to send a message out. That means we take *Atropos* along. Chris, you agree?"

"Yes, sir. If anyone can get a message out, they can, either *Atropos* herself or the longboat."

Bury asked, "Dr. Buckman, how big are the Motie ships? Tiny, are they not? Too small to fight *Agamemnon*, even all together. Yes, and thus unarmed. So, Kevin, what are you thinking?"

"I'm thinking Eudoxus could tell us more about what waits for us on the other side. Then ... we can maybe rendezvous with *Agamemnon*, leave you and Joyce—"

"Hold up, *Commodore* Renner—"

"*My* ship, curse your hullmetal-thick hide."

"Okay, okay. Do we want to put the servants off?"

Bury said, "Each lady so lovely, though all in their forties. Did you ever wonder why, Kevin? I test them in lesser positions. I send the weak and timid to other duties. With such companions near me I need never fear my own people. New Levantines would never suspect my harem."

"Good. They can fight? I was always a little afraid of Cynthia."

"With reason."

"We still can't leave. *I* still can't leave," Renner said. "Not till we know who's where. Not till things settle down." But Bury was shaking his head. "*What*, Horace? Eudoxus didn't seem to be in any hurry."

"Kevin, in negotiations only a loser reveals that he is under a deadline. Even so, I think Eudoxus flinched when you cut her off. It's hard to tell, of course. But do consider what may next emerge from the I-point if we do not allow Eudoxus to report back."

"Yeah. Well, we'll *wait* for her to tell us. Now I need a link to *Atropos*. Dr. Buckman, I hereby appoint you communications officer."

Buckman chuckled. "Navy personality always comes through, doesn't it? All right, Commodore, I'll try. Incidentally, they're nine light-seconds away."

"Commander Rawlins here. Balasingham tells me I'm under your orders, Captain Renner."

"Such is life. What's your status?"

"We're chasing down the largest of the Motie ships."

"How many can you see?"

"Five. One we're chasing. One is quite openly headed for the New Cal exit point at top speed, but *Agamemnon* will be there first. One's parked near you. Two more are headed off in opposite directions, and we'll lose at least one of those before we catch up to the one we're chasing."

"So we've lost two now. How long until you catch that Motie ship?"

"I'll be in gunnery range in ten minutes or less. Do I fire?"

Renner looked to the others on *Sinbad*'s bridge. "Blaine?"

"Warning shots, sir?"

Renner activated the mike. "Put a low-power laser dot on them and see what they do. If they won't stop, blow 'em up."

"And if they stop?"

"Stand by," Renner said. "Damnation. Horace, of course they'll stop. And talk, and talk, and delay."

"We have already lost track of two. By Commander Rawlins's own estimation, no matter what he does with the one he chases, he will not be able to intercept all that will remain. Three will have escaped, Kevin. Three."

"Only into this system. That big cruiser can stop their getting out," Joyce said. "Can't it?"

"I remind you, what may come through next could be enough to destroy *Sinbad*. Then *Atropos*. Perhaps *Agamemnon*."

"They'll have plenty of time to recover from Jump shock before engaging," Blaine said. "We've seen ships come through the Crazy Eddie point that could have slagged *Agamemnon* in single-ship engagement."

"*Sinbad*, this is *Atropos*. We are closing in range to Motie ship. We have a beam on her."

"They'll stop," Blaine said.

"I am certain you are correct."

"Eudoxus is signaling," Buckman said genially.

"Everything happens at once!" Joyce said.

"*Sinbad*, this is *Atropos*. As soon as we demonstrated that we could hit the Motie ship, it turned off its drive and is now hailing us in Anglic. 'We come in peace. This is the Motie ship *King Peter's Gift*. We come in peace. Do you have instructions?' Sir, do we have instructions?"

"God's navel."

"Suggestion," Blaine said.

"Talk to me!"

"Have *Atropos* put a prize crew on that ship and send it to rendezvous with *Agamemnon*. Then he can see if he can chase down anything else."

"Yeah. Rawlins, put a crew with a bomb onto that Motie ship and send it to *Agamemnon*. Then see what you can do about the other Motie ships."

"Eudoxus is signaling," Buckman said cheerfully.

"Of *course* Eudoxus is signaling. Let her wait. Rawlins, I'm wondering about landings. I'll send you design specs for *Sinbad*. Horace, I'm sorry, but he's *got* to have those. Rawlins, *Sinbad* can land on a habitable planet, but we'd have to find fuel to get off. Does *Atropos* have landers?"

"Three. Two cutters and a longboat. All functional, but one cutter needs work. I'll send you specs. The longboat could carry enough fuel for a cutter to regain orbit from Mote Prime, but can't get back up without refueling. *Atropos* can scoopdive a gas giant planet for fuel."

What have I forgotten? Oh, I'll get it later. "Buckman, put Eudoxus on. . . . Hello, Eudoxus, sorry I had to cut you off, but your ships have been keeping us fairly busy."

"I was glad of the nap time, Kevin. Have you given further thought to our invitation?"

Glad of the nap time, hnpf hnpf hnpf! "Further thought, sure. Nap time sounds wonderful. We've got to wait anyway. So. Are you short of anything? Air, food, water? We can lob you a package."

"Kevin . . . no, we have enough to last us."

"Okay. Tell me *anything* about what we can expect to meet us on the other side of the Jump point."

"Ye-ess. My Keeper is part of the chain of command of—the name would not translate, of course, so I will call us the Medina Traders. We are the largest trading company in our region. We're involved in dominance games with several other groups, all under truce of one depth or another. We expect to meet you in space and lead you to our territory, all in perfect safety. Nevertheless, surprise by a rival becomes more likely the longer we delay."

Bury broke in. "Dominance games. War?"

Renner looked for hesitation, and he saw it. "Nothing so large, Excellency, but Warriors do become involved from time to time."

"Battles, then. For what prize? Ourselves?"

"For resources, thus far. Your existence we have kept to ourselves."

"So. We might have to fight. What would be your status if you returned alone?"

Shrug. "I would have failed. My Keeper and her—superior—would make decisions on that basis, and so would other clans."

Renner said, "I'm putting you on hold."

The picture remained. Buckman said, "We've cut the signal. So?"

"Keepers?" Joyce asked. "Where have I heard that term?"

"Keepers are sterile male Masters," Blaine said. "Possessive but not aggressively expansive. Joyce, the group we dealt with on Mote Prime was headed by a Master calling itself King Peter—you'll recall one of these ships they've sent us is called *King Peter's Gift?*—and the Moties he sent us included a Keeper ambassador called Ivan . . . Captain? It feels funny."

"What?" Renner prompted.

"King Peter's Gift. It's too bald and not too accurate. That damn ship isn't a gift, it's a threat. Eudoxus speaks of different factions, different clans. She spoke of Warriors, but was that really a clever ploy? Sir, we have to suspect that they really don't know what all the expedition learned, and may not be part of King Peter's clan at all."

"Interesting," Bury said. "Of course they know everything I was told. Or think they do."

"Decision time," Renner said. "One of the Mote ships has to go back, but does it have to be *Phidippides?* Or has Eudoxus learned too much by watching us? Blaine?"

"No, sir, trust me on this. She's starting from too far back. She hasn't been able to interpret anything pointed; she's still correcting *egregious* assumptions. At worst she might finally know what destroyed *MacArthur.* Is there a strong reason why they shouldn't know that?"

"I don't know. Let's just say we'll keep all our secrets until we have a reason to give them up."

"Sounds right, sir. And of course we confirmed that we know about the Warrior class. Pity, but at least there won't be any more of the 'harmless Moties' game they played on my father."

"Yeah. Warriors. Horace, if there's anything I don't know about *Sinbad's* defenses, tell me privately, before we jump."

"Yes. Eudoxus is becoming nervous, Kevin."

"Yeah. So she's worried that things are coming unraveled at the other end. That's probably not good for us. It means we can ask for concessions, though, because she won't have time to dicker. What do we want from Eudoxus?"

Bury's eyes half-closed. "Yes. If we *knew*—"

"*Atropos* calling," Buckman said. "They've got a second ship. Middie going aboard with a bomb. The first prize crew reports that an Engineer reworked the air system to give them air to breathe. All very cooperative. Rawlins has a third ship at the edge of detection range, but it's deep in the asteroids and decelerating. He's sure it's already too late."

"Tell him to leave it alone. Ladies and gentlemen, do we go? Yeah, Joyce, I know. Blaine?"

"Go."

"Horace?"

"Go, of course, but something must be done first."

"Name it."

"We need trade goods. Specifically the magic worm that we presume Glenda Ruth Blaine is bringing."

"Bury, we can't wait for that!" Renner said.

"I do not propose to. I do say that you must order the Navy not to hinder Miss Blaine when she arrives in this system. If she thinks it best to come to the Mote system—and she will, will she not, after your message to her, Lieutenant?"

"Yes, of course."

"Then the Navy must not prevent her."

"They're going to think it odd," Renner said. "A lord's daughter going into a combat zone. Okay, I can leave those orders. Anything else? . . . All right. Buckman, do we go?"

"Certainly. I can get a second view of a protostar in process of collapse! Maybe they'll let me leave instruments."

Kevin Renner nibbled his forefingers for a moment. "It'd be nice to refuel first . . . ah, well. Put *Atropos* through."

". . . Sir?"

"Rawlins, we're going through to Mote system. You're going first. How much fuel have you burned up?"

"I've got half a tank. Enough to get anywhere if we don't have to fight. Sir."

"We're expecting to be met by friends, but it's not certain at all.

200

Battle stations. Prepare your ship, full sleep period included and I am *dead* serious, and then call me. *Sinbad* out." With his eyes closed Renner said, "Somebody check on dinner."

*　　*　　*

Will Rawlins turned to his executive officer. "General Quarters, Hank."

"Aye, aye." Horns sounded through *Atropos*. "What do you think we'll find?"

"God knows. Get me Balasingham, please. Maybe he'll have an idea."

"Not likely," Henry Parthenio said. "But what the hell. Here he is."

Balasingham was under three gravities and looked it. "Go ahead, Will."

"Sir, Captain Renner wants me to accompany him into the Mote system."

"Yeah. Have fun."

"You think it's a good idea, sir?"

"I haven't the faintest flipping notion of whether it's a good idea," Balasingham said. His voice came from deep in his chest as he fought the strain of high gravity. "What I do know is that he's the boss now."

"Yes, sir—a Reservist, pilot to an Imperial Trader. . . ." Rawlins's tone said it all: the Navy did not like Traders and never had, and—

"Will, Captain Renner has been to the Mote. A long time ago, but he's been there, and that's more than I can say for anyone else we know. Now switch off your recorder and make sure we're secure. Got it? . . . Okay. Bury and Renner have been Navy Intelligence for a long time, and Bury comes to this system with the personal recommendation of Lord Roderick Blaine. Will, they're the best people we've got for this job."

"We-ell, all right, sir. Okay, I'm sending two Motie ships with prize crews to rendezvous with you at the exit point. They're under way now, so there's nothing keeping me. I'll take formation with *Sinbad* and the Motie ship *Phidippides*, and I reckon we'll be going through when I've done that. God knows when I'll be back."

"Right. Remember your first duty is to get The Word out. Godspeed."

"Thank you, sir. Sir, can we stop them?"

"God knows, Commander. You've seen some of the ships they've sent out of the Mote, and from all we know they've had decades to prepare for this. They could have a whole fleet of dreadnoughts just waiting for orders."

"Ugh. Yeah. Okay, here we go." Rawlins turned to his bridge crew. "Let's do it. Hank, get us into place to enter Mote system. *Phidippides*, then *Atropos*, then *Sinbad*."

5
The Battle of Crazy Eddie's Sister

To delight in war is a merit in the soldier, a dangerous quality in the captain, and a positive crime in the statesman.

—George Santayana

A brown blur swept past his eyes, too close; came wobbling back, taking on definition. Arm, fingers; fingers searching, closing on his shoulder, a nose nearly touching his. "Kevin. Captain. We." Joyce Trujillo blinking, trying to work her mouth. "We're being shot. At."

Cameras had been pulled inside for the Jump. Through the viewport Kevin saw murky red light where he should have seen black. Enemy lasers must be bathing *Sinbad's* Langston Field. No hot spots.

"Yeah. Okay. Field's holding. You . . . recover quick . . . Joyce." Renner looked around. His head wanted to swivel too far. Buckman was cursing as he tried to get his fingers working, to poke a camera through the Field. Blaine's arms jerked as he tried to bring them to his instruments. Horace Bury was contemplating nirvana with vacant eyes and a trace of a smile.

His doctors had finally got through to him. *Stroke, heart failure, ulcers, ruined digestion, and you won't be through it a moment sooner. Don't fight Jump shock!*

203

"Got prr. Probe," Buckman said. A picture appeared in Renner's monitor, and wobbled, and hunted, and found a green glare. "There. One ship using lasers only. Who's gunnery officer?"

"Me." Renner couldn't trust Blaine to kill. Navy trained, but raised by Mediators. Blaine wasn't functional anyway, not even as much as Trujillo. And *Sinbad* didn't have much for guns: a signaling laser that was several thousand times more powerful than it needed to be, good enough to keep armed merchantmen at bay, nowhere near enough power to be useful against real warships.

How hardened a target was the enemy ship? Would it be worth firing back? And where was *Atropos*? *Sinbad* had gone through last. It should be Rawlins's job to protect *Sinbad*.

The green glare wavered. Lost focus. Now it was a green point ringed in red, a yellow-white halo, glare green and expanding, an inflating violet sphere, *poof*, gone in seconds.

And with *that* enemy gone, the sky cleared.

It was a birthday-party sky, a black starfield full of colored balloons linked by bright strings. *Sinbad* had fallen into a battle. Ships must number in the hundreds. No telling how many sides, or who was who. But *Sinbad*'s Field was murky red and darkening, shedding stored energy and no longer under attack.

"Buckman, get an antenna through that!"

"Done. We've got ships in all directions .. not so many toward the Mote . . . I think I see *Atropos*."

An orange blob, close, cooling .. . darkening to red, but not contracting. Definitely *Atropos*. The Moties' expanding Langston Field had revolutionized Empire warfare; but *Atropos* had been built for duty at the Eye, where an expanding Field only meant more surface area to absorb heat from the star.

"I have *Atropos* on the line."

"Good. Rawlins, what's your situation?"

"Stable. We were attacked the moment we came through, Captain Renner. Two fleets, one that shoots at us, one that shoots at the other fleet.

"When the Motie embassy ship, *Phidippides*, came through, one fleet started shooting at her. I moved in front of her and shot back. When I did, everyone else got in the act."

"How's *Phidippides*?"

"That's her on the other side of us, with an expanding Field, yellow and getting worse. The one that's not shooting back. Now that we're in front of her it's not critical unless they're hit by torpedoes."

"Can you protect them?"

"Yes, sir. We can't talk to the other fleet, but they cooperate. Between us we slagged one of the enemy just after you came through. Commodore, we haven't seen torpedoes yet, just lasers and particle beams. We're in a general fleet engagement, but beyond watching over you and the Motie ship I don't know the objective. It's all guns, all the ships have expanding Fields—"

"*Sinbad*, this is *Phidippides*. Are you unhurt?"

The Motie was speaking in Horace Bury's voice, blurred by noise, probably still affected by Jump shock despite having gone through well before *Sinbad*. Renner grimaced. He said, "Carry on, Commander Rawlins. You're doing fine. I'll try to get information."

It was pointless to remind the Moties that the passage was supposed to be safe. "Eudoxus, this is Renner. Who's shooting at us?"

Static made a ragged silhouette of the Motie shape. "Call them . . . Ghengis Khan and the Mongol Horde. They're bandits, a large, well-established group. We were under attack from the Khanate when the Crazy Eddie point moved, but we thought they were after our comet."

"Comet, Eudoxus?"

"Resources, Kevin. We moved a comet out of the Waste to feed the industrial needs of Medina's monitoring fleet at the new Jump point we were expecting. Dammit, most of them *are* protecting the comet—"

"Speed it up, Eudoxus. Who are we fighting? Do we have allies? How do we recognize them? How safe are you? *You* can't fight."

"Protection is coming. Don't try to fight, Kevin. I will lead you away to our base, to safety. Medina's Warriors are moving to protect us now. They'll guard our withdrawal."

Renner saw it quite suddenly. "You're not from Mote Prime at all."

"No no no," the Motie said immediately. "On Mote Prime they've blasted themselves back to the invention of the brick. Medina Trading is at present based in the Oort Cloud, with allies in the Mote Beta moons and other regions. We've been using that wonderful protection field of yours to scoop up mass and debris, but a comet is better."

The pattern of distant ships was changing . . . had been changing

205

for some time. Brilliant points and larger colored dots, ships under attack and ships not under attack, several hundreds of them, were converging into place between *Sinbad*'s position and the main congestion of warships. *Phidippides*'s Field was cooling, shrinking, as her allies destroyed the ships that were attacking her.

It wasn't easy to see what they were doing, until you remembered the lightspeed gap. Even the nearest ships hadn't been seen to move for the first half-minute. The battle must be scattered up to three or four light-minutes across, tens of millions of klicks. They were all . . . no, only the *nearby* ships were reacting to the sudden appearance of three ships in the new Jump point. Some had moved to protect *Phidippides* and the Empire ships she escorted; some to attack. But far beyond, other glare-white sparks swarmed around the cold white glow of a comet's tail.

It was war among the asteroid civilizations for possession of the I-point, the Jump point into Empire space. Kevin Renner had led them right into it. Asteroid civilizations . . . and all his preparations had been made for Mote Prime!

Bloody Hell! Renner raged at himself. He couldn't even claim he'd been lied to, though of course he had. And now he was being told to run . . . but without knowing who was who, how could he argue?

"Stand by," Renner said curtly. "Rawlins?"

"Sir?"

"You're better at analyzing battles than I am. Is there any way we can get a message back to *Agamemnon*?"

"No, sir. The longboat wouldn't have any chance to get back to the I-point, and *Atropos* wouldn't have much more. None unless we could coordinate with the Motie fleet that's not shooting at us."

"Thanks. That won't happen. Okay, follow us and watch our backs. We're not going to Mote Prime. We're headed for the comets, outbound from the sun. I'll send the course when I have it."

"Sir—"

"Rawlins, when I know more, you will! Now I have to talk to the Moties. Out."

"No rest for the wicked," Joyce said.

Renner grinned slightly and hit the control keys. "Eudoxus."

"Here, Kevin."

Bury smiled softly, but said nothing.

"There may be another ship coming through anytime in the next five hundred hours," Renner said. "A very valuable ship. With a"—he saw Chris Blaine easing into place off camera—"a human female Mediator aboard. Be sure your people bring that ship to us when it comes."

"We'll try."

"Do more than try. The ship is valuable, and two of the passengers are Imperial aristocracy. Influential. Very influential."

"Ah. I will convey the urgency of the request."

"Good. Now, where are you taking us?"

"Medina Trading is among the nearer comets, above the plane of the Mote planetary system. There is an intermediate base, closer, well defended. We'll go direct to Medina Home unless we're interrupted, but on a course that lets us get to the base at need. Here is your course vector. . . ."

Renner examined it. "About twenty-five hours to turnover at something near one and a half standard gee. Everybody okay on that?"

"It is better than being caught in a battle," Bury said.

Renner glanced at the telltales, then caught Nabil's eyes. Nabil nodded slightly.

"Fair enough. Lead off," Renner said.

Chris looked okay; so did Alysia. Bury was fully alert and mad as hell. Good: Renner could use their opinions. He said, "Buckman, I need *Atropos*, but maintain the link to *Phidippides*. I'm sounding acceleration warning."

He let *Sinbad*'s corridors turn raucous while he ran the thrust up to one gee. Nabil and Cynthia hovered around Bury like worker ants feeding a queen. Bury's medical monitors were drawing a forest of needles, but why wouldn't they? Horace Bury hadn't been shot at since . . .

The Outies at Pierrot? Rape my lizard, was it that long ago?

And Blaine and Trujillo were staying well clear of each other's privacy bubbles, and neither was saying anything. *There may not be as much help there as I thought.*

Phidippides was easing away at a gee and a half, almost two Mote gravities. Renner ran his thrust up to match.

Atropos was aglow, black to glare green in a few seconds. The Motie ships looked tiny compared to the empire cruiser, but they had expanding Fields and *Atropos* didn't. Not good . . . but somewhere behind them a red point blossomed into a violet sun and dissipated. *Atropos* began to cool. Rawlins was fast with his guns.

The battle was mostly behind them now. Friendly and enemy ships looked too much alike; in the telescopes each was unique; but one squadron was definitely deploying to form a barrier behind the three fleeing ships. Another group converged on a ship trying to get past the barrier force.

Renner sighed. Until he knew more, what the hell else could he do but run? He made eye contact with Chris Blaine: *Do you see anything I don't?*

Blaine shook his head and pointed to the battle screen. "Rawlins is right, it's unlikely we'd get a message back to *Agamemnon* even with help from Medina's fleet, and without *Atropos* we're in big trouble. Other than that, we're fine. Rawlins knows how to fight, and whoever our allies are, they're pretty good. And willing to take punishment for us."

"They'll be Warriors," Renner said. Nightmare creatures like those statuettes in the Moties' *Time Machine* sculpture, perhaps altered by selective breeding for life in low gravity. Warriors on both sides.

"Horace?"

"I think of nothing you have not. I feel as if I have deceived myself."

"Which you did," Buckman said, chuckling.

"Mote Beta?" Joyce asked.

"We called the main Mote planet Mote Prime," Renner said. "There's a gas giant we called Beta."

"And almost certainly another planet," Buckman said. "Mote Gamma. Almost certainly a gas giant. There are also two large clusters of asteroids sharing the orbit of Mote Beta. Nearly all of them were moved into place."

"Moved," Joyce said. "Isn't that a lot of work, moving asteroids?"

"Sure is," Renner said. "Enough. We're committed."

"*Alea jacta est,*" Joyce said.

"Onk?"

"The die is cast," Bury translated. "Indeed."

"Right. Okay, mike's live again. All right, Eudoxus," Renner said. "Keep talking. What in Hell is a Bury's Fyunch(click) doing in the Mote asteroids?"

✳   ✳   ✳

Freddy Townsend woke when Kakumi's voice barked at him from the intercom. He woke quickly as he always did when he slept at the bridge console.

"Freddy, there's a radio message. General communications band. Talk to them, Freddy. You there?"

Freddy reached tentatively for the console. The timer showed nearly an hour since the shift. His hand was steady, and his head felt clear. He flipped a switch to put the incoming message on the speakers:

"WARNING. YOU HAVE ENTERED AN INTERDICT ZONE. THIS SYSTEM HAS BEEN PLACED UNDER INTERDICT BY AUTHORITY OF THE VICE-ROY GOVERNOR GENERAL OF TRANS–COAL SACK SECTOR. THIS SYSTEM IS PATROLLED BY THE IMPERIAL NAVY. BROADCAST YOUR LOCATION AND IDENTITY ON THIS BAND AND WAIT FOR INSTRUC-TIONS. FAILURE TO COMPLY MAY RESULT IN DESTRUCTION OF YOUR SHIP. WARNING."

"Well, that's pretty explicit," Freddy said. He typed quickly on the control console. "Glenda Ruth, I think you should include something in your code so they can be sure its you. That message wasn't friendly at all."

"All right." She connected the interface cable into her computer and scribbled. "Clementine, code that with my private key."

"Yes, dear."

"I wonder about this," Glenda Ruth said. "That message sounds pretty positive."

"You think something has happened?"

"I don't know, but I bet we don't have long to wait."

The reply came four minutes later:

HECATE THIS IS INSS AGAMEMNON. REQUEST YOU RENDEZVOUS WITH US IMMEDIATELY. VECTORS FOLLOW. WE HAVE MESSAGES FOR THE HON. GLENDA RUTH FOWLER BLAINE. BALASINGHAM."

Freddy's fingers played. She'd seen him more tense, his fingers moving faster, during a Sauron Menace game . . . when the penal-

209

ties for mistakes weren't so high. "Not far. We can be there in ten minutes. Glenda Ruth, I can't find a blinker."

"A what?"

"Normally they'd give us a laser spot to follow. This close, with 100x mag, I should see something that big directly . . . unless the Langston Field is up. Nice that we were expected, though. And it's a request, at least so far."

"They've gone stealth," Glenda Ruth said. "And no comment regarding *Sinbad* or my brother. Freddy, I think it's happened. The Moties are loose."

"Uh-huh." He tapped at console keys. "ACCELERATION WARNING. Stand by for half-standard gravity."

✳   ✳   ✳

"The Fyunch(click)s of humans were very diverse," Eudoxus said, "and so were their various fates. Captain Roderick Blaine's went mad. Sally Fowler's remained sane enough to advise, but was rarely considered trustworthy. Jacob Buckman's never had a problem. Chaplain Hardy's played abstract intellectual games; even some of the Masters found them interesting. Kevin, yours won so many arguments that she was made a teacher, but always under supervision."

"Flattering," Renner said. "Did you meet her?"

"No. I know these things due to observations by Horace Bury's Fyunch(click). That individual—shall we call her Bury-One? She was young, male, when he studied Horace Bury.

"After *MacArthur's* departure he saw a ruinous war shaping itself. He made some efforts to avert it, then to shape any kind of refuge for knowledge that would be lost. When these attempts had clearly failed, Bury-One left her Master. With a tangle of alliances and bluffs collapsing about her, she built and provisioned a spacecraft, reached the asteroids, and announced that her services were for sale."

Eudoxus waited patiently through Kevin Renner's laughter. Others were laughing, too, and even Bury was smiling in . . . pride? Presently Renner said, "I take it your Medina Trading—"

"No, Kevin, Medina hadn't the wealth or position by then. A civilization we will call Byzantium won the bidding among those

210

who could not be driven off or barred by distance or shortfall of delta-vee."

Chris Blaine was listening patiently, taking it all in and giving nothing. Joyce huddled in one corner of the bridge, whispering frantically into her recorder. Bury was smiling, enjoying Kevin's discomfiture. Bury had played this game before.

None of Renner's crew were going to be any help at all . . . unless one of Cynthia's agonizing massages could put him back together, sometime in the indefinite future.

Byzantium? Renner rubbed his aching temples and considered ordering *Atropos* to blow *Phidippides* out of the sky. At least he'd know who his enemies were then. And the next alien who tried to parley might feel impelled to give him more information.

Some of this may have showed even through static, to a trained Mediator. Eudoxus said, "Please, Kevin, let me try to give you some picture of the extraplanetary civilizations."

"Try it."

"On Mote Prime they tend to big, sprawling cultures," Eudoxus said. "They use more intricate interlockings of obligations, bigger and more extensive families controlling wider, better-defined territories than we do. We don't go near Mote Prime. The planetbound are too powerful, and also not mobile enough to threaten us.

"In the asteroids and the moon clusters of Mote Beta and Mote Gamma—"

"Gamma," Buckman said. "So it does exist. A gas giant?"

"Yes, approximately twice the distance from the Mote as Mote Beta. It has an extensive system of moons. In those and Beta's moons the families are small, independent, and not inclined to trust outsiders to supply needed resources."

"Any idea why?"

"We can't make maps out here. There's no way to define a territory. Everything changes shape constantly. Trade routes depend on fuel expenditure, on position and energy considerations, and both are constantly shifting. Your Alderson Field has made it even more complex, because now even the waste areas may yield mass."

"I was going to ask, who is Byzantium? But rape that. Who are you?"

"Medina Traders. Byzantium is an ally."

"Yeah."

"An important ally. When *MacArthur* arrived in our system nearly twenty-seven Mote Prime years ago, Medina Traders was a family of . . . how to describe? . . . well, twenty to thirty Masters and equivalent subgroups, perhaps two hundred of every class excluding Watchmakers. Our position in Mote Beta's Trailing Trojans was gradually slipping. The geometrical relationship of the various rocks had gone through some crucial changes. Our lore included detailed knowledge of failed investigations of the Crazy Eddie Drive, and also of the Curdle in the Coal Sack. We recognized your ships for what they were, from your appearance in the Crazy Eddie point right down to the black-box glow of your Langston Fields."

"I expect you weren't born yet." Any Mediator alive then would be dead by now.

"Oh, no. I was taught these things because His Excellency would insist on knowing the flow of our politics. Kevin, may I talk to His Excellency?"

"For the moment, no." The Mediator would have more trouble reading Renner's thoughts and emotions. Bury, of course, was watching the monitor; he could interrupt if he saw need.

The Motie nodded brusquely. "The advent of interstellar aliens changed everything. We retreated from our position in the Trailing Trojans in good order. Medina lost considerable valuable resources, but we were able to hold on to some by going before there was need. The usurper family, call them Persia, were as eager as we were to avoid noisy space battles that might attract *Lenin's* attention. We may call this Period One, from the Empire's arrival to *Lenin's* departure.

"My Master established us in the inner halo of comets, beyond both the old and the expected new Crazy Eddie points. She had a gripping hand on considerable territory when she died, a vast volume enclosing little mass, near to nothing valuable at all. But in thirty years we would be just outward from the access point to the human-ruled Empire. You follow? We would command Crazy Eddie's Sister when the Curdle collapsed and the Sister appeared.

"Resources are thin where we settled. During the twelve years following *Lenin's* departure, we did well. Call that Period Two. We were able to expand Medina's base due to alliances formed with Byzantium in the moon system of Mote Beta. We shared our knowledge with Byzantium. The family Byzantium is large and powerful and can afford what she sends us, even though half of the resources they send go to support Medina Traders and to increase our strength. Of course they expect to share in the rewards, once our way opens to the worlds of the Empire.

"When Horace Bury's Fyunch(click) appeared, Byzantium was able to block other competitors and acquire her. This worked out well for us. With Bury-One to advise them, Byzantium felt more secure in our partnership."

Bury was nodding, smiling. Politics. Eudoxus continued, "Medina Trading spent Period Two sending ships to test the strength of the Empire's defense of the Eye. All the tricky stunts tried in that period were of our working, using resources that flowed from Byzantium."

"From what we saw, that was a lot of resources," Renner said.

"Indeed," Eudoxus said. "A great deal of wealth was lost forever." The alien conveyed sorrow and resignation. "So. We agitated for a Bury's Motie, but many years passed before Byzantium would release one to us. He was Bury-One's first apprentice. Of course Bury-One was already training a second, and the first began at once to train me. Call her Bury-2A, my teacher."

"I don't see where the fighting comes in yet."

"Am I to feel hurried, Kevin? You'll be two hundred hours en route. We don't intend to keep this acceleration any longer than we have to."

"Two hundred hours . . . okay. I'd like *Sinbad* and *Atropos* refueled as soon as we arrive."

"I'll pass the word. We will do other things for you, too."

"The war . . ."

"Yes. Certain power structures in the Mote Gamma clusters—East India Company, Grenada, the Khanate—watched us build ships, move them into finicky position, make them disappear forever; we even armed and launched a comet that way. Wasn't that why some ancient comic named it the Crazy Eddie point? These pirates coveted what we were destroying in what must have appeared to be a form of potlatch. They thought they must have better use for such vast wealth."

"Potlatch?" Renner said. "A Motie word?"

Joyce stage-whispered, "Human. American Indian. Conspicuous consumption. Humiliate your enemies by destroying your own wealth."

Renner nodded. "Mote Gamma. Eudoxus, we didn't know about a Mote Gamma."

"As I said." The Motie was all unhurried patience now. "A gasball planet, three times the mass of Mote Prime, twice as far from the Mote as the greater gasball you've named Mote Beta. Gamma is much smaller, with two big moons and some gravel, all chewed to death by a million years of mining. I'll send you the mass—" The picture went dark with a *snap.*

Renner said, "Buckman? What?"

"It just cut off. Maybe she doesn't want to answer," Buckman said.

"No, she's under attack." Lieutenant Blaine pointed out a score of stars blazing dangerously bright. "That's good targeting. The enemy's a good quarter AU behind us. *Sinbad* can't shoot back, Captain."

"Not at that range. We've got the overpowered signal laser. . . ." A glance at Bury: had he held anything back? "And the flinger, and they're way out of range for either of those."

The light wavered. It wasn't getting brighter. Probably a whole cluster of enemy ships was firing . . . and if those lasers were free to converge on distant *Phidippides,* then Medina's fleet must no longer be a threat.

Phidippides's drifting star thrust sideways; drifted behind *Atropos.* Now *Atropos* became dark red, then cherry red, while *Phidippides* cooled.

"*Phidippides* calling," Buckman said.

"Good. Eudoxus, what's your status?"

"Temperature down. Can your warship handle the flux?"

"Sure, *Atropos* has more mass and bigger accumulators than you do . . . and the enemy's breaking off. But dammit, there aren't any of your forces left at the comet, are there?"

Eudoxus shuddered. "Comet! We abandoned the comet as soon as you appeared. What need, when we had Crazy Eddie's Sister to find and protect? Let the Khanate have it. But a splinter group formerly belonging to the Khanate has virtually destroyed our main fleet and now holds the Sister.

"Call them the Crimean Tartars, for the moment. They're new to us. The Crimeans hold the new Jump point to the red dwarf, and there's reason to think they know what they have. They'll be hard to dislodge."

214

Blaine was radiating distress. Renner said, "If they're there when Glenda Ruth comes through, we will all regret it."

"I will inform Medina's Warriors. After that it is out of my hands. Give me a moment."

The picture went dark. Kevin Renner clicked off, then turned to his people. "Horace? Anything? I don't even have intelligent questions. It's frustrating."

"Kevin, I have a thousand questions, but none are urgent. You will note the selection of names for the various groups. All from classic history, all having one way or another impacted on Arab civilization, some like the Khanate quite devastatingly. It is cleverly done."

"Eudoxus fully understands *Hecate*'s importance," Chris Blaine said. "It's still worth remembering, Mediators don't do war. I'm not sure what they'll do now that their fleet is knocked out. Send an embassy group, probably including one trained by Eudoxus . . . hmm."

"What?"

"It seems probable that the Tartars will capture *Hecate*," Blaine said.

"You're calm enough about it," Joyce said.

Blaine shrugged without quite using his shoulders. "It's a problem that needs fixing, Joyce, not a bloody funeral. Yet."

"There's certainly nothing we can do about it," Renner said. "We're headed away from the Sister at high acceleration, and our friends don't have any ships left. So what happens?"

Blaine shrugged. "So the Tartars will take possession of *Hecate*. Medina will send Mediators, one of whom probably knows Anglic. We might be able to get a message to Glenda Ruth. At least tell—yes. Captain, assuming that the Tartars will not allow Eudoxus's friends to brief Glenda Ruth, have Eudoxus instruct his Anglic-speaking Mediator to use the expression 'rape my lizard'. Either in Glenda Ruth's hearing, or as an expression she will be asked to explain."

"What in the world . . . ?" Renner demanded.

"It is recent slang, not used before this generation."

"Ah," Bury said. "Miss Blaine will know that the Moties never learned to say that from the *MacArthur-Lenin* expedition, therefore that this is a message from us. Subtle, Lieutenant. My congratulations."

"Thank you," Chris said.

"What else?" Renner asked. "What use can we make of the Crazy Eddie Worm?"

"What's that?" Joyce asked.

"Later," Chris Blaine said. "I don't know, Captain. Glenda Ruth may think of something. She thinks more like a Motie than I do, and she's seen it."

"Allah is merciful," Bury said. "But He expects us to use His gifts wisely. Lieutenant, where did Eudoxus learn about the protostar's future? I am certain my Fyunch(click) knew nothing of it."

"Not when you knew him," Blaine said. "Later . . ."

"Perhaps so. But perhaps very much later," Bury said. "Perhaps not until leaving the service of Byzantium. I need not tell you there are complexities here."

"Yeah, you must love it," Renner said.

✳   ✳   ✳

Medina Trading's main base was a billion kilometers from the light and warmth of the Mote, and ten degrees up from the plane of Mote system. It was at the inner edge of the cold and emptiness that lie beyond the farthest planets: the inner cometary halo. Medina's Master could hold such a domain because there was so little of value. But Medina Trading needed a base nearer where the Sister would form.

But matter closer to the Mote moves in faster orbits.

In the thirty years since Empire ships appeared in Mote system, Medina Trading had claimed six comets as temporary bases.

Claim a comet; build defenses and a mining operation. Pressure domes would expand to become homes. Finished products would arrive from Medina Main Base: food, metals, technology for working hydrogen, energy-shield generators, in exchange for spheroids of refined hydrogen ice. Some of Byzantium's tribute to Medina would be diverted to the inner base, and that could include power in the form of a collimated sunbeam. The base would house Watchmakers and Engineers, many ships, a few Warriors, more Masters, and always, at least one pair of Mediators. More would be better.

Before the base could drift so far from Crazy Eddie's unborn

Sister as to be useless, the comet would be mined almost to nothing. Medina would claim another.

Ten years ago East India Company won the battle for the Crazy Eddie point. Medina's Master had been forced to make them a partner . . . but hardly an equal partner. East India Company used its own wealth to test the Crazy Eddie point, while they watched for the Sister in the wrong place. But they also demanded representation at Inner Base Five and, later, Six. Unwanted representatives to be housed at Medina's expense, a family and entourage of spies.

Therefore Inner Base Six became a peaceful industrial installation with a secondary purpose; eventual contact with the Empire through Crazy Eddie's Sister. Dozens of spacecraft were always about. These were harmless mining and transport ships, weaponless, with big bubble cabins. The Sister might open at any time, and then these ships must carry Mediators to meet the Empire of Man. Base Six's Master kept Mediators ready at all times; so did the East India presence.

But contingency plans were made that East India Company was to know nothing of.

6
Hostile Takeover

Power consists in one's capacity to link his will with the purpose of others, to lead by reason and a gift of cooperation.

—Woodrow Wilson

The great black blot must be *Agamemnon*. It was twenty klicks away and drifting closer, dead slow. Three much smaller ships were clustered nearby. Freddy expanded the view.

"Alien," he said.

"Moties," Jennifer Banda said. Her grin was enormous, red mouth and white teeth in a dark face lit only by starlight from the viewport. "Glenda Ruth, they look like the ships your father saw. At least, that one does. Those others . . ."

That one had a crude look. Most of it was a spherical tank. Forward, a smaller, more elaborate container (a cabin?) bristled with sensors; it looked as if it could detach. Aft was a fat doughnut and a spine like a long, long stinger, a magnetic guide for a fusion flame.

A second had a similar spherical tank and a smaller cabin, plus a tube that might be a cargo hold. A third was all tori and looked as if it would spin for gravity, but was attached to a round-bottomed cone . . . a lander?

"All different," Glenda Ruth said.

"Will the Navy let us talk to them?" Jennifer asked.

"I don't see why not," Freddy said.

"*HECATE* THIS IS *AGAMEMNON*, OVER."

"Frederick Townsend here. Centering communications beam. Locked on. Over."

"Locked on. I'm Commander Gregory Balasingham, Mr. Townsend."

"I take it the Moties have got loose," Freddy said.

"I wouldn't put it that way. There's a new Alderson path from this system to the Mote, but no Motie ships have got past us here."

"So far as you know," Glenda Ruth said.

"Ma'am?"

"I see three ships of three radically different designs," Glenda Ruth said. "The message here is that you can't predict what they'll send next, Commander. Maybe something with a lightsail and crew in frozen sleep. Maybe anything. And of course you didn't see all the ships that came through."

There was a long pause. "Miss Blaine, we have a recorded message for you."

"Thank you."

"Stand by to record."

"Standing by," Freddy said. "Got it. Thanks."

"Commander, can we talk to the Moties?" Glenda Ruth asked.

Another pause. "Yes, but I want to listen in."

"That's all right," Glenda Ruth said. "Maybe you'll hear something I haven't. We don't have a lot of time."

"I'll connect you after you've read your message."

"Thank you. We'll call you back," Freddy said. "Give us half an hour. By the way, what time are you on?'"

"It's seventeen fifty-two here."

"Thank you, we'll synchronize." Ship's time for *Hecate* was 1430, early afternoon. They'd been on a twenty-four-hour ship's day since they left Sparta. "Commander, would you or any of your officers care to join us for dinner?"

"Thank you, Mr. Townsend, but we're on general alert here. For all we know, there may be a fleet of Motie warships bearing down on us."

"Oh. Yes, of course. Thank you. Half an hour, then."

"Not much here," Glenda Ruth said. "Chris says the Moties came through, seven unarmed ships. One—hah."

"Hah?"

"One asked for Horace Bury. First thing they said."

Freddy chuckled. Then he laughed. "Wow. Glenda Ruth, I've listened to you and Jennifer trying to convince people how smart the Moties are—"

"Actually, it was the only thing to do," Jennifer said. "Now that I think of it. Look, if no one was waiting here, they'd go on into the Empire and—what? Who might be glad to see them? Traders! And Bury's the only trader they know about."

"Well, all right, but I still wish I could have seen his face when they asked for him," Freddy said. "What else do we have?"

Glenda Ruth hesitated, then said, "Jennifer, it isn't really. Obvious. They didn't ask for Imperial Autonetics. They asked for the oldest man on the expedition, a full Motie lifetime ago!"

"Mediator lifetime."

"Whatever. Have you considered who they *didn't* ask for? Dad. Mom. Bishop Hardy. Admiral Kutuzov! People who could exterminate them or save them from someone else. Oh, hell, I don't have an answer. Chris wants us thinking about it."

Jennifer was nodding. "A puzzlement. Hey . . . Fyunch(click)s to humans can go mad."

"Oh, come on! And *Horace Bury's* is the one that stayed sane? I just . . . Let's all keep thinking, okay?"

"Okay. The message?"

"Not much more. Kevin Renner's in charge of the expedition. I always thought—"

"Yes?"

"Let's say it doesn't astound me that he's in charge. Renner left orders to Balasingham to let us into the Mote system unless he has good reason not to. Freddy, he won't want to let us go."

"We'll see," Freddy said. "I sure can't fight him."

"Run away," Jennifer said. "He has to stay to guard the Moties, and he won't shoot at us."

"Don't be silly," Freddy said. "Loaded down the way we are, that cruiser's boats could catch us with a long head start. Glenda Ruth, are you sure we want to go to the Mote?"

"I'm sure," Jennifer said.

"Chris wants us. Freddy, what do they have to bargain with? The Crazy Eddie Worm might make all the difference."

"Shouldn't we leave a breeding set here?"

"Pointless," Glenda Ruth said. "It won't be *that* long before the Institute ship gets to New Cal. My parents, and all the worms you'd ever want. But meanwhile, Bury and Renner may need bargaining chips fast."

Freddy mulled it over. "Well, all right. Look, how big a hurry are we in?"

"The quicker the better. Why?"

"Then we spend some time here." Freddy touched the intercom button. "Kakumi, it's time to lighten ship. Strip down to racing trim. Leave that special cargo in place, but otherwise lighten ship's stores."

Jennifer caught his grimace. "What?"

"George. He didn't volunteer for this. I'll leave him with the Navy if they'll let me. I sure hope one of you can cook!"

Hecate was in shambles. Freddy and Terry Kakumi worked to strip out bulkheads, rearrange equipment, and neither wanted help from Glenda Ruth or Jennifer. Glenda Ruth watched Freddy connect a hose to the foam wall, suck the air out all in one *shoomph*, roll it up and expose the master bedroom to all and sundry. Kakumi moved in with the hose, mated it to the bed, and *shoomph.*

To Hades with it, she thought. *I'm going to take a shower while there's still a shower facility.*

She felt superfluous. The Navy had no objections to Glenda Ruth's talking to the Moties, but the Moties were taking their time about answering the invitation. Why? Motie Mediators always wanted to talk; the decision must come from the Master, the one called Marco polo.

Explorer and ambassador. The first expedition to the Mote had consisted of two Imperial warships, *MacArthur* and *Lenin,* with *Lenin* forbidden to talk to the Moties at all, and *MacArthur* greatly restricted in what information could be passed along. The Moties had obtained several books of human history from Chaplain Hardy of the *MacArthur,* but none covered events as recent as the invention of the Alderson Drive. That left them a limited number of human names and cultures to draw on.

They had chosen: Marco Polo, the Master. Sir Walter Raleigh, the senior Mediator. Interesting choice of names . . .

Glenda Ruth heard Jennifer's voice as she wriggled out of the shower bag. "Yes. Henry Hudson? Yes, of course. . . . No, I can't promise that, Mr. Hudson, but I can let you talk to my superior." Jennifer's arm semaphored in frantic circles.

Glenda Ruth slid quickly into a towelsuit and moved up beside her.

Henry Hudson was a young Motie furred in brown and white; the pattern didn't match Glenda Ruth's memories of Jock and Charlie. Family markings differed, maybe. The creature seemed both strange and familiar. This one was probably no more than twelve Mote Prime years old, but Moties matured much faster than humans.

And Mediators aboard the other Motie ships would be watching everything. Glenda Ruth felt a surge of stage fright . . . nothing to what Jennifer must be feeling.

"Good day to you, Ms. Ambassador," the Motie said. Brown-irised manlike eyes looked directly into hers. "Jennifer tells me you are Glenda Ruth Blaine, addressed formally as the Honorable Ms. Blaine. I call myself Henry Hudson, and I speak for Marco Polo, my Master. Might I know the nature and extent of your political power?"

Glenda Ruth smiled with the hint of a deprecating shrug. "Through family relationships, but none given formally. We came in some haste. I'll be granted some decision power just because I was here and others weren't, and my family . . ." She trailed off. It felt like talking to a squid: the creature wasn't reacting right.

She was vaguely aware that behind her Jennifer was speaking rapidly and quietly into a mike. A middie was in the second view-screen; then an officer; then Balasingham himself. *Good.* He didn't try to interrupt.

The Motie said, "It delights me to speak to you regardless." The creature's Anglic was textbook perfect. Her arms . . . "Your progenitors visited us before my birth! Including your—father?"

"Father and mother."

"Ah. How did it change them?" Arms, shoulders, head, moved wrongly, with a momentary illusion of broken joints, and Glenda Ruth was suddenly terribly aware of her own arms, shoulders, fingers, body language . . . moving without conscious thought, in a language learned from Charlie and Jock. And suddenly she understood.

"You were not trained by a human's Fyunch(click)!"

"No, milady." The Motie moved its arms in a pattern unfamiliar to Glenda Ruth. "I have been taught your language, and some of your customs. I am aware that you do not experience our cycle of reproduction, and that your power structures are different from ours, but I have been assigned no one human to study."

"As yet."

"As you say. Not until we meet the givers of orders in your Empire." It paused. "You do not speak for your Masters. I have been told that I would meet—humans—who were neither Mediator nor Master, but I confess that the experience is stranger than I had anticipated."

"You speak for . . . ?"

"Medina Traders and certain allied families. My sister Eudoxus returned to the Mote with your ships."

Glenda Ruth grinned. "Eudoxus. Medina Traders. For Mr. Bury's benefit, of course."

"Of course. The terms would be familiar to him."

"But that name would imply that you do not speak for the Motie species. Who are Medina Traders? Who must we negotiate with?"

"We are the family with the foresight and the power to be here in the moment after Crazy Eddie's Sister opened a path. You are surely aware that none can speak for the Motie species. It's a problem, isn't it? The Empire doesn't like that." Henry Hudson studied her for a moment. His own posture still showed nothing. "You have learned Motie customs, some of them, but from a group I have never met." It paused again. "I wish to consult the Ambassador. Forgive me." The screen blanked.

"What's happening?" Freddy asked.

"I'm not sure. Captain Balasingham, have you spoken with these Moties?"

"Only formalities, my Lady," *Agamemnon's* skipper said from the viewscreen. "We instructed them to take station here. They have requested to be taken to our seat of government, and we told them that would happen in due time. Not much else. There's something odd happening, isn't there?"

"Yes."

"Why did he have to go running to his superior?"

"He doesn't represent King Peter. Or anybody who knew King Peter's family."

"King Peter?" Balasingham prompted.

"King Peter headed the Motie alliance that dealt with *MacArthur* and *Lenin*. They sent us our first group of Motie ambassadors, the ones I grew up with. But these Moties don't represent King Peter or any large Motie group. He doesn't even know the . . . well, the signals, the body language that Charlie and Jock taught me." Glenda Ruth's arms, torso, shoulders, moved in twitchy intricacy as she recited, " 'Irony, nerves, anger held in check, you ask too much, trust my words, trust me fully.' Universal, simple stuff even a human can learn."

Jennifer Banda wasn't breathing. Behind her unfocused eyes she was trying to memorize what she had seen.

"I'm afraid that still doesn't mean anything to me, my Lady," Balasingham said.

"This Motie represents a group that has been out of contact with King Peter's group for a very long time," Glenda Ruth said. "Cycles. Several cycles."

When Balasingham frowned in puzzlement, Jennifer added, "But King Peter's organization was very powerful. Widespread. Very likely planetwide."

"Planetwide, indeed. They had to be," Glenda Ruth said.

"So any group out of touch so long . . ." Jennifer fell silent.

"I still don't get it, but I guess I don't have to. So what are they consulting about?" Balasingham demanded.

"I hope," Glenda Ruth said, "I hope he's getting permission to tell us the truth."

"I am instructed to invite you to the Mote system," Henry Hudson said. "To offer you any assistance we can to aid in that journey and thereafter terminate this conversation. I regret that this is necessary."

"I had hoped you would tell us much more."

"We will . . . explain everything, to those who have the power to make decisions," the Motie said. "My Lady, you understand, when we talk to you, we tell you more than we learn, yet if we convince you to aid us, we must also convince others."

"So you are still concealing Motie history," Glenda Ruth said.

"Details that might aid your bargaining position? Yes. Not the basics. It is clear that you now know we are capable of war. You infer our capabilities from the probes we have sent," Henry Hudson said. "But you conceal your recent history, your military abilities, your strategies, as is proper. Doubtless you will reveal these in due time. As we will reveal ours. My Lady, it has been delightful speaking with you, and I hope we will meet again after

224

we have been permitted to speak with those whom you obey. I will receive any recorded message you care to send. Good-bye."

✳   ✳   ✳

Commander Balasingham pulled his lips into a tight line. "Andy, I don't like this much."

Anton Rudakov, *Agamemnon*'s Sailing Master, nodded in sympathy.

Balasingham activated the mike again. "Mr. Townsend, it's not yet established that I should permit you to go, much less store your surplus gear and personnel!"

"Oh, well, that's all right, the Moties offered to take care of my gear if you didn't have room," Freddy said.

"Yeah, I heard that."

"I mean, George will have to stay with you, but he's a retired Navy cox'n, he won't be in the way. Good cook," the Honorable Freddy Townsend said wistfully.

Balasingham sighed. "Mr. Townsend, you want to go off to the Mote system. Your ship is unarmed. We've been shooting at Motie ships since before you were born!"

"We've been invited," Freddy said. "By the Moties, Eudoxus and Henry Hudson. We have recognition signals, and both say there won't be any shooting."

"They say it. And you're headed into totally uncharted areas. If you don't come back, the Blaines will have my head even if your parents don't. And to what end?"

Glenda Ruth's voice spoke from off camera, and Freddy was seen to wince a little. "Commodore Renner thought it was important. Mr. Bury thought it was important enough to send one of his ships to rendezvous with us and fill our tanks. It's important, Commander."

"Okay, I'll give you that, they think it's a good idea, but ma'am, that's a dangerous area."

"*Hecate*'s faster than most people think," Freddy said. "Now that we've taken out the luxury stuff."

"And you'll get lost—" Balasingham cut off the mike when he saw his Sailing Master waving. "Yeah, Andy?"

Anton Rudakov said, "Skipper, whatever happens to them,

they're not likely to get lost. I know you don't follow yacht racing much, but even you have to have heard of Freddy Townsend."

"Freddy Town— Oh. Invented something, didn't he?"

"Reinvented. In the Hellgate race he did a gravity assist around the star and then unfurled a lightsail. Everybody calls them spinnakers now, but he was the first."

"You sure that's him? He looks like a kid."

"He started racing as crew on his cousin's ship when he was twelve," Rudakov said. "Skippered his own at age seventeen. In the past eight years he's won a bunch, Skipper. He lost at Hellgate, though. The sun flared and the sail shredded."

Balasingham opened the mike again. "My crew tells me I ought to know who you are, Mr. Townsend. And that I should ask you about the Hellgate race."

"Well, I didn't win that one," Freddy said.

"Suppose I send one of my officers with you?"

"Thank you, no."

"Suppose there's a fight?"

The image on the screen changed. A surprisingly adult young lady, very serious. "Commander," Glenda Ruth said, "we do thank you for worrying about us. But we don't need help! Freddy's ship will be faster without any extra people. We have a good engineer, and if there's a fight, we'll lose, and it won't matter if we have one or fifty of your crew with us."

"Miss Blaine—"

"Warriors," she said. "They're a Motie subspecies bred specifically for war. Nobody's ever seen them in the flesh and lived. We have statuettes of them on record. Our Motie ambassadors tried to tell us they were mythical demons, and that's what they look like. . . ."

Glenda Ruth's prose turned rich and purple as she went into detail. Freddy found himself sweating. Given what she knew, why was she willing to face such creatures? But Glenda Ruth had never backed away from a dare.

"Exactly," Balasingham said patiently. "It's too dangerous."

"If we're attacked, we'll surrender," she told him. "And talk."

"Why would they listen?"

"We have something they want. We need to put it in Commodore Renner's hands so that he'll have something to negotiate with."

226

"What is it, Miss Blaine?"

"I'm afraid that's not my secret, Commander. My father gave it to me. I expect you'll find out in a few weeks. The trouble is, in a few weeks almost anything could happen. Commander, you're risking your ship, your crew, the whole Empire, on your ability to block the Moties from getting past you."

"It's not what I'd choose—"

"And we admire you for it. But we all know it may not work. Commodore Renner and His Excellency are trying their own approach, and they've asked for our help. Commander, some of the aristocracy may be riding on its privileges, but the Blaines don't!"

Then, more reasonably, but in a tone that did not even hint that it could be disobeyed: "We have a fast ship. Freddy's a racing pilot, his computer is better than yours, our engineer is first rate, and I can talk to Moties better than anyone including my brother. We thank you for your concern. Freddy, let's go. Thank you, Commander."

The screen darkened for a moment.

"She wouldn't dare," Balasingham muttered.

The screen showed the Honorable Frederick Townsend. "*Hecate* requesting permission to come alongside for fueling," he said formally.

Balasingham heard Rudakov chuckling. No sympathy there! He turned back to the screen. "Permission granted. You can turn your excess baggage over to Chief Halperin."

"Very good. Also, if you have chocolate or oranges aboard *Agamemnon*, we'll need it all."

Balasingham was beyond surprise. "I'll find out. Godspeed, *Hecate*."

"Thank you."

❋　❋　❋

"I-point dead ahead," Freddy said. "Jump in ten minutes. Terry, secure for Alderson Jump. Ladies, strap in good."

Hecate was an empty shell. The main cabin area was crisscrossed by nemourlon webbing. The elaborate shower was gone. Of the cooking gear, only a heater remained. With the walls gone, the oversize water tank made a conspicuous bulge.

Glenda Ruth and Jennifer used the harness attachments at the center of the web. Freddy typed instructions to the ship as Terry Kakumi went from system to system, manually shutting each down to prevent accidental activation following the Jump.

"We shouldn't find any trouble," Glenda Ruth said. "Henry Hudson said that Medina controls the space around the Jump point . . . Crazy Eddie's Sister. I have recognition signals."

"Why do I feel you lack confidence?" Jennifer asked.

"No messages," Glenda Ruth said. "Renner, my brother, Bury— they'd try to get a message through, and even if they didn't manage it, the skipper of *Atropos*—Rawlins—would have been ordered to get a message out. Freddy, doesn't *Atropos* carry a boat that could do that?"

"Yep. Longboats on light cruisers have both Field and Drive."

"Fuel?" Jennifer wondered.

"There'd be enough to pop through and squirt a message," Freddy said. "Clear enough they couldn't do that. We might guess that somebody won't let 'em."

"Which means—we're about to Jump into what?" Jennifer asked. "Maybe they'll shoot first! Like we do at the blockade!"

"Not likely." Freddy turned back to his console.

"He's right," Glenda Ruth said. "Look at it. They sent the un-armed embassy fleet. What could they gain by luring ships into the Mote system and destroying them? That wouldn't make sense."

"And we know Moties always make sense," Jennifer said banteringly. "Don't we?"

"Want to go home?" Glenda Ruth asked.

"Humpf."

"Here we go," Freddy said. "We'll go through at nine kilometers a second relative to the Mote. That's close enough to orbital velocity at the other end. Should keep us from running into anything. Other hand, it'll make it easy for anyone to catch us. That okay, Glenda Ruth?"

"Yes."

If the tiny note of uncertainty in her voice upset him, Freddy Townsend didn't show it. "Stand by, then. Here we go."

✳   ✳   ✳

Crazy Eddie's Sister was a hundred hours and more than a hundred million kilometers behind *Sinbad*. Almost everyone was asleep. Buckman was on watch, and Joyce Trujillo had wakened long before she wanted to. She saw it first.

Indicators blinking in the display in front of Buckman. Faerie lights glowing in the magnified display aft, colored balloons, a flash. "Jacob? Isn't that—"

"Activity at the I-point," Buckman said. His voice was thick with fatigue. "We're getting a relay. It's six light-minutes to the I-point, don't know how far the relay ship is from it. *Kevin! Captain!*"

Everyone crowded into the lounge. Kevin Renner blinked at the displays while Buckman spoke rapidly. "It's a battle, of course. Looks like a third fleet just arriving."

"See if you can get me Eudoxus," Renner said.

"There's a ship!" Joyce said.

"No Field. Not a Navy ship," Blaine said.

The ship's entry triggered events in ever-widening circles. Motie ships changed course. Some fired on others. Those near the intruder—

"Bombs," Buckman said.

The newcomer rotated, tumbled, rotated—

"That's *Hecate*," Blaine said.

"How do you know?" Joyce demanded.

"Well, it's an *Empire-style racing yacht*, Joyce."

Joyce was silent. Renner said, "I can't do anything about this myself. Chris, shall we tell them what the treasure is? It might motivate them."

Blaine thought about it. His lips moved rapidly, talking silently to himself; then he said, "No sir. Let me talk to Eudoxus; you're asleep. But we're in a better bargaining position if they don't know about the Worm. We'll let Glenda Ruth work her end."

"If she lives."

✳ ✳ ✳

The Master of Base Six, Mustapha Pasha as he would be called when the humans arrived, was lactating. With a babe cradled in his right arms and the urge to mate rising in him, he was not in a proper mood for crisis. Emergencies never happen at a convenient time.

He'd been given this much luck: East India Trading's Masters

229

had no wish to be in Mustapha's company at such a time. Most of them were keeping to their own dome and domains when East India's signal arrived. They must have heard in the same instant that Mustapha did: the Crazy Eddie point had moved.

If it was a false alarm, Medina Trading would lose much bargaining power. Mustapha Pasha would likely die, executed for murder.

Such was luck and such was life. Mustapha began issuing orders. Only details were needed; these plans were years and decades old.

First: bumblebee-sized missiles sprayed the East India dome. Four got through. Most of East India's Masters had been in the ruptured dome, and a third of their Warriors, too, kept as a guard.

East India's remaining Warriors reacted at once; but Mustapha's Warriors were already attacking. Bombs and energy beams tore the Base Six iceball and its fragile housing. Clouds of ice crystals exploded from the surface; colored flashes lit them from within. A kamikaze attack destroyed one of the farming domes. Without orders to guide them, East India's Warriors were going berserk. It didn't matter. They would have had to die, each and all of them, regardless.

Of other Classes, many died, too. Mustapha Pasha had enough of Engineers and Doctors and the space-specialized Farmers, who tended the agricultural domes. The remaining Masters of East India Company were held safe, and enough others to give them an entourage. They would serve as hostages until new terms could be made.

After all, East India and Medina were not in fundamental disagreement. They must redivide certain resources and assign access to the powerful aliens on the far side of the Sister; but this was best thought of as a gambling game waged with lasers and gamma beams and projectiles, technology and false maps and treachery.

7
Labyrinth of Lies

As for those with whom you have made a treaty
and who abrogate it every time, and do not fear God,
If you meet them in battle, inflict on them
such a defeat as would be a lesson
for those who come after them,
and that they may be warned.
For God does not like those who are treacherous.

—al-Qur'an

Freddy always recovered first.

And Freddy was swearing in a lurid mumble as his fingers wobbled over the controls. *Hecate*'s oversize attitude jets kicked the racing yacht about like a windball. Glenda Ruth surged in the elastic web, her vision wobbling about the cabin, uncontrolled. Jennifer was whimpering, trying to curl up. Terry offered no resistance to the turbulence, waiting until his body would obey him.

"Feddy lub," Glenda Ruth said, her tongue like a foreign invader in her mouth, "*Freddy!* Calm down and talk to me about it!"

"Talk." Another surge, milder this time. "We're surrounded. Embedded in an armada of teeny warships fighting another armada of teeny warships, Coal Sack direction. Nukes going *flash.* Radiation count is scary. I'm trying . . . I've got the water tank between us and that, if I can *stop the lizard-raping rotation!*" He was wailing like a child.

"That will do it?"

"Yeah. The water—the water tank. That's what it's for, partly, stop us from getting fried. Partly, when I dive near a sun—that's got it! And there goes another bomb, *flash*, wouldn't you know, but I think it's blocked, too." He bashed at keys again. "Damn!" Held one key down. "There. Now I think it's safe to wake up the computer, but I'll send it a test problem before I give it control. . . .

"Not yet. Another minute. Anyway, when we dive near a sun to get a gravity assist, I don't want solar radiation sleeting through *Hecate,* so I mounted this mucking great water tank alongside the cabin for a shield. And I freeze it. Then the hull's superconducting, of course, so I can cool the hull by running a wire into the water tank. I can do serious aerobraking or get awfully close to a sun because it can't fry us without first boiling all that thermal mass of water, and even then I can vent the steam—" Freddy sagged back. "And I guess the battle isn't going to fry us, but those ships might unless you talk to them. Computer's safe now. How are you doing?"

"How do I sound?"

"Lucid."

"I'll try talking to them. I don't think I want to move, though. Can you connect me?"

"Sure—one moment. Terry? . . . No answer. He stays out longer than me. All right, you're on the frequency Henry Hudson gave us."

She spoke the syllables she'd been told would show her to be an honored guest of Medina Traders. Nothing. She spoke again.

"That got a reaction," Freddy said. "Two of the ships out there—they've changed course. Others are shooting at them—Wups!"

"What?"

A fierce green blaze bathed Freddy's face, from a screen she couldn't see. "Someone just tried to boil us! No real damage, but I sure hope they don't do it again. And—look here. Can you see the screen?"

An alien face. A brown-and-white, a Mediator. It spoke alien words. Nothing she recognized at all. It spoke again—

"They hit us again!" Freddy said. "Not so hard, but do something!"

"Surrender," she said. "There's a word—"

"Use it! We can't take many more hits like that!"

"Right. Freddy, we'll have to open the airlock. Both doors."

He did things to the controls. "Whenever you say. Jennifer and Terry are sealed in, suit integrity checks. Yours too. Whenever you say."

"Leave the light on in the airlock. No other lights."

"Romantic."

She considered various answers and chose, "Yeah."

✳   ✳   ✳

"Let me get this straight," Renner said. "You want me to rig something that makes static and simulates a failure in the communication system."

"Only in the transmission system," Bury said. "Elementary politeness, Kevin. I wish sometimes to be able to observe the Moties while we are not ourselves observed. Let them see static, while we continue to receive their signals. Give the control to me, and do not use it except as I direct. Can you do this?"

"Sure. It *could* even be real, once or twice, but won't they be suspicious?"

"Of course they will be suspicious. Thank you."

"Need it right now?"

"It would do no harm."

"There are now three fleets at Crazy Eddie's Sister," Eudoxus said. "The new faction we will call the East India Trading Company, a group based in the Belt asteroids, but with many ships. East India was a nominal ally of ours until a few hours ago."

"What happened then?" Renner demanded.

"They will be allies again when we have negotiated new changes in status. I will explain later. In any event East India appears to be losing. So are we. The Crimean Tartars retain possession of your third ship."

"Three fleets. One's yours. Do you have any ships left?"

"One intelligence ship, with a Mediator aboard who is relaying data. Our other warships could do no good and have been ordered to retreat. No fighting ships remain near Crazy Eddie's Sister."

"Damnation. What can you do?"

"Inform my Master. Request means to communicate with the Crimean Tartars, learn what I can of their situation and goals, and

233

ask what I may offer in trade. You must tell me, Kevin, what must I ask for, what must we have, and what may they keep?"

"Mmm . . ." Kevin rubbed his face. Bristles. "The ship, *Hecate*, probably isn't worth saving. We want the humans, three to five humans back in good order. Tell them the Empire will be enraged if anything happens to those humans."

"It will, too," Joyce said. "They once sent a hundred ships to avenge the death of a Prince Imperial."

"I hadn't heard that story," Renner said. "Thank you, Joyce."

"Are these people that important?" Eudoxus demanded.

"Not quite," Renner said. "Next thing to it, though. Eudoxus, there are goods, including trade goods aboard *Hecate*. Some will be very valuable. Others—if possible, consult with the woman Mediator on *Hecate*. Her name is"—he glanced at Chris Blaine and got a nod—"the Honorable Glenda Ruth Blaine."

"Blaine. As I understand your naming conventions, she will be the daughter of a lord. A Lord Blaine. We know of a Lord Blaine."

"That's the one," Renner said.

"The commander of *MacArthur*. Second-in-command of your first expedition to us. You have not exaggerated her importance."

"Right. So get Glenda Ruth's opinion as to what to do with those trade goods."

"Their nature?"

"Not known to me. I'd expect them to carry chocolate, though."

"I never tasted chocolate," Eudoxus said.

"The Tartars can have this consignment. We'll get more for you when we can. There may even be some aboard *Atropos*. Okay?"

"Thank you. They will put restrictions on contacts with their— guests."

"Right. Stand by, I'll see if we have more instructions."

"With your permission I will begin making the Crimeans understand the importance of what they hold. Also to tell them of your life support requirements."

"Good. Thank you." Renner switched off. "Horace?"

Bury had watched in silence. He sipped at the coffee Nabil had brought. "One or another human might want to stay as liaison. Be prepared to give in on this, but ask for the return of all. I think it best not to mention the nature of the cargo."

"Chocolate?" Joyce asked.

Buckman said, "Signal from Eudoxus. Urgent message."

Chris Blaine inhaled sharply, started to say something, but didn't.

"Everyone ready? Here goes." Renner thumbed the communications controls. "News, Eudoxus?"

"Yes. Our observation ship reports that there are now two Crimean Tartar ships attached alongside *Hecate*. The ship itself does not appear to be harmed and was sending messages just prior to its capture."

Chris Blaine's relief was obvious. Captured was better than killed.

"One message was a broadcast of a Medina Traders hailing signal," Eudoxus said. "The rest were to Crimean Tartar ships and were not intercepted. Stand by a moment—here is one we recorded."

The viewscreen showed a human in full space gear, helmet closed, attached to a web of restraining lines. "We come in peace. *Fnamyunch(sniff!)*."

"That latter is a Medina Traders recognition signal," Eudoxus said. "She could only have obtained it by speaking with our embassy ship."

"That should help with your negotiations," Bury said.

"Ah? Ah, yes, Excellency, if they believe us, and they should. Thank you."

"Right," Renner said. "Stay on that. Anyone else? Good. Eudoxus, please call your Master and establish negotiations with the—Crimean Tartars."

"We are beginning that now. I will be needed shortly."

"Right. Then do something else for me. Call me back. And try to tell me who all these people are?"

Eudoxus nodded his head and shoulders, smiling, and vanished.

✳   ✳   ✳

The colored lights in the control display were the only lights in *Hecate*. *Hecate*'s four crew waited in a vast dark space, listening to clanking and thudding from the hull. They talked in whispers, and rarely.

With a sound like a gunshot, an elliptical section of hull blasted loose and into *Hecate*, edge on, straight toward Glenda Ruth. Jennifer shrieked, Freddy yelled warning. Glenda Ruth snapped her tether webbing loose and kicked herself clear . . . almost clear. The mass banged her flailing foot and tumbled aft, its course unaltered, and banged around back there where the cabin tapered to a rounded point. The cabin pressure fell rapidly, climbed, changed again, then stabilized.

Glenda Ruth's unladylike swearing fell into a sudden silence.

She hadn't seen the Motie enter.

Its gripping hand found a handhold. The crude-looking gun in its right hands was pointed at Glenda Ruth. She screamed and covered her face, then hurriedly grabbed a handhold and spread her hands wide.

Freddy asked, "Are you hurt?"

"It cracked me on the shin. Stay tethered, guys. The Motie might have shot me because I was moving. Just wait it out."

"It's a Warrior," Jennifer said.

"I think so. It's got toes, but . . . yeah."

Now the Warrior was gripping handholds with its feet, through digital gloves. A second weapon had appeared, a spiked club. The Warrior's head and shoulders swiveled rapidly. Its gun pointed everywhere. It leaped across the cabin, thudded against the wall, and scanned from there. When it was satisfied, it warble-whistled.

Another Motie came through. It was squat compared to the greyhound look of the Warrior. Its pressure suit hid the pattern of fur, but its behavior identified it: it was a Brown, an Engineer. Another Engineer followed and pulled a transparent balloon after it through the hole. Shapes moved within.

The Engineers converged on the controls, sliding past and around *Hecate*'s crew, ignoring them. One began to play with the controls. Freddy seemed braced for disaster, but nothing much was happening.

Another Motie entered. A pressure suit hid her fur; she was a bit larger than the Engineers. A Mediator? The Engineers huddled with the new one, then kicked themselves aft. One opened the balloon and released four Motie shapes each less than half a meter long. They began to work at the aft of *Hecate*'s cabin.

"Brownies," Jennifer said.

Glenda Ruth peered close. The little ones were chocolate brown, darker than an Engineer; and each of these had four arms. Watchmakers, "brownies," the Class that had destroyed *MacArthur*. All but one. The fourth was crawling carefully along the wall, toward the bridge. It was a different color, cream and pale brown, and it had three arms.

It launched from the wall, impacted against Jennifer, and clung. It chirped at her and waited for a response.

Glenda Ruth spoke to the big Motie. "Hello? Can you speak?"

The Motie watched her. "We come in peace for all mankind, and for your sake, too," Glenda Ruth said. "Can you understand me? We carry trade goods. We have the right to make binding treaties."

The newest Motie disappeared through the hole. Ignoring her.

"I can't really tell, but that thing doesn't move like it has anything to say. I don't think it's a Mediator," Glenda Ruth said. "Freddy, don't touch any controls."

"Brace yourselves," Terry said.

Glenda Ruth asked, "Why?" before she noticed that the Warrior had anchored itself with three limbs out of five. A moment later the cabin shuddered and rocked.

Freddy said, "That's torn it. Glenda Ruth, you—"

There was thrust. It built up smoothly over six or seven seconds to a tenth of a gravity and stopped.

Freddy said, "My readings don't connect to the rest of the ship. They've disconnected the cabin."

Jennifer began to laugh. "Maybe they'll bring the rest separately," she said, "and give it back."

"Oh, thank you very much. Nevertheless I fear *Hecate*'s racing days are over. Any idea what's happening?"

Glenda Ruth said carefully, "Ooyay ohknay apingtay us eythey areay."

"What? Ah. What else?"

"Henry Hudson and the Medina Traders believed themselves in control here," she said. "Clearly they aren't."

"Who is?"

"I don't know, but it changes everything, doesn't it? The Empire will make no important deals with anyone who doesn't speak for all of the Moties."

"Oh. All right. Now what just happened?"

"We've been captured by a warship. They don't understand what they have, but they can see it's valuable, so they'll be asking for orders. Eventually they'll send a Mediator. Who may or may not know Anglic, Freddy."

"There's air," Freddy said. "Best open up the suits to save the air tanks."

Jennifer tentatively opened her faceplate. "Smells all right—hey!"

Terry Kakumi swiveled toward her. "What?"

"It's a Mediator pup!" Jennifer said. "It has to be. Look, brown and white, and not much bigger than a Watchmaker, that's what it is. Glenda Ruth—"

"Figures," Glenda Ruth said. "As soon as they knew they'd be dealing with humans, they bred a Mediator. Jennifer, I think you've got a friend for life."

Jennifer and the Mediator pup considered each other wonderful. Jennifer cradled it in her arms and answered when it talked. The sounds it made were nonsense, but gradually they began to sound like Jennifer herself.

When she handed the creature to Terry, it cried and tore itself free and jumped off Terry's chin to reach her again. The pup wanted no part of other humans.

So the waiting was hard for the rest of them, and the entertainment thin. Glenda Ruth considered running a history flick on the monitors. Were the other classes, the Warriors and Engineers, really so specialized that they wouldn't watch?

"They've plugged all the holes in the cabin," Freddy said. "Near as I can tell, this is normal *Hecate* air."

"Temperature's all right, too," Jennifer said. She fondled the pups's ear.

"Obvious. They tore the cabin loose and sealed it and gave us our own life support system back. We're alive but helpless. They'll have time to copy our gear before anything stops working," Glenda Ruth said. "Air doesn't worry me as much as . . ."

"Yes?"

"Freddy, there may be more battles. Over us."

"Good news from all over," Jennifer Banda said. "I always wondered what the crown felt like when the lion and the unicorn fought over it."

238

Eudoxus seemed calm. "My Master has been informed. She will set other Mediators to the task of regaining your companions. Our observations show that the inhabited portions of *Hecate* have been detached from the rest of the ship. The life support systems appear to be intact. Meanwhile, there is heavy message traffic throughout that region. I'll pass on more information as it develops."

Renner said, "But you can at least tell me who's involved, can't you?"

"I can tell you what we have learned of the Crimean Tartars. They were among the powers in the moon system of Mote Beta until they were cast out in a complicated contest with the major Mote Beta clan we call Persia. The Tartar group then subsisted on trade and service to other powers until they were swallowed by the Khanate. They're much smaller now, of course, and as nothing has been heard of them, we thought they must have been successfully integrated into the Khanate families. In light of their capture of your ship we must conclude that they retained some independent identity."

Renner considered the death rate implicit in the phrase *they're much smaller now* among a people who die if they can't get pregnant. "Okay. East India?"

"Please reassure me that His Excellency is listening."

Horace Bury sighed. "Put me on."

Kevin turned off his mike. "You sure?"

"We will learn from each other. If I can't catch him in a lie, perhaps"—he jerked his head at Chris Blaine—"another can."

Kevin nodded and swiveled the camera. Bury said, "Greetings, Eudoxus."

The Motie bowed; the one ear folded flat, then extended.

"You spoke of the year we spent in Mote system as Period One. Period Two you spent sending ships to break the Empire blockade at Murcheson's Eye. Is it so?"

"Yes, Excellency. Period One began as *MacArthur* intercepted a miner belonging to Medina Trading. Thereafter a Mote Prime group headed by a powerful planetary Master who called himself King Peter took control of communications with the human expedition."

"Was there a battle?" Renner asked.

"None that you were intended to notice."

"I saw none,' Renner said.

"His Excellency noticed the change," Eudoxus said. "I know because—"

"Yes, of course," Bury said. "What I saw was that the Mote Prime group had no interest at all in the creature we had aboard— and although that Engineer had sent a message to its home, nothing came of that."

"Bloody Hell," Renner muttered. "The Skipper never thought of that, and neither did I."

"That also was clear," Eudoxus said. "Only His Excellency understood the true situation." He looked expectantly at Bury. "So. Period One ended with *MacArthur* destroyed and your battleship *Lenin* departing Mote system. The ship and its recorded observations sent back by our Engineer you took aboard gave Medina knowledge of how to build an energy shield . . . Langston Field? Name of a human inventor?"

Kevin said, "Right."

The Motie was amused. *Naming a tool for an Engineer!* "Our wanderings began shortly after. Our Master saw that there would be great changes, and Medina Traders would not be powerful enough to hold where we were. Thus we traded what we had to Persia: they would take our territory and give us ships. Then during our withdrawal from the Mote Beta Trailing Trojans," she said, "our Engineers developed a working Langston Field and traded it to Persia for more assistance in withdrawing to the comets.

"It was bad timing. If we had been larger and more powerful, we need not have abandoned our base at all. With what we gave them and what they had, Persia came to rule the Mote Beta moons. They didn't merely arm ships with your Field. They skimmed through the remains of the Mote Beta Ring. After a million years of mining, the planet retained only a narrow ring of dust, but that was megatons of dust. One pass and Persia had it all. We could have had that ourselves . . . but we were too far away and might not have held it, and in any case we had set our sights further."

Blaine caught Bury's eye. They exchanged nods. Blaine's voice came to Renner on the private intercom circuit. "Medina plans far and acts fast. And they've got some of the best Engineers in the system."

"During Period Two we tested your blockade at the Eye." Eudoxus said, "To do that we needed the assistance of the group we call Byzantium. This is a large and powerful coalition located in the Mote Gamma moons, far from Persia, far from our original home in Mote Beta's Trailing Trojans. I may give you details of our negotiations with them—"

"For the moment, continue your story."

"Well, then, various bandits had already noted our activity. East India Company was one of those. This is the group I spoke of, asteroid based, many ships, nominal allies of Medina until recently, and should be again if things go as planned.

"Still with me? The period during which the Curdle in the Coal Sack might be expected to collapse is Period Three. King Peter of Mote Prime gave you data we knew to be incorrect, data indicating that the Curdle would not become a star for some time. Incidentally, King Peter's data were incorrect also. They did not expect the star to ignite for another fifty of your years. We knew better, and we had the advantage of knowing what the Empire had been told. Of course we did not know *precisely* when the star would form, and indeed the date *we* expected was years too early."

"Wow," Joyce said. Her voice was barely audible.

Renner grinned slightly and looked to be sure that she was recording. *Good.* That gave them an extra copy for insurance. It would take study to be certain he understood everything Eudoxus was saying.

"Period Three opens around a hundred thousand hours ago," Eudoxus continued. "We prepared to exploit the new opening. Medina Traders began sending probes solely to determine whether the Crazy Eddie point had jumped. From your viewpoint these ships would still have come sporadically, and we still shaped them to shake the Empire's composure. You were not to notice a difference. We could afford nothing so flamboyant as the iceball fleet. . . . Did that have any success?"

Chris Blaine wiggled his eyebrows, offstage. Bury said. "Only in exciting our admiration."

"Our later probes were cheaper, but still our resources were not expanding to match our tasks. While our estimates were better than King Peter's, we made ready too early, and it was costly to remain in a state of readiness. Power shifted among the Mote Gamma families. Medina's behavior was becoming too conspicuous, our security was getting less attention than—"

Bury said, "You were expanding too fast."

Eudoxus—Bury3A—nodded reluctantly. "Wealth that should have gone to security went to feed our growing numbers. Eighty thousand hours ago, East India Company surged out of the Mote Gamma Leading Trojans and took possession of the Crazy Eddie point. They replenished the cost of that mighty battle by dismantling two of our probes already en route to the Eye."

"Where was your ally Byzantium?"

"Far around its orbit, too distant to interfere directly, preoccupied with local problems, and unable to send a large battle fleet. They were not happy, and they blamed us for our carelessness. But the Curdle's collapse was slow in coming, and nobody loves blockade duty."

That's for damn sure, Renner thought, and caught an answering nod from Chris Blaine.

"Having been dispossessed, we did what we could to recover our position. Medina Traders brought the East India Company in on part of the secret. Having taken the old Crazy Eddie point, East India Company was given the obligations, too. Byzantium gave them your Fyunch(click)'s second student's third apprentice."

Kevin said, "Just so I don't get lost . . ."

"Bury-One has died. Medina Traders has Bury 3A, me. Byzantium still has Bury 2 and Bury 3B. Byzantium's Bury 3C went to East India Company. Another family bought Bury 3D while they still had wealth; they may have sold some Bury-Fours. Byzantium may be training others."

Bury stared at the misshapen shadow in wonder. "Have I become the basis of your economy?"

"Not extensively, Excellency, not yet. Of course I am become immensely more valuable since I have had the honor of speaking with you directly."

"Wonderful."

"Our own problem was that East India Company sent the cheapest possible probes. You were bound to notice. I expect that was why you arrived so rapidly? . . . Yes. But having a Horace Bury Fyunch(click) made East India Company more confident than they should have been—as we intended. Their Bury student is not an astronomer. We gave them a wrong mapping for the expected new Crazy Eddie point, and they accepted it."

"They may be annoyed with you. They are attacking these inter-lopers, the Crimean Tartars, but whom were they sent to attack?"

"Excellency, you may well— Excuse me," Eudoxus said, and the monitor screen went dark.

Kevin said, "Blaine?"

Chris Blaine said, "The Motie ships got easier to hit nine years ago. Before my time, but the records show. The Crazy Eddie Squadron thought it was because we were getting better at it."

Bury was nodding, enjoying himself. "The word *Byzantine* might have been invented just for Moties," he said. "Well, Kevin?"

"We *can* make maps. Computer maps, holograms that move. We should."

"Yes. Jacob?"

"I've been doing that. Horace, I think your interests and mine may have converged at last. Have a look at this." All the monitors suddenly bloomed with an axial view of the Mote system. For a moment it held, then began turning like a sluggish whirlpool.

"Now, note." Buckman's pointer traced along the shaded ring of comets. "Mote Gamma is resources for anyone in this region. A better source than the nearby comets, right? Because comets are so far apart. Where Mote Gamma is passing, there's an economic boom. When Gamma's gone, there's a recession. Sanity check, Horace?"

"Very likely. The boom would stretch over perhaps twenty de-grees of arc before costs grow too great. Mote Beta would be too close to the sun for such an effect. And if . . . what are these marks? The old Jump point to the Eye, the new one . . ."

"Right."

They weren't moving. Matter flowed around and past them.

"The Crazy Eddie points. And the new Jump to the red dwarf, Crazy Eddie's Sister. Thirty degrees around from Mote Gamma, and up ten degrees along the Mote's axis. Medina Trading had no easy access to the Mote Gamma resources."

Renner watched the map display rotate. The Crazy Eddie point, not far outward from Mote Beta's orbit, had moved a few hundred thousand klicks when Buckman's Protostar (the Curdle) became Buckman's Star. But the Sister was a *billion* klicks away, above the plane of the system and well beyond Mote Gamma.

Eudoxus was back. "Excellency, Captain, my Master will act to recover your people and goods. Our bargaining position is worsening. *Hecate* is in flight with a Crimean Tartar escort, twelve ships of varying size, running out from the sun and wide of the Khanate positions. It seems the Tartars have severed relations with the Khanate. Thirty-six Tartar ships remain in command of the Sister. The East India Company contingent has fled."

Bury's eyes met Kevin's; he didn't speak.

The Motie said, "Your lost ship should be safe in the hands of the Crimean Tartars. No player in this game would risk harm to something so valuable, not even pirate groups like the Khanate, who can only guess *Hecate*'s value from the maneuvering of others. . . . We'll negotiate how to bring you together."

Of course a Mediator would negotiate, Kevin thought. She could hardly plan a war, though if she could estimate relative strengths . . . but if *Hecate* must be rescued, it must be up to the Empire ships.

"So you had East India watching the wrong part of the sky," he said. "And now they're pissed?"

"Just so. But they don't command the wealth they had when they wrested the Crazy Eddie point from us. They sent cheap token ships to the Eye, and they can't afford a real war fleet either."

"Tell me about the Khanate."

"Ah, yes, the Khanate. You see, Medina Trading's main base is deep among the comets, not conveniently close to the Sister. A succession of large comets have served as inner bases, generally a few light-minutes from the Sister. We're en route for Inner Base Six even now, and more of our ships will meet us there. But as an immediate source of volatiles and water and ores, we sometimes move a small comet head to pass very near the expected Sister.

"The Khanate is based in a cluster of comets outward and forward of Medina Trading. They expect wealth to surge their way when Mote Gamma moves into place in fifty thousand hours. Meanwhile they survive as bandits. They must have wondered at the mad placement of our small comet, but they covet the resources. But the Crimean Tartars seem to know *why* we wanted resources in place."

Bury asked, "Might they be working with someone else?"

"Instruct me," said the Motie.

"Merely a question, Eudoxus. Who knew of the Sister? Medina and Byzantium and East India, and whoever else might deduce the truth from observation. East India was given a false locus for the Sister, but were you truly prepared to deal fairly with Byzantium?"

"Of course," Eudoxus said.

"Any Motie family could learn the truth by observation and deduction," Bury said. "But Byzantium already knew. Perhaps Byzantium grew unhappy with the notion that Medina would command the Sister, so far from Byzantium's sway. Then Byzantium might seek allies easier to dominate."

"Ah."

"Only a passing thought. Finish your tale, Eudoxus."

The Motie needed a moment to react. "Tale? . . . Easily told. We were already embattled when East India signaled that a token ship intended for the Crazy Eddie point had failed to pop through to the Eye. We sent tokens along the arms of the arc where the Sister was to be expected. An expedition of ten ships was launched after, provisioned and manned well in advance, and all running from the firefight with the Khanate fleet. The rest of the Medina fleet followed in a guarded retreat, abandoning our little comet, intending to take possession of Crazy Eddie's Sister.

"By then East India Company's neutrino gauges and telescopes must have seen the action. They have reason for complaint, as you point out. They took our territory by force. Then they donated resources to the exercise: ten years' or more worth of their pitiful token ships. Now they learn that the Sister is not where they were told, but Medina's fleet is in place. *They* sent ships.

"None of this surprised us much. But when the Crimean Tartars fleet followed us, we were taken by surprise. Medina expected the entire Khanate fleet to remain with the comet. When our first ship disappeared, the Tartars were seen to correct course. They must have known what they were doing."

Jacob Buckman's head popped up at Renner's ear. "They knew better than Medina."

Renner turned. "Talk to me."

"Why did the Khanate attack *now*? *Now* puts the Tartars in just the right position to take the Sister. It looks like some genius among the Tartars—"

"Figured out exactly when the Curdle would collapse. Uh-huh. Eudoxus, you concur?"

"It's not my field, Captain Renner. I'll ask. Or they might have been told."

"By whom?"

"By anyone! Do you believe I have told you of all the families here?"

"Okay. Go on."

"The Tartars destroyed two of the ten Medina expedition ships. One missed the Sister. The rest of us reached the orange dwarf. Our fleet tried to hold the Sister until Byzantium's reinforcements could arrive, but these were not expected soon, or with confidence. Mote Beta is too far. But they held long enough for us all to pop through into an ongoing battle."

'But not long enough to protect *Hecate.*"

"No. And that brings us to present time. In ten hours we will reach Inner Base Six."

8
Medina Base Six

Rebellious angels are worse than unbelieving men.

—St. Augustine, City of God

Base Six had changed. Shaped charges blasted most of the un-worked mass of what had been a comet into shards. A snowstorm of dirty ice and ammonia and rock, all useful ores until the advent of the Sister, expanded in the direction of the battle raging at the Sister. If the detritus didn't shield Base Six from weapons, it would at least blind all watchers. Only Medina's Masters would guess what was happening here, and they only because they had shared in the planning.

The white sphere that remained was colder than a comet need be. East India had known of the refineries that made hydrogen and the ships that took it away, but had never known of the heat pumps. The hydrogen hadn't all been used to fuel ships, and most of the ships hadn't gone all the way out to Medina Trading.

Medina Base Six had become a compact hydrogen iceball with a shell of foamed hydrogen ice. Thus insulated and minutely cooled by evaporation, it would hold its cold for decades; possibly centuries. Buried in the iceball was an industrial-sized Empire-style shield generator that had served all six inner bases.

Base Six was too close to the action, too vulnerable.

Its three dozen ships were mostly disassembled. They always had been, always visibly under repair. East India's visiting Master had complained of this, but had never seen the significance of all those dismounted rocket motors.

Now Medina's Engineers mounted forty-one fusion motors in a

ring aft of the half-klick snowball. In hours, Base Six had become a warship. It began accelerating immediately, outward, toward Medina Trading.

Most of Base Six's ships, and the hydrogen they carried, had traveled only as far as the odd-shaped black bubble Mustapha thought of as the Storehouse: odd shaped to avoid detection by radar and other means. Within the Storehouse was a growing store of hydrogen, and a population of Warriors that did not grow because tournaments kept their numbers steady.

Now troopships full of Warriors moved to rendezvous with Base Six. Some would land, some would orbit.

Base Six was an armed carrier and fuel dump and warship, the heart of a fleet capable of defending whatever treasure had emerged from Crazy Eddie's Sister.

✳   ✳   ✳

Sinbad accelerated at .8 gravities, comfortable enough for Moties, not too great a strain on Bury. Behind them the Mote was not much more than a star. It had a barely discernible disk and was just too bright for unprotected human eyes. Murcheson's Eye was a dull red smear off beyond the Mote.

Four Motie ships, with Eudoxus in the lead; then *Sinbad,* closely followed by *Atropos;* finally, four more Motie warships.

"That's all I can detect, Captain Renner," Commander Rawlins said. "I have the general impression there are more ships moving around out there. We get a sudden detection flash, but nothing we can lock onto. Like . . . stealthed ships that change shape?"

"Thank you."

"Sir. We watched the Motie ships during the battle. This gives us another look."

"Have any conclusions?"

"They're pretty good. High performance. We saw nothing but gun actions, no torpedoes. Their ships tend to be small. We could certainly defeat any four of what we've seen so far, barring big surprises."

"I would *not* rule out surprises."

"No, sir, I sure don't. Captain, can you explain what's going on?"

248

"Do I detect a note of pathos? All right. It's time for a council of war while we have secure communications." Renner thumbed the intercom. "Please have Lieutenant Blaine come up, and if His Excellency is up to a conversation, he ought to listen in.

"Rawlins, we're not going to Mote Prime. They're out of it. The important players are all offplanet civilizations, and there are a *lot* of those. The one that was best prepared for the new I-point is Medina Trading, ruled by Caliph Almohad, and his chief negotiator is Eudoxus, the Mediator we're following, all names chosen by Eudoxus. Okay so far?"

"Yes, sir. Who are we fighting?"

"There are a whole bunch of factions." Renner's fingers danced. "I made notes. Here."

"Got it." Rawlins's eyes focused offstage. "Oh boy."

"And that's just the important ones."

"Khanate's got the comet . . . nobody cares . . . the Tartars hold the new Jump point, and a ship . . . oh, my God."

"Yeah. *Hecate* is a civilian ship piloted by the Honorable Frederick Townsend with Chris Blaine's sister, Glenda Ruth Fowler Blaine, aboard as passenger."

"Oh, my God. Captain, Lord Blaine isn't going to be happy about *that!* Are we going to rescue them?"

"Could we?"

Rawlins was quiet for a moment. "I don't know, but I'd sure as hell hate to go back without trying."

"I see your point, but Eudoxus doesn't think we have enough ships even with yours. Right now the best evidence is that they're safe, and our Motie allies are trying to deal with the Tartars. Meanwhile, we're headed for a Medina Traders base. Until recently it was a joint base with East India Trading, but apparently there's been a readjustment of that alliance."

"Readjustment?"

"That's the word Eudoxus used."

"Somebody else to fight?"

"Maybe."

Chris Blaine came to the bridge and took a place near Renner.

Commander Rawlins said, "Are things usually this complicated with Moties? Captain, what the hell is our objective?"

"Good question," Renner said. "First is to survive. Second, get Glenda Ruth Blaine back. She's got a cargo that may change things

249

. . . may affect our third objective, which is bringing order out of chaos."

"Cargo?"

Renner said, "Lieutenant Blaine?"

"Yes, sir. As Captain Renner said, there's another objective to consider. The Moties are loose, and that's got to be dealt with, by us or a battle fleet."

"Only there's no battle fleet." Renner sighed. "Okay, Chris. The cargo." Renner caught Cynthia's eye; he negotiated for coffee.

Blaine nodded. "Commander Rawlins, just how much do you know about Moties?"

"Not much. I skipped the classes on Motie society back in the blockade squadron. Studied their tactics, but I didn't see any need to understand them, since all we were supposed to do was kill them."

"Yes, sir. You must have a crewman who was that curious. Find him. Meanwhile, I lecture.

"To begin with, we all know Moties are a strongly differentiated species. Masters are the only Motie class that really counts; whereas the Mediators do all the communicating. Mediators are so likable that we tend to forget that they're not really in charge, that they take orders from Masters."

"But not always," Renner said.

"Okay, consider the three Moties sent to the Empire. Two of King Peter's Mediators, with an older Master related to King Peter but not previously in charge of Jock and Charlie. That gave Jock and Charlie some leeway. They didn't have to obey every order Ivan gave, although they usually did. There must have been rules, but I never learned them. Ivan only lasted six years, and then they were on their own.

"I once asked Jock what Ivan's last orders were. Jock told me, 'Act in such a way as to decrease the risk to our kind in the long term. Keep each other sane. Make us look good.' I think she left out considerable detail. And Mediators would lie to us if Ivan had told them to.

"So here we are back in Mote system and everything we know is a little bit wrong. We're dealing with a space civilization, not a planet. All the Classes will be a little different, some a lot different, even including the Masters. Motie civilization is *old*. The asteroids have been settled for over a hundred thousand years, time enough for *evolutionary* changes, and we know the Moties have used radical breeding programs on themselves as well."

"Like Saurons," Rawlins said.

"Well, not really," Renner said. "Different objectives, different reasons."

"Yes, sir." Rawlins didn't sound convinced.

"We've had one piece of luck, *maybe*," Blaine said. "Horace Bury's Mediator apparently left King Peter entirely and sold her services to the highest bidder. Bury-trained Mediators seem to be swapped around out here like money."

"Must make His Excellency happy," Rawlins said. "Is that the reason for all the Arab names they give themselves?"

Chris's forefinger wagged. "No, no! Skipper, these names were all chosen by Medina's Bury-trained Mediator, Eudoxus, probably for their emotional impact on Horace Bury. Tartars are enemies of Arabs. Medina Traders sounds good to an Arab. Eudoxus was a famous Levantine trader who operated out of the Red Sea and discovered the original Arab trade route to India."

"Ho, ho," Rawlins said. "And of course Bury knew that."

"Of course. There is another thing. Motie Masters don't really form societies the way we do. The subordinate classes generally obey the Masters, but Masters don't have any instinct to obey each other, and whatever it is about humans that makes us form societies is largely missing in Masters. Motie Masters will cooperate, and one will take a subordinate position to another, but as far as I can make out, the only loyalties are to a gene line. There's no loyalty at all to any abstraction like an empire, or a city. That's more like an Arab civilization than it's like the Empire, which may account for the popularity of Bury Mediators. Mister Bury is likely to understand things here better than any of us."

"Including you, Blaine?" Rawlins demanded. "The Word in the fleet was that you were *raised* by Moties."

"Somewhat," Chris Blaine said. "We were still in New Caledonia and my father was on the High Commission until I was six years old. It was when we got back to Sparta and my parents set up the Institute that I got to see the Moties every day. Ivan was dead by then, and Glenda Ruth was just born. She saw a lot more of Jock and Charlie and never met Ivan at all."

"Um. Now what about *Hecate's* cargo?"

Renner said. "Chris, let me. You've never even *seen* the Crazy Eddie Worm. You were on blockade—"

"*Hold* it, Captain." There was a snap in Blaine's voice. "Commander Rawlins, the Worm is a hole card of sorts. Sir, are you sure you want to know more?"

Though he was pretty sure lieutenants didn't talk that way to captains, Renner held his tongue. Rawlins said frostily, "Why wouldn't I want to know, Lieutenant?"

"If you know and you talk to Moties, they'll learn it," Blaine said. "Commander, until you've been around Moties, you just can't understand how quickly they learn to interpret *everything* you say or do."

"I may have an idea," Rawlins said. "A year aboard my ship and nobody in the wardroom will play poker with you."

"Yes, sir. They may learn from Captain Renner anyway, but probably not. He's had more experience dealing with Moties. They won't learn from His Excellency. Or me."

"Won't learn what?"

They turned to see Joyce Mei-Ling coming into *Sinbad*'s lounge.

"All right," Rawlins said. "I'll take your word for it, it's valuable, and it's better that I don't know about this Crazy Eddie Worm. Captain Renner, if the objective is to recover Miss Blaine and her cargo, how do we go about doing it?"

"That's the question," Renner said.

"We negotiate." Bury was onscreen. "Forgive me, I was invited to listen. Commander Rawlins, what is important now is that we appear to be ready to fight, and that the Moties believe that overwhelming Imperial forces will come to our rescue in the not too distant future, so that it is better for the Moties to conclude an agreement with us now while they still have strength."

"Yeah. And that they don't learn just how far the Blockade Fleet is from us. Only it's not so far, sir. Into the Crazy Eddie point and back with the Squadron."

"Except that whatever's left there will shoot before listening. There's no real way to tell a Motie ship from an Imperial," Renner said.

"Damn. Of course that's right. And we can't get a message back to *Agamemnon* either. Commodore, I'm *real* glad you're in charge and not me." Rawlins paused. "One thing, though. Admiral Weigle's in command of the blockade fleet. He's got to know some-

thing has happened. The Jump point back to New Cal has moved, he damned well will know *that,* so he'll send back for orders, fast. Also he'll look for the new Jump point to the Mote."

"What will he do if he finds it?" Renner asked.

Rawlins shook his head. "Stand guard over it, I suppose. But you know, sir, Weigle's an aggressive commander. He just might send a scout. We'd better watch for that. All right, Blaine, what else don't I know?"

"A lot, but we don't know it either," Chris Blaine said. "For example. These space civilizations are more like nomads than anything settled. No stable maps, no permanent homes. A few, like the ones in the big planetary moons, are relatively fixed, but mostly things shift and change. The value of . . . air, food, power, machinery, anything that has to be moved, it depends on distance and delta-vee. It changes every second. There must be ways to *sell* delta-vee."

"Hah," Rawlins said. "As if the old Silk Routes changed distances. One day it's like walking across a river bridge to get to Far Cathay. Next month it's thousands of miles away."

"It was like that!" Joyce exclaimed. "When things were stable and there were strong governments, it was only a few weeks from Persia to China, but when the nomads were strong and bandits blocked the passes, it could be months or years, or no land routes at all. And there were pirate empires in Viet Nam and Sumatra, so even the sea routes weren't stable."

"An interesting observation," Bury said. "Which may do much to give us new understanding of these Moties. Thank you, Joyce. Kevin, perhaps we should assume these Moties are more similar to bedouin Arabs than to your Empire."

"Wonderful," Renner said. "The only Arabs I know are you and Nabil."

"Face," Joyce said. "Arabs are concerned with saving face, even more than Chinese. Appearances are very important. Maybe to the Moties, too?"

"I didn't notice that on Mote Prime," Renner said. "But maybe I wouldn't have. But— You know, they did have stories about everything. The paintings, the statuary, they made up stories to hide their past, and they did put the best face they could on things. On the other hand it occurs to me that Chris and Glenda

Ruth, me, all of us only knew Mote Prime Moties. Which means none of us are real experts."

"Except His Excellency," Chris Blaine said. "Look at how valuable Bury Mediators are. Of course they're expecting the Empire to be much more like Mr. Bury sees it than as we do."

"As I saw it nearly thirty years ago, Lieutenant," Bury said.

"Damnation," Rawlins said. "Commodore, this is way over my head. Only thing I'm sure of, if we let something happen to Lord Blaine's daughter, my career is finished. Well, I guess I know what to do, keep the guns and torpedoes ready and wait for orders. Commodore, you tell me what to shoot at, I'll try to shoot it, but I sure don't know any more than that!"

"Join the club. Signing off." Renner thumbed the switch.

Joyce turned to Chris Blaine. "All right, what's the Crazy Eddie Worm?"

"I can't tell you," Chris said.

She turned to Renner. "The deal was, I learn everything. Now you're going back on that?"

Chris Blaine said. "Joyce, do you want to be forbidden to talk to Moties?"

"No, of course not. And you can't do that!"

"We can't do that. Joyce, we can't fall thirty stories unless somebody's pushed us off a balcony! There are things you can't know. If you know them, you can't talk to Moties because then the Moties would know them, too."

She didn't believe him, not even when Kevin nodded at her.

"Kevin!"

Renner vaguely knew he was asleep, and someone was trying to wake him, and he didn't care.

"Come on, Kevin. Come on, open the bloody circuit. Your attention please, Captain Renner. God damn it, Kevin—"

"Yeah? Buckman? What?"

"It's a message from nowhere, Kevin, nowhere we know about anyway. I just got it."

"Message from nowhere. Important. What is it?"

"It was a general broadcast, wide beam. Must have cost a lot of power to send. Kevin, there's a cover message and a complete library of astronomy for the past hundred thousand years! More, I think! You were asleep, so before I woke you I did some tests. I sampled their observations to see how they match the New Caledonia data base over the past few hundred years. It all verifies, all I tested does anyway. Kevin, I think you've got to *do* something about this. Oh, and *Phidippides* wants to talk. *Atropos* wants to talk."

"Yeah." Renner found his uniform and wrestled his legs into it. "Verification. Well?"

"Loci for some of the more obvious stars check out. I started a program to verify the orbits of Murcheson's Eye and the Mote. Then I came and got you. It should be finished by now."

"Okay, let's go." He squeezed through the curtain. "Hello, Horace. You're looking well this morning. Cynthia, we need breakfast, large, served at our posts." Into his acceleration couch. "Jacob, first show me that message. Then you can get me *Atropos*."

"It's this file."

The message was printed out on Kevin's screen, but it gave the impression of being written on a scroll:

"Greetings, O Caliph from afar, from the newest of your servants. You may think of us as the Library at Alexandria; our locus is described in this vector. We give you this record of all of our history's observations of this region of the sky. We have watched the skies for countless ages, and we offer all this to you that you will be pleased with us and know how useful we can be. Remember us, O Caliph, when you come into your kingdom."

Renner was at a loss for words. Not so Bury: "This tells us many things," he said, "not the least of which is that they have a Bury-apprentice Mediator."

"What else?"

"They know nothing of us. They're powerless and poor. They have no way to engage in dialogue with us, which may imply that they fear Medina, or that they are light-hours away."

"Both, I'd say," Blaine said. "But they're certainly a long way off towards Mote Gamma. They've got good detection. They broadcast across just over two billion kilometers. Even so, they must be poverty-stricken, or they would have sent *something*, if only a relay to project a narrower beam."

Bury dreamed, his face calm and perfectly still. "Yes. As is, look what they've done. They've spilled their secrets across the sky. They've given away all they had because there was no way to establish a trade. Perhaps the strangers are not strangers to gratitude. Exactly right, for those with no power at all."

"Thanks—"

"There is more. They believe we are powerful, or likely to become so. This argues that others do also. The question is, why? Certainly we are not now."

"Thanks, Horace. Buckman, what have you got?"

"New program just finishing. Their orbits for the Eye and the Mote check against what I've got, with a minor margin of error."

"A hundred thousand years of observations?"

"That, or two or three."

"Okay, get me—"

"Wait one, Kevin. This is finished. Mmm . . ."

Renner watched Buckman dreaming before his screen and presently said, "See if you can describe it," biting off the words.

"Yeah. It's a reiterative program to predict the collapse of Buckman's Protostar. Kevin, at first blush it looks like Medina Trading should have had this. It would have given them the right date . . . year. I mean this is really, seriously valuable."

"Okay. Get me *Atropos*."

"Yes, sir, we received a copy, too," Rawlins said. "It came from an asteriod that trails the Beta Leading Trojans."

"Onk?"

"Beta Leading Trojans, sir—"

"Right, I understand that."

"Well, there's an asteroid that trails that group. The group is sixty degrees in front of Mote Beta."

"Naturally."

"And this is maybe fifty degrees from Beta."

"Unstable. Had to be nudged, right, Jacob? Anything else, Rawlins?"

"Yeah, my Sailing Master is a science buff, and he hasn't stopped playing with that since he got it."

Eudoxus's sneer was clear and blatant, if hard to describe. " 'Library at Alexandria,' forsooth! Their claim would have been valid once. They're near broken, now. They still had some of their wealth ten years ago."

"That would be when they bought a Bury Mediator," Kevin surmised.

The Motie didn't visibly react. "Yes, they bought their Bury Fyunch(click) from Persia. They were maintaining their ancient tradition of collecting and codifying knowledge. Perhaps they still are.

"They're the oldest family we know of. They've traded in information throughout history. They've had to move countless times. They were in the Leading Trojans of Beta eight thousand years ago, at the killing of the Doctors."

"We heard of that," Renner said. Something made him add, "No, I guess we didn't."

"Was there a Killing of the Doctors on Mote Prime? I'm not surprised," Eudoxus said. "It must seem so obvious. Doctors make population problems worse, yes?"

"Obvious, right."

"Here it was very successful. Alexandria refused to participate and so did some other forgotten civilizations; they must all have been destroyed by the victors. Alexandria alone kept their Doctors. Afterward they bred a basic stock and sold crossbreeds and tailored mutations. But other cultures have sequestered their own breeding stock, Doctors and other rare castes, and Alexandria has fallen on hard times."

"Should we be dealing with them?" Renner asked. He noticed Bury's attention fully on the screen.

"It does no harm," Eudoxus said. "They are considered—a bit strange. But they're no threat, and they can be useful."

Bury was nodding to himself. When Renner broke the connection with Eudoxus, Bury said, "Interesting. Strange. No threat. Librarians. Kevin, this group is poor, but it is permitted to keep its resources." He smiled softly. "Whatever our final decisions, they should include Alexandria."

"Okay, we're closing on it," Buckman said. He enlarged the image on the screen: a dark object surrounded by a glare. "Ah. And now Eudoxus is relaying a better picture."

The Motie ship had run on ahead and was nearly alongside the Motie base. The screens showed a ring of fusion fire linking black candle flames: fusion rocket motors, forty or more, bright enough to wash out the sensors.

The light washed out some detail, but . . . the motors ringed one side of a highly regular iceball. Most of the iceball was webbed in colored lines and studded here and there with domes connected by bright bands on the surface. Some of the domes were transparent. There were ships, too, scores of them on the ice and in the space around it.

The instruments aboard *Atropos* were superior to what *Sinbad* carried. A man aboard *Atropos* was relaying data. "Mass: sixty-five thousand tonnes. One klick by half a klick by half a klick. Albedo: ninety-six percent."

"My God, it's huge," Renner said. "Not so bloody big for a comet, but it's not a comet anymore. It's a carrier spacecraft! Joyce, did the Empire ever build—"

The image became a black ball with only the engine-glare protruding. The proprietors had closed the Field.

Eudoxus appeared. "That's Inner Base Six," she said. "Maneuver to the gripping side in this plane."

From *Atropos:* "The surface is foamed hydrogen ice. We think the interior is hydrogen ice; the mass is about right. The jets are hydrogen fusion with some refinements."

Renner said, "The Crazy Eddie Probe looked bigger than that. Way bigger, but it turned out to be only a lightsail. I remember before we found that out, Captain Blaine was wondering if we'd have to land on it with Marines."

"This time we do land, I think," Horace Bury said.

Half an hour later, *Sinbad* was close enough to feel the iceball's minuscule gravity. "Here goes," Renner said.

"Yes, sir," Commander Rawlins said. "Sir, I agree it's best to get *Sinbad* under a powerful Langston Field, but I *won't* be sorry to keep *Atropos* out here where I can maneuver. Captain, they've got a lot of ships and guns in there. There's no way I could force them to let you out."

"Right," Renner said.

"We can presume that *Hecate's* crew are in similar circumstances," Blaine said.

"The Moties of Mote Prime were gracious hosts," Bury said. "We believe these Moties are even more similar to Arabs."

"Yeah. Well, it's one way to find out if Moties have the same ideas about hospitality that Arabs do," Renner said.

"As Allah wills. I am ready, Kevin."

The black shield disappeared. *Sinbad* sank toward Base Six. *Phidippides* moved ahead, veering away toward its own mooring.

Chris pointed. "I think that must be ours."

Renner laughed. "Yeah. My God, it's a *mosque*."

It was magnificent. It was *human*, the only shape down there that wasn't utilitarian and alien. Light and airy, a bubble of painted masonry afloat on the ice field. The structure couldn't have been marble; it might well have been carved ice. It was far more mosquelike than the castle King Peter's people had built them on Mote Prime, and considerably smaller. A mosque with a cavity in it . . . a vertical channel or well, from which cables were even now snaking toward *Sinbad*.

The black Field closed over the black sky: the stars disappeared. *Atropos*, on station well away from Base Six, was now out of communication. Renner felt *Sinbad*'s vulnerability.

Sinbad was winched toward the well in the Mosque. It would fit exactly.

"Close fit," Buckman said. "After what we saw on Mote Prime, there isn't much Motie Engineers can do that would surprise me—looks like they have transfer bays matching the airlocks."

Sinbad was pulled inexorably into the docking bay. Those transfer bays were unfinished, mere holes. And Motie Engineers were waiting in the bays, prepared to finish them on the spot.

Fuel began to flow into *Sinbad*. Good: they'd kept *that* promise.

It was nearly an hour before the Moties finished connecting *Sinbad* to an antenna extended through the restored Field. By then Renner was savage with impatience. He pulled himself under control—because if he didn't, *Rawlins* wouldn't!—and said, "*Atropos*, this is *Sinbad*. Testing."

"*Atropos* here, sir. Locked on. Stand by for—"

"I'm here," said Rawlins.

"Right. Commander, we can figure that anything said here is monitored by the Moties. I want you to keep testing this circuit. Be sure we have communications."

"Yes, sir. And if we don't?"

"Try to reestablish, but the instant you're out of touch with

Sinbad, you're in command. Do what you think best. You'll recall the last orders you got from Balasingham. Of course you'll stay at full-alert status unless I tell you to stand down."

"Yes, sir. Understood. Do you expect real trouble, Captain Renner?"

"Not from here. I think the Moties here will be perfect hosts. Of course they told us they had a major readjustment of their relationship with the East India Company. That sounded sticky."

"Yes, sir."

"And I'll try to find out what that involved. I'll leave the circuits open on standby." Renner touched switches. "And that's done. Horace, I think it's time. Joyce, do you really want to carry—"

"It only masses eight kilograms." Joyce hefted the gyrostabilized pickup camera. It wriggled within its sleeve like a thing alive.

Renner touched indicators: inner lock, override, outer lock. *Sinbad's* air-lock doors swung in and out . . . on a corridor decorated in Moorish abstracts, and good air with a trace of chemicals in it.

✳   ✳   ✳

Chris Blaine waited impatiently as Eudoxus explained to Horace Bury. "We really don't have room for your Warriors to accompany us," she said. "Of course you don't expect to be escorted by Warriors any more than I do, but a Master of your importance would. My Master will have his Warriors present when you meet."

"It is no matter." Bury waved to indicate Blaine, Cynthia, Nabil, and Joyce. "My friends will have to substitute. In future years we will find new customs for meetings between humans and Moties."

"Thank you." Eudoxus paused. "There's another small matter. We're hoping you won't need your travel chair, Excellency. But we can rebuild the corridors if we must."

Bury smiled. "You are gracious hosts. Thank you, but for the moment Nabil can carry a portable medical unit that will suffice for my needs. Lead on."

"All right. Kevin . . . ?"

"I'd better stay in contact with *Atropos,*" Renner said. He was captain; he could not leave his ship.

The corridors bustled with activity. There were Engineers and Watchmakers everywhere. Blaine glanced over Nabil's shoulder at

Bury's medical readouts. Calm. Total calm. Perhaps even frighteningly calm.

They entered a dome, a flattened sphere. Through a forest of vines they looked out on the surface. White snow, pastel domes, lines in primary colors. And—Joyce looked behind her, then dashed that way and pointed her pickup camera between two masses of dark greenery.

The Mosque was magnificent. Joyce held for a moment, then zoomed on *Sinbad*, its single minaret, the piece that made it an artistic whole. She said, "We'll want to go out."

"No problem," Eudoxus said. "Your viewers would feel cheated if they couldn't see it all. Sensory deprivation?"

Joyce only nodded. An instant later she stumbled . . . as she saw how much she was telling Eudoxus about herself. Chris let his grin show through.

Now the corridor dipped beneath the ice. Branches ran off to the sides and up. Here and there were discreet vertical slits, like arrow notches in an ancient keep. Narrower tubes crossed the corridor above head height. Moties popped through these like leaves in a storm.

Down they went, deep into the interior of Base Six.

The corridor opened into a large chamber. Two grotesque shapes stood by a door at the far end. Chris saw Eudoxus's tension as they passed inside. He looked behind him and was not terribly surprised to see two more of the spiky horrors.

"Warriors," Joyce muttered. "Frightening efficiency, almost beautiful." She waved her pickup.

Nabil and Cynthia were on hair triggers.

One of the Warrior shapes moved to open the door. They were escorted into another large chamber. A white Motie nursed a pup at the far end. To that one's left stood two Warriors, and to their left was another white and a brown-and-white.

Eudoxus spoke rapidly in a language the humans didn't understand. The other Mediator instantly interrupted with splayed arms and an angry bark.

"*Hracht!* Our Masters spoke that this talk will speak in Anglic," that one said. He seemed unaware that he had the full, dangerous attention of every Warrior in the room. "Then we speak these same thoughts in the trade language. Need is sorrowful, but given recent change in levels, we demand. Else East India Trading Company will not act for you or with you."

Eudoxus gave the impression of bowing. "Very well. I have the honor to present His Excellency Horace Hussein al-Shamlan Bury, Magnate of the Empire, director of the Imperial Traders Association. Your Excellency, my Master, Admiral Mustapha Pasha. Our associate Master of the East India Company, Lord Cornwallis. The young mediator who speaks for Lord Cornwallis may be called Wordsworth." Eudoxus gestured to his master.

Mustapha spoke slowly and carefully.

"Excellency, welcome to Inner Base Six," Eudoxus translated. "In the name of the Caliph Almohad, who sends her greetings. This is your house."

"Thank you," Bury said. "You are gracious hosts." He bowed slightly to both Motie masters, then nodded to Chris Blaine.

"I will speak for His Excellency," Blaine said. "We wish again to thank you for your hospitality, and to assure you we understand that the need for haste was the cause of our coming here with less than full understanding."

Joyce moved to one side so that she could see everyone. Her pickup wriggled in her hands and made a tiny whirring sound. One of the Warriors started a rapid movement that was halted by a short bark from Admiral Mustapha.

Chris Blaine turned to the other Mediator. 'Wordsworth, please assure Lord Cornwallis that we are pleased to meet him."

"Her," Wordsworth said. "Medina speakers tell humans are usually hurrying. Is true?"

"Often," Blaine said.

"Then forgive me if we talk important things now," Wordsworth said. "Do you know what your hosts do to us? We were guests, and betrayed. The half of us are dead, torn by flying bits of metal, ripped apart by no air—"

"You were not guests by any choice of ours," Eudoxus said. "As all here are well aware. You forced yourselves into an alliance, and you did not do your part. Your incompetence has brought the Empire here. I will demonstrate." Eudoxus turned to Blaine. "Tell us how your Empire knew to come to Crazy Eddie's Sister when you did."

"The token ships. Mere shells," Blaine said. "They could have but one purpose."

"Exactly," Eudoxus said. "Had East India sent substantial ships, the Empire would not have guessed, and our ships would be well into Imperial space."

"Where are the ships now?" Wordsworth asked. "Our embassy to humans, do they live or die? I ask the humans to answer."

"No Motie ships have been destroyed," Blaine said. "One hides in the asteroids of the red dwarf. The others wait with an Imperial cruiser for escort by the main battle fleet."

"And East India's representative?"

"You will forgive us, but until this moment we did not know that East India had representatives aboard those ships," Blaine said.

Eudoxus spoke slowly in a language of emphatic consonants: like popcorn popping. Her white-furred Master listened carefully, then spoke in the same language.

"Admiral Mustapha says that both the East India Mediators are safe. There would be no reason to harm them. The Mediators aboard our ships had orders to keep contact with the Empire to a minimum until they could speak with someone in high authority. At that time the East India Mediators will be given the rights we agreed on."

Wordsworth looked to Chris Blaine. "Does he tell true? No powerful Empire person was there, far side of Sister?"

"Captain Renner and His Excellency were the highest authorities present."

"Thank you. I must ask now, what have you agreed with Medina?"

Blaine looked to Bury, then back. "We agreed to come with them. I think it is no secret that we expected to be taken to Mote Prime. Before we could find our balance"—he had almost said footing—"one of our ships and the Sister had both been lost to the Crimean Tartars. Medina has agreed to assist in rescuing the crew and passengers of *Hecate*. This seems fair. Their duplicity caused our loss."

"Can you speak for your Empire?"

"No, but if all of us here are agreed, that will have great influence. I am Kevin Christian Blaine, son of Lord Roderick Blaine. Commodore Renner has influence with the Navy. His Excellency controls the directors of the Imperial Traders Association. Joyce

Mei-Ling Trujillo speaks for the news services, Empire-wide. What we agree to will be heard at all levels of the Empire."

Wordsworth asked, "How do we stand, measured along Medina Trading? Have Medina told you? Is there agreement about us, you and Medina Trading?"

"No. We were told that you were partners with Medina, and that a readjustment of status was being negotiated."

"I do not understand."

"That you and Medina are partners now talking about changes in agreements."

"That is spoke with massive delicacy," Wordsworth said. He spoke slowly to his Master and received a lengthy reply. "We can agree to readjustment," Wordsworth said. "We know we do not have equals with Medina, but we insist we be heard in all discussions."

"You are not in a position to insist," Eudoxus said.

Wordsworth gave the Motie equivalent of a shrug. "For us has been worse. Crimean Tartars flee from their former ganglords. They need to know. They need friends. How if they come to us for refuge? If they carry to us human guests and gripping hand on the Sister to trade? We—"

"You could not."

"Medina lost the Crazy Eddie point because too many Masters, too little wealth, move in awkward orbits." *Resources badly handled*, Chris translated . . . tentatively. "Was bad mistake. Do not do it again. East India yet has wealth like yours in mass. Crimean Tartars do not know value of what they took. East India can work with Crimean Tartars and humans, or we can work with humans, or we can work with humans and Medina. What do you wish?"

The silence that followed was not empty. Warriors and Mediators and Masters shifted constantly: handholds and footholds, positions, flickering fingers and arms. Chris let it run for several seconds; but he couldn't read the silence, so he broke it.

"What is it you're dividing? Do you know?"

"Access to the Empire and the stars beyond our own," Eudoxus said instantly.

"Your Fyunch(click)'s student's third student tells us Empire would agree with *all* Moties," Wordsworth said. "All, never less. A stepping . . . a hierarchy of sorts would look good to you, yes? So, we speak, we mediate, we argue for command over Mote system, too. Some Motie families will control Mote system. We wish will be part of families."

"The highest possible stakes," said Eudoxus. Before Chris or anyone could answer—if he had *had* an answer—both Mediators had turned to talk to their respective Masters.

Joyce whispered, "At least they agree on *that*."

Blaine nodded. He was more interested in getting Horace Bury's reaction. Bury caught the query (eyebrow lift, tilt of head) and said, "There's motive here for an arbitrarily large number of murders."

Eudoxus's head and shoulders suddenly snapped around to face Joyce Trujillo. "What do you know of our breeding habits?"

Chris considered throwing his arm across her face. Too bloody late . . . and it would have told the Mediators what *he* knew. Eudoxus didn't even wait for her answer, only for the emotions that chased across her face. "So. You would deal with the Moties united. How can you expect us to stay united? Our histories tell that we've tried to unite before, and failed always."

"Neither problems nor opportunities last forever," Bury said. "And what neither Moties nor humans can do, Moties and humans together may accomplish. Allah is merciful."

"King Peter's ambassadors must have told you much," Eudoxus said. "What happened to them?"

"They were well treated," Joyce said. "One was still alive a few years ago, as I remember. At the Blaine Institute. Lieutenant Blaine could tell you more."

"As His Excellency says, everything has changed," Blaine said. "When there was one point to blockade, and that one easily defended, blockade was an effective way to gain time. Now there are two paths to block. There must be a better way, better for humans and Moties. If not . . ."

"Your battle fleets will come," Eudoxus said. "War in the Mote system, and you to exterminate us. Bloody hands forever, but else we escape to the rest of the universe. That is your terror." She had spoken truth; she must have seen it in their faces. "Our numbers increase. Our domains. In a thousand years we enclose you. Yes, we must seek a better answer."

265

PART 4
THE CRAZY
EDDIE WORM

Take up the White Man's burden—
Send forth the best ye breed—
Go bind your sons to exile
To serve your captives' need;
. . . .
The ports ye shall not enter,
The roads ye shall not tread,
Go make them with your living,
And mark them with your dead!

—*Rudyard Kipling*
"The White Man's Burden"
"The United States and
the Philippine Islands, 1899"

1
The Tartars

Knowledge is valuable when charity informs it.

—St. Augustine, City of God

Through the windows they could see the beheaded corpse of *Hecate*.

A scar gaped along half its length: the gap where *Hecate*'s cabin had been. The rest of the hull had been mounted alongside a silver sausage, one of their captors' ships. It flew three hundred meters distant, keeping pace with their own captor. A slender spine projected aft. The drive flame was a faint violet-white glow running along the spine.

Hecate's severed cabin rode the flank of another such sausage. From inside they could see almost nothing of that: just a silver membrane bulging with fluid, centimeters away, and a rigid cabin forward.

But they saw *Hecate*'s host ship well enough. Freddy had set their remaining telescope to following it. The sausage was banded with color-coded lines and chains of handholds and catwalks, and Moties. The maze ran round *Hecate*, too. Moties in pressure suits moved over the hull like lice.

They found the lightsail, Freddy's spinnaker. In minutes they had spread several acres of silver film to inflate ahead of the nose.

"That won't add much to the thrust," Jennifer said. "Why . . . ?"

"Why not? It's there," Terry Kakumi said. "Blink and it's a signal device, blink again and it's heat shielding. They do *love* to fiddle."

"It'll heat their cabin some," Freddy said.

269

Hecate rotted before their eyes. Engineers and tiny Watchmakers stripped away sections of hull and plated them over their own ship. They found automated cameras at nose and tail and amidships, an officially approved model, all identical, which the Moties seemed to find confusing. *Hecate*'s fuel tank they studied and then left intact. They worked inside the cut end until the Engineer was able to pull loose a glass tank festooned with tubing—

"Dammit. That's our sewage recycling system," Freddy said. "We'll starve."

"We have the goodies locker," Jennifer said. "A week's supplies, maybe."

"It's a double time limit. Will the sewage crowd us out before we starve for lack of basic protocarb? Stay tuned."

The men were edgy, talking to distract themselves. But Jennifer was calm, even happy, cradling a six-kilogram alien who clung to her with three arms, watching her face intently, sometimes trying to imitate the sounds she made. And Glenda Ruth . . . was frightened when she thought about it, and frustrated, and uncomfortable; and alive as never before, playing a game she'd begun learning in the cradle.

She worked on Freddy's back, running her thumbs along basic shoulder muscles, probing deep. Freddy subsided with a grunt of unwilling satisfaction. He asked, "Do you suppose they'll keep the data cubes? I've got some good recordings of the battle."

Hecate dwindled. They took half the hull to make a curved mirror to relay light from the light-sail. Kilometers of wiring went into the nose of the captor craft. A small craft arrived from somewhere else; some of the wiring, four cameras, and all of *Hecate*'s little attitude jets went aboard; the Engineer pilot traded places with a replacement, and away it went.

The Moties exposed *Hecate*'s drive; moved it aft; set it to firing. Then they were all over it, tuning, testing. Presently their own drive went off, leaving *Hecate*'s running.

"Something of a compliment," Glenda Ruth said. Freddy nodded.

Jennifer asked, "Does it bother you? *Hecate* . . ."

Freddy's shoulders set hard. He said, "Not all that much. A racing yacht, we change *anything* at the slightest excuse. The idea's to *win*. It's not like"—to Glenda Ruth—"not like your dad losing his battleship, his first command."

"He still flinches if you mention *MacArthur*." Glenda Ruth resumed trying to soften the knots in Freddy's shoulders.

They could hear the rustling. Engineers and Watchmakers were moving over the surface of their own life bubble. What was happening out there?

"Then again, *Hecate* is where you and I got together. I do hate—"

"The bed's quite safe."

His tension softened. "We get it back from Balasingham, we can build a ship around it."

The Mediator pup looked into Jennifer's eyes and said, distinctly. "Go eat." Jennifer let go, and the pup pushed off from Jennifer's chest, setting her rotating, sailing unerringly to impact the Engineer.

The cabin was aswarm with Moties. The Warrior would remain in place for minutes at a time, then bound about the cabin like a spider on amphetamines, and presently come to rest again. The Engineer and three skinny half-meter Watchmakers, and a slender creature with a harelip and long, delicate fingers and toes, had reshaped the hole in the cabin wall into an oval airlock. The Engineer had found the safe near the cabin's forward cone, tapped at the code readout, then left it alone. Now the Moties had peeled the cabin walls away and were going through the air and water regeneration systems. From time to time there came a whiff of chemical strangeness.

"Too many of them. They'll strain the air changers," Freddy said.

"I think that one's a doctor," Jennifer said. "Look at the fingers. And the Motie nose is in the roof of the mouth. That thing's got enhanced smell and surgeon's fingers. There was a Doctor caste on Mote Prime."

"Maybe several."

"Right. And between them, the Doctor and the Engineer are going to decide how to keep us alive. I've got to say I don't like that."

Now the three Watchmakers were moving about the cabin drawing green lines. They squeezed the stuff out of what the Navy would have called *ration tubes*. The patterns weren't complex enough to be writing. The Watchmakers covered the walls with

271

lines and curves, and presently converged where the sewage recycling system had been.

Freddy asked, "Why not, Jennifer? The way you and Glenda Ruth talk, these Moties can do anything, including keep humans healthy."

"But it's all very *basic*, isn't it? Nothing like the castle they built for us on Mote Prime."

"It's a battle fleet, not a city," Glenda Ruth said.

Terry Kakumi snapped, "It's a poor little pathetic battle fleet. Look at them, Jennie. Tiny little ships, mostly tank, big cabins because there are too many of the buggers, motors that do a meter per sec squared at best. What's left for weapons? Are they supposed to make them on the spot?

"What would a real fleet be like, Jennie? Rape my lizard, what *couldn't* we build with Motie Engineers at the Yards? They're church-rat poor. We've been captured by BuReloc transportees! They're stripping our car and fixing our life support with borrowed chewing gum and string!"

Jennifer giggled. "Bag ladies with borrowed chewing gum. I love it!"

Glenda Ruth felt herself bristling, as if these were *her* Moties. But she could feel it: Terry was right. "What can we do?"

"*Talk* to them, Glenda Ruth. Tell them we're worth the price of their last coin," Terry said. "Tell them to pull the pea out from all those mattresses, I'm just a pathetic mass of bruises. Explain *ransom* to them. Or they'll let us strangle."

She said, "These don't talk. We'll have to wait."

※　　※　　※

The new East India Mediator was old, as old as Eudoxus, with gray streaks at the muzzle and along the flanks. She was escorted into the chamber by a Warrior and a younger Mediator, who both left quickly.

When she was presented to Horace Bury, the trader flinched. Chris Blaine moved closer and saw what the Motie was carrying. "A newborn?" he asked, and watched Bury relax. *Of course Bury took it for a Watchmaker.*

The aged Mediator examined the humans and turned toward Bury radiating delighted surprise. "Excellency! I had never dared hope to meet you in person, even when it became known that you were again in the Mote system. I have thought long on the name I would give myself and have chosen Omar rather than something more pretentious. It is my greatest pleasure finally to meet you."

Bury bowed slightly. "I am pleased to have had such apt students."

"And my new apprentice. We have not chosen a name, but—"

"You presume," Eudoxus said. "We too have new apprentices, and we are eager to introduce them to His Excellency."

"Of course." Omar turned to Wordsworth and began to speak.

"Hracht!" Eudoxus looked pleased. "We agreed that all conversation will be in Anglic. This means yours as well, does it not?"

Wordsworth was about to speak, but some gesture from Omar silenced her. "I would prefer rigid rules to no rules," Omar said. "Very well, I will receive my information for all to hear. Where do matters stand now?"

"Not good not bad," Wordsworth said. "We make progress, agree that East India will have honored place, second to Medina but only to Medina."

The Mediator pup was staring intently at Horace Bury. The trader was not annoyed. Interesting . . .

"Progress indeed," Omar said. "And how will all this be accomplished?"

Chris Blaine smiled thinly. "Not all details have been resolved," he said. "Yet we can agree, there has never been a better time to unite all Moties. Mote Prime is not a factor. The Empire has many ships. With Medina and East India, and allies you may bring . . ."

Omar moved closer to Bury. The Mediator pup stretched toward him. Absently Bury's hand reached out, touched the pup's fur, drew back.

"Excellency," Omar said. "Let us speak seriously. Medina and East India are powerful if united, yet it must be obvious to all that even united we are not the greatest power among the space dwellers."

"King Peter wasn't the most powerful Master on Mote Prime," Chris Blaine said.

Bury spoke softly. "Medina and East India were the first to understand the implications of the protostar. Your ships even now negotiate with the Empire. Why should you not have the rewards of prescience?" He deliberately scratched behind the pup's oversize ear. "May I choose a name? Ali Baba, I think." Bury smiled. "Of course there is a small favor we require."

Eudoxus said, "We have begun to speak with the Crimean Tartars. It goes slowly. They know only obsolete languages."

"Obsolete to you," Omar said. "Not to us. One of my sisters has spoken with the Tartars, and I received word moments before I landed here. Excellency, the Tartars are afraid. They find that every Motie's hand is against them, and they do not know what they have. Only that it is important, and holding it is dangerous."

"They're holding a wolf by the ears," Joyce said.

The hull *clonked*.

In *Hecate*'s cabin, they waited.

A Warrior bounded through the new air lock, scuttled about the cabin, and presently settled. It exchanged words with the Warrior already present. It emitted a warbling whistle.

Other Moties entered: a Master, a meter and a half tall and clad in thick white fur, and a smaller Motie furred in a dense brown-and-white pattern: a Mediator.

"We're in business," Glenda Ruth said.

Two Engineers followed, towing a glass cylinder with green goo sloshing in it: *Hecate*'s sewage recycler. Six-fingered hands had been at work on it, but it didn't seem greatly changed.

"Another compliment," Freddy said. "Given what that cost me, I'd have been surprised if they could make it much more efficient."

Glenda Ruth felt Freddy's relief; she even shared it. Their life spans had just been extended by several weeks. More important was the timing.

"We thank for glorious gift," she said in the language Jock and Charlie had taught her, King Peter's language, from Mote Prime.

The Mediator's stance indicated receptivity but no understanding.

Damn! But free-fall might alter a Motie's body language. (Stance, indeed!) Or her words might be wrong, or her own gestures. How would a crippled Mediator speak, one with a missing arm?

Two of those little Moties with the Engineers weren't Watchmakers; they were Mediator pups. Jennifer waved. The larger pup jumped across ten meters of space, impacted, and clung. *Jennifer* wasn't having trouble communicating.

Okay. Glenda Ruth released her seat belts to give her body full play, worked her foot under a strap for anchorage, and said, palms facing out, regal-but-unarmed. "Our lives much improved by generous—"

The Moties converged on her.

Glenda Ruth had to remember to resume breathing. She was very aware of the spiky Warriors. They shifted constantly to keep a free path between prisoners and weapons. The four humans held quite still as six-fingered hands moved over them.

They had guessed this might happen. Glenda Ruth's mother, the only woman aboard *MacArthur*, had stripped so that Moties could learn something of human anatomy. Jennifer wanted that slot for herself.

It didn't matter. The caste that Jennifer thought was a Doctor moved in with the Engineer, and they peeled *Hecate*'s crew like bananas. The humans had to help in self-defense. The Doctor shied back from waves of alien pheromones, then sniffed dutifully. It had been many hours since there was a shower aboard *Hecate*.

Jennifer blushed and twitched at tickle points. Freddy thought it was funny and was trying to hide it. Terry's rounded nudity didn't bother him, but his hyperawareness of the Warriors' guns was driving Glenda Ruth nuts. She tried not to flinch at the touch of Motie hands. Dry. Hard. Right hands felt like a dozen twigs gliding over her face, seeking the muscles that make the front of a human head into a signaling system. The left hand clamped like a vise to hold her arm or leg or torso to be probed.

They turned and twisted for the Doctor. The Mediator and Master hung back, watching.

Human vertebrae fascinated them, as they had thirty years before, when *MacArthur*'s crew met Moties from Mote Prime. Evolution had not taken that path on the Mote. Motie life-forms had spines of solid bone and heavy, complex joints.

The brown-and-white pup jumped from human to human, sniffing, feeling, comparing. Even the Master, judging it safe, moved forward to run its right hands along Glenda Ruth's spine. Jennifer collapsed in giggling that was half sobs, sandbagged by everyone's favorite memory from *Summer Vacation*.

(Outside the museum on Mote Prime, a Master's dozen fingers

explored Kevin Renner's back. Renner shifted in delight. "Right! A little lower. Okay, scratch right there. Ahh!")

They couldn't talk under such circumstances. Glenda Ruth tried. They *had* to educate the Mediator, give it words to learn . . . but the others' embarrassment was just too strong. Glenda Ruth quickly gave up.

The Doctor and Engineer began talking to the Master. Pointing, demonstrating, explaining. The white-furred Motie took it all in. It asked short questions (that one inflection, *query*, brought verbal responses, where another, *command*, caused action), and the Moties resumed their examination. One question sent the Engineer to join its Watchmakers at work in the air recycler. Another had it comparing Freddy and Terry, Jennifer and Glenda Ruth. Hands. Hair. Toes. Spines again. Genitals (*will* you stop that giggling?)

The Mediator watched.

And finally they were allowed to put their clothes on. They found it hard to look at each other. The Master and its attendants were still talking.

"We should have guessed," Glenda Ruth said. "Masters do talk. It's different from the Mediator skill. They have to organize data from a dozen different castes . . . professions."

Clothed, it was all right to speak again. Jennifer said, "I think the Doctor's nearsighted. In a surgeon that's probably good."

The adult Mediator took the second Mediator pup from its Engineer parent. She crossed to the bridge, caught herself, and offered the little Motie to Freddy: clearly an offer, not a demand.

Freddy looked at Glenda Ruth. He was showing surprise, no distaste, and a touch of hope. She said, "Take it." *Why Freddy?* Freddy immediately reached out, smiling, and accepted the thing into his arms.

Why Freddy? Why not me?

It clung with five limbs, its hands exploring Freddy's head and shoulders, where his skin was exposed. Presently it pulled back to watch his face. Moties caught on to that one quick, the notion of a mobile face. *Why not me, or Terry?*

The Master spoke. The Engineer led the Mediator to the safe door. The Mediator began playing with the code readout.

"Damn," Glenda Ruth said. The others looked at her.

If she let the others know exactly what she had in mind, a Mediator would know it now or later. Could she get some help on this? She pointed at the safe and shouted, "Show signs of distress, dammit! It's too soon!"

Distress, right. Freddy spasmed, pointed to the safe with an outflung arm, and flung the other across his averted eyes, crying, "Weep! Wail!" Glenda Ruth choked back a laugh. The pup was trying to imitate him, right arms pointing, left across its eyes.

Terry's hand closed on her ankle. "The Warriors."

"They—" She looked. They *would*. "Freddy love, cut it."

"What was that about?"

She shook her head. "Anyway, you made the point."

One of the Warriors scuttled forward and anchored itself next to the safe, gun pointed back toward the humans.

The safe door slid open. A Watchmaker scuttled in. It handed out a laboratory sealed-environment jar as large as itself, then a plastic jar of dark powder, a stack of documents, a roll of gold coins.

The Engineer examined the gold and said something to the Master. The Master answered.

The Engineer put the papers back, and the cocoa. It examined the jar.

"Don't touch that!" Glenda Ruth shouted. No Motie would understand, but the Mediator would remember.

The Engineer opened the seals.

There was a *pop*. The Warrior's head snapped around to catch the same puff of gas that caught the Engineer. Glenda Ruth wondered if they would be shot.

The Warriors didn't shoot. The Engineer took a scraping from the sludge in the jar, then resealed it and put it back. It left the door open. It spoke a word and tossed the gold at one of the Watchmakers, who caught it and jumped through the new airlock.

The other Engineers had reattached the sewage recyling system where six lines of graffiti-green met in a sunburst. They continued to work on it, add a pipe here, bend, constrict. The Warriors maintained their stations. When Glenda Ruth kicked herself forward to the safe, she could feel phantom bullets. The Warriors came alert; the Master gave no signal that she could recognize; but no Motie stopped her.

Thanks to the Moties' parsimonious lowering of cabin pressure, the canister's pressure had sprayed perhaps 10 percent of the encysted eggs of the Crazy Eddie Worm into the cabin as an aerosol.

Most of the contents were intact. There was a mild odor of petroleum and other pollutants, the natural state of water on Mote Prime, fading rapidly as the air filters did their work. The Moties clearly didn't like the smell any more than the humans did. It wouldn't have bothered planet-dwelling Moties.

They've evolved in space, Glenda Ruth thought. *Space-dwelling Moties who don't detest pollution will die of it.*

Glenda Ruth carefully wiped the rim and resealed the canister, and glared at the Engineer. It might be vital to be able to claim that the Moties had been infected by accident.

Then she suppressed a shudder: a hundred wormlets would hatch and die in her lungs.

Thirty years before, Whitbread's asteroid-mining Engineer had been infected with the parasitic worm. *MacArthur*'s biologists determined that it couldn't infect humans and labeled it Form Zeta, the sixth living thing they'd found during autopsy on the Engineer. Present, not in large numbers, but present.

Jock and Charlie and Ivan carried it in greater numbers, and they didn't care any more than humans care about *E. coli*. Parasite Zeta did no harm beyond consuming a few calories; which was why the Blaine Institute biologists had used it as the base for their genetic engineering experiments.

It would be interesting to know if the parasite was normal among these space-evolved Moties. Not that it mattered: surely it would live, and this worm was different. And it would not survive in human lungs, but just the *thought*—

The Mediator spoke at her shoulder, and she jumped. It said, "Mediators talk. No Horace Bury Fyunch(click), but we talk."

"Good," said Glenda Ruth. "Let's talk. Please leave our trade goods alone. This is all we have to bargain with. It should not be ruined."

And now the Crazy Eddie Worm was growing in an Engineer, a female. Had the Warrior been female, too? Would it affect these Watchmakers?

How many Masters were aboard? Too many, of course, more than their captors would actually want, but . . . three? Four? And the clock was counting down.

❋　❋　❋

"Your Lordship's presence is requested," the voice said. "My Lord. My Lord, I must insist. Rod Blaine, wake up, dammit!"

Rod sat bolt upright. "All right, already."

"What is it?" Sally asked. She sat up with a look of concern. "The children . . ."

Rod spoke to the ceiling. "Who?"

"Lord Orkovsky. He says the situation is urgent," the telephone said.

Rod Blaine swung his feet over the edge of the bed and found his slippers. "I'll talk to him in the study. Send coffee." He turned to Sally. "Not the kids. The Foreign Secretary wouldn't call us in the middle of the night about that." He went across the hall to his study and sat at his desk. "I'm here. No visuals. All right, Roger, what's up?"

"The Moties are loose."

"How?"

"Actually, it's not *quite* that bad." Lord Roger Orkovsky, Secretary of State for External Affairs, sounded like a diplomat under stress. "You'll recall there was some question of when Dr. Buckman's protostar would collapse."

"Yes, yes, of course."

"Well, it's happened, and the Moties were ready for it. Due to some clever thinking—Chris is mentioned in the dispatches—Mercer had sent everything he could scrape up out to where the new Alderson point would form, so we were ready, too. Almost ready.

"Details later. We got a whole bunch of reports at once, about stellar geometry and such. You'll have to read them all. What's important is that there are some Motie ships with an ambassador on board cooling their heels under Navy detention while we decide what to do about them. And Mercer wants a battle fleet."

Rod was aware that Sally had come up behind him. "Roger," she said.

"Good morning, Sally. Sorry to yank you up like this—"

"Are the children all right?"

"I was just getting to that," Orkovsky said. "We don't know. Chris volunteered to be Navy liaison aboard Bury's ship—*Sinbad*. Commodore Kevin Renner commanding."

"Commodore."

"Yeah, that's complicated, too."

"So they went into the Mote system," Rod said.

"Right. *Sinbad*, a light cruiser—*Atropos*, Commander Rawlins—and a Motie ship. The reports say the first person the Moties wanted to talk to was Horace Bury."

"Roger, that doesn't make sense," Sally said.

"Maybe not, but it's true. Look, I better give you the rest of this. There'll be a cabinet meeting in the Palace in two hours. We want you there. Both of you. Matter of fact, we want you back on the Motie Commission. You were going back to New Caledonia anyway, now the government will pay for getting you there. The Navy will have a ship ready by the time you get to the Palace."

"We can't leave so soon!" Rod said.

"Yes, we can," Sally said. "Roger, thanks. You mentioned Chris. What about Glenda Ruth?"

"That was the last message in the stack," Orkovsky said. "Sally, a hundred hours after *Sinbad* went into the Mote system, Freddy Townsend took his yacht through. Glenda Ruth was aboard."

"I want his name," Sally said.

"Huh?"

"Whoever let them through. There's got to be a Navy man in charge out there, and he let our daughter go into the Mote system in an unarmed yacht. I want his name."

"Sally . . ."

"Yes, I know, he thought he had a good reason."

"Maybe he did."

"It wouldn't matter, would it? When was the last time you won an argument with her? I still want his name. Fyunch(click)!"

"Yes, madame?"

"Is our car ready?"

"Yes, madame."

"Tell Wilson we'll be leaving in an hour. Get clearances for the west entrance to the Palace."

"Yes, madame."

"So what do we take?" Sally said. "Jock. Fyunch(click), we want to talk to Jock. Wake him up, but check with the doctors first."

"Good thinking," Rod said. "Sally, we can't take him with us."

"No, but we can get him to record something to prove he's still alive," Sally said.

"What?" Rod held a sheath of facsimile papers. "The last report says, and I quote: 'The Hon. Glenda Ruth Blaine, on the basis of brief conversations with the Motie representatives, has concluded that although these Moties know Anglic and have some familiarity with the Empire, they are not part of any Motie group previously encountered.' I don't think they believe her."

"More fools they."

"Madame," the ceiling said. "Jock has been awakened. Do you want visuals?"

"Yes, thank you."

Brown and white fur streaked with gray. "Good morning, Sally. If you don't mind, I'll have chocolate while we talk."

"By all means. Good morning. Jock, the Moties are loose."

"Ah?"

"You knew about the protostar."

"I know what you have told me about the protostar. You said that it would collapse within the next hundred years. I take it that was wrong? That it has already happened?"

"You got it," Rod said. "Jock, we have a problem. Moties that Glenda Ruth believes aren't part of King Peter's group have got out of the Mote system. So far they appear to be stuck in a red dwarf backwater, but we all know the Empire can't keep up two blockades."

"And you and Sally have been given the problem of what to do about the Moties," Jock said. "Have they made you an admiral yet?"

"No."

"They will. And they'll give you a fleet." Jock's hand moved expressively. "At least it's not Kutuzov. Of course they want you to leave immediately. I am afraid I cannot accompany you."

"No, the Jump shock would kill you."

"Are the children well? They must have involved themselves by now."

Sally said, "They've gone to the Mote."

"I did not think you could surprise me," Jock said, "But you have. I see. Give me an hour. I will make what records I can."

"In what language?" Rod asked.

"In several. I will need recent pictures of Chris and Glenda Ruth, as well as of myself."

"We have a meeting."

"Of course. We will discuss this when you're done with that."

The Motie paused, and somehow the Motie smile was a grin of triumph. "So the horse learned to sing after all."

※　　※　　※

"I hadn't expected *this*," Jennifer said. "We're infested with Moties! Freddy ... Freddy, I can't keep thinking of this ship as *Hecate!*"

Freddy Townsend looked around. "Yeah. *Hecate's* cabin mounted on a ship of unknown name. *Bandit-One?* And we'll just hang numbers on the rest of the fleet."

Glenda Ruth said, "We could ask—"

And she shied back before he snarled, "I *won't* ask Victoria. She'd give us the name of this Motie ship, like we're strap-on cargo."

Jennifer said, "A two-headed ship. Two captains. We've never seen the Master that gives the orders. *Cerberus?*"

Five Watchmakers, two Warriors, three Engineers nursing two Mediator pups, the old Mediator they now called Victoria, a Master, a Doctor, and a lean, spidery variant that scuttled back and forth through *Cerberus's* big new airlock, perhaps bearing messages, had all made their nests in the cabin.

The change had come gradually, while they slept. Glenda Ruth remembered waking from time to time in a shifting pattern of variously shaped Moties. Twelve hours of that, then she woke choking and weeping. The Doctor had examined them and then meeped at the young male Master they'd named Merlin, who warbled at the engineers, who readjusted the air and sewage recyclers until the air was back to standard ... but it was still thick with Motie smells, and every human's eyes were still red.

The green strips painted along the walls had grown into vines, furry green tubes as thick Glenda Ruth's leg. The various Moties used the lines to mark off their territories.

They'd turned *Cerberus's* original airlock into a toilet: one toilet with a variety of attachments. The Engineers had worked on *Cerberus's* original toilet, too. It worked better now.

"They've put screens up. Both toilets," Glenda Ruth said. "We're *talking* now."

"Can you tell them to leave us some room?"

"I'll give it another try, but you can guess the answer. This much is more personal room than they've ever seen in one spot."

An Engineer arrived with food. All of the Moties converged except one Warrior. Glenda Ruth said, "Jennifer, go and see what they're eating."

The meal was democratic: the young Master called Merlin supervised distribution and sent a Watchmaker with food for the Warrior on guard. Merlin looked around when Jennifer came near. Victoria said he was a young male; this was not obvious, given he was helping to nurse the Mediator pups. The human presence didn't disturb him. Jennifer looked about her; spoke a few words to Victoria.

The Mediator swam to join Glenda Ruth. Victoria had been learning Anglic much faster than Glenda Ruth could learn Oort Cloud Recent.

She said, "About food? I think, *thought* you have your own."

"I'd like to know if this is like what we eat," she told it.

"Will ask Doctor and Engineer."

"I would like to feed you cocoa."

"Why?"

"On the planet they liked cocoa. If you like cocoa, we have something to trade."

"You said, what is in safebox is trade goods. We should not take without giving. Cocoa in safe?"

"Yes."

Victoria brought her flat face close. "Trade space with us! Past the starhole is all the worlds, all within your gripping hand. Give us the worlds, take what you want. Take tools you see, tell tools you want, Engineers make that. Take any caste of us, tell what shape and kind you want, you wait, your children will have."

Glenda Ruth said, "This is not so simple. We know how your numbers grow."

Stillness.

"We think we have an answer, but it's still not easy. Many Motie families will need to work together. As Moties do not always do."

"Glenda Ruth, who is Crazy Eddie you speak of?"

Glenda Ruth was only surprised for a moment. "Planet-dwelling Moties told us about Crazy Eddie. Maybe you know him with another name."

"Maybe."

"Crazy Eddie isn't one person, he is a kind of person. The kind who . . . who tries to stop change when change is too massive to stop."

"We tell children about Sfufth, who throws away garbage because it smells bad."

"Something like that." Sfufth? Shifufsth? She couldn't quite make that sound.

Jennifer had rejoined them, and now she carried the older pup. She said, "We had a very powerful Master, long ago. Joseph Stalin had the power of life and death over all of his people, in hundreds of millions." Jennifer glanced at Glenda Ruth: stop or go? Uncertain, Glenda Ruth nodded.

Jennifer went on, "Advisers told Stalin that there was a shortage of copper tube in his domain. Stalin gave his orders. Everywhere across a tenth of the land area of our world, what was made of copper was melted down to make tubes. Communication lines disappeared. Tractor parts, other tools. Wherever copper was needed, it was made pipes instead."

"Sfufth. We know him," Victoria said. "Sfufth is found everywhere, in every caste. Sfufth breeds Watchmakers for sale to other nests. No need for cage, they take care of selves."

Jennifer was delighted. "Yes! There's a painting in a museum on Mote Prime." She was about to convey an unfortunate nuance, and Glenda Ruth couldn't stop her. "A burning city. Starving Moties in riot. A Mediator stands on a car to be seen and heard and shouts, 'Return to your tasks!' "

Victoria nodded head and shoulders. "When possibilities close, Crazy Eddie doesn't see."

Glenda Ruth said, "In Stalin's domain, fifty years after. Things changed. More communication, better tools and transport. Their Warriors ate half their resources for all that long time, but the weapons they made were second best. Lesser domains began splitting off. Some older Masters acted to take charge of the domain and turn it all back. The Gang of Crazy Eddies."

Had she got her point across? Years of watching Jock and Charlie weren't helping enough. Too much of Mediator body language was conscious; was arbitrary. She said, "When possibilities open, Crazy Eddie doesn't see."

The Mediator thought that over. She said. "Make cocoa to look at first. For safety."

For poison, she meant.

So Freddy made cocoa for the four of them—"Make it hot," Glenda Ruth whispered—and an extra bulbful for analysis.

"Too hot," Victoria said when she touched it. She gave it to the Engineer, who carried it into the hidden part of *Cerberus*. The human crew huddled with their heads together, sipping, their shoulders shutting out the aliens around them. Freddy had a crime drama running on a monitor; Victoria might have been watching it, and Merlin watched intermittently, but no human was.

"How are you doing?" Freddy asked.

Glenda Ruth said, "I'm dancing as fast as I can, but the pace is too damned slow. Jennifer, what were they eating?"

Jennifer was running her hand along the pup's back as if it were a cat; but her hand kept stopping to feel the weird geometry. She said, "Just one dish. A gray crust around gray-green paste that looked a lot like basic protocarb."

"Jen, did it steam? Was it hot?"

"It wasn't hot. What do you want to know?"

She dared not tell them too much, but she had to know this. "Do they cook?"

"Glenda Ruth, the air coming through the new lock is warmer than it is here, but there's no smell of cooking."

"Okay." She looked at the faces around her. Open, honest faces shadowed by every passing thought. Did they understand, would they reveal, too much?

Engineer and Warrior were certainly infected. The worm eggs might well infect every Motie form in *Cerberus*'s cabin. If that didn't reach a Master, then an Engineer might have passed it on by now. But if a Mediator wasn't infected soon . . . there wouldn't be anything to talk about. Just a Master turned sterile male, and other forms showing the same symptoms, and the blame very clear.

2
Vermin City

And in that state of nature, no arts; no letters; no society; and which is worst of all, continual fear and danger of violent death; and the life of man, solitary, poor, nasty, brutish, and short.

—Thomas Hobbes, Leviathan

From the beginning Freddy Townsend had been concerned about his equipment. "I know we're prisoners," he told Victoria as soon as the Mediator would understand. "I know you can take what you want."

"Leave your stuff alone if play to win," Victoria said. "Need some stuff for now."

"Good. You think about future. You want us happy for future?"

"Say instead we want you not hating us for future."

"Good. Good. Then get them to leave my telescope the hell alone! It's this whole complex, here and here, all of this stuff—"

"Engineers make it better."

"Don't want better. Want this stuff the way it is," Freddy said distinctly. He had watched what happened to *Hecate*. He believed—and so did Glenda Ruth—that the Moties would strip the telescope of anything they wanted, leaving a tube and two lenses to be improved to their hearts' content.

They must have convinced Victoria; Victoria must have convinced one of the Masters. Days later, the scope and its computerized direction-finding and data-recording systems still matched Empire racing specs.

— — —

Freddy's fingers behind her ear teased Glenda Ruth awake.

The smaller pup was clinging to his back, a tiny skewed head above his left shoulder, wearing the generic smile; but Freddy looked quite solemn. Glenda Ruth followed his pointing finger to a screen and . . . what? Display of a broken kaleidoscope? Numbers indicated that she was looking aft, under one-hundred-power magnification, via Freddy's telescope.

"We're decelerating. Whole fleet. To that," Freddy said.

A shattered mirror on star-dusted black . . . mirrors, lots of mirrors, circles and ribbons and scraps and one great triangle. The mirrors weren't rotating, but some of what they illuminated was, on an eccentric axis. Sunlight off the mirrors set it to glowing like the City of God. . . .

"Schizophrenia City," Jennifer said.

Glenda Ruth winced. "Pandemonium," she said. John Milton's capital of Hell. If this was Captor Fleet's home base, they were indeed mad.

Pandemonium was backlit, showing mostly black, but she could see the lack of pattern. There were blocks and spires and tubes, considerable fine structure, very spread out. As an artistic whole . . . it wasn't whole.

Jennifer said, "Cities do grow this way, if there's no street plan. But in space? That's *dangerous.*"

"Dangerous," her pup said emphatically. Freddy's pup peeked out of his arms and nodded wisely.

Glenda Ruth called, "Victoria?"

"Something's happening," Terry Kakumi said.

Light flashed here, there. A chunk of Pandemonium City broke free, 6 percent or 8 percent of the whole; rotated to use its section of mirror as a shield, and pulled away. Ruby light sputtered at it, belatedly.

"Civil war, maybe. Maybe a lifeboat running away from us. I don't think they see Captor Fleet as friends."

"Yeah, Terry. Maybe it's how Motie cities breed? But whose city? *Victoria?*" No answer came. Glenda Ruth said, "Likely she's asleep." Moties needed their sleep, or at least Mediators did.

Terry said, "We've been decelerating for two hours now. Matching velocities. Glenda Ruth, we have to *see* this—" Terry's arm flashed up to block her eyes. A ruby glare filled the cabin. An instant later all screens were black.

"Langston Field," Terry said. "Ours. Don't think that place has one. Sorry. Are you okay?"

Freddy said, "Hell, we're under attack!"

"But by what?" Jennifer asked.

"Good question."

When nothing further happened, Terry presently cut bricks of basic protocarb for their breakfast. They watched the screen, but it remained dark.

Victoria emerged from the airlock. The Mediator skimmed along one of the big vines, picking red berries, then veered to join them. She asked, "Do you take chocolate for breakfast?"

Glenda Ruth spoke before Terry Kakumi could. "Sure. Freddy? Make it lukewarm, then we can heat ours. Victoria, does your Engineer say it's safe?"

"Yes."

Terry couldn't stand it. "We're pulling near a large structure. Is it your home?"

A moment's pause, then Victoria said, "No. Chocolate?"

Freddy didn't move until Glenda Ruth opened the cocoa and pushed it into his hands. No, he couldn't read minds, but she made eye contact and thought hard: *Yes, Freddy, Victoria's trying to distract us, yes, she's hiding something, Freddy love, but we want the lizard-raping chocolate!*

Freddy set to work, meticulously measuring powder, shaking it with boiled water, adding the basic protocarb product most crew called milk. He poured it into squeezers and handed one, lukewarm, to the Mediator. The others he set heating in the microwave.

Victoria sipped without waiting. Her eyes widened. "Strange. Good." She sipped again. "Good."

"This is the least of what the Empire can offer. More to the point is the meeting of unlike minds."

"And elbow space."

Terry's patience was short. "The city?"

"It's resources, Terry," Victoria said. "We will take them."

"Uh-huh. We want to observe the battle on-site," Terry Kakumi said. "If—"

"Not a battle, Terry. Pest control. No Master in there, no Mediators, not even Engineers."

"What are they, then? They're shooting at us."

"Watchmakers and . . . I don't know your word. Only animals.

288

Destructive small animals, dangerous when cornered. Use resources we need."

"Vermin," Glenda Ruth said.

"Thank you. Vermin. Yes, they're shooting, but we can protect ourselves. What is it you want?"

"I want to go in with you, with a camera." Terry took the bulb Glenda Ruth handed him, but didn't drink. She sipped the chocolate: a bit too hot, and that was good. Heat would kill what her fingertip had added to the cocoa powder.

"You would see our weapons in use. I know your nature, Terry Kakumi. Warrior-Engineer, as close as your generalist species comes. But able to talk well."

Freddy suppressed a smile; but Terry showed his teeth. "You wouldn't use your serious weapons for varmint control, Victoria. Whatever it is that has you so embarrassed, it's something we have to know. Later would be worse. Nasty surprises breed nasty surprises."

The screen cleared. Pandemonium glowed before its mirrors. *Cerberus*'s Watchmakers had pushed a probe through the Field.

Victoria sipped, and thought, and said, "I will ask Ozma."

Merlin nested in the forepart of the cabin. He was young, with clean white fur you ached to touch; he had never been female. He spent much of his time watching the humans and—if Glenda Ruth was indeed learning some basic captor language, if she'd correctly judged his body language—discussing them with Victoria, the Doctor, the Engineers, the Warriors. Masters asked questions and gave orders. They did not seem inclined to needless conversation, even with other Masters. But they did talk.

Ozma, an older and clearly superior Master to Merlin (parent?), lived somewhere out of sight beyond *Cerberus*'s big new airlock. Thence Victoria went. An hour later, the spidery Messenger scuttled through and summoned Merlin from his place in the forecabin.

Terry Kakumi slept curled in his couch like an egg in an egg cup. Glenda Ruth watched for dreams to chase themselves across his round features, but really, he was remarkably relaxed for a man who was about to enter mystery.

"He does that better than anyone I know," Freddy said. "If he

289

knows nothing is going to happen for twenty minutes, he's out like a light. I guess that's what they mean by *old campaigner*."

"You think it's a warrior's skill?"

"It never would have occurred to me before. Sauron, heh?"

The chaotic industrial complex was considerably closer now. Its shape had changed, had closed around the gap left by the one departing section, which was still in view a few kilometers away, under desultory thrust. There was motion on the surface, a doubly silent rustling: windows glinting (not many), small vehicles racing along wire tracks, mirrors rippling as they swung to block a laser spear, a sudden spray of . . . missiles? Tiny ships?

Sporadic ruby beams bathed *Cerberus* with no effect. Just once the entire mirror-sail complex focused white light with enough energy that the cameras had to be pulled in. Several minutes later the screen was glowing with just a touch of red heat. More minutes later the probe was out again, and Pandemonium showed almost unchanged.

"They ran out of power," Jennifer surmised. "What do you suppose is in there? Watchmakers and *what*?"

"Maybe nothing we know about," Glenda Ruth said. "Watchmakers alone might have built this. You saw Renner's recording: they ran riot through *MacArthur* and finally turned it into something alien."

A tube poked from near the center of the structure, and extended, longer and longer. Like a cannon. "Grab something," Jennifer said, and reached to tighten Terry's straps. His eyes opened; with a shrug he freed his arms and folded Jennifer into his chest.

The screen went dark. In the airlock Merlin snapped some command; every Motie form snatched for handholds. *Cerberus* torqued about them. In the screen was a red glow . . . orange, yellow . . . holding.

Victoria popped up beside Merlin, with several other Motie shapes behind her. They all held close to their handholds. A Messenger was towing one of their pressure suits.

"Terry, you may travel with us, unarmed," Victoria said. "You'll want hands for your camera anyway. We have restored it to the state you are accustomed to. Don't try to leave your escorts."

Terry took the camera from the Engineer. He made adjustments. One of the screens lit with a close view of Victoria, blurred, then sharper. Terry said, "How long?"

"Suit up now."

The Field was orange and cooling.

Terry and Freddy examined the suit, whispering. *Hecate*'s pressure suits had been confiscated and stowed on the other side of the oval airlock. They were hard suits, rigid pieces shaped to slide over one another, with a fishbowl helmet. Now green-gray sludge in a flaccid plastic bag rode the jet pack on the suit's back. The helmet's view had been expanded; the sunblind visor was gone; the helmet itself was no longer quite symmetrical.

"You trust it?"

"No choice, boss. I'm *bored*." Terry worked his way into the suit. Before he'd finished, the Engineer and three Watchmakers were already at work on him. Freddy and Jennifer smiled to watch. Glenda Ruth's stomach was a hard knot.

He could *die*.

Terry was zipped up when the alarms sounded again. He knew that one: *Anchor against attack!*

When the screen cleared, Pandemonium was very close. The pipe still protruded near the center of the complex, but it pointed askew of *Cerberus*. More conspicuously, the mirrors were gone . . . shredded, trailing outward in comet's configuration.

"It was a double attack on us," Terry said for his companions' benefit. "The laser cannon isn't maneuverable, but you had to take out the mirrors, too, right, Victoria?"

She waved it off. "Battle is no skill of mine."

Motion swarmed around the shreds of mirror. Glimmers and flashes: they began to re-form. The laser cannon jerked into sudden motion, too slow to catch *Cerberus* drifting around the city's edge. Others of Captor Fleet were moving into position.

"Come," Victoria said. She leapt for the airlock, and Terry, almost as agile, followed.

The Moties could hardly be unaware that they were showing him *Cerberus*'s Motie sections for the first time, and on record. Terry waved his camera where he would. He was not trying for detail, but rather looking for whatever would bear further investigation.

He didn't get much of that. He was in a tube that curved like a loop of intestine. Here a dark opening, here a bulge and an armed Warrior clinging to handholds, here a lighted opening and a first glimpse of an older Master. "Studying me. I'd better not stop," he said. "Victoria isn't."

The tube ended in a canister full of Warriors in armored pressure suits.

Victoria waved him in. The Warriors watched him, every one. "Forty armed and armored Warriors, no two weapons alike, no two suits alike, and . . . that one's pregnant, and that one." Distinct bulges in the armor, where a human heart would be. Terry let the camera hold on four others: "And I don't know what to make of those."

There was a couch just for him. It had an orthopedic look and a plenitude of straps. Terry gave the camera a good look before he strapped in. "Looks like an Engineer and Doctor tried to design this for a human spine. Let's see . . . Not bad. Not many humans build chairs this good."

The airlock was sealed and Victoria was gone.

"Three windows, one fore and one aft . . . whichever . . . and this. Considerate bastards." The amidships window was right before his face. One of the odd ones handed Terry a big folded umbrella, nearly weightless. "They've taken me for a Pom."

He was being judged. He chattered because of nerves.

The tradition of Terry Kakumi's family was never to dwell on tradition. Flexibility was a virtue. Landing on one's feet was a graceful thing to do. In anarchy and in war and in the Empire's peace, on Tanith and a score of other worlds, their numbers had grown. But he and they knew their ancestry.

The Kakumis were of Brenda Curtis's line.

Brenda Curtis had lived nearly four hundred years ago. She'd had six children of her own, and over two hundred had passed through her orphanage farm on their path to adulthood. They tended to intermarry because they understood each other.

Brenda Curtis had been a Sauron superman.

Current tales of the Sauron breeding centers were entirely imaginary. Terry had no idea what his ancestor had escaped from. Only the bald fact of her origin was known, and only to her children . . . and their fathers? Who could tell, now?

But twenty-four gene-tailored Motie Warriors were about to learn whether a child of Brenda Curtis could take care of himself.

He was not required to fight, Terry reminded himself. He would be judged by whether he survived.

The canister surged. Aft defined itself: the window was wreathed in pale flame. Terry's chair rotated; the others didn't. "They're pampering me, I think."

His eye and camera found a broad patch of black against the stars, and a scattering of blunt cylinders accelerating alongside his own. The black edged across the stars. The troopship struck it with a surge and an ominous crunch.

The troopship turned powerfully. Thrust distorted Terry's voice. "We've punched through the mirror. It's stronger than I expected. Maybe they reinforced it after *Cerberus*'s attack. I can see a ragged black hole—ooppshit!" Pellets blasted through the cabin.

Terry hadn't even had a chance to curl around himself. He took a moment to understand that he was alive, unhurt. The rest—

"Some Warriors are hit, but they're ignoring it." He let the camera watch Warriors place meteor patches in a tearing hurry. "The ship's decelerating hard. The hailstorm isn't over. Maybe you can hear the impacts, but the pellets aren't hitting the life support system anymore. We're thrusting, too. Something—" Terry grabbed handholds.

The ship smacked nozzles-first into a wall, with a booming recoil.

Terry's vision cleared quickly. One of the odd ones had already cut the ship's hull wide open, and the Warriors were pouring through. Terry searched for a strap release.

The four odd ones moved last.

Terry cut himself free and followed them out. "I'd bet anything that one's a Warrior-Doctor," he told his audience. "Those two are officers: better armor, and the widgetry they're carrying looks like communications, not weapons." The officers separated quickly. The last Motie was more compact, larger head, the hands more delicate. "That one looks like a cross between Warrior and Engineer. I'll follow it."

The starscape was gaudy, but the mirrors were brighter yet. Terry opened his silver umbrella . . . his laser shield.

Pandemonium was brilliantly backlit by the mirrors. The troops were jetting into a madman's maze. One and another Warrior flashed red, then puffed neon-red gas. Answering fire made actinic flares among the spires and blocks. Warrior troops swarmed from other directions. The ships of Captor Fleet were on all sides of Pandemonium.

Once Terry looked back. He reported, "The troopship's wrecked and nobody cares. They must be counting on their Warrior-Engineer to build them a way home. They'll guard him pretty carefully." But Terry was no longer sure of that. Pandemonium was very close.

They were approaching a windowless wall. The lasers that menaced them were suddenly unable to reach them, except for stragglers . . . such as Terry Kakumi, crouched behind his umbrella. A red dot played across it, and then he, too, was out of the lasers' view. He moved his umbrella-mirror and saw a bulging crater in the wall, and Captor troops diving through.

Too fast. He activated his backpack jets, then swore luridly for his audience and posterity. "Sorry. I'm getting low thrust. Watchmakers must have fixed my bloody jet pack." The crater came up, too fast, and he steered to miss the edge. "Must think I don't mass that much after all." He clutched his camera to his chest, pointing down into the dark.

*　　*　　*

A racer's crew must see what's going on. A warship is a different matter, and most of *Hecate*'s window space had disappeared . . . but not all.

So *Cerberus*'s human crew had three views of the battle. There was Freddy's telescope, and the window, and Terry's camera. Mostly they watched the feed from Terry's camera.

Thirty-four black-armored Warriors had plunged through a black wall, and the camera POV plunged after. Mirrorlight glowed through from behind, illuminating a honeycomb structure too small for humans or normal Moties. Ruby and green flared within the structure. An explosion ripped open a score of rooms. Then tiny forms in silver armor were jetting among the larger Warrior shapes, riding bullet-shaped rockets no larger than themselves, swerving at terrific accelerations, or just blasting through walls and Warriors and into space carrying dead passengers.

Terry's voice said, *"Watchmakers, I think."*

Jennifer said, "Right. It's like films from *MacArthur*."

294

Terry's voice ran on. *"They're using projectile weapons, and so are the Warriors: spray guns with tiny bullets."*

Jennifer clutched Freddy's arm and pointed through a window. Glenda Ruth didn't turn around. In a moment Freddy touched her shoulder and said, "Somebody's arrived, some other ship. Real Moties, not—vermin. We can see the ripples in the skin of *Cerberus*. Maybe your brother's arranged something."

"Great," Jennifer said. She started to say something to Glenda Ruth and fell silent.

"Glenda Ruth?" Freddy said. "Are you—"

"Not okay, Freddy. Not. He's so scared!"

"Traces of the original structure here, I think. Nickel-iron being shaped on site. This may have been an icy asteroid rather than a comet, closer to the sun before all these mirrors altered its orbit—"

"I never saw you like this. How do—"

"Can't you hear the fear in his voice? He could be *killed*. That's why Mediators can't stand battle. They're all trying to chew each other up, the Warriors and those little Hell beasts and whatever's out of sight and—*oh God!*" The view jerked and skewed, and Terry's voice stopped. Her hands clamped hard on Freddy's arm.

Freddy didn't speak. Glenda Ruth saw that her nails had drawn blood. Her voice rose into a hysterical whine. "They shot him!"

✳   ✳   ✳

This looked solid, some kind of support strut. Terry had dodged behind it when the bullets sprayed across him. He huddled behind it, reaching. Engineers and Watchmakers had been at work on his suit, and he could only hope—*there*, the pouch of meteor patches.

He pulled one open. His fingertip traced three tiny holes across his chest carapace, between his right nipple and right shoulder. They'd nearly closed themselves; the hiss had dwindled. The patch covered all three.

But the hiss continued, and he wondered how he would reach his back. The pain and wet were just over his shoulder blade.

The Warriors had gone on. A big Motie head poked around a partition (big was friendly), looked him over (officer?) and withdrew. Another such shape floated nearby, leaking fog through scores of tiny holes, its laser weapon spinning nearby. Maybe the little demons had gone after it deliberately. It was the Warrior-Engineer.

"Doctors probably aren't intelligent." Terry had forgotten his audience; he was talking to himself. "Probably. One to treat any Class, but none to treat a human. Who's going to treat me? Three bullets through my right lung."

With his fingers on the edge of the second patch, he reached behind him, forced it past the pain, then rubbed his back across the support strut. The hiss stopped.

A cough would have worried him. He'd be coughing blood before this was over. Meanwhile, for his audience: "These were high-velocity slugs intended to penetrate armor. Fast but small. No tumble. No stopping power. They're for Watchmakers or something not much bigger. Infections aren't any danger out here. Ronald Reagan was shot through the lung with a bigger bullet than these, seventy years old in FDA-era medicine, and he went on to finish two terms as president of the United States of America." And Reagan hadn't had Brenda Curtis for an ancestor.

"I'm going for the gun," Terry said, and leapt. Turning, he snatched the Warrior-Engineer's laser rifle and impacted his feet against a wall, the camera and gun turned down. The wall shuddered, and his camera caught six silver shapes plunging through.

His gun caught them, too, in a spray of projectiles. There was no answering fire, only a twinkling of edged weapons. His tiny bullets were cutting them up good, but six had become twenty jumping in pursuit as Terry Kakumi's recoil and suit jets hurled him up through the crater hole. And now they were all bright in mirrorlight and starlight, and Terry held his camera on the swarm.

A fireball blasted out of Pandemonium, half behind an angular bulge. Terry didn't bother with it. The camera recorded the shock wave surging through the city.

His breathing was going ragged; he'd have to stop talking soon. But: "They don't fit the suits. There are slack parts. Six-limbed suits, Watchmaker suits, with one limb tied down, and—" He coughed and stopped trying. Let the camera speak for him.

They wore borrowed pressure suits with the lower left arm tied down. Half of them had used up their jets and jumped anyway. Animals. Others were fleeing the light; but three turned and made for Terry. He held the camera on them and slashed them with high-V pellets.

Nice. Two merely died, but one silver suit, filleted, puffed its occupant thrashing into space. They weren't Watchmakers at all. They were something nastier.

*   *   *

"I never saw . . ." Freddy peered at the display. "Victoria? What in Hell—" Victoria was missing. "Glenda Ruth? I've seen 'em before."

She didn't want to look. She made herself look and considered what she was seeing. She said, "The Zoo on Mote Prime," and watched them remembering.

Fourth floor: a Motie city, struck by disaster. Cars overturned and rusted in littered, broken streets. Aircraft had embedded their wreckage in the ruins of fire-scorched buildings. Weeds grew from cracks in the pavement. In the center of the picture was a sloping mound of rubble, and a hundred small black shapes darted and swarmed over it.

Every student at the Institute had studied that scene. The Motie cycle of boom and bust was so dependable that plants and animals had evolved specifically for ruined cities!

One had a pointed, ratlike face with wicked teeth. But it was not a rat. It had one membranous ear, and five limbs. The foremost limb on the right side was not a fifth paw; it was a long and agile arm, tipped with claws like hooked daggers.

"But those were quite different," Jennifer said. "Look, these are *all* hands, and longer, leaner. Freddy, can you summon up a copy of *What I Did on My Summer Vacation*? I think the skulls are bigger, too!"

"They're changed," Glenda Ruth said. "Evolution must have moved much faster for them. Shorter generations, bigger litters. Why not? Freddy, I've got to get Victoria."

Terry Kakumi's voice was much weakened. *"I don't know how to tell Warriors that I need medical help. Freddy, if you're still hearing me, s-s-s—"* Coughing.

Freddy nodded. He floated toward the airlock, slowly, hands visible for the Warrior on duty. When Freddy reached the lock, the Warrior put his gunpoint in Freddy's ribs.

Freddy put his head in the lock and yelled, "Victoria! Now! Terry's been shot! Do you hear me?"

A lopsided face wreathed in white fur confronted him. Freddy wondered if he was seeing Ozma. The Master spoke a word to the Warrior, who pointed its gun elsewhere. The Master turned full away and hiss-whistled.

Victoria came. Freddy explained rapidly; Victoria translated; the Master went away; so did Victoria. The Warrior reached, turned Freddy around, and pushed him back to the control center.

On-screen, a pair of Warriors had retrieved Terry. Freddy could glimpse them at the screen's edge, towing him. Voiceless, Terry pointed the camera to pick up:

A snowstorm of dead war rats, big as greyhounds and small as puppies, all armed with edged weapons, some armed with guns.

A factory, empty, scaled down. That looked to be a distillery; that, a smelter. Even in the asteroid mines of most systems, humans would align their furniture. Here boilerplate-bulky machines pointed off at all angles, leaving almost no waste space.

A sudden firefight receded as Terry's escorts made for safety. A Warrior's grenade opened a wall to space. War rats blew past them toward the stars. Warriors picked off the few in stolen suits.

Victoria was back. "Ozma has told the Chief, but—" She saw the screen. "That's better. Your friend was inside too many walls. Ozma has also summoned a hybrid who might help your friend, an interbreeding of Doctor and Master. We only have one."

Freddy nodded and said appropriate things. Glenda Ruth only watched. The camera didn't seem to be pointing at anything interesting anymore.

3
Chocolate

And there're a
hun-dred-mil-lion-oth-ers, like
all of you successfully if
delicately gelded (or spaded)
gentlemen (and ladies)

—e. e. cummings

When the Doctor-Master arrived, Freddy had anticipated him. He had library medical tapes already running. The long-fingered almost-Master watched for a few minutes, looked the three humans over, decided Freddy was the male, peeled him, and began comparing him to what he was seeing on the screen. The Anglic commentary ran at low volume while Victoria spoke a running translation into the fleshy trumpet of the Doctor's ear. She was frequently baffled.

The Doctor was a young male, Victoria told them. "Doctor Doolittle," Glenda Ruth named him, and saw Jennifer smile. Freddy's face remained a rictus of discomfort.

Glenda Ruth wondered why Captor Fleet had chosen to feed such a peculiarity when they were so obviously short of resources. As if they had known aliens were coming . . . known ten years ago. *Where the hell was Terry?*

Terry was alive, technically, when they brought him in nearly two hours later. A misshapen Warrior was pumping his rib cage, breathing for him. Glenda Ruth looked at him and gave up hope.

Doctor Doolittle spoke rapidly.

The Warrior slashed the front of Terry's suit and pulled him out. A pair of Watchmakers pulled a black pressure balloon open and fished out transparent tubes and a canister. The little Doctor-Master wrapped itself around Terry's head and shoulders, planted his ear on Terry's torso, and listened. Then it pulled his head far back and fed the tube into his nose.

Terry thrashed weakly. Red flowed down the tube. The Motie watched for a few minutes, then spoke. The Warrior had gone back to breathing for Terry, flexing his chest, on and on, without fatigue. The Watchmakers fished out a squeezebulb of clear fluid.

Glenda Ruth stopped watching. She couldn't stand it.

Freddy pulled his shorts on and left it at that; the Motie Doctor might need to compare again. He caught her eye as she turned away, and she knew another moment of dread.

"Glenda Ruth—"

She turned away as the strange doctor spoke softly to the Warriors.

Captor Fleet was at work beyond *Cerberus*'s windows. From all they could see, the War Rats and Watchmakers were no longer to be feared. Larger ships had moved in. Altered troopships and tinier ships yet moved in a cloud around Pandemonium. An Engineer with a crew of Watchmakers worked on one of the damaged troopships. Large Moties from time to time came out of the ruins with—things. Broken machinery. Tankage. Plastic bags.

Jennifer said, "Remember the battle? Just before we were captured? Just lasers, no projectiles. In Pandemonium the Warriors used bullets, but only inside walls. But the rats and brownies were shooting everywhere."

"Your point?"

"Well, Victoria keeps calling them animals. She especially likes the word *vermin*. Maybe because they don't care how much stuff they throw away, even if it can be recycled. That's what all those little ships are doing, chasing down stuff that got loose during the fight."

Glenda Ruth nodded. "Yeah. How's Terry?"

"Breathing on his own. I want a human doctor."

"Hang in there. Terry's tough."

Silence.

"I couldn't watch."

"I noticed," Jennifer said.

"You think he's not feeling anything, and you're almost right, he won't remember how bad it is. But his body, his nerves, he's *hurt*, Jennifer, and I can *feel* it. Oh, hell, don't you leave me, too!"

"Too?"

"Freddy saw me! He saw me turning away from Terry. Squeamish. I'm going to lose him, Jennifer!"

"Not if he watches you save our asses. But you're juggling priceless eggs in variable gravity, girl."

Glenda Ruth only nodded. She couldn't answer that at least they were right on schedule.

✳   ✳   ✳

"I hope you're not overly tired, sir," Chris Blaine said.

"Not yet, not in this gravity," Bury said. He looked across the room to Omar, who once again held Ali Baba. "Against all reason I find myself attracted to the pu—to Ali Baba. An unexpected pleasure. But I fear we are away from the comforts of *Sinbad* to no great purpose. Except, of course, to reassure our hosts." It was an awkward situation, made more so because no one wanted to talk about it. It was the one thing East India and Medina Traders agreed to completely: neither would allow the other to talk to Horace Bury alone. "They cling to me as to a talisman," Bury said.

"Or a credit card," Blaine said, and Bury glared.

The outer door opened and a thin, spidery shape entered. The Motie went to Omar and waited patiently as Omar and Eudoxus gathered around it, then chattered excitedly.

"Something important," Blaine said. He thumbed the microphone of his communicator. "Captain, an East India messenger just came in. Whatever it's saying has got both the Mediators listening hard."

"Could it be about *Hecate?*" Renner's voice asked.

"I don't—"

"Stand by one," Renner said.

"What?" Joyce demanded. "What's happening?" She edged closer to the Moties, pickup camera whirring softly.

"Rawlins has spotted a fleet," Renner said. "A big one, coming from in-system. Hyperbolic orbit, accelerating like they've got lots of power."

"Warships," Blaine said.

"Sure sounds like it," Renner said. "Don't know whose, but they're heading this way."

"Excellency, we have news," Omar said.

"Thank you."

"Excellency, the humans are all safe. One, the ship's engineer, was injured in a way that I do not quite understand, but I am assured it was through no fault of the Crimean Tartars, who have been persuaded of the value of their guests. One of my apprentices, very young and inexperienced but fluent in Anglic, has been accepted by the Tartars and will presently be allowed to speak with the humans." Omar beamed. "He will, of course, be pleased to invite a representative of our Medina Allies, as soon as one arrives."

"This is splendid news," Bury said. "We are in your debt. I wonder if we might prevail upon Medina's hospitality for one more favor."

"You have but to ask, presuming it is possible," Eudoxus said.

"A message," Bury said. "It would be well for all concerned if Lord Blaine were informed that his offspring are safe."

Eudoxus and Omar looked at each other. Ali Baba's attention remained fixed on Bury. "An interesting notion," Eudoxus said. "But one that presents considerable technical difficulties. Neither East India nor Medina controls Crazy Eddie's Sister. Nor do the Crimean Tartars. The Khanate now holds that point and even now gathers more warships to consolidate their hold. Their own, and others. We fear they have created a formidable alliance, one which may even now be growing."

"A combined action of Medina and East India might suffice to escort one ship to the Sister," Omar said. "But as East India has more ships in that area, our losses would be the greater. We would require compensation."

"I had in mind something simpler," Bury said. "Send a message through the Crazy Eddie point to Murcheson's Eye. Take one of your flimsy token ships. Wrap a transmitter in a thick layer of suitably ablative material with a mechanical device to turn it on once through. Let it broadcast its location. Message cubes inside should survive long enough to be retrieved."

"Simple mechanical device," Omar said.

"Jump shock is an experience previously described to us, which I have now twice experienced," Eudoxus said. "It is—formidable.

Excellency, I need hardly point out that the contents of a message to your blockade battle fleet will be of great interest to all of us. Will you summon that fleet here?"

"I think not," Bury said. "But surely it would be to our advantage to have those not inconsiderable resources at our disposal?" He looked significantly at the Motie Warriors. "And of course we will continue to enjoy your gracious hospitality as we negotiate."

Eudoxus and Omar exchanged looks, then Eudoxus began to speak, slowly and carefully, in the glottal language the Moties had been using to speak to their Masters. Both Masters replied, each to a Mediator, never to each other. The messenger was sent out. Two came back; they delivered messages to each of the Mediators. The Masters spoke quickly and curtly, the Mediators at greater length. The discussion continued for a long time as Joyce's pickup whirred.

Bury waited with a look of serene calm. Ali Baba aped his look, a study of serious concentration. Blaine reported developments to *Sinbad* and Renner.

Finally Eudoxus spoke. "It seems you are correct, Excellency. We may have need of your fleet. We count five fleets probably converging on us. One is from Byzantium. We have reports that the Masters of the Mote Beta moons, the group we have called the Persian Empire, are gathering a fleet. The Khanate has summoned allies to their aid in holding the Sister. There comes another large group from sunward."

"In other words, everyone who has warships is becoming involved," Joyce Trujillo said.

"Just so," Omar said. "And thus our Masters are agreed. The partnership between Medina and East India shall be renewed. When that is accomplished, it would be well to summon whatever resources your Empire can bring."

"Before they kill us all," Joyce said.

Omar bowed. "Just so."

Engineers had erected a screen around the area where Dr. Doolittle and his aides worked on Terry. Freddy was back there for ten hours, while Jennifer and Glenda Ruth waited alone. Finally he came out.

"I'll have to go back presently," he said. "They want my opinions. Mostly I don't know, but I can work the data retrieval system for Dr. Doolittle. It's mostly in charts. Some of it I have to read to him, with gestures. He learns fast, numbers he understands already. Got any coffee?"

Jennifer handed him a bulb. "I should heat that."

"Heat the next one. I'll drink this."

"All right." Jennifer put a bulb in the microwave and started it. "Freddy, I haven't heard Victoria back there?"

"She's been gone for hours. One of the others, I think the Engineer that's been . . . improving *Hecate,* came and got her, and that was the last I saw of her. Sometimes I talk into a mike and Dr. Doolittle listens to what has to be a translation, but I don't know who's on the other end." Freddy sipped the lukewarm coffee. "Good stuff. Thanks."

"When can I see him?" Jennifer's cry was more nearly a wail.

Freddy looked to Glenda Ruth.

Glenda Ruth dropped her pensive look and shuddered. "I think you should wait to be asked. Something odd is happening."

"I'm scared," Jennifer said. "We talked about—he grew up on Tanith, you know. Freddy, he will be all right!"

"If the Moties can manage it, he will be," Freddy said. "They're going all out. They have some instrument the size of a spatball racket that puts a three-D image of Terry's insides on our tri-vee screen. They've got him stabilized. Blood pressure has been the same for hours now."

＊　　＊　　＊

It had not been instantly obvious: the looming bulk of the Mosque had been a block of water ice permeated by tunnels when Sinbad docked. But Engineers had been at work, carving rooms out of the ice, insulating, decorating. The lounge, located just outside *Sinbad's* airlock, had been growing during the negotiations. Now there was a small kitchen, a wardrobe, and a half-completed mini-gym besides the conversation pit with Motie and human chairs and couches. Chris feared it would be the size of Serpens City before they accomplished anything.

Eudoxus spoke long and earnestly to the Master called Admiral Mustapha Pasha. From time to time Omar spoke to the East India

Master in the guttural language Chris Blaine had learned to recognize as the Motie trade koine. Ali Baba moved from Bury to Omar and back, but his attention was always on Bury.

Messengers went to and fro like big-headed, lopsided spider monkeys, beautiful only in their agility. Mediators and Masters took frequent rest periods and returned always together, sometimes with Motie pups. The Mediators were talking now, briskly, as if it hadn't all been talked to death long since.

Chris watched and listened and presently offered to speak for Joyce's pickup camera. Joyce tried to find an excuse to refuse and gave up almost instantly. "Thank you, Lieutenant Blaine," she said most courteously, and posed him in a corner of the new lounge.

So: scholar's pose, no sexual signals, and give her his best. "A pidgin is needed to bridge two languages because shadings and nuances and background assumptions don't work. You need it *whenever* nuances don't work. But Motie language is inflections and body language and even scent, and any of that might have to be dropped for a telephone, or pressure suits, or video with a bad connection. The weird thing is just how *easily* these Moties use what they can and drop everything else. It isn't just the flexibility of the trade language. They generally have to create a trade language on the spot." Chris saw goblin ears focused on him and wondered how much they would understand. How much *he* understood.

"We're watching a parallel here. Ali Baba, not yet at the age of reason, clearly understands the concept called Fyunch(click) in the Mote Prime language. We're watching him learn both Anglic and the new pidgin simultaneously, and in hours he has learned what a bright human child might pick up in days or weeks. Biological specialization at work. And of course we've seen that in the other specialties.

"We're learning a lot about Moties, and that's important."

"Can you say more about that, Lieutenant?" Joyce asked. Her tone was richly professional.

"We've no choice, this time," Chris said. "Blockades just aren't going to work. We'll have to learn to get along with the Moties—"

"One way or another," Joyce said, but her own pickup mike wasn't on. "Lieutenant—" She stopped.

Here came the paired messengers again. Chris watched them scamper along the chamber's multicolored rock, breaking stride and zigging into channels and depressions. He'd watched them several times, and this time he was sure: their fur changed color to match the rock. Piloerection was doing that, exposing different layers, but the effect hid them like chameleons. They reached their respective Masters, clung to their fur, and whispered briefly.

The Masters had one final exchange with their Mediators, and all four Mediators came to the human group.

"Excellency," Omar said. "I am pleased to inform you that Medina and East India are agreed, in principle and in all essential details." He bowed; his feet left the rock and returned when he straightened.

"This is pleasing," Bury said.

Eudoxus bowed, too. Nobody laughed. "We have agreed on our status and domains, but more important is that we have agreed about you. We tell you nothing new when we say our choices are limited, and our greatest asset is your friendship."

Bury nodded. "More pleasing still. We are honored to be your friends."

"Thank you," Omar said. "We perceive that even if we watch you compose the message you will send to your colleagues in the Crazy Eddie Squadron, we must still trust you to tell us its meaning. Before you send this message you will naturally wish to speak with crew aboard your ship, and it is pointless to detain you here. When your message is complete, East India will deliver it. A suitable ship is being readied."

This time Bury's smile was warm and genuine. "Our thanks. Your hospitality has been admirable, but perhaps my friends would be more comfortable aboard our own ship."

"There is one matter," Omar said. "My colleague at the Crimean Tartar fleet reports his own observation that all the humans aboard *Hecate* are alive, and only the engineer-warrior has been injured; but for reasons that the Crimean Tartar Mediator will neither explain nor discuss, he has not been permitted to speak with them. We have been promised that this will change soon.

Bury acknowledged with a nod.

Damned odd, Chris thought. Something has changed, something happened that the Tartars don't want us to know. What? But Eudoxus and Omar knew that as well as he did.

"Do you wish to return to your ship now?" Eudoxus asked.

Bury nodded gravely. "It would be convenient."

"Medina and East India have come to another agreement, Excellency," Omar said. "But one which requires your consent. With your permission, Ali Baba will become your companion. An apprentice. Of course he will spend only part of his time with you, as he must learn our languages and customs as well."

Bury bowed slightly. "I am flattered. I find him an agreeable companion. However, you will understand, there will be times when I must be alone with my friends."

"Of course, Excellency."

"Meanwhile, this is satisfactory. We go now to draft our messages. We will, of course, read and explain to you any message we compose."

"Thank you. We will provide you with an escort," Eudoxus said. "Joyce, your viewers may be interested in this base. If you would care to see more of it, I am available to conduct you on a tour. We'll have you back on *Sinbad* in, say, two hours?"

"Perhaps another time," Chris Blaine said. What did they have in mind? Nuances here, subtle, ominous.

Eudoxus spread her hands slightly. "There may be no other time when we are both free, but of course it will be as you wish."

"No, I want to go," Joyce said. "You can tell me about the message later when we finish the interview. Eudoxus, I'd love to see the rest of your base."

"Very good. Join us when you can, Joyce," Bury said affably.

Chris as a Navy officer knew that he didn't have Bury's authority. If Bury saw no way to stop her or them, how could Chris? He'd have to use persuasion—

Outmaneuvered. Joyce was gone, Eudoxus leading and a Warrior behind. Bury and Omar followed at a leisurely pace, chatting, Bury carrying Ali Baba. They left Chris and Cynthia to bring up the rear.

※　※　※

After fifteen hours in the hidden depths of *Cerberus*, Victoria arrowed through the airlock with the agility of a Messenger. Glenda Ruth was jolted.

"*Victoria?* Victoria, what are th—"

"We have to talk. Ambassadors are arriving."

"Ambassadors from where?"

"Second, from the kingdom that allies with your ships called *Sinbad* and *Atropos*, henceforth Medina Trading Company."

Jennifer smiled acknowledgment. "Medina—"

"Later," Victoria said. "The Medina ship will rendezvous here; Vermin City makes a convenient target. But the first is already aboard. He speaks for former allies of Medina, henceforth East India Trading Company. The two are now involved in a dominance dance. We must settle certain matters before he may see you. We've been verbal-dancing for some days."

Glenda Ruth looked at the screen that hid Terry and Doctor Doolittle. "Can we summon a human doctor?"

"He is in no more danger than you are," Victoria said. "How is it that one of our Engineers has turned male without first giving birth?"

"Oops," Jennifer said.

"And so has one of our Warriors," Victoria said, "and although Watchmakers are difficult to keep track of—"

"How do you feel?"

"We must settle this now. Have you brought alien death among us? *What* did you say, Glenda Ruth?"

"How do you *feel*, Victoria?"

The Mediator tasted the question, as if she found the flavor novel and fascinating. "I feel good. Motivated. The air is sweet, our food seems up to specs, my appetite—" Victoria suddenly reached between her legs. "Talk fast," she said. "For your lives."

"I have a recording to play for you."

BLAINE INSTITUTE REPORTS, Volume 26, Number 5, Imperial Library number ACX-7743DL-235910:26:5

Approaches to Stability of the Mote Civilization

Ishikara, Mary Anne; Dashievko, Ahmed; Grodnik, Vladimir I.; Lambert, George G.; Rikorsky, W. L.; and Talbot, Fletcher E.

"The C-L Symbiote."

Research reported in this document was funded by grants from the Imperial Ministry of Defense, the Imperial Select Commission for Governing Relations with Aliens, and the Blaine Foundation.

Summary

The Blaine Symbiote or C-L (Contraceptive-Longevity) worm is bio-engineered from a Motie benign parasitic organism similar to platy-helminths. The resulting C-L organism is a symbiote that lives in the Motie body and produces the same hormone that the male testes produce.

The original symbiotes were universally present in the intestinal tracts of all Moties studied. The first forms were detected in the Motie Engineer taken aboard *MacArthur*, but none of those specimens survived. The current C-L symbiote has been bred from a strain taken from the Motie known as Ivan. It is known to survive in Mediator castes, and there is no reason to suppose it will not thrive in all Motie castes.

In all Motie castes so far examined there has been one testis, and the documents brought by the Motie ambassadors, and the Moties themselves, do not contradict this. This testis normally withers. Hapgood et. al (1) have speculated that this withering is triggered in part by pheromones given off by a pregnant female, but it is known (see Ivanov and Spector, (2)) that the process is more complex than that.

Upon withering of the single testis, the Motie turns female. Pregnancy must follow soon after or the Motie sickens and dies, with symptoms not unlike vitamin deficiency. See Renner, K. (3), Fowler, S. (4), and Blaine and Blaine (5), as well as *The Report of the* MacArthur *Expedition* (6), for details. The process of giving birth excites cells in the birth canal, and more male testes form.

The C-L symbiote normally sites itself anywhere in the body cavity and does not wither. Present data indicate that several C-Ls have no more effect than one. It is believed that this is due to excretion of surplus hormone via Plumbing-Six, tentatively the kidney.

We have observed no signs that C-L will breed in a host Motie, undoubtedly due to inhibition by the hormone itself. Consequently C-L must be bred externally in an environment that provides sufficient fluid around them to flush the hormone.

Video Report (Reuters)

Blaine Institute Announces New Developments in Bioengineering
(Film clip: Lord and Lady Blaine, the Hon. Glenda Ruth Blaine, students at the Blaine Institute, and His Excellency the Ambassador from Mote Prime, announcing publication of results of bioengineering development.)

"Of course that record could have been made at any time," Victoria said.

"It has me in it."

"Or a very good double, Glenda Ruth. It would take much forethought to plan far in advance to deceive us into believing that a Mediator can survive this long—but your Empire has both means and motive."

"I'm in the pictures, too," Jennifer said.

"Yes. You would require two doubles and two surgical alterations of adults. Is this beyond your capability?"

Freddy's eyes wandered from the screen to Glenda Ruth to the screen . . . and he shook his head.

Victoria, watching him carefully, said, "Jock's survival surprised you, Freddy, when you learned of it from Jennifer and Glenda Ruth. With her training, could Glenda Ruth deceive you? And Jennifer?"

"It's not that. Think, Victoria. If that's not Jennifer and Glenda Ruth, then it's two actors just out of surgery who have to fool Motie Mediators, and know they've done it!"

Good, Freddy! "This game gives us no profit," Glenda Ruth said. "Victoria, you already feel better than you have in years! And your Engineer, and your Warrior, are they sick?"

"Is this reversible in fertile castes?" Victoria demanded.

"Probably. With difficulty, but very probably. Is the native parasite endemic to space civilizations?"

"If so, I do not know of it. It is no skill of mine. Would I be infected with a parasite and not know?"

"Why not? People often are," Freddy said.

"Even those who live in isolation? I see you believe so." The Motie paused, and whatever expressions Glenda Ruth had been able to read were replaced by a different mask. "I must think on this."

"Wait. *There.*" She could have remained silent—

Too late. Victoria turned. "What?"

"I don't *have* any better argument than *that.*" Glenda Ruth pointed. "On the screen, Victoria."

The busy spacecraft of Captor Fleet had torn away a tremendous strip of the city's skin. Pandemonium lay exposed, a hive of cells still sparking with defenses. Corpses floated away in a pestilential cloud of black dots. The ships pulled a square kilometer of transparent skin over the wound and moved inside to work. Nothing was to be lost.

"That's your past, a million years or more of your past. Breeding yourselves into a starving cannibal horde, then tearing your numbers down in blood. Vermin City. That's your future, forever, without us." Glenda Ruth waved at the screens. "It's Vermin City or the Crazy Eddie Worm."

4
Messages

Three may keep a secret, if two of them are dead.

—*Benjamin Franklin*, Poor Richard's Almanac

Chris, it's time," Kevin Renner said. "Tell me about you and Joyce."

Blaine looked from Renner to Horace Bury. No help there. *Sinbad's* lounge had grown larger yet; it seemed very large, and very empty.

"All right, Captain, we were sleeping together, so to speak, and then we weren't. I'm more worried about what the Moties might get out of her."

"So am I. Try again."

Chris Blaine saw no point in pretending to misunderstand. "I got to know her. I could see what she was looking for in me, in a man, and when I got some free time, I, hell. I let her see it. But when we reached MGC-R-31 and Motie ships came spitting out . . ." How to put this?

"She wanted you to keep your promises."

Chris gaped. "Well, but I never—"

The Captain said, "What she wants from a man is knowledge and power. That was what you let her see. But when Moties appeared, she wanted in on the action. You couldn't give her that. You couldn't even let her keep interrupting you while you were on duty. What else couldn't you give her?"

"Aw, hell. Captain, she wanted to know what my sister's bringing. I don't *know!* Not certainly, I only know what Dad and Mom, what the Institute, *wanted.*"

312

"Which is enough," Renner said.

"Well, no . . . well. That was the trouble. I couldn't tell her as much as I do know because the Mediators would read her. They'd be doing that now if she knew anything. Now she won't talk to me at all."

"Chris, you *did* make promises. You used body language and nuances and all the things Jock and Charlie taught you. You've got to be more careful of how you use people."

Chris's ears burned.

"If you told her anything, if she *learned* anything that the Moties shouldn't know, tell me now."

"Captain, she heard *you* talking about Crazy Eddie's worm. She was sure I must know all about it. There was nothing I could do to tell her different."

"She's a reporter. She must have met every brand of liar there is."

". . . Yeah. I thought it must be Mom's C-L worm. I didn't tell her that. Now she thinks I'm dirt. Yes, she's right, I lied to her. I had to."

Captain Renner studied him and presently sighed. "All right, Lieutenant. Now what the hell *else* is going on? What's your reading of this situation with the Crimean Tartars?"

"I think Omar is as confused as we are," Blaine said. "Glenda Ruth must have done something to shake them up."

"We may well be able to guess what it is," Bury said. "Which could leave her in some danger."

"Whether or not the worm works as advertised," Chris said.

"Yeah, I'd thought of that," Renner said. "But so far—"

"So far no harm has come to them," Bury said. "And time is very much on our side. The Empire, for all its divisions, remains a nearly unified force. We have no need to negotiate alliances to gain great strength. With the Moties it is not so."

"Horace, what will happen to the Moties?" Renner demanded. "What *should* happen to them?"

"I truly do not know."

"You'll pardon me, but you don't seem quite the fanatic you used to be."

"Kevin, how could I be? I see here a tragedy, a people not unlike my own, with few resources, divided against themselves."

313

"Finding the whole place shot through with Bury Mediators might have changed your perspective?"

"Don't miss the implication," Chris said. "They can swallow His Excellency's views and not choke. That tells us a lot about them."

"Yeah, but does it tell us enough? Horace, I can't believe you've changed that much."

"I bow to Allah's will. Kevin, the Empire barely had the resources to guard one gate, and that one through a sun. Shall it now have two blockade fleets, one to hold a volume of normal space? Perhaps, but at great cost, and for how long? Kevin, the Moties are no less a threat than ever, but our ability to contain them is not adequate to the task."

"So now what?"

Bury looked through the Mosque's picture window and made a face. Somewhere on the pale face of Base Six was Joyce Mei-Ling Trujillo, unreachable.

He said, "One day's work at a time. We are to compose a message, which the Moties will attempt to send for us. What shall we say?"

"Think we're secure here?" Renner asked.

Bury shrugged. "All of Nabil's skills were unable to detect listening devices. I do not believe the Moties can be so confident that they could plant a device with the *certainty* that we would not find it. If we found one, it would very much affect our relationship. Let us act as if there are no Moties listening, but not act as if we were certain of it."

"On that score, what happens when Ali Baba's with us?" Renner demanded.

"Then we are faithful allies of East India," Bury said. "Motie Mediators serve their own Masters."

Renner nodded. "Blaine. Message."

"A quick description of the situation, with all of the Alderson geometry data we have," Blaine said. "Including all that data from the Alexandria Library. That will make it a lot easier to get the Fleet in here. Of course there's not much chance it will happen. Admiral the Honorable Sir Harry Weigle. Sent out after Joyce Trujillo's first articles. Assigned to clean up the corruption, put some discipline back in the Crazy Eddie Squadron. He's doing a good job at that, but he's not big on disobeying orders."

"And his orders are to maintain the blockade," Renner said.

"Just so."

"What can we do to convince him?"

Blaine thought for a moment. "He'd have to be convinced that he had a higher duty than carrying out his orders."

"Could *you* persuade him?"

Chris thought that one over. "Possibly. I can't reach him. You can. So let's look at what he knows. The Alderson point back to New Cal has moved. So has the Jump to the Mote, and he'll know that, but he probably hasn't found it. It's dancing around down there inside a red giant star."

"*MacArthur* found it easily enough thirty years ago," Bury reminded them.

"Different geometry. No jittery new star to distort the path," Renner said. "Not that bloody easily, either. Trust me."

Blaine nodded. "*MacArthur* and *Lenin* were specially equipped and had some of the Empire's best scientists aboard, along with a top navigator. Even then it took them a while to find the old one. So. We're going to help him find the new Crazy Eddie point. That will start him off thinking right. We give him information that helps him in his mission."

Renner's nod prompted Blaine to continue: "The tricky thing is to be sure we don't ask him to violate orders. Such as letting anything get out of the star and through to New Cal."

"So if we ask him to listen before he shoots."

"He might do that," Blaine said. "It's worth a try."

✳   ✳   ✳

Eudoxus led her down and slantwise from the lounge. Vacuum gear waited in an alcove a hundred meters below the Mosque. Joyce was taken aback. This hadn't come from *Sinbad!*

Eudoxus was watching. That irritating smile . . . hah. Joyce recorded, "The Motie smile is rigid. It's always there. You don't *see* it on a Mediator unless she's not sending any other signal."

Joyce donned a skintight pressure suit (it felt funny, comfortable though), fishbowl helmet, thermal oversuit (lighter than she'd expected) and mirror cloak. They looked archaic: they almost matched Empire Navy specs of thirty years ago, altered to alien tastes.

"Comfortable?"

"Yes," she told Eudoxus. She was relieved. She'd thought they would have to return to the Mosque. The helmet would reveal her face for the pickup camera.

Two of the little Messengers joined them. The party returned to the tunnel as five puffy silver dolls. They passed through three doors of a massive airlock and out onto an icy surface.

Frozen hydrogen, she remembered: fluffy, loosely packed, not visibly different from water ice. Maybe crusted in water ice. How could you tell? She didn't feel the cold.

"These are handholds, all but the green and red," Eudoxus said. "Don't lose your grip, Joyce. The Base is under acceleration."

Joyce gripped a yellow-and-orange line. "Green and red?"

"Green is superconductor cables. Red is fuel." Eudoxus was already moving, jumping along the surface, the cable sliding through her hands. "And the big translucent tubes are for transport."

The gray ice curved sharply. The top of a dome showed beyond the curve. In another direction, the Mosque cradled *Sinbad*. A bright red spark looked over its shoulder: the Eye. In another, a violet horizon-glow that had to be the fusion motors pushing Inner Base Six.

Fabulous pictures! The kind of thing careers are founded on! She chuckled to herself. Chris Blaine's frantic look! *As if he'd told me anything to begin with. As if the Moties could read my mind . . . or my face. What could Eudoxus see, anyway? I'm a big silver pillow.*

But if Joyce could see the Motie smile . . . less irritating, now that she understood it . . . then Eudoxus could see *her* face, too.

Eudoxus was taking them away from the motors: forward. Joyce followed. The Warrior followed her, and the Messengers.

The cable split; they followed yellow. It led over a small dome. Moties looked up at Joyce through a glass bull's-eye and a forest of dark green moss: three Whites, a Warrior, a Messenger, some Watchmakers.

Eudoxus asked, "Joyce, what's with Horace Bury?"

"What do you mean?"

"Thirty years ago, he thought the Mote system was the way to get rich. He couldn't see enough of *anything*. Now he seems much calmer, less ambitious, more like a Keeper. But—"

Joyce was amused. "He was already older than a man can get without serious medical help. It's thirty years later."

"There's more. He flinches when a Warrior comes near. All right, so do you, I can understand that." Eudoxus had lost all trace of accent, Joyce realized suddenly. "But he flinches from Watchmakers. Even from the newborn, until he knows they are not Watchmakers."

"They blindside him. His eyes can't be all that—"

"No, Joyce, it's not their size. He likes the little Mediator pups, once he knew what they are."

Bury's attitude toward Moties was no secret within the Empire. Rather the opposite. "He has always been afraid of you," Joyce said. "Terrified, even. Since he returned from the first Mote expedition. But that's changing. I can see it."

"Why?"

Joyce thought it over. Bury's attitude toward Moties was no secret, but the cause of *MacArthur*'s death was a Navy secret; secret from the Moties, by order of the Privy Council. It was a good question, though. What was changing Horace Bury? Greed, probably. "There are still vast fortunes to be made. Power and influence, for Bury and his relatives."

Three dissimilar spacecraft nursed from red cables that dipped into the ice. Each ship was built as solidly as a safe. A transparent tube ringed the ships; canisters and Moties of several sizes flew along inside it.

Eudoxus didn't try to stop Joyce from circling the ships with her pickup camera running. Others—Chris, the Captain, Dr. Buckman—would understand more than she did. She pointed her pickup along the tube, watching the Moties fly. Warriors, four Engineers, a Messenger . . .

Eudoxus said, "We don't have to move this slowly, Joyce. The tube is faster and you would still have a view."

No accent, but an irritating richness, an overemphasis on consonants— *My voice!* Eudoxus spoke with Joyce Trujillo's voice, exactly as she sounded on video. "No, this is fine," she said. "I'm getting great pictures."

The Mediator led off. Aft, the glow of jets had faded to black sky.

Eudoxus stopped. Joyce and the Warrior caught up; Eudoxus

spoke briefly to the Warrior. Then her upper right arm pointed ahead and up. "There, Joyce, what do you see in the sky?"

Joyce followed the creature's long upper-right arm. "Just stars."

"The Warrior says he's spotted it, the locus of your friends."

"Do Warriors have good eyes?"

"Yes."

Joyce tapped at the pickup, instructing it to find and fix on the brightest spot in its field, narrow the field, zoom in. She raised it by its sleeve, aligned along Eudoxus's arm, and set it going.

The camera wriggled in its sleeve, gyros whirring. A wide field of stars showed on the monitor screen. There: crumpled tinsel reflecting dim sunlight, just bigger than a point. Joyce set the camera zooming. Structure began to show, crumpled mirrors, a beehive torn open, violet points that might be fusion torches or spacecraft.

"Do you have it? It's a nest of war rats and Watchmakers. It's being harvested by the Crimean Tartars.

"Now follow my finger down to the horizon. A scattering of blue points?"

Joyce shook her head. Again she worked with the pickup.

"I don't see it either, but Warriors can. That's a war fleet bearing down on the nest."

"Got it." It was as Eudoxus had said, a scattering of blue points and no more.

"Mostly Khanate ships. In four hours they will arrive at the rat nest, but in twenty minutes the Tartars will be running. It's being negotiated now. They'll rendezvous with Base Six as we pass, and they have your friends."

"Great! I should tell the Captain."

"We will do that," Eudoxus said.

"Good." Chris should have been here, she thought with satisfaction. A sudden thought. "Have the Tartars become your allies?" *And thus ours . . .*

"Perhaps. For the moment they are in mortal danger, and we offer them refuge. For the future—what is the future, Joyce? The question is not what place the Tartars have with Medina and East India, it is what place have Moties in the universe."

"I can't answer that."

"No, but you must have thought about it."

"Sure. A lot of people have." Interest in Moties flared and died and flared again through the Empire, and the latest news would cause the biggest flare of all. What to do about Moties would be the topic of discussion everywhere. The Humanity League. The Imperial Senate. The Navy League. The Imperial Traders Association. The editorial board of her own news syndicate. Little old ladies at tea parties.

She was beginning to notice the cold . . . or was it the dark? Her body wasn't cold, she was sweating with the exercise, but the black sky and gray ice pulled at her mind. They'd left the domes and ships behind.

Eudoxus bounced alongside her, talking, with the Warrior at the lead. "We've taken a great gamble, you know."

"Yes."

"If we could only understand one thing, we would feel far less at risk. Your superiors seem to expect . . . what shall we call our gathering of alliances? . . . expect the Medina Consortium to remain stable, ultimately to speak for all of Mote system. How can they expect that?"

"I don't know." The Motie was too distant: Joyce couldn't see her face. She wouldn't be able to see Joyce's either. But all discussions of Moties came down to the same thing: there was no central Motie government, and it didn't look as if there ever could be. How could there be stable relations with a caldron of Motie families? Even the real Genghis Khan hadn't been able to form a stable empire of Mongols. . . .

They'd reached a ring of domes wreathed in cables of all sizes and colors, with a great ship rising out of the center. In the minuscule gravity Joyce bounded to the crest of a dome and caught up a handhold line. Joyce considered herself to be hard and fit, but this was hard work . . . and the Warrior was alongside her in an instant, and here was Eudoxus, too. Didn't Moties get tired faster than humans?

Eudoxus spoke to the Warrior, who said little, and then switched to Anglic. "A Master's ship is bigger, to house an entourage, and is built for intelligence and communications and defense, and never for stealth. In battle a Master may be left alive for later negotiations."

"Uh-huh." Joyce was filming the huge ship, retractable antennae, the long cylinder that must be a weapon: ram tube, rocket magazine, laser, whatever.

"I have heard that your Empire prefers not to interfere with its member cultures, but sometimes it must. Is that our fate?"

"I don't know that, either, but it's got to be better than what you've been doing." Joyce was surprised at her own vehemence. *I sounded just like my father, and I never thought of myself as an Imperialist.*

"Joyce, we have a great deal more to see. Shall we take a tube?"

Fatigue made her irritable. "Eudoxus, they're too small. Anyway, why would that be easier? We'd still have to move!"

"No. Difference in air pressure moves us. To fit inside we must deflate our oversuits. Let the Messengers follow with them."

"Done."

❋   ❋   ❋

Victoria came into the humans' area of *Cerberus.* "Representatives of houses allied with your Empire await you," she said. "Gather your possessions. Particularly your trade goods. You will not be returning here, and we may not be able to save this ship."

The humans stared in astonishment. "What's happening?" Glenda Ruth demanded.

"The Khanate comes. We have formed an alliance with Medina Trading. Their representatives await you. They call themselves Mentor and Lord Byron and you must assure them that you have been well treated. I trust there will be no difficulty with that."

"That's not a problem," Freddy said. "And I can afford to lose *Hecate,* but just what's about to happen to us?"

For answer Victoria pointed to an image on the telescope screen. Vermin City continued to change, to dwindle . . . was rapidly melting away, Glenda Ruth saw, leaving long bulges . . . slender spacecraft emerging from the wreckage.

"Looks familiar," she said.

Freddy laughed. "They're oversize copies of *Hecate!*"

"You'll board the fastest of those. We're running away. Warriors will delay the Khanate as long as they can, others will try to save this ship and any others, but we will be matching velocities with your friends, who appear to be aboard a sizable traveling fortress."

"How fast will we be going?" Jennifer demanded.

Victoria frowned. "As swiftly as possible. Three gravities—Mote Prime gravities."

Mote Prime was a lighter world. Freddy said, "Call it two and a half standard gee. Terry—"

"Terry can't take that," Jennifer said.

"No. Victoria, thanks, but—"

"You will not save your friend by being captured by the Khanate," Victoria said. "And they might not be quite as understanding about the benefits of your cocoa. I am afraid I can leave you no choice here. Your friends will forgive us for leaving behind one human, wounded in activities he insisted on joining. They will not be so kind if we abandon you all. Come."

"I'm staying," Jennifer said. "Glenda Ruth, you and Freddy go. Victoria's right, you're important, and it won't matter how it happened, the Empire won't accept it if you're lost. But someone has to take care of Terry, and you can tell them I insisted. Pollyanna—"

"Stay with Jennifer," the Motie said. Her voice was Jennifer's accent but in a lower register.

"Whatever we do, it must be done quickly," Victoria warned. "A Khanate battle squadron approaches, and your friends are impatient to talk to you."

"Battle squadron. How reasonable will they be?" Glenda Ruth demanded. "Would they talk?"

"Mediators will always talk when there is not active fighting. Sometimes then. Whether the Mediator with this expedition can speak your language is another matter, of course. You will have Pollyanna to help."

"I will help you talk," the Mediator pup affirmed. Jennifer hugged her. She said, "You're not trying to talk me out of staying."

"I had hoped you would stay," Victoria said. "Your Terry might then survive until Medina can buy him back from the Khanate. Without your help I do not think so."

"I don't like this much," Freddy said. "Glenda Ruth?"

"Victoria, *how* will you leave them?"

Victoria chattered rapidly to a Warrior. The Warrior answered briefly. Victoria said, "We can leave you *Cerberus*, minus our own life support segments, and a Warrior pilot and motors to give half a gee . . . in fact, you should have *Hecate*'s motor of alien design, to indicate your nature. Jennifer, you might be overlooked, and if so, Medina will find you. I regret we cannot allow Dr. Doolittle to accompany you."

"What are their chances of escape?" Glenda Ruth persisted.

"Not good," Freddy said. "Stealthing is fine, but *Cerberus* needs thrust to get away from here, and they'll see that."

Victoria shrugged. "This is likely. If we delay much longer, none of this will matter. I will also leave recordings in the trade language, informing the Khanate that they have a valuable possession which those more powerful than the Khans will wish to buy back, but only if intact."

"Go on, Glenda Ruth," Jennifer said. "It's the best we're going to get."

"Come," said the Mediator. "Come meet the representatives of your friends."

✳ ✳ ✳

The Warrior led; then Joyce, then Eudoxus, all in skintights and helmets. Air pressure wafted them down the tube. Their insulating oversuits followed, collapsed, with two little Messengers to tend them.

Eudoxus said, "Bury's Fyunch(click) brought us tales of swimming. Is it like this?"

"A little," Joyce said. The currents kept her from brushing the sides. She drifted like seaweed, in a dead man's float.

An industrial complex wafted by, brightly lighted. Where the tube curved, she could see Watchmakers following her, a swarm of them bracketed by two Engineers.

"Crazy Eddie always misreads the turning of the cycles," Eudoxus said. "Crazy Eddie tries to arrest the turning, to make a civilization that will last for all time. What do humans think of Crazy Eddie, Joyce?"

"I suppose we think he's crazy." Silence prompted her to continue, "Not all that crazy, though. Our cycles of history, they go up and down but generally up. A spiral. We don't just go round and round. We learn."

"So you use the term without embarrassment. Crazy Eddie point . . . our term, yes, but you don't flinch from it. Crazy Eddie Squadron. Joyce, you've studied the Crazy Eddie Squadron?"

"My views are on record, Eudoxus, and you can't have the records. Navy matters." How the hell had Eudoxus learned that? Was there a hole Chris hadn't plugged? So to speak.

322

"We are allies. It seems unfair that we cannot know what you have told every casual inhabitant of the Empire."

"Unfair. Yes, it is, but it's still not my decision, Eudoxus. I took an oath."

The Motie said, "Yes, of course. Joyce, nobody loves blockade duty. The Squadron is crumbling, isn't it? The opening of the Sister is not a bad thing for you, but how can your companions expect to create stability here?"

Good question, and Joyce didn't know. The Empire had *something*, though. Something to do with the Institute, Joyce thought, and the Crazy Eddie Worm. Joyce knew only the name, and even that she must keep secret. *Why?* But the Mediator was behind her; her view was of Joyce's feet, not her face.

"Mote Prime sent you ambassadors," Eudoxus said. "A Keeper and two Mediators. You've had thirty years to study them. We've studied billions of ourselves for millions of years. What can you possibly have learned that we could not?"

"Eudoxus, I am not supposed to talk about this."

"The Imperials have told you very little, haven't they, Joyce? As if they didn't trust you to keep secrets."

"That's right. So there's not much point in this, is there?"

"Yet you are a public opinion specialist. You are heard throughout the Empire. Joyce, it is clear that your Empire is united as the Moties have never been, but not every family is obedient. Has your Empire the strength to exterminate us? Is this your real plan?"

"No, we don't plan that!"

"Are you so sure? No secret weapons? Ah, but they would not tell you. Joyce, look ahead and up."

The ball of crumpled tinsel was a larger point among the stars. Violet sparks were rising from it. Joyce trained her pickup and spoke for continuity. "Spacecraft are rising to meet us, bringing the human hostages captured by the group our Motie allies call the Crimean Tartars. The humans are Glenda Ruth Fowler Blaine. The Hon. Frederick Townsend. Jennifer Banda of the Blaine Institute. And an engineer crewman, Terry Kakumi. . . . Eudoxus, when can we talk to them? To the people who were in that ship? Did they get any pictures of the war rats? What are war rats?"

"In due time. When your friends arrive. For now—we should show you the motors."

Joyce looked up. The crumpled ball and its sparks were setting, and the violet-white glow of Base Six's motors was coming into view ahead. "Yes," said Joyce. "Please."

Eudoxus spoke into his hand. Mediators ruled all transport, Joyce remembered. And sometimes sat in judgment. . . . The wind that moved them almost died; then the tube branched, and pressure wafted them left.

"We knew that Glenda Ruth Blaine must be daughter to Sally Fowler and Roderick Blaine, and the Honorable Frederick Townsend son to another powerful master, but we don't know of a Blaine Institute."

"It's a school, but it does research."

"I thought you called such organizations 'universities.' "

"Yes, that's right, the Blaine Institute is like a university, it was deliberately located next to a university, but universities study everything. The Blaine Institute has only one purpose. To study Moties."

"Ah. Was this Institute responsible for the blockade?"

"No, that was Imperial policy. Although Lord and Lady Blaine helped set the policy even as they were founding the Institute. And Lady Blaine's uncle. But the blockade was proclaimed before I was born." Instead of an extermination fleet. The Mediator still couldn't see her face: right. "You can't imagine the impact you made on the Empire. Just your existence."

"Do you have children?"

"No. Not yet."

"You will have?"

"Let's leave it at 'not yet.' "

"Neither do I, of course. But I'll *see* your Motie impact on the Empire and *raise* you not getting pregnant until you happen to feel like it!"

Jennifer's ears felt scorched.

Eudoxus said, "Never mind. I might guess the Empire's reaction, knowing that we've solved *your* inbuilt reason for making war and then invented our own."

"How so?"

"Mediators prevent misunderstanding," Eudoxus said. "Moties will fight for territory and power and resources for their descendants, but if there's a way to avoid fighting, the Mediators will find it. You fight because messages are badly worded."

"Oh. And invented your own, yes, of course. If you don't get pregnant, you die. And Mediators don't get pregnant." I should just shut my face and give it a vacation, Joyce thought.

"The Institute, is it considered a success?"

"It gets the best minds in the Empire."

"Yes. But such structures always freeze up, don't they? They get old and can't react anymore, like the Blockade Fleet."

"Oh . . . generally." But she hadn't heard that about Blaine Institute. "Ossified is the word you want."

"So they study Moties and nothing else, and they have not yet become ossified. Will they study ways to kill Moties?"

"Don't be absurd! You've met Chris Blaine. His parents own the Institute. What do you think?"

"I think he has secrets, some terrible," Eudoxus said.

So do I. Maybe enough of this. But . . . she can't see my face, so what is she reading?

But I'm a reporter, I'm as good at controlling my face as any politico or poker player. But they put me in a silver balloon and let me get complacent and then snaked me out of it, and who ever taught me to control the muscles in my damn feet?

✳   ✳   ✳

"Joyce, it's important. What did you tell them?" Renner asked.

"Nothing at all," she said, and laughed. "Look, you don't have to keep asking. I taped it all. Here."

"Thanks. Blaine, let's look at this."

The voices were identical: Joyce Trujillo's voice, recognizable Empire-wide. The only way to tell them apart was through context. This was the alien speaking: "I think he has secrets, some terrible."

"What do you think she meant?" Renner asked.

Chris Blaine frowned. "I don't know. But notice the context, just after Eudoxus asked if the Institute was set up to find ways to kill Moties. If I'm reading Eudoxus right—pity the camera wasn't on her much—"

"How could it have been?"

"I know, Joyce. Now, if I read this right, Eudoxus is convinced that Joyce doesn't believe the Institute is for making Moties extinct, but that hasn't laid all suspicions to rest."

"Anything we can do about that?"

325

"I'll think on it. I have some general recordings about the Institute, mostly promo stuff, but they might help. We'll give them to Eudoxus."

"Better review them first."

"Sir, I did already. There's nothing about the Empire they won't already know. I was holding off in case I might be wrong, but now . . ."

"Okay. Sounds reasonable. Anything else?"

"Only the message to Weigle. It should go while East India is still willing and able to deliver it."

✳   ✳   ✳

"That should do it," Chris Blaine said. He held a message cube. "All the Alderson data we can find including the stuff from Alexandria. The Admiral shouldn't have any trouble finding the new Crazy Eddie point. Now it's your turn, Captain. Remember, heavy on duty. You can't lay that on too thick."

Renner took the cube. "Thanks. I'll be a while, and I have to be alone." He waited until the others had left, then inserted the cube into the recorder and began to dictate.

"And that's the situation as we see it," he concluded. "The Moties are ripe for an alliance. It's dicey, but there may never be a better chance.

"I don't believe we have the power to exterminate the Moties. There are too many of them, too many independent families, scattered through the rocks and the moons and the comets.

"We can't exterminate them, and we never expected to maintain the blockade forever, and now we'd need two blockades. My assessment is that we'd do better to try for an alliance using the Crazy Eddie Worm to help control Motie breeding. Of course we don't know what the Motie reaction to the worm will be, and we won't know for another forty or fifty hours. I don't think I should wait that long. Right now Medina Trading and East India are cooperating to send this, and they have the means to get the message through. God knows what can happen in fifty hours.

"Kevin J. Renner, Captain, Imperial Navy Intelligence; Acting Commodore, Second Mote Expedition. Authentication follows."

The authentication was more trouble than the message had been. Renner stretched a metallic band around his forehead and attached

326

its cable to a small hand-held computer. Then he plugged in earphones and leaned back to relax.

"Hi," a contralto voice said. "Your name?"

"Kevin James Renner."

"Do you eat live snails?"

"I'll eat anything."

"Where were you born?"

"Dionysius."

"Are you alone?"

"Quite alone."

"What's the word?"

"Hollyhocks."

"Are you sure?"

"Sure I'm sure, you stupid machine."

"Let's try it again. What's the word?"

"Hollyhocks."

"Sure it's not rosebuds?"

"Hollyhocks."

"My instructions are to be certain you are calm and uncoerced."

"Damn it, *I am calm and uncoerced.*"

"Right. If you'll attach me to the message cube recorder . . ."

"You're on."

"Stand by. This may take a while."

Renner waited as seven minutes went by.

"Done. You may disconnect."

Renner took out the message cube. It was encrypted in a code that could only be read by an admiral or at a Navy Sector Headquarters; and the authentication code identified it as coming from a very senior official of Imperial Naval Intelligence. The only way to get that authentication was to convince the encrypting device that you really wanted it done. Any deviation from the script would have produced an authentication sequence that proclaimed the sender was under duress or wasn't the proper sender. Or so Renner had been told.

Renner punched the intercom. "Okay, Blaine, here it is. You sure the Moties can manage to duplicate this at long range?" If the Moties couldn't do that, the cube itself would have to be sent, and that would take days, if it got through at all.

"They're sure. We sent the details of the message cube system to the East India group at the Crazy Eddie point. They've built a recording device. Now we send the encrypted message, they record it onto a cube, and pop it through."

"Fine."

"Now what?" Joyce asked.

"Now we wait," Renner said. "For the Tartars."

5

The Guns of Medina Mosque

Diplomacy is the art of saying "Nice doggie" whilst you find a rock.

—Attributed to Talleyrand

A day or three ago, the Great Hall must have been solid ice. This day it occupied half the volume of the Mosque. It was lavishly decorated: Renner recognized a modified illustration from *A Thousand Nights and a Night*. Tapestries with fantastic decorations: a djinn, a roc, Baghdad as it might have been in the twelfth century. The carpets were soft with unmistakably Saracen designs. There were also certain anachronisms: the big viewscreen on one wall, the opposite wall a vast curve of glass looking out onto the ice.

The screen showed another region of Inner Base Six, and a ship dropping through the iceball's black Langston Field sky.

Horace Bury paced, looking very relaxed, bobbing as if underwater in the low gravity of Base Six. He hadn't noticed that Joyce's pickup camera was on him. Ali Baba bobbed along beside him, a perfect half-scale mime.

It was a funny sight. Kevin Renner saw that, but he found that command has its own emotions: he had to look beyond humor, and beyond calling attention to humor. There was a lot at stake here, and the responsibility fell squarely on Kevin Renner. *And that's what Captain Blaine felt, back at the Mote. That, and his reluctant tolerance for the smartass Sailing Master....*

"Almost neutral territory," Eudoxus said. "Our base, but your part of it, a place where Commodore Renner may come and yet retain control of his ship. Excellency, this is to be a formal reception. Are you certain you will not invite any of the crew of *Atropos*? To act as entourage. Warriors, for instance."

"Is that really important?" Renner asked.

"It is important," Horace Bury said. "But it is also important that all Motie groups understand us as we begin to understand you. Moties and humans must modify their customs when they meet. Let us begin now."

Eudoxus bowed. "As you wish."

Chris Blaine watched the alien ship descend. "Looks like a racing yacht," Blaine said. "But bigger."

Eudoxus said, "I had wondered at the strange design. The Crimean Tartars must have taken considerable resources from the vermin city."

And your Engineers will already be examining everything about that ship, Renner thought. *Moties aren't just innovative, they're adaptive.*

The ship docked in a pattern of concentric scarlet circles, onto a platform that began to descend at once. As it sank from sight, Eudoxus listened to a handset. "They're down. Do you wish to see your friends disembark?"

"Of course," Renner said. Bury and Ali Baba turned as one.

The screen blinked, then showed an opening airlock. A Warrior emerged into the pressurized reception lock, then a Mediator with an odd marking pattern. Glenda Ruth Blaine followed, clutching a sealed carrying case to her chest. After her came a young man in space coveralls who carried a Mediator pup in his arms. Two Warriors and a young Master followed them.

"Only two." Bury and Ali Baba were bristling. "We had understood there were four?"

"Yes, Excellency. We are only now learning the details. One of the four insisted on filming the cleansing of Vermin City. He was hurt. His wounds were serious, life threatening. The Tartars have not ceased to tell us of the resources expended in saving his life.

"But when the Khanate ships were seen to be attacking, all realized that Terry Kakumi would not survive the acceleration required to escape. He was cast adrift. His female companion insisted on accompanying him."

"And thereby hangs a tale," Renner said. He looked at Blaine and got a slight nod. "And what has happened to them since then?"

"I have not been told," Eudoxus said.

The handset squawked. Eudoxus listened for a moment. "Your friends seem to be of two minds. They wish to see you immediately, but they are concerned that their appearance might lead you to suspect they have not been well treated."

"Tell 'em we've already seen them on-screen," Renner said. "With war fleets coming at us from all directions I don't think we have a lot of time to waste washing up. Eudoxus, can Medina Trading send someone to rescue the other humans?"

"I will learn."

" 'Adrift,' you said," Joyce noted.

Eudoxus shrugged. "What better word?"

Blaine said, "Cast loose at low thrust, concealed but with a transponder beacon that will answer if pulsed with the right signals. Right?"

"I have not been told, but I assume so. We will do what we can to rescue them, but I suspect we must simply buy them from the Khanate."

"Buy how?" Joyce demanded.

"A matter for negotiation," Eudoxus said. "And not yet."

Renner prompted her. "Why not yet?"

"Kevin, the Khanate Axis cannot themselves know what they will want. You have seen the pattern of their movement as well as I." She gestured toward the screen, which now showed points of light clustered around nothing whatever. "They wished to control the Sister. This they attained. Now they assemble their strength so that they can send through their war fleet. They wish to escape into your Empire, as we would have done if you had not been present to meet us, but the Khanate will not talk or bargain first. They have this advantage over us: they know that ships went through and lived to return, something that no ship ever did before. Now they believe that surprise is their best weapon, victory their best bargaining tool. Is it not clear to you?"

Blaine nodded. "Clear enough."

"But that's horrible!" Joyce said. "Captain Renner, shouldn't you be doing something?"

Renner's eyes fell on her without interest; wandered back to the screen. Mediators ruled information flow; this would be as good as anything *Atropos* could tell him. The Khanate was gathering. They would involve all the allies they could persuade to break free into the wide universe: every family within a billion miles, likely, excepting those who flew Medina's banner. All ready to flash through to MGC-R-31, where Balasingham waited with *Agamemnon* and whatever reinforcements might have reached him. If they broke past *Agamemnon*, they would be loose in the Empire.

The Khanate Axis. How would they work it? By long odds, they would soon have Jennifer Banda to describe *Agamemnon* and MGC-R-31 as she'd last seen them. Terry Kakumi might be used to persuade her. By now one of their allies might have brought a Bury Fyunch(click) to read her face. Jennifer could translate, could convey surrender terms . . . in either direction.

But what was Commodore Renner to do about it? He must talk to Glenda Ruth, soon. Was *Agamemnon* holding the MGC-R-31 system alone, or did other Navy ships arrive before *Hecate* came through? What had she done with the C-L worm? "Eudoxus . . . "

"We will fight, of course," Eudoxus said. "All of the strength of East India and Medina assembles. We have sent messages to Byzantium, and their war fleets are gathering. The Khanate Axis will send their Warriors through to fight whatever they find on the far side of the Sister, but they must leave their Masters safe on this side. Those ships we can attack, but we must know what contributions you humans can make."

"War for the stars," Joyce said, awed.

"Here are your friends," Eudoxus said. The outer door of the Great Hall opened. It had been made wide, so that a number could come through it at once.

Warriors streamed in and took places along the walls. They were followed by Admiral Mustapha Pasha, Master of Base Six. Behind that group came new, strange Moties, and two humans; and with them were other Mediators, a small group of Warriors who huddled around two Masters, and a scattering of other forms including a Doctor.

That must be Freddy Townsend, with a Mediator pup riding his shoulder. The box in Glenda Ruth's arms threw her balance off. She settled it and stepped away. She was radiating joy like a summer day as she turned to her brother; but Lieutenant Blaine was entirely absorbed by the Moties.

Eudoxus spoke slowly, formally, in the trade language. The visiting Mediator answered. "Victoria," Glenda Ruth said, and waved, but Victoria didn't notice. East India spoke. Blaine was trying to follow it, and so was Glenda Ruth . . . and then brother and sister grimaced at each other because all the Mediators were talking faster and faster. Twisted bodies shifted, danced. Renner was awed. Before his eyes and Joyce's camera, they were turning the skeletal trade koine into a language. The Mediators broke off to speak to the Masters, then resumed their gabble. The Masters spoke, first one of the newcomers, then Admiral Mustapha.

And every Warrior jumped straight into the air.

Glenda Ruth screamed, "No, no, it's a gun, Victoria! You point it!"

The Warriors ringed the ceiling and their weapons ringed the humans. They could fire, now, without hitting each other. Two Engineers and a dozen Watchmakers scrambled forward. Victoria shouted at the Masters, at the other Mediators. They gabbled, while Watchmakers surrounded Glenda Ruth's box and began spraying it with plastic foam. Every Motie Warrior held a weapon, and every weapon was pointed at a human.

Kevin hadn't gone for his pistol, and neither had anyone else. His only real weapon was *Atropos*. If the Masters had cut his communications, then *Atropos* would be on alert status *now*.

"I presume there is an explanation for this rather startling behavior," Bury said.

"Your Crazy Eddie Worm," Eudoxus said. "A boon to Mediators! But terrible for Masters. You knew of it and did not tell us. Joyce knew and would not tell us."

Joyce drew in a breath to speak but held it in. Her neck and cheeks flushed pink, then red.

"Our natural suspicion," Eudoxus continued, apparently to all of them, "is that your altered parasite is a means of making Motie life extinct. You would not consider this suggestion insane, would you, knowing what Victoria has just told us? Kevin, you did not instantly describe the Crazy Eddie Worm. You were much disturbed when you knew that you were going not to Mote Prime, where winds might distribute your parasite, but to a domain where spacecraft must bring the worm to an infinity of closed environments—I see my point is made. So. I fear some tension remains, Excellency, until we again reach understanding. It is, after all, not too late for us to join forces with the Khanate."

"Endless war," Chris Blaine said.

"Preferable to extinction. Glenda Ruth, what did you mean—"

She cried, "But it's for you! It doesn't reproduce except under controlled conditions. You can *point* it, like a gun. You win a battle, you don't have to kill your enemies. You give them the Crazy Eddie Worm instead, and now they're Keepers, conservative—"

Eudoxus waved her silent. He spoke rapidly to Victoria. They gabbled. A Master spoke. Eudoxus asked Glenda Ruth, "Do you wish to change anything you told Victoria? . . . So. Lieutenant Blaine, tell me what you know of this. Quickly."

"His Excellency knows more than I do."

"Excellency?" The tone held respect; but the Warriors clung to the roof, their weapons tracking back and forth among the humans.

Quietly, calmly, moving slowly so as not to startle any Warrior, Bury had linked himself to Nabil's medical package. The displays were alive and the lines they drew were turning jagged. Bury wasn't as calm as he looked. Ali Baba regarded the displays with interest.

Bury said, "I know this. One of King Peter's Mediators was alive when I was last on Sparta. Less than a Mote year ago. Alive. I was told that this was due to the action of a genetically altered parasite."

"And you believe this?" Omar asked. "Truly, Excellency?"

"Certainly those who told me believed it, as do all those here. Yes. I believe."

"You fear Moties," Eudoxus said. "The Bury who came to Mote Prime did not, but you do. When we first spoke to you, I was surprised to see that. Yet since you came here, that, too, has changed. What has happened to change you, you of all humans, not once but twice? Speak truth, Excellency."

"The first is a Navy secret," Bury said.

Enough. Kevin Renner said, "Watchmakers destroyed the battleship *MacArthur*. Civilians had to be evacuated by lines across vacuum to *Lenin*. Horace was almost there when he realized that the man crawling up behind him was a pressure suit full of Watchmakers. He fought them off with his suitcase and his oxygen tank. Okay, Horace?"

"No longer secret, then." The lines were turning choppy. "There was worse. I had intended to bring Watchmakers to the Empire,

334

to aid in building my fortune. Then I saw the danger. The war of all against all, and I nearly caused it."

"We have pictures to top that," Glenda Ruth said. "Wait'll you see Vermin City, Your Excellency!"

Bury looked at her. "Wonderful." To Eudoxus: "You must understand, I enjoy the company of Mediators. Even half-grown Mediators, yes, Ali Baba?"

"Certainly, Excellency—"

"And Watchmakers would be fantastically useful, fantastically valuable in Empire space. But that was not to be. Your society— is much like that of the Arabs before the Prophet. Infanticide. Genocide. No other way to control your population. And after the Prophet, we burst forth to conquer, but we had not learned how to live with other cultures." Bury shrugged. "Nor had others learned to live with us, and this was still true when I last visited your star system."

"And you have learned now?" Eudoxus demanded.

"Yes. We have learned, the Empire has learned. The Arabs have found a place within the Empire. We are not yet as honored as we would wish to be, but we have a place that is not without honor. We are free to govern ourselves, and we can travel among the Imperial planets. As you see that I do."

"You are tolerated."

"No, Eudoxus, we are accepted. Not by all, of course, but by enough, and that, too, will change."

"And you see us in that role?"

"Provided that you accept our terms."

Eudoxus turned and spoke slowly in the newly adapted trade language. Admiral Mustapha spoke briefly. Eudoxus turned. The Warriors had not moved.

"Your terms?" Eudoxus demanded.

Bury smiled. "Of course we cannot speak for the Empire, but I know what those terms will be. First, there is to be one Motie government. That government will see that no Motie leaves the Mote system without carrying the stabilizing parasite. Within the Mote system—well, I suspect that is all negotiable. Kevin, would you not agree?"

"Mmm . . . yes. The notion is generally that you keep your own house clean. Mote system is to be one government, kept that way by Mote citizenry. We've had at least one piece of luck, Eudoxus.

Mote Prime is . . . eighty, ninety percent of your population? But they're not a consideration because Medina Concordance can keep them bottled up. That is, if you can hold the rest of the system in your gripping hand."

A Master spoke. Six Watchmakers finally ceased spraying foam plastic on a sphere that was now two meters across. Moties resumed their rapid conversation. Abruptly Eudoxus turned to Renner. "The worm is the heart of your strategy. Must we examine it?"

"We have holograms," Glenda Ruth said. "Victoria has records, too. Why not save it? You don't have anyone to use it on yet."

"Victoria tells us different, Glenda Ruth, and I'm amazed that you could forget. For Mediators, the Crazy Eddie Worm extends our life span at least twenty years. We're being very careful not to let that sway our judgment."

"Judgment," Bury said. "That is your real purpose, isn't it? Not mere obedience, and more than negotiation. Judgment. In your zeal for fairness, think on a Mote society in which Mediators live long enough to learn for themselves."

"We have," Omar said. "Excellency, you speak of holding the Mote system. Will the Empire help?"

"Of course," Renner said.

"Defending system unity is Imperial policy," Joyce Trujillo said. "They're already keeping the Blockade Fleet. Expensive, with no return. Trade with the Moties will be so profitable that the costs of helping you to keep order in here won't matter. His Excellency can tell you—"

"None of this requires extraordinary intelligence for understanding," Bury said.

"True," Omar said. "Excellency, it appears that your Crazy Eddie Worm truly is the key to human and Motie cooperation."

The Mediators began their gabble again, each to his own Master. Admiral Mustapha listened, then spoke rapidly.

"The Admiral agrees," Eudoxus said. "The question now becomes, what shall we do about the Khanate?"

Kevin Renner thought hard. "Horace—do we trust them, Horace?"

"They trust us." Bury swept a hand to indicate the Warriors who now hung relaxed, their weapons holstered, though still in place. Ally had turned enemy had turned ally, and no Warrior seemed surprised.

336

"Right. Glenda Ruth, what was the situation beyond the Sister when you left?"

"Not much different from when you came through. *Agamemnon* was on guard at the Alderson point leading out of the red dwarf system. There were three Motie ships waiting there with *Agamemnon*. Reinforcements from New Caledonia were expected, but hadn't arrived. But that was hundreds of hours ago."

"Thank you," Renner said. *But they didn't have any ships to send. Meaning we better assume there aren't any.* "They'll send their fleet through. What happens if we attack the Masters that stay behind?" Renner asked.

"They'll send for their Warriors."

"The whole fleet?"

Eudoxus spoke with the Master of Base Six. Another Master got involved, then two Warriors and an Engineer. Ultimately Eudoxus said, "As I surmised. Dividing one's forces is rarely a good idea. They will bring back all of their fleet."

"Nothing to gain. Why did they try it at all?"

"We surmise that they did not anticipate our use of Inner Base Six. We've already built up a respectable velocity for several hundred ships and an enormous fuel dump. They believe they have time to clear a path beyond the Sister. We can deny them that time. Still, Kevin—"

"Good. Then what we do is get in position, wait until their battle fleet goes through the Sister, and pounce."

"And when their fleet comes back?" Omar asked. "Several *thousand* ships."

"We cross that bridge when we come to it," Renner said.

"And hope the horse can sing," Glenda Ruth added, but she spoke so softly that no one but Renner could hear her.

6
Judgment

First ponder, then dare.

—*Helmuth von Moltke*

No," Kevin Renner said. "Damn it, we're going into a battle!"

"I'm the only correspondent present," Joyce said. "An opportunity of a lifetime, and you can't say no!"

"You'll slow us down."

"Not I, Commodore Renner. With His Excellency aboard you're limited in how fast you can go to begin with."

"Horace . . ."

Bury was pacing a contorted path through *Sinbad*'s crowded cabin: his last chance to inspect his altered ship. "Ms. Trujillo is correct, of course. Yet I must come. This is my ship, and I have messages to send, orders to give, that I can only give personally." Bury waved toward the new control panel. "*Sinbad* is better defended than she has ever been. And all that is irrelevant. Kevin, if we do not win, no one in the Empire is safe. Having Joyce aboard will not change that and will not lessen our chances."

"So who do we leave behind?"

"Jacob, I think. Nabil—"

The old man hissed in surprise. "Please, Excellency, I have served you for all of my life."

"Serve me now. Hold this message cube in safety aboard Base Six," Bury said. "Cynthia—"

"I think I should be with you, Excellency."

"Then we agree, because that was what I was about to say."

"All touching, but we have no time," Jacob Buckman said. "Horace, I think you're crazy, but good luck." He shook Bury's hand and held it an instant longer. "We—"

"Good-bye, Jacob."

"Um. Yes." He turned and joined Eudoxus and the others who would stay on Base Six.

"Mother isn't going to like this," Chris Blaine said. He took his sister by the shoulders. "Commander Rawlins is right. They need one of us here on *Sinbad*, and I'll be more useful on *Atropos*."

"If we don't bring this off, nobody's safe," Freddy Townsend said. "Anywhere. Not even Sparta."

Renner nodded to his new copilot. "I'm afraid you're right, Freddy. Okay, secure the airlocks. Everybody strap in."

Sinbad was intensely crowded. The Motie Engineers had re-worked *Sinbad*'s interior and added a fuel tank outboard, where the add-on cabin had been. The control bridge held two couches for humans. It was bounded by collapsing doors that opened onto the main lounge. There they had built shaped acceleration couches for two Mediators and two Engineers, each with a Watchmaker, as well as couches for the other humans. *Sinbad* looked cluttered, with incomprehensible gadgetry attached at odd angles wherever there was space for it.

Cynthia had Bury tethered into his water bed. Bury watched the Moties settle in.

"They've all got the worm," Kevin said.

"Yes. And how does it affect these cursed little Motie brownies? We test it here for the first time!"

"We may need them for damage control," Renner said. "Omar, can you keep them from mucking about with the ship? The last thing I need is to have the control system rebuilt."

"They will do nothing without orders." Omar took his place next to Victoria of the Crimean Tartars. "Your *MacArthur* was safe until the Engineer died. A Medina Engineer, Kevin. Even then a Medina Master or Engineer could have saved her. But—"

"But we didn't allow any communications with the Engineer or the Watchmakers, and Medina was already fleeing from King Peter," Renner finished.

"Precisely. It was not all your doing. After the arrival of King Peter's ship it would have been very difficult for you to communicate with Medina."

Renner nodded to himself. Even then, thirty years ago, the Moties had known more than the humans suspected. And what did they know now? But there was work to do.

"Rawlins?" A screen showed the commander of *Atropos* watching *Sinbad*'s chaos with concealed disapproval. "Let us get well clear before you move in and refuel," Renner said.

"Aye, aye. Godspeed, Commodore."

"Thank you."

Refuel only. No Motie would ever touch *Atropos. Paranoid, but am I paranoid enough? After thirty years with Horace Bury?* Renner said, "All right, Mr. Townsend, let's launch."

An hour after *Sinbad*'s departure, Rawlins called to report launch from Inner Base Six with full tanks.

One of Renner's screens displayed *Atropos* as a black dot on a violet-white glare. Another display, unmagnified, showed violet dots weaving a slow pattern about *Sinbad*. Another showed Commander Rawlins sprawled in his acceleration chair, and Chris Blaine behind him in a similar couch. The strain of three-gee acceleration showed in both faces.

"First things," Renner said. "The Moties report that our message to the Crazy Eddie Fleet went through as planned. No way to know if the Admiral got it."

"But he ought to," Rawlins said.

"And no way to know what he'll do about it. Right," Renner said. "Anyway, for once things are pretty simple."

Rawlins lifted an eyebrow with some effort. "If so, it's the first time."

"Yeah. Bury and I have discussed the Khanate's options with the Moties, and we're all pretty much agreed on how things have to be. They've got two options. Plan A, they go through the Sister with everything they've got, hit whatever's waiting, and get through into Empire space, where they scatter. The Khanate is used to living off slim pickings: give them any kind of a system, and they'll soon be breeding like mad, if they can get their colony ships through."

Rawlins said, "What's to stop them? Why have a Plan B?"

"Well, they don't know they can get through," Renner said. "Or what they'll find when they do."

"They're risking everything they have," Glenda Ruth said. "Those colony ships *are* the Khanate. Everything they have, and they don't really know what they're facing. By now they'll have Terry and Jennifer, so they'll know *Agamemnon* was all there was a couple of hundred hours ago."

"Pity that engineer didn't just get himself killed," Rawlins said.

Freddy bridled; Renner spoke quickly to head him off. "What they don't know, because nobody on *Hecate* could know, is what reinforcements *Agamemnon* may have picked up."

"It won't be a lot," Rawlins said. "But maybe something. We did have some ships under repair, and this wouldn't be the first time Sinclair and his crew at the Yards passed a miracle."

"We're presuming they can talk to Terry and Jennifer," Freddy Townsend said. "The first Tartar group couldn't."

"The Khanate is richer than the Tartars," Glenda Ruth said. "They could have bought a half-trained Bury Fyunch(click) by now. I hope so."

"Why?" Rawlins asked.

"Jennifer admires Bury," Glenda Ruth said. "And she's impressed by the Empire. She'll be sure there'll be a big fleet with *Agamemnon* because she's got a romantic view of our competence. If they could talk to Joyce, it would be a different—"

"Now, Glenda Ruth, I don't—"

"We can hope," Renner said. "It may have happened that way. Whatever the Khanate learned from Jennifer Banda and Terry Kakumi, they're playing it plenty cautious. They're sending their warships through, but so far they've left their Masters behind. Those are still in Mote system with nothing but a corporal's guard."

Renner touched the screen controls and brought up images of the remaining Khanate ships. They were big ships, like civilian cruise ships in the Empire, and not one resembled any other. They were accompanied by a score of smaller ships.

"Two dozen—actually twenty-six of the big ships. That's the target. The thing is, a Master's family and entourage *are* a colony. Those are all the Masters and everything they need to survive, plants, symbiotes, useful Classes, everything. Each family a little colony.

"We go after those. Medina is vectoring everything onto those ships. So are East India and the Tartars. Byzantium has agreed to help. In about twenty hours, things are going to be plenty hot for the Khanate Masters."

"That part I understand. Fine by me," Rawlins said.

Blaine said, "It won't be a surprise attack by the time we hit them, but right now they don't know how fast we're coming. They won't have factored in the boost from Inner Base Six. The Medina Alliance is bigger than they thought, too, as they'll soon find out. So—what choices do they have? Either they pop through to get support from their war fleet, or they send for help. Quite possibly both, that is, they go through and then yelp for assistance, which means recalling the war fleet. That should buy some time for *Agamemnon*."

"Yeah, it just might," Rawlins said. He looked thoughtful. "If they do that, maybe we can reinforce Balasingham in time to do some good."

"Good thinking," Renner said.

"What's Plan B, Commodore?"

Renner said, "Our best guess is that the Khanate's Plan B is the same as Medina's. If they can't blast past *Agamemnon*, then they come back here, put together a big alliance that can defeat Medina, and offer to negotiate with the Empire."

"So the important thing is to see they don't get past *Agamemnon*. Other than that—do we care who wins?" Rawlins asked.

Kevin Renner had never thought of that at all.

"The Empire may not care," Bury said. "But we do."

Rawlins frowned.

"I'll second that," Freddy Townsend said.

Both men were civilians. Rawlins couldn't quite suppress a patronizing tone. "Now, I know you like these Moties, but Imperial policy is not to get involved with the internal affairs of candidate systems."

"We all know it happens," Freddy said.

"Maybe, but this is at a policy level a hell of a lot higher than any of us," Rawlins said. "Even with the Blaine heirs aboard."

"Rawlins—" Renner began.

"Commander," Glenda Ruth said. "We're only speculating on what the Khanate might do. The fact is, they haven't tried to negotiate with us. They have taken two Empire citizens captive, and they won't even talk to us about it."

"Hell, your friends took you captive."

"And are doing their damnedest to make restitution," Freddy said.

The two Mediators were listening intently, but neither spoke.

"Medina has earned our trust," Bury said. "Should we not earn theirs? Then there is a matter of property rights. Medina knew that—"

"Property?" Rawlins demanded, his reply delayed by the light-speed gap.

"Yes, Commander. They knew that the protostar would collapse, that the Sister would open. They bought that knowledge with scarce resources. Including the life of an Engineer we allowed to die aboard *MacArthur*."

"Be damned," Renner said.

"Yes." Bury's voice sounded labored. "The situation is not quite what happened to Mr. Townsend, but there are similarities. And from that little store of knowledge they guessed what we would do, and they bet their survival on being right. I have done the same myself. Do you not regard ideas as property? In a sense, Medina Consortium holds copyright on the Empire."

A beat. Then, "Copyright. Thank you, Trader. Commodore?"

Renner said, "We'll fight alongside Medina Trading. I'll take the heat. You've got your orders, Commander. Go hit those colony ships. We'll be thirteen hours behind you."

"Yes, sir." Too late to be of any help, but they both knew that.

"You're an unknown to the Moties," Renner said. "They won't know what your ship can do. I don't know if that means they'll concentrate on you or try to avoid you. Be ready either way. We're going to need your protection when we get closer, so try to stay alive."

The delay was longer this time. "We'll try."

"Any more questions? . . . Right. Let's get to it. Godspeed." Renner switched off, to find Bury chuckling.

"Yeah?"

"I was thinking," Bury said. "I can envision a trial. With Miss Blaine's parents presenting our defense."

✳   ✳   ✳

Sinbad was accelerating at 1.2 standard gravities. Glenda Ruth Blaine was using the cramped space of the galley area to do slow stretches. She asked, "Have you ever had a pet?"

"My dad had a pair of Keeshonden," Joyce said.

"They died, though. You knew they'd die someday and they did." Glenda Ruth didn't wait for a response. "It was like that with Jock and Charlie. They told me themselves. Charlie died. We, my folks had a version of the C-L worm by then, but it was too late for Charlie, or it wasn't quite right. No, Joyce, you leave the camera where it is."

Joyce hadn't moved. "I can't help what I'm thinking, Glenda Ruth, but if they were about to shoot me for knowing too much, I'd still be listening."

"I'm not sure what I want to say for the press. What I did, it wasn't honest and it wasn't simple and it would be insanely complicated to try to describe. What I'm getting at is that the C-L worm pulled my oldest friend off death row. Hello, Freddy."

Freddy had popped out of the pilot's enclosure. "Hi. Being interviewed?"

"Off the record. Coffee?"

"Bless you." Freddy Townsend turned to Bury. "Gravity all right, sir?"

Bury looked up at him. "It is no worse than Sparta. I am quite comfortable. Thank you. It is harder on Ali Baba and our friends." The Mediator pup was huddled into Bury's armpit; it didn't seem unhappy.

"I came back to show you something," Freddy said. "We've got cameras outside the Field." He indicated the lounge screens. Bright flashes and softer glows, the intricate light threads of a space battle.

"*Atropos* group?" Glenda Ruth asked.

"They're still a couple of hours short of the Sister. That's the Tartar fleet. They were closest. Victoria, I'm afraid it's not going well for your people."

"We did not expect it to," Victoria said.

"A fearful consumption of resources," Omar said.

"An investment," Bury said.

"With potentially unlimited returns," Omar said. "We have had years to contemplate, but this is the first generation of Moties to see the universe as a place of real opportunity. So. How soon will we be there?"

"It's a bit under two light-minutes," Freddy said. "Call it twenty-six hours at our present rate."

"Won't it be all over by then?" Glenda Ruth asked.

"Possibly not," Victoria said. "Space battles take time."

"And this is a battle such as few have ever seen," Omar said. "A battle of Masters, the final failure of the Mediator class."

"One thing I don't understand," Joyce said. "Why won't the Khanate negotiate?"

There were new flashes of light on the screens.

"More ships," Glenda Ruth said. "Whose are those?"

"Hard to tell," Freddy said. "But they're shooting at the Khanate, so they're on our side."

"Enemies of our enemies," Bury said. "We can but watch with patience. Allah has been merciful."

"Joyce, there are many answers to your question," Victoria said. "Their history. The Khanate has had few successes with alliances."

"Given their record this is not surprising," Omar said.

"All true. They treat their allies with contempt. They did not honor the terms they had made with us. And now they see unlimited potential if only *one* of their colony ships survives to roam Imperial space."

"Unlimited," Glenda Ruth said. "Crazy Eddie. An entire clan."

"We see it, too," Victoria said. "As do Medina and East India. Call it an entire culture."

Sinbad's control bridge was dark except for the navigation screens. Freddy had closed it off from the lounge. He had set the pilot's couch for massage mode.

Glenda Ruth noted Freddy's relaxed posture. "Hi."

"Hello."

"I saw some activity on the screens."

Freddy nodded. "The battle's started up again. I told the Commodore. There's not much we can do about it, for another fourteen hours, so there wasn't any point in rousing the others."

And you're not saying why you didn't call me. "What do we do when we get there?"

"Good question," Freddy said. "On this course we'll shoot past at about two hundred klicks a second."

"That's not much use."

Freddy showed some irritation. "If we slow to match velocities, we'll be forever getting there. The idea is that we can boost our thrust at the end if somebody needs our firepower. Otherwise it's safer to go through fast and backtrack."

"Good news from all over," Glenda Ruth said.

The main screen flared, a blue flash. She stared at it. "Freddy—"

"It's all right. You don't have to watch."

Her voice was almost patronizing, though it came three seconds later. "Freddy love, there's not much point anyway. All I'm seeing is colored lights. Why don't you tell me what's happening? Pretend it's a race."

"Race. Okay." A touch zoomed the picture, expanded the center of the maze of colored lines. Lasers were splashing across black and coal-red balloons of varied size. One was inflating, green, blue, a white flash like a nova. "They began with twenty-six big ships. After twelve hours of fighting it's twenty-three. They're not moving much, but your brother would recognize that dance they're doing. Ship A floats behind Ship B. Ship B takes the heat for a while. You can't do it unless the enemy is all in one direction. Ship A sheds some energy, then drops the Langston Field just as it passes from the other ship's shadow. Fires everything. Turns on its Field again . . . oops."

"Doesn't always work?"

"No. Twenty-two."

"Uh-huh. Freddy, that was twenty-six clans of the Khanate. Each ship is an extended family. The ships are different sizes because some families are bigger, or richer. It's worth remembering that Moties don't flinch at extermination."

Freddy looked at her.

"What are they doing now? Freddy, there goes another one!"

"Caught you looking." He turned. "Where's the cloud?"

"No, it just winked out. There, another one."

"No, my love, that one's not dead." He slapped at the intercom keys. "Commodore! Mister Bury!"

Bury's image appeared on the intercom screen. "I saw. Kevin? Two ships have fled through the Sister. I think they are all in motion. There goes another one, yes, Freddy?"

"Yes, and another one just died. Five down, three gone through, and the rest are converging on the Sister."

"O-okay. *Atropos* won't have to fight." Renner sounded tired, and there was no image on the screen. "Freddy, we'll have to go through, but that won't be for fourteen hours. You have the watch.

346

I'd appreciate it if you'd work the navigation problem. It lets the rest of us get some sleep." There was a moment of silence. "Horace, we've got to talk to the Moties. We can't go through the Jump alone."

"So I had surmised. Go to sleep, Kevin. I will negotiate."

Kevin Renner set his couch to full recline and closed his eyes. He heard Bury's voice, brisk but with a thread of fatigue in it. "Omar, we will need as many warships as can be assembled to accompany *Atropos* and *Sinbad* through the Sister. . . ." And then it all faded out.

*   *   *

"Urgent message," the computer announced.

Renner sat up at the console. "Put it through."

Eudoxus showed on the screen. Renner punched in questions: Base Six was a bit under four light-minutes behind him.

"Kevin, the fleets of Byzantium are delayed. They will not reach the Sister in time to accomplish anything. Shall we send them elsewhere? Also, we have detected objects on an intercept course with *Sinbad*. Three unidentified ships on this vector." There was a twitter of binary data. "They should be twenty-six minutes from intercept when you receive this."

Renner thought it through, then sent, "I assume Byzantium is still your ally. Ask them and any other allies to join you at Base Six. Help to secure the Sister. We will look at your unidentified ships. Our present plans are unchanged. We will follow the *Atropos* group through the Sister. With luck you will secure the Sister from this side." Kevin thought for a moment and shrugged. *Why not?* "Godspeed." Renner clicked off. "Mr. Townsend?"

Freddy Townsend's picture said, "What's up?"

"Screen two." They studied the screen together. Black space and stars, and three dots approaching from low and thirty degrees off the port bow, a degree below the Pleiades.

"*Sinbad's* detectors haven't seen them yet," Freddy said. "Maybe now that we know where to look . . ."

"Right." Renner punched in commands. "Three targets acquired. Constant bearing, and closing, thirty thousand klicks. They're not throwing anything at us yet, Freddy." He watched violet-white lights weaving about him and said, "I'd say our allies are already alerted, but call them anyway and make sure Rawlins knows, too."

"Wake anyone else up?"

"Call Joyce." Bury was fast asleep. His readouts were a little jagged, a bit disturbing. The Moties slept, too, and Kevin considered. "We don't need a translator, do we?"

"Let her sleep. Death makes Glenda Ruth twitchy."

Joyce Trujillo was awake: Kevin could see her screen alight past the back of her head. "Hi, Joyce. Battle shaping up. Freddy, have you got any of the other ships?"

"Signal from Ten, but I can't read it. Warriors. I'm waking Omar."

"Swell."

Omar uncurled and sat up. What followed was a rapid exchange between *Sinbad* and its twenty small Motie Warrior fighter escorts. Omar said, "You are to be protected."

Irritating. Kevin said, "If I tell you that I am a Mediator-Warrior—"

"Ships Six through Twenty deployed between us and Bandit Cluster One. Ships One through Five in reserve. Expected attack at high velocity, two clusters of fighters around a fuel tank, expected to separate, plus a Master ship. These are some random ally of the Khanate, arriving late but obliged to protect the Sister from capture by East India and Medina."

"*Much* better, Omar. Might they be aware that the Khanate has abandoned them? Give me your best guess."

"They will not guess that, because the Khanate need not have told them what the Sister *does*. Ship One suggests you activate your Langston Field now."

Renner did that. Screens went black, then lit one by one as he raised cameras.

Violet lights were diminishing toward the Pleiades. "Omar, did *all* of our escort go off to fight?"

"Omar's off," Freddy said. "I see four Warrior fighters still with us, not holding any special position. Dammit—" He didn't have to finish. Glenda Ruth was watching Joyce's screen with bright eyes.

Joyce spoke to her, a near-whisper in the dark cabin. Kevin wasn't meant to hear. "Are we going to fight, do you think?"

"To fight, or to timidly hide behind our allies? Hmm." If Glenda

348

Ruth hadn't meant him to hear, Kevin didn't believe he would have. "Joyce, we tried to put everything we know in the message to Weigle. We even duped your tapes as a supplement."

" 'Even'?"

"Barring that message, whether or not it went through, everything mankind knows about Moties is right here in *Sinbad*."

Three enemy dots had become a spray of lights. *Sinbad*'s Warrior fighters were dancing, an unpredictable pattern. The enemy began to dance, too. When the enemy is light-seconds away, it is possible to dodge laser beams.

"The thing is," Glenda Ruth said, "if *Sinbad* has to fight, it'll be a very bad sign."

"It's likewise true that my holos may be the most important thing to emerge from Mote system."

"Point."

"I've read about space-fleet engagements," Joyce said. "They all say the same thing. They'd be boring if they weren't terrifying. I didn't really believe that before."

The weaving lights of the enemy ships had converged to one blurred point and stayed that way. Renner frowned. What did they think they were doing?

They were withdrawing, the Warrior ships protecting the Master. *Sinbad*'s entourage were too many for them.

❉   ❉   ❉

Bandit Cluster Two was bigger. They went past at six hundred klicks per, firing once. Cluster One's beams impinged on *Sinbad* at the same time, the attack easily absorbed by Langston Fields. Cluster Two decelerated to join One.

Atropos reached the Sister and took up station there, without incident, surrounded by East India Trading's Warriors and the remnants of the Crimean Tartar war fleet. The Medina outriders were already arriving.

A third Bandit Cluster arrived, too. With Cluster One/Two they gathered their forces into a complex pattern half a million klicks out and forward of the Sister, then held station.

Freddy Townsend recorded that and later played it for Renner at high speed. "Sir, it ought to make a pattern, but I can't see it."

"Omar, who are these?"

"Three families, one local, none of any consequence. The Khanate's contract to depart Mote system must leave enough wealth behind to back any number of alliances."

"Okay. There aren't enough to attack us. They're expecting the Khanate to come surging back through the Sister. Then when we flee, these guys block our path."

"What's in that direction?"

"It doesn't matter. They're not between us and what we want. They only think they are. Freddy, how close are we to the Sister?"

"Three hours, but we'll be going through at two hundred klicks per, unless we increase thrust. Another three hours if we miss the pass."

Bury was asleep. His telltales seemed to have settled down: he was resting well. *Give him another hour,* Renner thought. "Belay thrust increase. Omar, we need a conference with our escorts and allies. Freddy, please call Commander Rawlins."

"Let me be sure of this," Rawlins said. "We're going through the Sister. Me first, and I'm to try to protect the lot of you. What from?"

"Whatever the Khanate has left as doorkeeper," Renner said. "Opinion is divided on just how much that will be."

"Okay," Rawlins said. "Standard convoy escort through a Jump point. I can do that, but the Moties will have to cooperate. Shall we work out the courses, or will you?"

"Your job," Renner said. "I've been away from it awhile. You'll do it better. Now, we're six hours behind you if Townsend's maneuver works, thirteen if it doesn't. You'd better not wait. We'll follow you."

"Yes, sir. Okay, I go in and cover the forty-seven Motie alliance warships you're vectoring in. Then when we're all through, we make for *Agamemnon* at flank speed."

"Everything that gets through," Renner said. "You've got a copy of my report to *Agamemnon*. Relay that if you can. The important thing is to keep the Khanate from getting out to the Empire. Don't you agree?"

"Yes. All right. Sir. Okay, but there are too many ships for me to cover them all. I'll have to send some through in a dispersion pattern. I'll work out the course vectors and send them over within an hour. As for *Sinbad*, you're moving too fast, it would take hours to match velocities."

"We don't have hours. We're too slow anyway, with Mr. Bury aboard."

"Exactly. We'll fight what we find there while you and your escorts go right on past. They won't be expecting that."

"That's the way I see it," Renner said.

"Then we all go on. Commodore, I suggest you work on the message to Balasingham. He isn't going to like seeing a bunch of Motie ships coming at him."

"Right. Thanks," Renner said. "Omar, make sure your people understand. Commander Rawlins will have his computers work out a course for every ship. It's important they follow directions exactly."

"Understood," Omar said. "Thank you."

"Okay, Commander, we'll wait for you to call. Thanks." Renner turned to Freddy Townsend. "So. Still think we can get through at two hundred klicks?"

"Piece of cake."

"Just what is happening?" Joyce asked. "Freddy?"

"Give me a minute," Freddy said.

"Omar," Renner said. "When you can spare a moment, we have a job for your Engineer." He tapped furiously and a series of diagrams appeared on the screen. "I need this set up."

"The Flinger, Kevin?"

Bury. "Yeah." Renner glanced at Bury's medical readouts. They'd settled to normal. "Glad you got a good rest. We're going through, and we don't know what's on the other side. I want to erect the Flinger."

"Indeed." Bury sighed. "In that case—Cynthia, I believe you should open the sealed locker in Compartment Eight. We may need its contents."

The brown Motie Engineer had been studying the screen. Now she chattered to Omar.

"Problem?" Renner asked.

"No, she understands the mechanism and its purpose. It will be done in less than an hour. Indeed, she says she can make considerable improvements—"

"No!" Bury said. "My ship, and by the Prophet, no! Leave it as it was designed."

Renner was chuckling, but stopped when he saw the medical readouts. "Omar, I think it will be best if the system works as I expect it to. We can leave the improvements for another time."

"Very well." Omar spoke rapidly. The Engineer and Watchmakers went aft to find their pressure suits.

"Please," Joyce said. "Won't somebody tell me what's happening?"

"What's happening, or what we think is happening?" Glenda Ruth asked.

"Both!"

"I would appreciate the information myself," Bury said.

Kevin kept an ear cocked. Freddy, too, was listening, though he had his own work.

"Not for the record, my opinion only." The screens showed a chart of the Mote system. Glenda Ruth said, "The Khanate sent its main war fleet through the Sister while the Masters and their colony ships stayed behind. East India and Medina made it too hot for them, and they fled through as well. We figure they'll be headed for the Jump to New Cal, but they'll have to find it first.

"Meanwhile, our group is heading toward the Sister. There's another squadron of alliance ships that can work it so they get there just ahead of us. *Atropos* goes in with those. If there's nothing there to shoot at, they'll head directly for *Agamemnon* at the exit point. We'll follow at our own speed."

"Oh," Joyce said. "Of course. We know where it is."

"So we ought to get there first . . . *Atropos* and the Medina fleet, that is. Rawlins goes directly there, so the Khanate won't know just how strong we are."

"But we're expecting trouble."

"The Khanate is entirely likely to leave a sniper or six," Glenda Ruth said.

"But they know how many ships we have. Don't they?"

"How could they possibly know what we'll take through? Anyway, that's why *Atropos* goes first. He goes through and we follow, as many as we can. Some snugged up behind *Atropos*, the rest in a crazy-quilt pattern. The notion is that some get through. A lot get through."

"Oh."

"Something else they won't expect," Freddy said. "Or rather they *will* expect—"

"Jump shock," Omar said. "They will have experienced it. Eu-

352

doxus says it is formidable—but less so for you than us. They will not expect you to recover as quickly as you will. Our Warrior officers agree. It is a good plan."

Atropos went second. First there was a fan of twenty East India warships not much larger than Imperial corvettes traveling at high but different speeds. Their mission was to distract whatever enemy waited on the other side of Crazy Eddie's Sister.

Freddy Townsend watched in appreciation. "Any regatta commodore would be proud of that performance."

"Or fleet admiral for that matter," Renner said. "All right, there goes *Atropos*." Alliance warships huddled close behind the Imperial cruiser, in what would have been called "line ahead" in wet-navy days. Now they vanished one by one as *Sinbad* hurtled toward the Jump point.

Sinbad's Warrior entourage would have been visible if the Field were not up. They were needed for more than protection. Freddy Townsend was using them for triangulation.

The Sister was thirty seconds away.

"If we make this, it'll be a record," Freddy said. "Will I be allowed to file it?"

Kevin said, "Not my decision. And if we miss, we can try again, of course, but that's three hours down the recycler, Freddy, and I don't know how important three hours is. Give it your best."

"Always."

Victoria and Omar concurred: any decent Warrior pilot could do this. With twenty Warrior pilots to triangulate, even a human pilot had a chance.

Kevin never saw Freddy hit the switch.

7
Jump Shock

Among other evils which being unarmed brings you,
it causes you to be despised.

—Niccolo Machiavelli

In the two days before the Khanate ships found them, Jennifer
had little to do but watch Terry, and talk to Pollyanna, and pray.
The God of mankind was God of the Mote, too. She prayed for
solutions that would bring peace to both kinds of mind.

When the Khanate ships approached, Jennifer looped Freddy's
stored data on the Contraceptive-Longevity Worm. The Khanate
Warriors found it running when they burst through the wall.

For a time they ignored it. Two Engineers, four Watchmakers,
and a Warrior searched once for booby traps, then in leisurely
fashion for anything of interest. A Mediator and a Master arrived,
discussed, examined. *Cerberus's* cabin was again infested with
Moties.

The Mediator listened to the recording Victoria had made, the
notice in trade Koine that the ship was salvage but that Medina
Alliance would pay well for Jennifer and Terry. The Mediator
turned to the Master and spoke. The Master spoke curtly. Both
ignored the humans.

The Warrior went away. The Mediator examined Pollyanna
without waking her, then took position in front of a monitor recently worked over by an Engineer. Watchmakers scurried about
like big, helpful, curious spiders.

Over the next several hours *Cerberus* changed again. A pity
Freddy couldn't see this. The Khanate found his drive, *Hecate's*

drive, pushing too light a load. They added a truss to hold cargo, fiddled with the drive to get yet more thrust, added nets of spheroids, as if *Cerberus* had sprouted clusters of tremendous grapes. More cargo . . . and weaponry? Jennifer couldn't tell. Terry would have known, but Terry wasn't talking.

Terry dozed most of the time. Something would get his attention: Jennifer caressing his neck or ear, or a Watchmaker running across his back. His eyes would open; maybe he would smile, maybe he would drink some water or broth, speak a few words, and presently go back to sleep. He wasn't keeping good track of events. Jennifer had to keep her own counsel.

Help would come. Jennifer waited.

Inside, the Moties were at work. This time there was no stopping them. Their interest was in the screens, cameras, computers, communications. They didn't touch the air system. Perhaps the Tartar Engineers had sufficiently altered that.

Pollyanna woke. She and the Khanate Mediator chattered as they watched the monitor.

The Master came back with a Doctor and another Engineer. Pollyanna jumped to her at once and began to nurse.

The Khanate's Doctor was distinctly different from Dr. Doolittle, smaller, frail seeming. She did little to disturb Terry, though she examined Jennifer in detail.

Pollyanna, well fed now, returned to Jennifer's shoulder and stayed there while she chatted with the Khanate Mediator. Her toes clutched Jennifer's shoulder now, while her arms waved in flamboyant gestures. The adult's answers were more concise, a flip of the wrist, right elbows rapping each other: how the hell would a human copy that? Jennifer tried to concentrate. An infant Mediator was teaching a mature one to speak Anglic! The recording would be fantastically valuable, but it would miss things, nuances . . . that head-and-shoulder tilt, "not quite" . . .

Terry stirred, and Jennifer looked into his eyes. Was sense returning to him?

And everything went blurry.

Jennifer recovered slowly. It struck her that if she were Terry Kakumi, and uninjured, she could take the ship from these wailing, kicking Moties. But lack of sleep had done Jennifer in, and the Moties were already gathering themselves. She moved hand over hand to the telescope controls.

Cerberus had jumped, of course. The Frankenstein's monster of a spacecraft was nearly the first through to MGC-R-31. Ships were pouring through aft, accelerating, sweeping past *Cerberus* and leaving it behind, a crippled hybrid. *Cerberus* limped behind the Warrior fleet at about one Mote gravity. The drive flames of a thousand small ships retreated ahead.

And the Mediator spoke to Jennifer for the first time. "You are Jennifer Banda? Call me Harlequin. I serve the Master Falkenberg." She must have seen Jennifer's reaction—*Oh, really?*—but she did not try to temper the arrogance of her claim. "We must discuss your future."

"Surely yours, too," Jennifer said.

"Yes. You are ours now. If all goes best, we break free from the Empire to seek our own stars. You and Terry Kakumi with us. When finally we must confront the Empire, you or your children must speak for us."

It was hardly the future Jennifer would have chosen. But the Mediator was speaking: "Barriers wait before us. Where will the next bridging point lead us? What stands to block us?"

"The Empire of Man," Jennifer said. Terry smiled, barely, and she saw bright glints: his eyes were open.

"Detail," the Mediator said. "We find one tremendous ship and several much smaller."

"There'll be more. We got the jump on you. More ships will be coming through from New Cal, any hour. You don't know what you're facing. This is the Empire."

When Jennifer Banda was six years old, the Navy had declassified certain holo recordings. The whole school assembled to watch them.

That was twelve years after the Empire fleet had assembled off New Washington before the final Jump to New Chicago, a world that had seceded from the Empire and renamed itself Freedom. That world had been restored to the Empire, its name restored, too. There had been battles, but what Jennifer remembered was the massed might of the Empire of Man, ships the size of islands passing at meteor speeds and higher.

No Motie Mediator could see all that in her eyes. Still, Harlequin would see nothing to deny what Jennifer believed: that the power that held a thousand worlds in its gripping hand was coming down the Khanate's throat.

Harlequin said, "If we could reach the new bridging point in time—"

"You'd find our battleships just the other side. You felt the Jump shock. And they'll be waiting."

"I will show you what we plan."

Warrior and Engineer and Mediator huddled, and Pollyanna with them. On *Cerberus*'s screens the gory details of an Engineer's autopsy were replaced with . . . something astronomical. The colors were poor, but this was MGC-R-31, *there* the little red star, *there* the blue sparks of Warriors retreating well ahead of *Cerberus*, *there* a lozenge next to concentric circles: undoubtedly *Agamemnon* and the Jump to New Cal. And *there*, popping out of the other target area aft: more ships, bigger.

"The Masters come before it was intended," Harlequin said. "Never mind. What waits beyond"—she indicated the outward target—"this?"

"Classified," Terry said.

"Oh, good! Terry, how are you feeling?"

"I might live. Won't like it at first. Thanks for staying."

"Oh, no! How could I leave you?"

"Don't tell them details. Sleep now," Terry said, and closed his eyes.

Jennifer nodded. She'd expected him to speak earlier.

Harlequin said, "What system lies beyond the bridge? There must be other bridges."

"I'm going to stop talking now," Jennifer said.

"Not a problem." Harlequin pointed at the cluster of large ships aft. "I will tell *you*. Twenty Master ships have come through. Our Warriors will prepare the way through to the Empire. There must be bridges to other stars. We seek the one that departs the Empire. So do you, Jennifer, for my life and yours, and to save the lives of any in our path."

"You shouldn't be running from the Crazy Eddie Worm," Jennifer said. "You can surrender. Don't you understand, you don't have to *die!*"

The Warrior made a sound, and Harlequin turned. On the

screen other ships were popping through behind the Khanate Masters.

✳　✳　✳

Something big was crawling across Renner's chest. A monkey . . . or a big spider, injured, missing limbs. "Ali Baba is sick," it said. "His Excellency is sick. So is, am I. Sick in the head, concussion, scrambled brains and wobbly eyes. Kevin?"

"It'll be all right." Renner hugged the little Mediator. Craning his head around made him dizzy and sicker. "Just wait, it'll get better."

Bury was on his back, toes pointing slightly apart, hands apart and palms upward. Yoga corpse position: he was calming himself the only way he knew how.

The screens were blurred. A voice was shouting from the background, shouting for the Captain. *I'm too damned old for this.*

Renner popped his restraint belts. "Townsend?" His balance was still screwy. He pulled himself around to where he could see Bury's monitors. The medic array had turned itself off at the Jump. Now it was running a self-test loop. But here came Cynthia, moving quickly on hands and knees. She crouched above Bury and began a medical inspection, pulse, tongue, eyes. . . .

"Townsend!"

"Here."

"What's—" Renner couldn't say it properly.

"*Atropos* on line. We can receive."

But no transmissions yet. Renner slapped at the keys. The screens were still dark, but a voice was saying, "*Sinbad* this is *Atropos*. *Sinbad* this is *Atropos*. Over."

Renner stretched experimentally. *Integral e to the x dx is e to the x* . . . He'd found that the computers recovered quicker than he did. *Should be safe enough to test now.* He woke the communications computers. A snarl of static. "*Atropos*, this is *Sinbad*."

"*Sinbad*, stand by."

"Rawlins here."

"Status report?" Kevin croaked.

"Critical. We're under attack by half a dozen ships. One of them's a big mother. Sir."

Green lights showed on one corner of Renner's control board. "Freddy! She's waking up, see if you can see anything."

"Right."

"We're recovering," Renner said. "How bad is it?"

Rawlins: "We're peaking in green. I won't last forever, and I can't shoot back. No chance to send a message to *Agamemnon.*"

Renner shook his head. Critical. Can't shoot back. Why can't he shoot back? Energy. Energy control. More green lights on his console.

Bury's machinery started suddenly: displays hunting, then drips to adjust his chemical balance.

The Mediators were thrashing feebly.

A screen came to light. Then another.

"Rawlins," Renner said. His voice was still thick. "Hang in there. We're going past."

"Here's a battle picture. I'll relay as long as I can."

The enemy fleet was a scattering of black dots across MGC-R-31's orange-white glare, visibly receding with *Sinbad's* velocity. They'd positioned themselves well, Renner thought. Just sunward of the Sister, to foul an intruder's sensors; near enough to blast them at point-blank.

Atropos was glowing far brighter than the little sun. Nothing smaller than *Atropos* would have survived this long, without *Atropos* itself as shield. Too few Medina ships were adrift behind *Atropos,* firing around the shield, easing back. When *Atropos* went, they'd go, too.

It was going to be tricky. The Moties aboard were no use at all. *Sinbad's* computers were Navy quality, three independent systems, each working the same test problems until they all got the same answers—and they weren't getting them.

"Townsend!"

"Sir?"

"Get the Flinger going! Hit that Motie fleet. Especially the big ship."

"Will do. Launcher self-check. In order. Erecting." The Field blinked for a second as the loops of the linear accelerator eased up through the black energy shell. "Launcher outside Field. I'm getting direct camera information. Trajectory analysis—"

Sinbad was flashing past the battle. They had almost no time.

"Trajectory computers give divergent answers!" Freddy shouted. "Rape it. Launching. Stand by!"

Sinbad recoiled. Then again. "On the way. Automatic loaders are working," Freddy said.

A muted keening sound had to be coming from Glenda Ruth.

"Stand by," Freddy said. "On the way. Dispersion pattern. Continuous fire, stand by!"

There was a floodlight glare from every screen, then all screens went dark. "They hit us. That's it for the cameras," Freddy said. "Captain, the Flinger's dry. We'd have to bring it in to reload."

"Never mind."

Bury was trying to crawl up Kevin's ankle with just one hand. "Bring it in. Kevin, bring it in!"

"Okay, I'm doing it. Lie still, Horace." Unseen, the loops of the Flinger were sinking through the Field into the hull.

"Superconductor," Bury said.

"Ah." *Sinbad*'s flinger was a linear accelerator made with Motie superconductor. That was why it hadn't melted in the glare of Khanate lasers. If it wasn't withdrawn, it would conduct the energy of the laser attack into *Sinbad*.

"We're still getting relays from *Atropos*," Renner said. The relays would be progressively out of date as *Sinbad* moved away from the battle. "And I've got a camera on-line."

Someone, human or Motie, made a strangling sound. Glenda Ruth wailed again. The black beyond the windows began to glow dull red.

An image formed on Renner's screen, a composite of the relay and direct observation. It showed a cluster of Motie ships receding as *Sinbad* moved past the battle. Beams reached from three smaller Motie ships toward *Sinbad*. Six others held *Atropos* pinned like a bug. One of the Motie ships attacking the Imperial cruiser was nearly as large as *Atropos*.

"Blue field," Renner muttered. *Give him another five minutes. Then he's gone and so are we.*

"Five. Four," Freddy counted. "Three. Two. One. Zero. Maybe the timer's off. Or the trig—"

Something flashed intolerably bright beyond the larger Motie ship. The larger Motie ship went from green to bright blue, expanding. Another flash. Another. The blue shaded toward violet.

360

"Jesus, Horace," Renner muttered. "Fifty megatons? More? How long have we had those aboard?"

"You would not . . ." Bury's voice was weak but held a note of ironic triumph. "You would not have approved. At what those cost I nearly did not approve myself."

"It's working!" Joyce shouted. "They're not attacking *Atropos* anymore. They're—"

She fell silent. Two of the Motie ships flashed violet and beyond and were gone. The largest ship was now glowing blue-white, and *Atropos* was firing at it. "He can't last," Joyce said.

The big Motie ship flashed and vanished. Now a score of bright dots clustered around the fading glow that was *Atropos* and accelerated toward the remaining Tartar ships.

"*Sinbad,* this is *Atropos.*"

"Go ahead, Commander."

"Well done, sir. We've won this battle," Rawlins said. "The Moties can clean up the rest of their blockade fleet. Sir, there was no opportunity to contact *Agamemnon.* I suggest you do that."

"Right. Carry on, Rawlins. Townsend!"

"Here."

"Find *Agamemnon.* Send that message."

"On it."

✳　✳　✳

"You fight like vermin," Harlequin said with contempt.

Jennifer flinched at the insult, then wondered at its meaning. But the Mediator had kicked himself aft without giving her a chance to reply. Now the Moties huddled, chattering, and Jennifer turned back to the display.

There had been a battle. Ships had died. It looked as if the intruders had won.

Harlequin was back, with the Warrior hovering behind her. "I apologize," the Motie said. "I understand now. You throw away resources like vermin, but it is not that you are animals. You have endless resources."

"If you win everything you want, your descendants will think the same way," Jennifer said.

"Yes. Our battle plan has changed, Jennifer. We no longer believe we can pass to New Cal."

"Surrender," Jennifer said. "Accept the Crazy Eddie Worm. No Motie need die because there are too many."

A wave dismissed the notion. "We have considered this. There are domains to be fought for, and we may yet win."

And Mediators speak for the Masters. "You can't win. The Empire has—you've seen the resources we have. This hasty little expedition. A *civilian* ship was enough to harm your war fleet and alter your plans, and you haven't seen what the Empire can do! Harlequin, talk to your Masters!"

"I have done so. You have none of your altered parasite. There is no time to test it, and your altered parasite might well be fiction." Harlequin might not even have seen her reaction. "In any case, our options are not ended. Your representatives have made agreements with our rivals. Medina Consortium, Pollyanna calls them. Very well, we need only conquer Medina and take their place. Then we will have a gripping hand on the vast resources offered by your Empire."

This at first seemed ludicrous to Jennifer. "All Moties look alike?"

"We must assume that you passed messages describing your situation, describing promises made to Medina Consortium, describing battle plans. But if we silence every human voice, and if we make our rivals extinct, who will tell your Masters which of us was Medina Consortium?"

Jennifer sensed that her answer would be taken very seriously; so, very seriously, she thought it through.

"What if you fail? One voice could destroy you all."

"Humans are conspicuous. They require their special life support systems. We will find you."

"What are you going to do?"

"It is done. Our Warriors will follow your human-built ships and destroy them. Others may remain on Medina's major carrier, but my Warrior adviser calls it a mere hydrogen snowball, conspicuous and slow, easy to capture."

She's crazy! But all Moties look different. It's no better than looking all alike. It could work, Jennifer thought. *And Harlequin knows I believe it might work. Damn.* "What of us?"

"We may have need of you."

362

"Of course." If the Khanate failed, she or Terry would convey surrender terms to the Empire. So, they would be the last to die. *I have to think. There must be some way to convince them that this is madness.* "Crazy Eddie."

Harlequin had not mastered the art of appearing to shrug, but her inflection conveyed the same sentiment. "As you say. These are Crazy Eddie times. But time is short, and if we seek this option, we must seek it now. We will speak later."

✳　✳　✳

Freddy Townsend said, "Sir, I have some other ships in view. Interested?"

"No. Find *Agamemnon.*"

"Waiting."

"Making coffee," Joyce said. "Strong, with hot milk?"

Freddy said, "If *Agamemnon* has shields up, I won't find it, period. What if we just beam your message at the Jump point?"

"*Good*, Freddy. Do that. Then keep trying."

"Aye, aye."

Lights dimmed. All of *Sinbad's* power was going into that one blip.

"Oh, Lord," Freddy said.

"Talk to me, Townsend."

"More ships under acceleration. Fusion drives, high acceleration. I count sixteen no more than five million klicks away, all with a redshift and no drift, and I don't know where they're aimed but it isn't at the Jump to New Cal."

Renner brought the images in closer.

"Kevin, what is it?" Joyce demanded.

"Not enough data."

"There's more," Freddy said. "A whole sparkling *field* of drive lights at maybe sixty million klicks, all of 'em between us and *Agamemnon.*"

"They've cut us off," Joyce said.

"That they did," Freddy said. "Skipper, I've got four minutes integration on them now. They're showing a *decreasing* redshift and no drift."

"Thrust?"

"Close enough to three standard gee."

"Bound to be Warriors."

"All redshifted?" Joyce asked. "That means they're going away from us."

"Decreasing redshift," Freddy said. "Going away, but they're thrusting toward us. An airplane would be turning around, but you can't do that in vacuum."

Renner touched the intercom buttons. "Omar, have you been following this?"

"Yes, Commodore."

The Motie's voice conveyed weariness, confusion, and determination at the same time. *Never off duty*, Renner thought. "Watch. That group I just marked. That's the main body of the Khanate fleet. Best estimate is that their Warriors were going all out toward *Agamemnon* and the Jump point to New Cal until the Masters popped through."

"That is reasonable."

"Okay. But *now* the Masters are all moving away from the Sister, and the Warriors are slowing, probably coming back. What are they likely to think they're doing?"

"The Warriors are swarming back to defend the Masters from us. The Masters have many options. Their target may be a place of hiding, perhaps the comets around the brown dwarf star. They seem to have given up the Jump point out of the system. Something has convinced them that your defense at the Jump is too formidable."

"Jennifer," Freddy said. "She must have convinced them."

"Those bombs did not weaken her arguments," Omar said. "Whatever else you have done, you have shown that you are willing to expend resources."

"Resources to burn," Joyce said. "Which we quite literally—"

All the screens whited out. Kevin moved two dial displays, in haste. The screens dimmed to a scattering of laser-green points. *Sinbad* was under attack.

"Whatever. Now what's happening?" Renner mused. "Omar, that Warrior fleet is aimed right at us. Or at the gate back to the Mote system. Which is it?"

"Why not both?"

"Both."

Omar and Victoria conferred briefly. Then Omar said, "If we threaten the Khanate Masters, they will attack us, of course. But consider this. If they have abandoned the notion of forcing their way past *Agamemnon*, then the Khanate may have instructed their Warriors to return through the Sister to prepare a path of safety for their return to Mote system."

"They're giving up?" It was the first time Glenda Ruth had spoken since the battle.

"Perhaps." Omar shrugged. "Or they may attack Medina, to soften our power for later negotiation. Or something else. This is a matter for military strategy."

Victoria said, "They'll kill or capture the humans if they can. If your Empire has only the Khanate to negotiate with, any contract would favor the Khanate."

"Bet?"

Victoria answered in Motie. Glenda Ruth laughed as their speech became faster and faster. She said, "Uncle Kevin, they're betting! Descendants for their Masters! Victoria's giving four to one—"

"Later, Glenda Ruth. Omar, it looks like their whole fleet of Warriors is coming straight at us."

The cabin went dark. "I've found *Agamemnon*," Freddy reported. "I'm beaming your message again."

"Good. Very good. Now we've got to get out of here. Suggestions?"

No one answered. "Freddy, turn us around. Get us on course to go back through the"—hell—"through the Sister."

"Through the Sister. What thrust?"

Renner let the computer work for a moment. "That's a god-awful amount of radiation they're aiming at us. If it keeps up, we'll have to duck. What are they trying to do?"

"Kill us?" Freddy suggested.

"Well, if they can, but what else?" Renner studied the screens. If the Motie fleet continued on course, it would get to the Sister in about twenty-five hours. Another moment of indecision. Then, "Keep it reasonable. Say point three for now." The Field was dull red. Not bad, but they'd be bathed in that green laser glare for hours to come. "I want to see what those Warriors will do."

"What of our ships?" Omar asked.

"I'll keep *Atropos*," Renner said. "Have all your Motie ships reinforce Balasingham. Look, he's going to be a bit wary of them."

365

"We have discussed this," Omar said. "Our ships will position themselves to aid your warship without threatening it."

Horace Bury's voice trembled with exhaustion, but there was triumph, too. "Mercy of Allah! Kevin, we have sent our message to the Empire, and the Khanate has turned back. We have fulfilled our mission, whatever happens. Now we survive if Allah wills it."

"We may have fulfilled the mission," Kevin said. "It all depends on that Khanate Warrior fleet. We don't know what they're going to do, and as long as they're in this system, they're dangerous. They could still batter their way past Balasingham." Renner studied the screen again. "Well, as long as they're chasing us, they're not doing that. If they're back in Mote system, they're for sure not doing that. Maybe we can lead them there."

"Good," Bury said.

Kevin thought, *Can you take another Jump?* and didn't speak. What if he said no? "I'll tell Rawlins."

"My viewers may not understand," Joyce said. "I'm not sure I understand. First we come through to the red dwarf system. Then we fight. We win. Now for the past four hours we've been slowing down, and we're headed back the way we came." She looked at her screens, noted the yellow glow of the Field. *Sinbad* was under continuous attack.

"It's all part of the same battle," Freddy Townsend said.

"The important thing is that the Khanate fleet is moving toward the Sister, not going after *Agamemnon*," Glenda Ruth said. "We have to keep them heading toward us."

"But are they after us, or would they go back to the Mote anyway?"

"It doesn't matter, Joyce," Victoria said. "Anything that gets them back into the Mote system."

"So we're bait," Joyce said. "I guess that wouldn't be so bad—but to be bait when you don't even know it's you they're after!"

"They're after us," Freddy said.

"How can you be sure?" Joyce demanded.

"If they're not, they're sure wasting a lot of energy," Freddy said. "They can't spare the fuel. I think it's this way. If they can

366

kill us, they won't go through, but if we run through, they'll follow us. Glenda Ruth?"

"Best bet," Glenda Ruth said.

Joyce said, "And there you have it."

"Situation unchanged, Commodore," Rawlins said. "They haven't tried to intercept the allied ships we sent to reinforce Balasingham. It's us they care about, all right, and there's too many to fight. Our only chance is to run. I suggest we increase acceleration. The less of this fire we take, the better chance we'll have once we're through."

"Agreed. Take it up to one point five gee."

"One point five, aye, aye." Rawlins's image turned away for a moment.

"Once we're stabilized in the Mote system, thrust along this vector," Renner said. There was a twitter of data. "And I had the Moties record some orders. You'll recover before we do. Send these messages to Base Six as soon as you can."

"Messages to Base Six. Aye, aye."

"Keep the comm link," Renner said. He sighed and touched the intercom buttons. "Stand by for increased gravity. One point five g." He touched another button. "Horace—"

"I will survive."

"Yeah. If they keep that beam on us too long—"

"Kevin, you will do what you must do."

Renner had been at work. Sailing Master aboard *MacArthur*, Bury's pilot for thirty years: this he could have done in his sleep. "Horace, can you take one point seven gee for eleven minutes?"

"Yes, of course, Kevin."

Of course. The danger to Bury wasn't from another increase in thrust, but from Jump shock. "Townsend, do it."

Ali Baba's eight kilograms hit him in the chest. The pup cried, "No, Kevin! Not again!"

"Here, Ali Baba," Bury said, and the Mediator went, fearfully.

Freddy said, "Aye, aye. Done. Any margin of error there?"

"We'll be violet when we go through the Eye."

Freddy shuddered.

The Engineers were up and crawling; the Mediators watched.

Kevin bit back his questions and presently understood. The Moties had Cynthia's couch disassembled and were putting it back together next to Bury's water bed. That crowded Glenda Ruth, so they had to move her couch before they could return to their couches and collapse.

"Commodore? I've got the Master ships' target. It's the brown dwarf. Maybe they expect to take cover in the ring."

"Once they kill us."

Cynthia had finished her exercise set in the kitchen space. The view through the window was a uniform cheerful green.

✳   ✳   ✳

On the enlarged screen that the Watchmakers had finished erecting, one blazing point reached the Sister and disappeared without exploding. Then the second. Jennifer heaved a great sigh of relief. "They're through," she said.

Terry squeezed her foot. She reached around to pat his cheek. "How are you doing?"

"Healing. You?"

"Just waiting. Harlequin's up front getting battle data. Should I really stop talking, or try to talk them into something?"

"Talk. They'll read you anyway."

But it was over an hour before Harlequin rejoined them. "The Sister hides your ships for the moment," he said. "We did not expect they could survive our barrage."

"That's another thing about resources," Jennifer said. "Our ships are bigger, better defended, more powerful."

Harlequin laughed in great amusement and some scorn: Freddy's laugh. Harlequin must have had it from Pollyanna. "Another thing about our breeding problem: our ships are more numerous by far! Jennifer, our intentions are not your concern. We will discuss strategy. These two ships—"

"I must stop listening—"

But the Mediator's big left palm was out, *pause a minute*, while the Warrior spoke.

They finished. Harlequin said, "Jennifer, we sent most of our Warriors to chase your two Empire ships down, under the command of our junior Master. Medina's lizard-raping Warriors managed to destroy that command ship as they passed, but our Warrior ships are nearly untouched. They will follow your Empire-built ships through the Sister to Mote system. They can't hide, Jennifer, their drives are too peculiar."

In fact, the blue sparks of the Warrior ships' drives were disappearing even as Harlequin spoke. Other, larger sparks had flown past: the Khanate Master ships were on their way to Bury's Star. "Where will your Masters hide?"

"In the rocks. Does it matter? We've given up hope of bursting through the other bridging point into your Empire. We must wait until our Warriors report success at the Mote."

"You intend to kill us all?"

"Yes. Your ships will have the advantage in the first instants because they will go through first and recover first from the shock. Unless humans tolerate the shock worse than we do?"

Jennifer laughed.

Harlequin frowned. "No? We watched you. You recovered very slowly."

"Harlequin, I'm half-dead of fatigue. Poor Terry's half-dead, period." An instant later she could have bitten her tongue off. Too late: Harlequin was leaping aft.

Terry's hand closed on the Motie's ankle and yanked him backward. Jennifer shrieked, "Kill him! Kill him, Terry!"

The Warrior was arrowing toward them.

Terry's arms closed around the Motie's head and shoulders. He twisted. "Dammit!" he muttered, and set himself and twisted much harder. The lopsided head turned with a pop like a branch breaking, and then the Warrior was wrapped around Terry like strangler vine, with his gun in Terry's ear.

Terry let go. Harlequin floated loose, still screaming thinly.

Under the Warrior's gun, they watched the Doctor pull and twist the Motie's head back into place. Harlequin's screaming died to a moan.

"No good," Terry said. "I forgot. No vertebrae, just that kind of handle that connects the skull to the shoulders. I only dislocated it, and the spinal cord isn't even in it, it's underneath. He'll talk."

"Jump shock. It hurts them much worse than it hurts us. They didn't know it."

"Yeah. But that was the last Warrior ship going through. I'm right, aren't I, Jennie?"

Jenny looked. "Yeah. Those other lights are all big Master ships, and they're all past the Sister."

"Hah. Slowed Harlequin down just enough. Now their whole Warrior fleet is in Mote system chasing down *Sinbad* and *Atropos*, and no Master to tell them different. Isn't that interesting? I wonder what a Navy man can do with that."

"We may not live to see it."

"Jenny, that took everything I had. If they decide to shoot me, don't bother to wake me." Terry's eyes closed.

8
Stern Chase

Retreat, hell! We're just attacking in the opposite direction!

—*U.S. Marine Corps commander, Changjin Reservoir, Korea*

I'm just too damned old for this. Renner gradually became aware . . .

. . . Cynthia was swearing in a loose-lipped mumble. Her body covered Bury's, obscenely, kissing . . . breath for him, squeeze his rib cage closed, blow into his mouth, squeeze . . .

Freddy said, "*Atropos* calling."

"Put'm through. . . . Hello, Rawlins."

"Commodore, you're a flawless diamond on black velvet. Brilliant blue-white."

"Flattering. Ss'a quote—" From a historical novel, *The Taking of Serpens Peak,* just before the ship exploded. "Any threats here?"

"We're clear. Bandit Group One-Two-Three pulled well back from the Medina ships. East India is still holding the Crazy Eddie point for us, but not with enough ship to defeat what's coming here. Byzantium hasn't got here yet. Nobody's shooting at us. What's our move?"

Renner's eyes were properly focusing now.

"General order: Make for the Crazy Eddie point. Keep station with *Sinbad.* Are we in communication with the Motie fleet?"

"Yes. I'll relay."

Bury was trying to sit up. Cynthia braced him.

Renner didn't recognize the Motie on-screen. A young Mediator, presumably male. "Commander Rawlins has informed us that a large Khanate war fleet, too large for our power, will arrive here through the Sister within the hour," the Motie said. "I am ready to convey your instructions to our Master."

"Avoid combat with the main fleet," Renner said. "Preserve your power, but we want you to take out any command ship that comes through. We expect the main Khanate fleet to chase us. As long as it does, leave it alone, but we don't want that fleet to get new instructions.

"Same for the Jump point. Make it expensive to go back through the Sister. Their main war fleet can do anything it wants to, and you can't stop them, but you can stop them reporting back to the Masters on the other side with anything short of a real battle group. Do that, please."

"Instruction received. Stand by for acknowledgment."

What else? "Townsend, get us moving toward the Crazy Eddie point. Cynthia, how much can he stand?"

"Pulse is strong."

"Anything," Bury said. "Kevin, do what you must. It is now in the hands of Allah."

"Yeah." *And I think I'm too old for this.* "Run up to one gee, Townsend. There's a stunt I want to try."

The communications screen lit again. "Your instructions will be obeyed," the Mediator said. "We will do what we can."

"Thank you. Rawlins, you stay with us."

"I can boost harder than you can."

"I thought of that, but no. I need you with us."

"You're assuming they're sending their whole fleet."

"I sure hope so," Renner said. "The warships anyway." His last observation in the red dwarf system was of the Master ships making for Bury's Star at low thrust. It didn't look as if they'd be coming back to the Mote system soon. And as long as the Warriors were chasing *Sinbad*—

"We're bait," he said to no one in particular.

After Rawlins rang off, Renner looked around his ship. Horace was breathing by himself, eyes open, jaw slack, full of funny chemicals. Borloi extract, no doubt: no prohibition in the Koran against borloi. It was amazing that he could talk at all.

Freddy had recovered from Jump shock with stunning speed. Renner resented that. Glenda Ruth Blaine still looked as if she'd been blackjacked. The Moties were worse off, still keening in pain and angst. That couldn't last. Renner needed them.

The Empire ships fell toward the Crazy Eddie point at zero gee, following forty-five minutes of thrust. Renner couldn't tell them how long that would last. Cynthia was leading Horace Bury through a program of stretches. Joyce was preparing a sketch lunch. Nobody had ever asked if the reporter could cook. She could.

Telescopes aboard *Atropos*, then aboard *Sinbad*, observed small hot ships emerging through an invisible hole at high velocity and high acceleration. They dimmed, reducing thrust while they sought their targets. Presently they flared and moved at low acceleration toward the position of Bandits One-Two-Three.

"It worked."

"Why are you whispering? Call *Atropos*."

Freddy cleared his throat. "Yessir."

"They can't have taken time to refuel," Renner told Rawlins. "They're burning fuel they can't spare. Which means we can beat them to the Crazy Eddie point at anything above one point one gee."

"If they chase us."

"Yeah. Assume they will."

"Then their best bet is to take it easy," Rawlins said. "A stern chase is a long chase. Easy to use all your fuel in the chase and have none for the battle. Of course, they won't know where you're headed." Pause. "Or if they do figure it out, they won't know why."

"Okay. All we have to do is make sure they don't cripple us. I want to beat them to the Crazy Eddie point, but not by much, and I want to make sure we have plenty of maneuvering fuel when they catch up to us. Meanwhile, maintain your watch. You, too, Freddy. I want to know instantly if large ships with cooler exhaust and lower acceleration come through."

"Aye, aye, sir." Rawlins signed off.

At least he didn't ask if I know what I'm doing.

An hour later Freddy saw the Khanate Warriors turning. "They've found us," he said. "Somehow."

Renner grinned widely. "They've found us and they're chasing us. Stand by for acceleration. Horace, how does one standard gee sound? We'll take it up slowly."

"Heavenly," Bury said.

"Stand by." Weight returned slowly.

"There," Freddy said. "You can unstrap now. It should be steady enough."

Behind *Sinbad*, little dots of fusion flame now numbered over a hundred and rising. As many more Khanate ships had *not* turned: they were still on route toward the massed Khanate allies, Bandits One-Two-Three. Other lights . . . what were they doing? Converging, then going out one by one.

Renner said, "Omar, get on the horn to our forces around the Sister. Orders unchanged: leave the main fleet alone, but watch for stragglers. Keep it expensive going through the Sister, but stay alive."

"Fleet in being," Victoria said.

"Right—where did you learn that phrase?"

"It was in one of the books *MacArthur* left behind. The reference was to sea power, but—"

"Mahan," Joyce said. "He wrote before space travel."

"Oh. Victoria, I need your help."

"Yes, Kevin."

"I need some work done. Get the Engineers on it. We need some alterations in *Sinbad*'s Langston Field. Townsend can show you what we need."

"Right away."

"Horace, how are you feeling?"

"I've been better, Kevin. I've been altering my will. I will need you to witness that it is my work, and that I am in my right mind."

"Bizarre. You never were before."

"Kevin, you will need to be convincing. Truly. Now say, 'Horace Bury was in his right mind,' without smiling."

"Maybe another approach. Tonight, Igor, we must build a convincing duplicate of Kevin Renner."

"May we have doglike devotion this time, Master? I wanted doglike devotion last time."

Glenda Ruth was staring. It was something, to have shaken Glenda Ruth Blaine.

"But it might interfere with his sense of humor, Igor!"

"Yes, Master, yes, yes! Please may we interfere with his sense of humor. . . . I don't have the energy, Kevin."

"Yeah. Give me a sanity check, Horace. Glenda Ruth, listen up. Here's what I have in mind. . . ."

Joyce's hand was steady as she poured tea into Cynthia's cup. Acceleration was down to one-half gravity for the moment, but she didn't expect that to last. For the past ten hours there had been sudden and random accelerations as *Sinbad* avoided different attacks from the hundreds of ships following.

"If someone tells me that 'a stern chase is a long chase' one more time," Joyce said, "I'll scream." She sipped carefully, then looked at the older woman, not bothering to conceal her curiosity. "You've been with Bury a long time. Is it always like this?"

Cynthia's smile might have been painted on. "Not precisely. When my uncle Nabil offered me service with His Excellency, I knew we would face many enemies, but few of them had warships. Mostly we are concerned with assassination."

"What's it like, working for a man who has that many enemies?"

"He has enemies because he is a great man," Cynthia said. "I feel honored to serve him. When I graduated from medical school—"

Joyce was startled and showed it despite her news training. "You're a doctor?"

"Yes. Does that seem so unlikely?"

"Well, no, but—yes, actually. I thought you were a bodyguard."

Cynthia's smile softened. "I do that as well. But you were supposed to assume I am a concubine. Thank you, I will have more tea."

"I'm supposed to think you're a concubine. Are you?"

"The appearance is a professional duty. Nothing else is required."

Which could mean anything. "It must be a strange career for a doctor."

"Call it my first career. I will have others after I retire from His Excellency's service. And think of the stories I can tell my children!" Cynthia's laugh was almost inaudible. "Of course first I will have to find a father for them."

Joyce laughed. "Looking at you, I wouldn't think that would be so hard to do."

375

Cynthia shrugged. "I have no difficulty finding lovers. And our culture is changing. Not just on Levant."

"That's for sure." Joyce looked around *Sinbad*'s crowded lounge, humans and aliens, magnate and aristocrats and naval officer, and grinned. "That's for damned sure."

The Empire ships fled across the Mote system. For Joyce it had been three days of trying to make sense out of myriad details.

Sinbad and *Atropos* had jumped into Mote system, then accelerated toward the inner system for forty-five minutes, then coasted. Minutes later the Khanate Warrior ships had poured through an invisible hole, paused, then blasted away in the wrong direction. They'd used up an hour's fuel—but at low thrust—before they found *Sinbad* and *Atropos*.

Since then it had been a race; but there were nuances.

Bury's couch was located near the door to the control cabin. It made a convenient gathering point when the cabin door was open. When Freddy went over to tell Bury what was happening, Joyce went to listen—and noticed that Glenda Ruth didn't come over until after Joyce had joined the party.

"We laid low. Got them moving in the wrong direction for a while," Freddy said. "Odds are they can recognize our exhaust, so we didn't give them one. Maybe they found *Atropos*'s old-style Langston Field. But this much for sure, they're chasing us."

"Flattering," Glenda Ruth said.

Freddy didn't answer.

"Getting all our enemies into one bunch," Bury said. "It is not the first time. On Tabletop—but that was a long time ago."

"Yeah. Well, it isn't quite working," Freddy said. "We've got maybe a hundred twenty on our tail, out of a thousand. Three hundred kept going; they've just about reached the Bandit cluster. We still don't know what they think they're guarding, but never mind *that*. I've lost five hundred of the buggers."

Kevin Renner said, "They haven't disappeared. It only means they're not under thrust."

"What are they doing?" Glenda Ruth asked.

Freddy shrugged. Kevin said, "Something else. Something interesting."

Horace Bury spoke suddenly. "The thing to remember is that we've won."

Joyce said, "I beg your pardon?"

"The Khanate Axis will not pass *Agamemnon*. Will not burst free into the Empire. They can never reclaim that option. Now their only hope is to replace the Medina Alliance. Well, what of that? They must reproduce Medina's agreements and fulfill them as best they can. They must even be overcooperative, to cover promises they might be expected to remember."

Joyce thought that through. "But they'd have to kill us all. And our friends."

"Silence every voice, yes. But the Empire of Man is safe *now*. The Mote will be organized according to our wishes and custom. We have won that war *now*," said Horace Bury. "We have protected the Empire of Man, indeed."

And Kevin Renner was trying to swallow a laugh; but why?

Wait— "You could do it!" Joyce cried. "I mean, I'm being very unprofessional here, but—if push came to shove, if they've got us in a box, you could still negotiate. The Empire could get what it wants from the Khanate instead."

They were looking at her. Joyce was sorry she'd spoken. Nobody spoke until Renner said, "Yup."

"Would you? Rather than, um, die?"

"No."

Now the eyes turned away, and only Glenda Ruth sighed in relief. Joyce thought, *Why not?* and said, "Okay."

"We don't want to teach the wrong lesson here, Joyce. Treachery can become habit-forming."

Five days: part acceleration, part coasting, Sinbad and Atropos led the enemy fleet across Motie space. Five days to observe, not just the battle, but the people.

Freddy Townsend was busy, too busy to talk . . . but it was more than that.

Freddy was avoiding Glenda Ruth, just a bit. Joyce was willing to learn why, but she hadn't thought of an excuse to probe. And Freddy would clam up a bit when Joyce was wearing her "reporter" hat.

But he would talk to both women. Joyce found herself coming on to him a little; when she caught herself at that, or when Glenda Ruth did, she would back off; but she could loosen his tongue that way. There was so much to understand, and Freddy was her best source of information.

"But this is the part we're wondering about," Freddy said, and with a woman peering over each shoulder, he moved his cursor about the screen. "Here, a quarter of the fleet turned around to chase us. Another third went on to join the Bandit cluster, the Khanate allies that never went through. What are they after? Why did they think they'd find *Sinbad* and *Atropos* in that direction?"

"Fuel," Kevin Renner said without turning around. "They must be desperate for fuel by now. They're trading time for fuel."

"The rest of them turned off their drives. That lasted for hours. Then we got *this*." Freddy put the cursor on a tight pattern of blue-white points, like a cityscape or the work lights on a half-built factory. "And that's been following us, changing as it goes."

Again Kevin spoke without turning. "We think those ships are all linked up into one framework. They'd have broken up some ships to build it. It took them ten hours. Then they came after us."

"If Empire ships tried that, they'd come apart like nose wipes in the rain," Freddy said. "Even so, they're only doing a fifth of a gee. Hundreds of ships are following them from Bandit cluster, linking up."

"Fuel ships, of course. I bet they're dropping stuff on the way, too. Empty ships. Spare troops. They'll keep some framework to make their structure stronger. Unless I'm crazy. Jesus, Freddy, I wish we could see that thing better."

"It looks a lot like Vermin City, backlit," Freddy said. "Not much pattern, and that changes every minute. Okay, Joyce, Group A is still in the lead. They'll reach us first, yes? We have to outrace *them*."

"First, but with dry tanks. Group A can't maneuver," Kevin said. "That's not going to hurt them, unfortunately, because they've guessed where we're going. Group B might get to us late, but with fuel to maneuver."

"You're guessing, Commodore."

"But it's what Moties would do," Glenda Ruth said. "The ships they start with won't be the ships that attack you."

"Keep a watch. I want to close my eyes for an hour."

"Yessir. Hold it! Commodore?"

Drive lights flared where the cursor lay. "I see it," Kevin said. "See if you can get a better picture. I have the watch."

"What is it, Kevin?" Bury demanded.

"Won't know for an hour," Renner said.

They were building a sketchy dinner when they heard Freddy whoop. Joyce reset the oven before she followed Glenda Ruth.

Freddy was grinning. "Sanity check. We've been right all along. What do you see?"

Behind the tight pattern of blue lights that was Khanate Group B was a looser pattern, a score of drive lights well spread out and shifting in intensity. Kevin said, "Two of those just went out. Shot down by our guys?"

Freddy looked. "Our allies aren't anywhere near. It's possible, of course. Warriors are just bloody damned good at killing. . . . Enhanced view, Screen Two."

"Right. Khanate rescue ships, Freddy. They're towing that cylinder now. Rescue or salvage. And the rest are still coming . . . and there goes another pair. They're merging. Group B must be leaving garbage and personnel clear across the sky."

"That'll hurt 'em."

"It will if our allies have anything to say about it. They're losing mass, losing numbers, losing firepower, all to get the fuel to reach us. You agree? It's us the Warrior ships are after. The Empire ships."

"Yessir."

"I should talk to *Atropos*."

Joyce found the next hour even more confusing. It was frustrating: she had her news equipment, nothing was being kept from her, but she wasn't getting a story she could tell.

"The only thing that still concerns me is this," she heard Renner telling *Atropos*. "When we go through the Crazy Eddie point, we have to know that no Master ship has given the Warrior ships new orders. Otherwise we'll be abandoning the Mote system to the Khanate."

And that made sense, but how to lay it out for a viewer? *If we lose, you'll never know it. Even we may never know. If we returned via New Cal and that little orange star, a year from now we could be talking to a replacement Eudoxus speaking for a replacement Medina. All Moties look alike, but these are the good guys and—?*

379

"Maybe later," she said to Bury. "Maybe I'll understand later."

"And perhaps you never will," Bury said.

"If we lose—"

"Yes, of course, but even if we win. It has happened to me." And he launched into another tale of his terrible past, a skewed view of Empire history that Joyce could never have bought with pearls and rubies.

There had been incidents. Sometimes the Khanate fleet beamed laser light at them, forcing *Sinbad* and *Atropos* to take turns shadowing each other. Renner and Townsend had at first considered this a mere annoyance.

"Probably tryin' to distract us," Freddy said in one of the rare intervals he was off duty. Commodore Renner kept Freddy Townsend busy. When he did get a break, he often used the opportunity to talk to Horace Bury; and when that happened, Joyce invited herself into the party.

"They've scattered their fleet," Joyce said. "Some of the ships used all their power and now can't keep up. Why would they do that, Freddy?"

Freddy said, "I can tell you what they're doing, but why is out of my department. You'll be famous even if you don't know why."

Horace Bury chuckled. "I should instruct my brokers to invest in your network. You will have the highest ratings in Imperial history, I think."

"A few weeks ago I would have resented your saying that," Joyce said. "And even more resented it if you'd actually bought stock in IBC."

"And now?"

Joyce shrugged. "It's your ship, and we're all on it."

"Besides, his brokers will already have made the investments," Glenda Ruth said.

"Cautiously. They'll buy too little," Bury said. "After all, it was not certain that we would be bringing Miss Trujillo to the Mote."

"Or that we'd come out alive," Joyce said.

"Well, if we don't, it won't matter if the investment's no good," Freddy said.

380

"Oh, Freddy, that's silly," Glenda Ruth said. "His Excellency—"

"*Acceleration warning. Action stations.*"

"Oh, Lor', what now?" Freddy demanded.

"It's a big mess of junk under high velocity," Renner said.

Most of the leading Khanate ships were in deceleration mode at high thrust. Most of them. A few were burning fuel at a prodigious rate and converting that to energy beamed at *Sinbad*; and out of the glare of that beam came a dark mass on a collision course.

"We'll have to dodge," Freddy said. *Sinbad* began to turn.

"Yeah. Horace, Group A ran up to maximum velocity and then stripped their ships. It could be mostly fuel tanks. Freddy's turning the ship."

"It won't cost us too much fuel."

"No, but I should— *Atropos* calling, good." Joyce heard Renner setting a direction for the other ship. *Sinbad* and *Atropos* would diverge.

Four minutes later—the lightspeed gap—Group A's junk pile pulled into two masses. They'd armed it with motors. Freddy spoke of raping his lizard; Renner called *Atropos* and ordered a laser barrage.

Four minutes later the junk pile flared with the light of *Atropos*'s barrage. An instant later it flashed a hundred times as bright! The camera overloaded and burned out before Freddy could enfold *Sinbad* in the Langston Field. Glenda Ruth was cowering with an arm over her eyes, and Joyce was waiting for glowing spots to disappear. She knew better than to interrupt Freddy or Kevin.

Freddy spoke anyway. "They had a mirror. The clever little . . . nightmares waited for our beam and then threw it back at us. It's way dimmer now, but they're still throwing sunlight at us. It's nothing, Glenda Ruth. Just another goddamn nuisance attack."

And more to understand. Medina Alliance ships trailed the Khanate fleet, darted in toward it with a reckless expenditure of resources, fired lasers and missiles, then darted away again, fuel gone, coasting away from the battle to be rescued by unarmed ships from other clans.

"Another major development," Joyce dictated. "There's a big fleet, two hundred ships and more, trailing the Khanate war fleet. They're rescuing ships that run out of fuel. Khanate and Alliance ships alike, they're retrieving stragglers. We thought they were Khanate allies, but they're not. They're neutrals.

"We've changed Mote politics like nothing else in their history. A hundred families and clans in cooperation, hundreds more gathering their strength, but all of them staying uncommitted.

"Our Motie allies say this is a good sign.

"Joyce Mei-Ling Trujillo, Imperial Post-Tribune Syndicate."

"We are ninety minutes from the Alderson point everyone calls the Crazy Eddie point. The Moties are getting nervous. No one likes Jump shock much, but our Motie friends really dread it. We can hope the prospect makes the Khanate Warriors nervous.

"The situation is this: *Sinbad* and *Atropos* are on course for the Jump point and decelerating. The leading elements of a war fleet from Byzantium, the most powerful of our allies, have already reached the Crazy Eddie point and are standing by for orders.

"Meanwhile, things are happening in the pursuing fleet." Joyce zoomed in on a screen.

The structure they'd been calling Khanate B was under heavy deceleration. The tremendous junk pile was no longer a single object. The bright sparks of fusion drives were separating in pairs.

Another screen showed a blurry picture relayed from *Atropos*: two Khanate ships docked and remained docked until one reconstructed ship began to decelerate, leaving part of its mass as debris.

"We don't know what this means," Joyce said. *Reporterspeak for I don't know*. Kevin and Freddy had given over arguing about it, but Renner had taken time off to talk with Bury. Marooned face-up in a water bed at high gee, Horace Bury could at least use the entertainment. Joyce turned the camera on them; they didn't notice.

"So what have we got?" Renner said. "Group A boosted to high velocity, coasted, and is now under deceleration. Classic. They'd get to the Crazy Eddie point about the same time we do, but we can fix that."

Bury wasn't asking, so Joyce did. "How?"

Renner's glance showed his irritation. "Low thrust deceleration now, high thrust later, brings us in sooner. They can't play that game. They're at max thrust with no spare fuel."

"But high thrust—"

"As Allah wills, Joyce. What of Group B, Kevin?"

"Aye, there's the rub. They never turned off their drives. They did low thrust forever, right up to midpoint turnover, and dropped mass every step of the way. Fuel tanks, Engineers, that mirror thing, who knows? It looks like they'll get to the Crazy Eddie point just behind Group A, but with plenty of fuel to spare. If we miss our Jump, I'd say we're dead. So, we're forced to jump."

"If so, Kevin, they've made themselves very vulnerable to Medina. The Medina forces will face seven hundred Khanate ships strung in a long line. Is this a winning strategy? They must do more than silence all human voices. They must control the Sister. When the Empire comes again, the Khanate must speak first."

"You're missing something," said Glenda Ruth Blaine.

An odd source, but— Kevin said, "Okay. What?"

"I don't know." She perched on the edge of the water bed and scratched behind Ali Baba's ear. "But they're Warriors. They're following a Master's orders, but that doesn't make them silly. Remember their mission and look again."

Cynthia knew how to prepare Turkish coffee. Bury sipped his and said, "Fuel matters here. The Khanate ships are depleted. Are we? Base Six is following us, of course."

"They'll be a hundred and ten hours late. They can rescue any ship that ran dry, but that doesn't help us fight. Still, we could refuel from a Medina ship. I don't think we even need to. And we'll go through the Crazy Eddie point at three hundred per, just like last time, with the East India ships to triangulate for us."

"Ah!"

Cynthia snapped alert. "Excellency?"

"I'm all right, Cynthia. Kevin, the debris. The mass, the junk left over when two ships merged at a thousand klicks per second. Set *Atropos* to tracking the course of the junk. You'll find that a mass equivalent to over a hundred spacecraft is on course to pass straight through the Crazy Eddie point just when *we* would like to do that."

"Okay, lie down already. Freddy?"

"I'm on it." Freddy Townsend was working his control board hard. A screen lit: Rawlins's talker.

Now why am I less scared than I was? Renner wondered. *Because my people are getting the right answers?*

No, more: because Horace Bury's mind is alive and alert.

While Freddy was at work, Renner said, "Omar, I need that

debris blocked somehow. The only ships that have to go through the Crazy Eddie point are *Atropos* and *Sinbad*. Will you inform Medina's Masters?"

"I will learn," Omar said.

Now no one had time to explain things, and her questions were distracting. Joyce could only record everything and hope to make sense of it later. "We've heard about the 'fog of war,' " Joyce dictated. "It's all too real. I don't know what's going on, and neither does anyone else, not really. Sometimes you just have to make choices and stick with them."

With twenty minutes to go, Kevin gave the order to strap in. The Khanate ships' stream of high-V debris couldn't be far away.

"I have a feed from *Atropos*," Freddy said. "On Screen Three."

Star-sprinkled black. Kevin said, "I don't . . ." One bluer than the others. That stellar background . . .? "Freddy, it's a Master ship that's just popped through. Now prove me wrong."

Medina called. "We have a Khanate Master ship just emerged from the Sister. One ship only. It made no attempt to communicate, so our man has fired on it. He reports an overpowered shield."

"One lousy Master. That's all it takes," Renner said. "We're dead."

Bury was chuckling. "Why, Kevin?"

"This whole thing falls apart if the Khanate Warriors get the right orders. Here's a Master, just in time, and hell, it's even too late for us to abort!"

Bury was laughing with some effort. "Yes, Kevin, they can send orders to their Warriors, but what would they say? What can they learn in time, across a lightspeed gap of thirty-eight minutes?"

Medina was still speaking, had said something about the barrage. Renner hadn't caught it. "What did he say, Freddy?"

"The Warriors will solve it. Hold to the plan."

Pity Omar hadn't been at the comm. The lightspeed gap was already too great to get any answers. Eight minutes. Everyone strapped in? "Joyce! Strap in!"

"Okay, Skipper." She'd been standing on her chair to get altitude, photographing them at work. She dropped and strapped in, cheerful as hell, hugging the camera like her own baby.

The Khanate Master ship was still in view, glowing fiercely

bright in green. Medina's forces must be bathing her in energy. She'd never get a message through that.

The feed from twenty East India ships was providing good triangulation: he would hit the point dead center. Bury was doing *sava-sama*, but his heartbeat and brain-wave displays were all over the place. Scared. Calling his attention to it would be worse than useless. Behind *Sinbad* a darkness was growing . . . black dots crowding out the stars. What the hell?

Two minutes. And weird lighting effects among the black dots, sparks in rainbow colors.

The Byzantium fleet! They were blocking the Khanate barrage, catching the stuff with their Langston Fields.

And the Crazy Eddie point was here, now, unseen, passing at three hundred klicks per second as Freddy touched the contact.

✳　✳　✳

Orange murk looked in through the screens. Renner, bemused and groggy, enjoyed the appearance of a mechanical hell in which men and monsters writhed in torment and confusion. But his memory was already organizing itself, and he barked, though it came out a croak, "Townsend."

"Renner. Captain. Get us behind *Atropos?*"

"When I start the drive."

Sinbad was coming alive again, but slowly. Now *Atropos* was a black near-circle against white light, unmistakable, a few hundred miles distant . . . almost toward the core of Murcheson's Eye, according to *Sinbad's* instruments.

Fifteen minutes. Fifteen minutes to get ready, then all hell. There was a lot to do, but some of it would have to wait for the Motie Engineers, and they were flat out of action.

Communications. "*Atropos*, this is *Sinbad*. *Atropos*, this is *Sinbad*, *Sinbad*, *Sinbad* . . ."

It would just be dawning on Joyce Mei-Ling Trujillo that they were inside a star. Wonder and terror and a reflex reach for the camera. Glenda Ruth was a basket case, no better off than the Moties. "*Atropos*, this is *Sinbad* . . ." Others were moving. Renner craned his head around. At least Bury wasn't thrashing. "*Atropos*, this is *Sinbad* . . ."

Bury was too still. "Cynthia!"

She was already loose, pulling herself against him, fingers on his throat. "No pulse."

"Do something. Sorry, of course you will." The drive test lights blinked green. Renner enabled the drive. "Move her, Townsend."

"Aye, aye. Acceration. Stand by."

"*Sinbad*, this is *Atropos*."

"Blaine. Good. Situation unchanged as of our Jump time."

"Unchanged as of your Jump time. Acknowledged, sir."

"Report."

"Yes, sir. We're broadcasting on Fleet hailing frequencies. Nobody's shot at us yet. That may be a good sign."

"Not shooting, but not answering."

"No answer yet, Commodore."

Where the hell was Weigle and the Crazy Eddie Squadron? Silly question. Weigle could be anywhere. "Keep trying. We'll hide behind you when we get there."

"Right. I'll leave the channel open."

More movements behind him. Cynthia had reattached the medical systems to Bury. He thrashed suddenly, and quieted. Electric shock. Still dead. Skeletal metal arms lifted from the box, for the first time in Kevin's memory, and began to work on Horace Bury.

Ali Baba howled in terror.

"Victoria. Glenda Ruth. Anyone," Kevin shouted.

"Yes, Kevin." Renner turned joyfully. It was Bury's voice! It was Omar.

Not Omar's fault. Renner said, "When the Engineers recover, make sure the Flinger is ready and loaded, and keep double-checking the Field generator." They had rebuilt the Field generator, altered it so that it would not expand and present a larger surface area to the wispy superhot starstuff around them. Now it matched all the Crazy Eddie Squadron ships, including *Atropos*.

"Stand clear!" Cynthia shouted. "Glenda Ruth, take Ali Baba! Clear!" Horace Bury thrashed again. Once more.

Glenda Ruth made crooning noises. The medical-panel lights glowed, but no sign of heart or brain activity. Dead panel, or—

Glenda Ruth said, "Kevin, Cynthia, my God, stop! He's dead!"

You never know— Kevin bit it back. She would know.

They were alongside *Atropos* now. Townsend matched velocities.

"Stay alongside," Renner said. "Blaine."

"Sir?"

"I'm changing the plan. If I'm going to use the Flinger at all, it'll have to be before we build up too much heat, so we'll stay alongside you for the first phase of the battle."

"Yes, sir?"

"Keep relaying data."

"Aye, aye, sir. Data relay set," Blaine said.

"Got it. Any luck contacting the Fleet?"

"Not yet. Any further orders, sir?"

Renner looked back into the cabin once more. "Yes. I'm canceling the instructions on avoiding high gees. Use any acceleration the tactical situation demands."

They saw through the eyes of *Atropos*. A black dot popped into place, then another, then two more. A green thread from *Atropos* to one of the intruders. The intruder's Field flared, expanded.

"It's working," Renner said. "The Khanate ships have an expanding Langston Field, which is great for most battles, but in here when it expands, it picks up even more heat."

"Could they have done what you did?" Joyce asked. "Got their Engineers to rebuild it?"

"Omar?"

"No data. I would not have thought of it."

More black dots. "Freddy, stand by the flinger. We'll aim for the center of the cluster."

"Right."

The black dot expanded, ran through colors, and vanished. *Atropos*'s green thread moved to another ship.

"*Atropos*."

"Aye, aye, Commodore."

Not Blaine. "Tell your skipper we'll commence firing when we have twenty-five targets. Watch the data link for exact time."

"You will fire when you have twenty-five, that's two five, targets. Observe data link for exact time. Aye, aye, sir."

Joyce's camera was running. Why not? What could it matter now if everyone learned that *Sinbad* carried nuclear weapons?

"We've got another edge," Renner said. "Imperial Autonetics has developed a ship's coating that only becomes a superconductor at forty-four hundred Kelvin. That's two hundred degrees cooler than what it takes to soften the hull. I can run a superconducting wire into *Sinbad*'s water tank and then vent the steam.

387

"In short, we can stay alive a long time."

"We may need to," Freddy said. "Twenty-four."

"Load."

"Erecting the Flinger. Loading. Wow, it's *warm* out there. Fire. Retracting the Flinger into the Field."

A timer began on Renner's console. Twenty-nine seconds. Twenty-eight . . .

A bright star within the star. Twenty black dots expanded, stretched, added their stored heat to the white glare. Green lines converged on another. It flashed and was gone.

And thirty more ships appeared.

"Stand by Flinger," Renner said.

Scattered across a brilliant orange sky were sixty to seventy colored balloons. The eye couldn't tell their distance: sizes varied too widely. Most were red. Fewer were orange, and those faded into invisibility until they grew hotter. A handful were green and blue, inflating as their temperature rose, until one or another made a brief nova. It was a kindergarten astronomy class, the stars color-coded to their places on the Hertzsprung-Russel diagram.

". . . Three. Two. One. Bingo," Freddy droned.

Another flare. Red and yellow bubbles inflated suddenly, green, blue, *flashflashflash*.

"How many is that?" Joyce demanded.

"Counting what *Atropos* bagged, over a hundred."

"Should we be cheering? Sorry, Glenda Ruth . . ."

"It's all right. They're only Warriors. To the Moties they're valuable property, but—"

"Retracted. Seven warheads left," Freddy said. "Timing's about right, we'll be too hot to use it pretty soon. Captain, I have to say this is easier than I thought it would be."

"Too easy," Renner said. "*Atropos*, let me speak with Captain Rawlins, please."

"Rawlins here."

"This was Group A, agreed?"

"Yes."

"I think it's time to get the hell out of here before the B group arrives."

"Agreed. What course?"

388

"Out of the star. Head for the Jump point to New Cal. I'll lead. And keep calling for the Fleet."

"To New Cal. Damn right we'll keep calling! Acceleration?"

"Two gee's?"

"Good enough."

"Here they come!" The *Atropos* talker was shouting. "Hundreds of them!" Then in a calmer voice, "*Sinbad*, this is *Atropos*. Enemy fleet coming through the Alderson point. The count is three hundred ships. We are firing torpedoes."

"Maybe this would be a good time to use our last loads," Townsend said.

"I hate to fire ourselves dry, but, yeah." Renner touched keys. "*Atropos*, designate us a target group, please."

The screen jumped, and a ring appeared indicating a cluster of ships moving together at high velocity away from the Jump point. Other ships were appearing every second.

"Hail Mary," Freddy Townsend said. "Okay, I've got a solution . . . erecting . . . on the way. Eighty-nine seconds." The timers began the countdown. "Of course you know we can't fight all those ships."

"All true," Renner said. "Of course we don't have to."

"They're not going to give up," Joyce said. "Omar, Victoria, can't they see they've been defeated? It won't do them any good to destroy us now!"

"They have their orders," Glenda Ruth said. "Victoria, do Warriors ever question a Master's orders? Joyce is right, this can't do them any good, not now. Whatever they do to us, they get back to the Mote overheated and out of fuel, and the Alliance fleets will be waiting. Do they know that?"

"They know it better than you," Victoria said.

"And they have their orders." Glenda Ruth shuddered.

"I think it is more than that," Omar said. "If they return, it will be the first time that Mote ships have done that. Many neutrals will join them just for that reason. And if a sizable group comes over to them—"

"Bandwagon," Joyce said. "Glenda Ruth, you agree?"

"I guess I have to."

"I have a new target group for you," *Atropos* said.

"Engaging."

"Rawlins here. Commodore, we're getting no answer from the Fleet, and we're going to be overwhelmed."

"Suggestions?"

"Run for it while we can. Pop back into the Mote system, where we have allies."

"It's not much of a chance."

"More than we have now," Rawlins said. "Sir."

"Actually, it's a good plan, for you," Renner said. "It won't work for us, we don't have the acceleration, but— Yeah. You do that. Commander Rawlins, I'm ordering you to detached service. Your mission is to survive and report to any Imperial fleet."

"Just a minute—"

"No, we don't have any time at all. I'm staying on course. You run like hell. Rawlins, somebody's got to survive this. Our Moties analyze it this way. If the enemy gets back alive, the neutrals will join the Khanate. We can't let that happen! Rawlins, you get back into the Mote system and let everyone know the Empire is coming!"

There was a long pause. "Aye, aye, sir. Godspeed."

"Godspeed. Freddy, get the Flinger ready."

"*Sinbad*'s last stand," Freddy said. He nodded toward Bury. "I guess he deserves a Viking's funeral. Only there's no dog at his feet."

The cameras went dark. "We've lost the link to *Atropos*," Joyce dictated quietly.

"No shadow from *Atropos* now," Renner said. "Our field temp's going up. Stand by, you'll have to fire blind after I get a quick look."

"I've got a tentative target group. Give me a look to be sure. Right. Launching. Retracting. Captain, I think that's it for the Flinger."

"Agreed."

"I hate being blind!" Joyce shouted.

"Who doesn't?" Freddy said.

"In the days before superconductors, we'd be getting burn-throughs now," Renner said. "I recall the battle off New Chicago. Captain Blaine—Commander then—got his arm half-burned off. Now we sit here comfortable."

"Whoopee. How long do we have?" Glenda Ruth asked.

"Hour anyway," Renner said.

"The Engineers are rebuilding cameras," Victoria said. "And I am informed there is a new antenna ready that might be able to communicate with your other ship."

"Bless you," Renner said. "Antenna, Freddy. I don't much like blind either."

"Identify yourself."

"What the hell? God damn! Imperial Fleet, this is Imperial auxiliary destroyer *Sinbad*, Commodore Kevin Renner commanding."

A short delay, then the regular communications screen lit. "Imperial Fleet, this is INSS *Atropos*, William Hiram Rawlins. We are part of the task force *Agamemnon*, detached to duty with Commodore Renner."

"Are there other Imperial ships with you?"

"None. *Atropos* and *Sinbad*," Renner shouted. "Get us a data link and I'll prove who we are."

"I may have a better way. Put Lieutenant Blaine on."

"*Atropos* here. Here's Blaine. Admiral, if you're going to help us, you better be damn quick about it! We're in trouble."

"We can see that. Blaine, who am I?"

"Captain Damon Collins," Blaine's voice answered quickly.

"Right. Blaine, tell me something a Motie wouldn't know."

"Poker. That first game. I know how you beat me, Captain."

"Remind me."

Renner made sure the mike was off. "I hope it's not a long story."

But Blaine was talking fast. "I'd never played Big Squeeze before. High-low, six cards plus a replacement. We had our six. I was showing two little pair up, and two down cards. You had three hearts and a something, club six maybe—"

"It's coming back."

"—nothing bigger than a nine. I threw a down card. You threw the nine of hearts. Pulled the jack of hearts. We declared, both high. You had the flush."

"You swore you'd never figure out how I did that."

"I worked it out after the next game. What happened was, you already had your flush, but you had a shot at low hand, too. I was betting like I had a full house. You believed me. You threw your flush away and got it back with your low hand ruined. 'Rape my lizard,' you said to yourself—"

"And beat you for the very last time."

"Fyunch(click)."

"*Enough*," another voice said. "Is it Blaine?"

"Definitely, Admiral."

"*Sinbad* and *Atropos*. Converge on the Flag. We're sending escorts. All squadrons, engage enemy closely."

Epilogue
Endgame

To travel hopefully is a better thing than to arrive,
and the true success is to labour.

—*Robert Louis Stevenson*

Inner Base Six had lost 80 percent of its mass. Its skin was wrinkled and folded. Despite the Engineers' busy maintenance, pipes and lines were bent in curves and loops, and domes edged against each other. The sky was clotted with spacecraft waiting to be refueled.

From the stretched-taffy look of the ice around the Mosque, it must have been twisted almost horizontal, then later pulled back to true. No damage showed. If anything, it had been improved.

The tremendous space of the Great Hall now sprouted semicircular balconies at every level. Men and Moties clustered on the balconies in groups of three or ten, sometimes shouting or even jump/flying from balcony to balcony. Diplomacy moved at a breakneck pace here, slowing down at times to accommodate human minds.

What Joyce was doing wouldn't have worked in the older Mosque; wouldn't have worked without the gyrostabilized camera either.

In the diminished gravity Joyce Mei-Ling Trujillo was leaping from balcony to balcony, stopping to swing the camera at Nabil and a handful of Moties, again with Glenda Ruth and her brother to do a short interview, then leaping on. She looked like some lovely goddess moving from cloud to cloud, gradually approaching earth.

She reached the floor flushed with the exercise, started to say something to Kevin, then swung toward the great monitor screen.

The great blue-and-white sphere filled most of the view. Cloud patterns streamed sluggishly across continents whose borders were marked all in circles. "That's Mote Prime! Isn't it, Kevin? I can see the craters. I came to see Mote Prime, and we've been here seven bloody months without coming anywhere near it!"

He put a hand out to steady her in the minuscule gravity. "You won't get any closer this trip. The good news is, they still don't seem to have any kind of access to space. That footage was taken from a Medina ship skimming just above the clouds, pole to pole, and nobody tried to shoot back."

"I would have loved to see the Zoo."

"Probably gone by now. Things don't last among Moties."

Joyce and camera faced him. "So it's a blockade again, but with Moties in charge."

"Subject to approval from home."

"Of course." Joyce switched off the camera. "Off the record? You don't have any doubts, do you, Kevin?"

"Plenty. How do we use the worm here? We could pick a faction on Mote Prime—maybe King Peter's family survived—and distribute it. Or not. Or not yet. The Crazy Eddie Worm is still experimental. Say . . ."

"What?"

"Bear with me a second, Joyce. Victor! Dammit, that worm's done it. Mediators really do all look alike now. Victor? All just out of adolescence."

The Mediator who had been the Tartars' Victoria bounded toward them in a low arc. "Kevin?"

"Yeah. Victor, sooner or later you'll be in contact with Mote Prime. We want certain bodies returned to us for proper burial. Three human males, Midshipmen Potter, Staley, Whitbread. They may have been dissected, God knows what, but please retrieve them at your earliest convenience."

"It will be done. If there is any successor to the group that held them. Things change rapidly there."

"Some don't. Try."

"Yes. Anything else?"

". . . Yeah. Joyce, guess what the Bandit Group was guarding?"

"Some weapons cache that was too far away to use," Joyce said promptly.

"No. It was the Khanate's main base, including all their wealth. They offered it all as bribes to their allies, and the allies have turned it all over to Medina. Victor, did your people find any surprises?"

"Not to us. We'll make holos, Kevin. Their Engineers are ingenious; you'll see some interesting innovations in the hardware."

Joyce considered the nuances. She turned the camera on Victor. "Then it's over? The Khanate didn't just surrender, they meant it."

Kevin caught Glenda Ruth Blaine's semaphore wave, halfway up the Great Hall's curved roof, and her all-too-knowing smile. Kevin grinned and waved back. No hiding anything. Dammit, Joyce had caught it, too.

"We control all of what was Khanate wealth," Victor answered. "The families have returned from hiding at Bury's Star, and all of them now carry the worm. I see no way in which they could harm us or you, ever again. Their line is at an end, unless we choose differently; would not that satisfy Horace Bury's anger?"

Joyce answered carefully. "As much as I came to know Bury, I think he had no anger left for Moties. This was his last corporate war. I believe he enjoyed it very much."

The Motie smiled and moved on. Kevin felt his eyes begin to sting. He said, "That was wonderfully well said."

"Thank you. I actually miss him, Kevin. Not like you, I expect. Almost thirty years."

"Yeah. But he did go out a winner, and ... I can't seem to decide *how* to feel about finally being free of the old man's power games. Life is about to turn simpler."

"What was the smirk about?"

"Smirk?" Joyce's black eyebrows came together and he said, "It's a secret. There are still secrets. Dammit, Joyce, is every woman going to go around reading my mind for the rest of my life?"

"This isn't any diplomatic secret, Kevin. And it isn't a scandal because you'd never be stupid enough ... you wouldn't."

"Joyce, there is a secret you should not hear. Just like last time, when Eudoxus read your feet."

She swallowed her first answer. "Maybe, but I have to have it."

"Okay." Kevin Renner began to talk.

Inner Base Six had been following the Empire ships. Renner took his own sweet time returning thence, sending the Blockade Fleet ships on ahead, thrusting at half a gee while he and his people healed. It still took him only eight days.

On the afternoon of the sixth day he found Glenda Ruth perched on the arm of his chair with a tray in her hand. He settled in with his lunch and said, "Talk."

She didn't seem able to.

"Freddy," he said. "Aristocrat. Just a touch lazy by my admittedly rigorous standards. Didn't want to join the Navy. He'll have precious little choice now. They'll hit him with major medals and a Reserve commission."

"Good motivation," Glenda Ruth said. "Put him in charge of avoiding a war so he won't have to work."

"He tenses up when you're around. What's he afraid of? You're too sensitive?"

"Squeamish," she said. "Whoever gets hurt around me, child or adult or cat or Motie, I feel it. But I had as much to do with saving us as he did. More. Kevin—"

"Glenda Ruth . . ."

"Oh. Sorry." She shifted to the navigator's empty chair and slumped a little and smiled at him.

"I was going to say . . . oh." That wide, her smile looked a little vacuous. "You got it."

Glenda Ruth said, "Please turn down the sex appeal because it makes me uncomfortable."

"Yeah. And I don't doubt you could turn it up again if I need to remember what gender I am."

"Maybe not. Kevin, you've stopped thinking of me as not quite human."

"Don't test that out, okay?" *Unless you mean it . . . no, dammit, seducing Lord Blaine's daughter is one of the many things I'm going to skip in this life.* "Sure you're human. You may be a great many humans. Every child does a lot of role-playing. You and Chris would do it better than most. What kind of role have you been playing with Freddy?"

"I haven't been playing! Uncle Kevin, I was running a game on the Tartars, for our lives and the Empire. There wasn't room to play that many games. He's seen what I am. I'm squeamish. When it all gets too much for me, I hide."

"You could get him back. He can't drop you, he's got obligations, and if you work on him for an hour, he'll never want to again. So what's really bothering you, Glenda Ruth? *Turn it off!*"

She shifted in her chair. The blood was thundering in Renner's ears. To his skewed perception she was going off and on like a light bulb. She asked, "What if I'm serious?"

"Get frivolous!"

"You're so *wary* of rubbing up against a lord's daughter. I can talk anyone into anything, Kevin. I can make mistakes and damage people, and I've done it, and so's Chris. You'd think I was a real fool, wouldn't you, if I weren't testing my limits?"

Kevin considered retreating to his own cabin and locking his door. But first he said, "I'm not just your randomly chosen dirty old man. I'm the junior officer who ordered Lady Sally Fowler to Captain Roderick Blaine's room when I felt it necessary to their survival. You're my responsibility."

She stared, then burst out laughing. That was better. He asked, "What do I have to do to get you to turn off?"

She was off. She said, "I'm sorry."

"I'm human. You don't need proof."

"I've been in Freddy's bed. He'd have gone crazy . . . well, antisocial, at least, if I hadn't. But I've only just got some freedom. What I think I want to do is turn Freddy loose with the option to marry him later. But he saw me do something he didn't like, and now I could lose him."

"Let's see. He'd marry you—"

"Because he'd have to."

"You're a nineteen-year-old girl. Being confused is part of the game. But look: he thinks he'd like to avoid you for a while. Let him. You free him of all obligation, you make it clear you mean it, and you're not mad. He'll be meeting you for years, lady! You're the heroes of the Mote Conquest! When you want him back, flash him. Agh! Not me!"

"Yes, Uncle."

"I think you'll want him. Good genes, good attitude, your families will approve, and in a pinch you're both survivors. Finding that out can be *very* expensive."

"Still breeding Blaines, are we, Uncle?" And she'd gone away. And Kevin Renner was suddenly very tired. . . .

✳   ✳   ✳

"So I went for a nap. And two hours later you were at my door—"

"Horny as hell."

"Suddenly taken horny, and curious, too. You wouldn't let me get back to sleep after—"

"We didn't just talk."

"No."

"And nobody smirked when I moved into your cabin."

"They were much relieved. Two extra cubic inches for everyone aboard *Sinbad*. Luxury beyond your wildest dreams. But—"

"I can't think what took me so long," Joyce Mei-Ling said. "I guess I was still mad at Chris. No, he didn't lie to me, I guess—"

"Sure he—"

"But this is no secret, Kevin! You and Glenda Ruth *know* something."

"But do you remember what *I* asked *you*?"

Her brow furrowed. She said, "Where did I just come from? I was in the galley with a tea bulb. Where was Glenda Ruth Blaine? Having tea with me. You laughed. Then I rubbed up against you and the conversation went all to hell."

"She sent you. She was grateful, so she sent me a gift."

"Oh, the hell she did! Kevin, all we talked about . . ."

He waited for her to finish. Presently he said, "All I had to ask was, 'Who were you talking to a moment ago?' "

"But I just . . . came to realize. You're the quintessence of availability. No visible ties, wealth, heroism, and you know more about current Mote affairs than any other human being in the Empire of Man! Glenda Ruth didn't . . . we only talked about . . . dammit."

"I don't really know if you'll ever want to see me again, Joyce. But if you do, there are secrets that you should not know, and by God I will keep the next one."

✳   ✳   ✳

There were two message cubes labeled and dated. One had been given to Nabil for safekeeping aboard Base Six. The other was dictated during the long chase across the Mote system and completed just before *Sinbad* jumped across into Murcheson's Eye.

"Should we be looking at this?" Renner asked. "I thought we were supposed to wait for lawyers."

Nabil's leathery face was a mask. "Commodore, His Excellency has instructed on the package that you review this immediately." He pointed to a scrawl in Arabic. "This is your name."

"Okay."

"It also instructs me to invite witnesses, specifically Glenda Ruth Blaine and Frederick Townsend, and as many alliance Motie Mediators as may conveniently be assembled," Nabil said. "Beyond that I know nothing."

They began with the cube dictated aboard *Sinbad*. It showed Bury in his couch. His face was drawn and his voice exhausted. The authenticity of the cube was witnessed by Joyce Mei-Ling Trujillo and Glenda Ruth Blaine.

"That's one picture of me I'll never put on the news," Joyce said.

"I am Horace Hussein al-Shamlan Bury, trader, Magnate Citizen of the Empire of Man, pasha and citizen of the planetary principality of Ikhwan al-Muslimun, known commonly as Levant.

"This is a codicil to my will and testament left in the safekeeping of my true and faithful servant Nabil Ahmed Khadurri. I hereby confirm all bequests made in that previous testament, except as may be directly and explicitly contradicted in this codicil. I dictate this document in the full knowledge that neither it nor this ship is likely to survive our present mission; but Allah may will differently.

"I hereby name Kevin Renner, commodore of the Imperial Space Navy, as executor to my will and confer on him full executive power to execute my wishes and dispose of my property in accordance with my original will as amended by this codicil. This supersedes the appointment of ibn-Farouk named as executor in the original testament. Kevin, I suggest but do not require that you delegate the detailed implementation of my will, and particularly supervising the bequests of entailed property on Levant, to the law firm of Farouk, Halstead, and Harabi, and I commend to you its senior partner, ibn-Farouk, as a longtime friend and counselor. I believe you will recall meeting him from time to time.

"I confirm the bequest of my house, my lands, and all entailed properties on Ikhwan al-Muslimun shall be divided among my blood relatives by the laws of my home planet; except that to my great-nephew Elie Adjami I leave the sum of one crown and what he has stolen from me. It is less than the law would have given him, but the choice was his.

"It is my strong recommendation to the Empire that Kevin Renner be appointed the first governor of the Mote system, and it is my belief that the Empire will make that appointment."

"Great Ghu," Renner said.

"My God, Kevin, I think they will," Joyce said.

"Governor or not, I know that Kevin Renner will be ridden by demons if he cannot observe future events in the Mote system. I confess I wish I could be there myself. To aid Kevin Renner in satisfying his compulsive curiosity, I bequeath to him my personal ship known as *Sinbad*; and since I know that he has not stolen any of my money, and certainly has not enough to operate my ship, I leave to him the sum of ten million crowns in cash to be paid after liquidation of assets other than Imperial Autonetics as described in the main body of my will, such to be deducted from the residual properties; and also I leave to Kevin Renner ten thousand and one shares of voting stock in Imperial Autonetics. Kevin, that's five percent plus one share of the company, and there's a reason I want you to have it.

"The balance of my holdings of Imperial Autonetics, amounting to an additional sixty-five percent of the total voting stock, shall be divided as follows:

"To my oldest living grandson, thirty-nine thousand nine hundred and ninety-nine shares. To Eudoxus as representative of the Motie family known as Medina Traders, thirty thousand shares. To Omar as representative of the Motie Family known as the East India Company, twenty thousand shares. To Victoria as representative of the Motie Family known as the Crimean Tartars, five thousand shares. To the Motie Mediator known as Ali Baba, thirty thousand shares."

Bury's image chuckled. And well he might, Renner thought. "The remaining shares are held by partners, banks, business concerns, and other humans scattered through the Empire. If you care to contemplate the possible voting blocks, you will find the combinations interesting. Kevin, Allah has willed that you shall live in interesting times, and I do no more than abet His will.

"One final bequest: to Roderick, Lord Blaine, onetime captain of the Imperial cruiser *MacArthur*, I bequeath the personal sealed files designated with his name. They contain information about agents who have been useful to the Empire of Man, but who may now be dangerous. I know that Lord Blaine will satisfactorily carry the moral obligations of this knowledge.

"As for the rest, you will find the details in the cube I have entrusted to Nabil. I have provided generously for those who have served me faithfully. I believe that I have faithfully discharged my duties to Allah, to my compatriots, and to the Empire; and whatever Allah wills for my future, I am content that we have done all we could do.

"Witness my voice and signature, Horace Hussein al-Shamlan Bury, aboard the ship *Sinbad* somewhere in the Mote system."

Look round our world; behold the chain of love.
Confirming all below and all above.
See plastic nature working to his end,
The single atoms each to other tend,
Attract, attracted to, the next in place
Form'd and impell'd its neighbor to embrace.
See matter next, with various life endu'd
Press to one center still, the gen'ral good.
See dying vegetables life sustain,
See life dissolving vegetate again;
All forms that perish other forms supply,
(By turns we catch the vital breath and die)
Like bubbles on the sea of matter born,
They rise, they break, and to that sea return.
Nothing is foreign; parts relate to whole;
One all-extending all-preserving soul
Connects each being, greatest with the least;
Made beast in aid of man and man of beast;
All serv'd, all serving! nothing stands alone;
The chain holds on, and where it ends, unknown.

—Alexander Pope, An Essay on Man